About Sisterland

Martina Devlin

WARD
RIVER
PRESS

Published 2015
by Poolbeg Press Ltd
123 Grange Hill, Baldoyle
Dublin 13, Ireland
www.wardriverpress.com

A catalogue record for this book is available from the British Library.

ISBN 978-1-78199-913-4

Printed and bound by CPI Group (UK) Ltd, Croydon, CR0 4YY

www.poolbeg.com

Acknowledgements

Sincere thanks to all those who read drafts of this novel at different stages of its genesis. Each one made helpful suggestions, particularly the people who came from the future (just checking who's still reading).

They are Justin Blanchard, Tonia Blanchard, Lia Mills, Betty Murphy, Jerry Murphy, David Murphy, Mary Pearson and Sarah Webb. I recruited them as unofficial members of Team Sisterland, and they all deserve medals.

Thanks to the unsung heroes at Ward River Press who made a valuable contribution to the book. In particular, I would like to acknowledge Gaye Shortland, a generous and tireless editor, as well as publisher Paula Campbell for her unwavering support.

Finally, thanks to my agent Lucy Luck of Aitken Alexander Associates, who keeps on keeping on for all of us scribblers.

For Mary Carr, with thanks

Sisterland

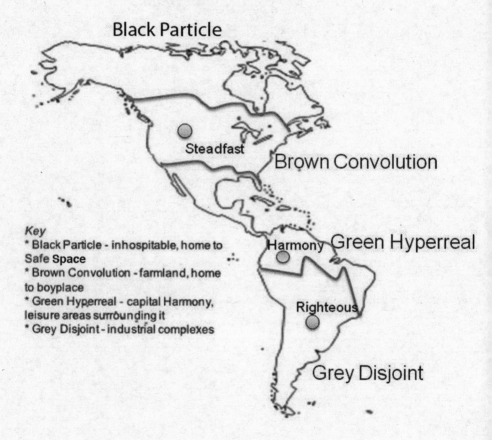

Black Particle

Steadfast

Brown Convolution

Harmony · Green Hyperreal

Righteous

Grey Disjoint

Key
* Black Particle - inhospitable, home to Safe Space
* Brown Convolution - farmland, home to boyplace
* Green Hyperreal - capital Harmony, leisure areas surrounding it
* Grey Disjoint - industrial complexes

"It will be like a nunnery under an abbess – a peaceful, harmonious sisterhood."
Herland by Charlotte Perkins Gilman

Chapter 1

Constance 500 pushed through the air-swamp, following a tree-of-life etched on the pavement. She had a faint recollection from babyhood of air tickling her body – a reminder that, once upon a time, it came in different consistencies. But gloopy air was normal now in Harmony. She had learned as a girl about different climates throughout their great state, but she hadn't yet been awarded a permit to visit anywhere else in Sisterland. The pavement pattern led Constance past Beloved Park, with its giant statue of Sisterland's founder. A good Sisterlander would detour in, and pay her respects to Beloved, but Constance was on a mission. It led her to Moe Express.

Outside, she paused to watch the hologram sign change colour, as it did every twenty seconds to follow the palette of the rainbow. Just now, it was shading from indigo to violet, and she took a moment to admire the transition. Fearless use of colour was a celebration of nature: that's what Sisterlanders learned in girlplace, and practised in their dress code. Except they all wore uniforms at work, and working hours were long, so platforms to showcase personal preferences were rare. Still, the uniforms were tasteful.

The shop door split horizontally across the middle, one

half lifting and the other lowering, at Constance's approach. A perfume of roses wafted out. At least, it was the fragrance which represented roses, because flowers no longer produced their own scent. Sometimes, Constance wondered if the smell of pink roses had differed from white back in the Pre-Sisterland Era – the PS days. Once, she had put the question to a memory-keeper, who had stared at her before admitting that she didn't know.

So, the true memory of rose scent was lost. What Sisterlanders smelled now was an approximation. And if that was the case with roses, perhaps it applied to other flowers. Such doubts overtook Constance occasionally, even though nobody was supposed to feel sceptical any more. It was counter-productive. Its moe[1] certification had been withdrawn.

Inside Moe Express, a flicker waited behind the counter. At Constance's approach, she smiled brightly through her glossy skin – the mask moulded precisely to the contours of her face. Constance could tell this was a cheap skin: the smile quality didn't convince. It took an expensive skin to pull off a smile.

"How may I help you, sister?"

"A U, please, sister."

"Excellent choice."

The flicker pulled on a pair of elbow-high gloves and approached a tall unit, from which a background hum flowed. Like all who practised the flicker trade, her movements were nimble and economical. Her fingertips pecked at a keypad on the left side of the unit, and its front changed from ice-white to smoky. A diamond-shaped cavity appeared at eye level, with a corresponding holder an arm's length below. A whoosh was followed by a thud. Into the padded holder was deposited a jar, also diamond-shaped, and glowing.

The flicker set it on the counter, and took up a close-woven silk net attached to a length of bamboo. An air of concentration transfigured her. She pressed the lid of the container, which

[1] See glossary at end for explanation of words such as *moe*

flew open, and out floated one of the tiny clouds causing the jar to shine. It shut tight again at once. With a fast-forward jump, the flicker gave a spin of the wrist and trapped the cloud, dropping a flap over the top of the net. Still holding the net, which had taken on a luminous primrose tint, she replaced the jar in the holder, tapped another code into the keypad, and the moes were whisked back into the unit.

"One portion of U, sister. Such a pretty moe."

Simply looking at the U almost made Constance feel its Upbeat lift – impossible, of course. Moe spontaneity had withered away. Moes were reined in and managed.

"I'd be worried about letting them float away if I did your job." Constance nodded towards the net.

"I'm careful. A friend of mine let her attention wander, and an entire jar of Exes flew into the street. They caused mayhem. Some kids on an educational trip inhaled them, and their teachers couldn't control them. They wouldn't sing their obedience song, or march in step, or stay in pairs. They wouldn't do anything they were told."

"I suppose the moes wore off after a couple of hours."

"Took longer than usual – the kids were underage. My friend was re-assigned. They sent her to Brown Convolution."

"Ouch!"

"At least it's a middle belt. She was landed with boyplace duties. Doubt if I'll ever see her again. Don't get me wrong, I'm sure she's proud to do it for Sisterland. But I don't envy her spending all day surrounded by boy-men!"

Another twist, and the U was transferred from net to bag, and sealed airtight. Constance admired the dexterity.

"Remember to use this within four hours for best results. Can I interest you in anything else? An N, maybe? A new batch was just delivered."

"Better not."

"Of course. Unchecked moes held us back for centuries. They're an indulgence – we can enjoy them best in

3

moderation." The flicker parroted a lesson from *Beloved's Pearls*, the small, circular book with a pearlised cover given to every newborn Sisterlander. "I see from your sig you're a shaper. What an honour to be chosen."

Constance glanced down at the signifier embedded onto the outer wrist of her right hand: Constance 500 φ – the φ stood for thought-shaper, and had been added last year. She read the flicker's wrist: Fidelity 81026 ⇔ .

"I dreamed of going forward for shaping but I wasn't selected," continued the flicker.

"I was fortunate to be singled out," said Constance.

"What's it like to travel outside Harmony? I don't suppose I'll ever earn a permit. I'm glued to the entscreen when there's a travel programme shown."

"I haven't been sent on a posting yet."

Constance couldn't admit that she wasn't working as a shaper, despite her qualification – she was among the first intake on a new training course. And she was forbidden from talking about it. Recruits to the programme hadn't even been allocated a replacement symbol for their wrist stamp. "Time enough when you take up your new roles," they were told. "The fewer questions, the better."

She changed the subject. "Do you have a favourite moe? You must be a connoisseur."

"I find a Co helps me to relax. Much more efficient than old-fashioned aids like alcohol, with all those harmful side-effects."

What a pearl, thought Constance, who liked the odd glass of sunset wine. Silence had been fond of it, too. Don't think about Silence, cautioned a voice in her head. With an effort, she concentrated on what the flicker was saying.

"That blast of contentment is a treat worth waiting all week for. Forty els, please."

"Forty? Last time it was thirty-five."

"They're becoming trickier to manufacture. When you're

ready, sister." The flicker turned the pay console towards Constance.

Constance held up her wrist, sig side out, and her image appeared on the screen. A twang of authorisation, the purchase was debited from Constance's elements' account, and marked on her moe chart.

A light, inexpressive voice spoke. "This uses up your moe quotient for the next seven days. You have eighty-five elements remaining. Kindly practise economy."

Constance pulled a face. She intercepted an admiring glance at her skin from the flicker – although high-sheen, like all skins, it was a flexible model, and had been expensive. "I'm on a spending spree at the moment," she admitted. "As a distraction. I had some bad news recently."

Dutiful, the flicker said, "We must guard against mindless consumption."

That's enough of *Beloved's Pearls* for one day, thought Constance.

She slipped the purchase into her leggings, and stepped out onto the street. The U had to be inhaled someplace quiet, where its buoyant properties could be absorbed fully. There was nothing worse than losing part of a moe before it was ingested properly. She looked left, towards the twoser she had shared with Silence. Not there. It had a lingering sense of emptiness. Was emptiness a moe? Not exactly. But it penetrated like one.

She looked right, towards Eternity Square, where Shaperhaus stood. It was some distance off, but easy to spot. Above the building soared a pair of giant wings, studded with pieces of glass which trapped and reflected the light. These wings, added for aesthetic reasons, lent it dramatic impact. They also meant space had to be left around it: the architectural equivalent of a pair of elbows sticking out. Constance had graduated from there as a shaper almost a year earlier, but instead of being sent out into Sisterland to promote approved thoughts, she had been chosen for additional training. A new role, and patriotic. But confidential. Just thirteen newly licensed shapers had been selected to participate. Now, they were nearing the end of the theory stage, and a practical apprenticeship was due to follow soon. Today was their weekly rest day.

Constance had been flattered when the Shaper Mother had told her she was to be groomed for new duties. But the reality of what Sisterland proposed disturbed her, a shadow-moe increasing in intensity as the course progressed. It wasn't that she had reservations about the job itself. She understood why alternative arrangements were necessary. But what she was learning to do seemed manipulative and – she hardly dared to let herself think it – dishonest. Constance was becoming infected by misgivings which she could not express openly.

Doubts about Sisterland itself.

Chapter 2

Constance decided to go to Beloved Park to ingest the U. It was choreographed round a pearlised statue of Beloved – all images of the founder were pearlised, because she had expressed a preference for it in life, and over time her wishes had acquired the status of commands. Her vision and charisma had guided Sisterland in its formative years. Sisterlanders left flowers at Beloved's feet, so that there was always a festival of colour surrounding the statue's base, sometimes blocking the lettering: *Not me but US*.

Already, Constance was fired up from the moe throbbing in her pocket. After she took it, she might dance through the streets. No, of course she couldn't – it would be frowned on as unruly. The peers would tick her off. Perhaps she could buy a hoop of little bells and shake them – their sound pleased her. Silence had worn an ankle chain with a bell which tinkled when she moved, like the bell that used to hang from a cat's collar.

No-one had seen a cat in years. Like dogs, they were extinct. Which meant a vermin-extermination patrol had to be set up to deal with the rat problem. Constance was relieved she hadn't been reassigned to those duties. She always admired images of cats in books, when she came across them

– attracted to their elegance and air of detachment. Silence called Constance 'Kipling's cat' because she liked to walk alone. Silence was fond of poetry. Everyone in Sisterland was meant to be in favour of it, because it was not just beguiling but functional – verses promoting public spirit and cohesion had a purpose. But few people bothered with it. Silence had said poetry would be banned, too, if the Nine who ruled Sisterland realised how moe-rich it was. But hardly anyone read any more. Books were decorative objects rather than wellsprings of information. There were no buildings given over exclusively to books, as there had been in PS days.

"No more about Silence," whispered Constance.

She looked up as a sleek, metallic Buzz train hummed overhead on its elevated tracks. Passing a flower-basket attached to a lamppost on the corner of Virtue Boulevard, the scent of jasmine enveloped her, and she picked up her pace to escape it. The gardening teams which injected the perfume daily sometimes laid it on with a heavy hand. She avoided the congested area near Beloved's statue, instead choosing a bench beside the fountain. It spouted peach-coloured water, and a sign invited sisters to vote on the following day's dye. She decided against voting. A dereliction of her civic duty, but so be it.

A man was sucking scum and algae from the fountain with a disposal unit, which vacuumed up objects and compressed them into molecules. Constance was resigned to his company. No woman in Sisterland enjoyed proximity to a man, but it was less unpleasant in the open air because his physical presence was diluted. Not that he was threatening – from birth, men were injected with drugs to reduce testosterone production, making them docile. It was for their own good, otherwise they were inclined to be disruptive.

She watched him working, while he studiously avoided looking at her. He was more blur than flesh, taught to be inconspicuous. His smoke-grey, hooded, one-piece garment left only a few inches of face visible. The stiff collar reached up to the base of his nose, and the hood ended at his eyebrows. The patch of flesh exposed to the air had a scraped texture – no wonder, when men didn't wear skins. Only women slotted on the feather-light, transparent masks which covered faces from hairline to throat, protecting them from environmental damage. It meant even elderly women had scarcely a wrinkle.

When he moved away, Constance took out the bag containing her moe, lowered her head, and tapped the seal. It flew open, the U wafted upwards, and she inhaled. At once, a sense of possibilities suffused her. Optimism swelled, the way sunshine strokes chilled flesh, until a peak was reached. And retained. She raised her arms high above her head, face upturned to the sky.

How wonderful it was to live in such an enlightened community! One where all women were equal members of the universal sisterhood. *Not me but US*. She was lucky to belong to such an advanced society. And to be entrusted with a special job. She must forget her silly qualms, no more than the wheeling of a tired mind still struggling with what Silence had done. Silence's act of disloyalty shouldn't be interpreted as evidence of misgivings about Sisterland. After all, Sisterland was a perfect state, a state of perfection.

"*I am a wave sweeping in with the tide,*" Constance sang out. "*I make a difference as part of the whole.*" She laughed aloud, quoting Beloved, and the water splashed in the fountain, laughing along with her.

The following day, shadow-moes nipped at Constance. Experience had taught her that taking a moe released all sorts of shadow-moes, which might resurface intermittently for days. It was like seeing something you recognised, but through a misty windowpane. They ambushed her now as she descended the steps from the Eternity Square Buzz station, and approached Shaperhaus – its frontage mirrored, like the iconic wings above it, to present a constantly moving surface. Many of Harmony's buildings were mirrored on the outer façade, to lend an illusion of space – and because Beloved had deemed it beautiful.

Constance was reluctant to enter her workplace, uncertainties about the test programme fluttering. She knew she was out of step with her sisters: none of her fellow trainees ever betrayed reservations, by so much as a sidelong glance or an intake of breath. At least Constance had the sense to keep her questions to herself. Even to Silence, she had never said a word, and Silence had noticed nothing. But there had been an absence about her, in those final weeks, which Constance had attributed to babyfusion.

She passed through the main entrance, the comtel on her thumb, which covered it from nail to base-joint, chirruping to authorise entry and register her arrival. Once inside, she cut through the foyer to a staircase at the back.

SMILE ALL THE WHILE

was painted on the wall.

Her lips thinned.

As she began climbing, Constance wished she could be out in the field, shaping. Why did she have to be chosen for the new programme? Sometimes, she wondered at the waste of drilling her in the art of silkenspeak as a shaper – skilled at minimising the downside and maximising the upside of Nine policy – if the training was not going to be put to use. Her new role would mean working with children rather than adults, a drawback as far as Constance was concerned – she knew no children, and consequently was wary of them. But she had to do her best. After all, the initiative would safeguard Sisterland's future, according to her teachers.

Constance was plucked from her shaper graduation class after a mindmap reading carried out by the Shaper Mother. But that was last year. She knew she would not pass mindmapping today.

She climbed past floors given over to administration and recruitment, floors devoted to operations, where shapers in the field were handled, floors housing lecture rooms. "A thought-shaper is permanently on message," she heard spill out from the trainee shaper floor. Finally, she arrived on the ninth floor, reserved for special projects, and again used her comtel for admission. The device had gouged a groove in the fleshy place on her hand, between thumb and index finger, but she no longer noticed its weight.

Without stopping to chat, she nodded at a couple of colleagues drinking ocean tea at their workpoints – everyone consumed rivers of Sisterland's national brew. She counted none of her workmates as friends. Constance was a loner. It was only with Silence that she had enjoyed true Togethertime. But Silence was gone. And she had to stop thinking about her.

Constance slid into her workpoint, where she took off her skin and set it in the container kept in a drawer. From habit, she ran a finger along her hairline where the skin rested, reclaiming her face. Next, she took a spray from another drawer and misted the plant on her desk. Everybody was allowed one personal item. Most chose images, but Constance admired her fern's delicacy. Now to check her lecture schedule.

Just then, Patience 9603 approached. Like Constance, her progress-monitor was wearing the Shaperhaus uniform of hip-length turquoise tunic with lime-green leggings. "Good morning, sister. May I have a word with you?" She could have messaged through to Constance's comtel screen, but the emphasis on courtesy in Sisterland made her put the request in person. *It's Nice To Be Nice*, as *Beloved's Pearls* put it.

Constance followed Patience to her elevated workpoint

with its clear view of the room, and a solitary personal item on the desk – a porcelain goosegirl which looked as if it would shatter should someone breathe heavily on it. She often wondered about that ornament. Patience didn't look the type. Even her rounded number didn't seem to belong to her wiry frame.

"The Shaper Mother wishes to see you at once."

A pit opened in Constance's stomach. "Have I done something wrong, sister?"

"I've uploaded temporary entry authorisation onto your comtel. Don't keep the mother waiting. It's impolite."

Patience was young to be a progress-monitor, and masked it with a stern manner. Constance knew better than to argue. Instead, she consoled heself by looking at her sig: Patience 9603. With 9602 Patiences who were still alive registered ahead of her, she wasn't well-connected.

Constance returned to the staircase to access the tenth floor: top of the building. Taller structures, inherited from PS generations, had been lowered – a ceremony made of the event. Cloud-scrapers had been a hubristic, male affectation. Just as lifts had been conceits, devised by men because they could, when everyone knew stairs were healthier. Sisterland declined to worship gimmicks. That didn't mean it was opposed to gadgets: everything in moderation. But unnecessary technology had a dehumanising effect. Sisterlanders valued the personal touch, as urged by Beloved. Between her *Pearls* and her entscreen chats, which continued to be repeated in a weekly show called *Make Time for Togethertime*, Sisterlanders were in no danger of running short on Beloved's advice.

Constance had been on the top floor only twice before, meeting the Shaper Mother. She saw her from time to time in the distance, naturally: the mother often strolled about, creating a crackle of electricity. After she passed, people felt capable of working harder, longer, better. Perhaps the mother intended telling her there had been a mistake, and she was unsuited to the new programme? That would save Constance from asking to be excused. Which she lacked the courage to do. It would earn a blot she could never scrub out.

She couldn't even let herself think it in the Shaper Mother's presence. The mother was skilled at penetrating thoughts. Constance knew thoughts could be hidden from those able to decipher them – parked in the mind's curves – but it took singular reserves of willpower to engage in such a joust against a mother. She must be vigilant.

She stepped into the mother's reception area, which bore no resemblance to the environment on the floors below. Entering it, Constance was engulfed by a wave of sultry heat, along with a musky scent. Primitive wooden carvings lined the room, drums were remodelled as occasional tables, and the walls were papered in leopard-print.

The mother's assistant, Modesty 2724, was fanning herself with a thunderous air, stirring a flyaway scrap of ponytail high on her head. Modesty was stumpy. Her size in general, her nose and fingers in particular – all stubby. Even her earlobes were practically non-existent. Constance was convinced that was the reason for her ponytail – it extended her length, if only by a fraction.

"It's ridiculously hot in here. One day, I'm going to be the decision-maker and not the decided-for," said Modesty.

"But we're all decided-fors. Apart from the Nine," said Constance.

"Don't be such a pearl!" Modesty's dark eyes flared. "Of course there's a pecking order below them. The Shaper Mother has choices, doesn't she? You ought to mop off before you go in to her."

Constance touched the damp sheen on her leggings. "Patience sent me up before I had a chance to do it."

Modesty rummaged in her desk, producing a palm-sized vac-pump.

13

Constance selected the setting marked D for delicate, to protect the lime-green embroidery on the wrists and hem of her tunic, and passed it across her body. "Don't you think it's odd, Modesty, that our scientists haven't come up with an anti-fungal solution by now? The life expectancy of clothes is getting shorter and shorter."

Modesty lowered her voice. "Some think they've been diverted into a secret programme."

Not more secrets, thought Constance. "Do you know what it is?"

"Maybe."

Constance shrugged, still preoccupied by this unexpected interview with the mother.

Modesty leaned forward, whispering. "The ultimate phase of women's evolution. That's what I heard the mother call it. Something that overrides the mating process."

"Mating is a necessary evil. We do it for Sisterland."

Modesty snapped back to business. "The mother's waiting."

Constance returned the vac-pump, and approached the leopard-printed wall. The paper peeled back in a long curl, so theatrical it deserved a clap, to reveal the door. She stepped through, to find the Shaper Mother waiting on an ornately carved mahogany throne, its back soaring to an arch and its feet ending in hooves.

"Sweet child." Leisurely, her voice trickled out. "You've been on my mind." Arms extended, she shaped her mouth into a dazzling beam of welcome.

It sent a shadow-moe of trepidation quivering through Constance.

Chapter 3

The Shaper Mother was a statuesque woman, exuding a vitality that created a force field about her. Her head was shaven, its terracotta-coloured surface lightly coated in oil. She wore the same uniform as everyone in Shaperhaus, but her position as a mother allowed her to customise it. Over the turquoise tunic, a peacock-print shawl trailed its feast of colours, a match for the substantial earrings shaped into feathers which stretched her lobes out of shape.

Constance bowed her head, and remained standing, since she was not invited to sit – indeed, the throne-like chair appeared to be the only seat in the room.

"Constance, you're one of our most promising students. Your teachers have high hopes for you. But lately, sweet child, you've shown signs of losing your focus. Naturally, there are reasons for it. Those charged with treasuring you are not blind to a recent event in your personal life. It's understandable that your spark may have dimmed. What happened was so volatile. So violent. So vicious in its abdication of loyalty. Who wouldn't be affected?"

She paused, and Constance realised she was expected to answer. "I try not to let it interfere with my work, mother."

"Come closer, Constance. We're not machines. It's natural

to veer off-course sometimes. How could the loss of an other make no difference? When I lost mine, it was months before I could carry out my duties to the proper standard. Doubts must have cropped up in your mind, sweet child. And no wonder, in view of the circumstances. The manner of her discontinuation was particularly regrettable. It defies logic. You might almost call it –" she expelled a breath that set the metal feathers swinging – "moe-driven."

Again she drew to a halt, waiting. But Constance was unable to respond. The mother stood and came towards her. Putting an arm about her waist, she led her to the throne-seat. One foot hooked out a footstool from underneath, and she pressed Constance onto it before resuming her previous position. This time, however, she leaned down, her face only two hand-spans away. Constance noticed it still wore its glossy, protective skin indoors – the mother was known to be forgetful. Equally, she could be shielding herself on purpose. Skins didn't only protect against climate.

"Sweet child, I see you have an unusual capacity for shadow-moeing, just as your teachers guessed. You feel something approaching grief – some version of regret, perhaps? – for the loss of your other."

Constance nodded. Let her call it regret, if it suited her, although she herself knew it was grief. Even if it was her first experience of it.

"Ah, you believe it to be grief? An unhealthy moe that's been deselected by the Nine? I see you're more receptive than we suspected."

Constance steadied herself. She mustn't let thoughts flare.

"I don't mean to invade your privacy, Constance. But Sisterland has a clear policy on moes. The clampdown was necessary because some moes are simply too troublesome – they lead to morbid states of mind. You must have cared dearly for your other to feel the vestiges of such a disturbing moe."

"I keep thinking I must have failed her in some way. I

16

should have been able to talk her out of it. Except I didn't know what she meant to do."

"It's not your fault Silence 1999 chose to discontinue. The report from the listeners said you'd come to terms with it. They said you didn't need advanced listening treatment. Perhaps you do require it, after all."

"No!" Constance collected herself. "I mean, please, no. I cooperated fully, mother. I was obedient. I listened. I'm sure advanced listening would help if it was recommended for me but I find keeping busy is the best way to deal with what happened."

"You mustn't blame yourself. Silence's behaviour was extreme. I agree, hard work is often the answer, it stops us brooding. I know that from my own experience." She rested a speculative glance on Constance, who trembled beneath its weight. "What troubles me is Silence had everything to live for. She was babyfused. Yet she chose to discontinue. It's baffling. Most worrying, though, is her betrayal of the Sisterland ethos. She discontinued in a way that sent a direct challenge to the State. We must assume the balance of her mind was disturbed. That's what the peers' report concluded. Don't you agree?"

Constance knew it would be easier if she said yes. Or even just nodded, if the word was beyond her. After all, Silence's discontinuation had cast suspicion on Constance. But unable to defend Silence, unwilling to criticise her, she remained mute and motionless.

"Ah, you continue to deny her mental instability." Constance's internal struggle had allowed the Shaper Mother to mindmap her.

"I don't understand them, but I believe Silence had her reasons."

"But why? It was such a drastic gesture. She allowed no room for compromise."

Constance hung her head. The mother stretched out a hand

weighty with rings, and laid it on her forehead. At her touch, the compulsion to speak was overpowering. Constance tried to keep the information terse. "Perhaps it was because she knew she was babyfused with a boy."

"It's natural to feel a sense of failure. But we need boy-babies, as well as daughters. It's a dutiful act, whatever the gender – the Nine says so. If Silence couldn't handle the disappointment, she shouldn't have put herself forward as a candidate. No sister is forced to become a source. There are alternative ways of making a contribution. But once babyfusion was achieved, she had no right to retreat from her responsibilities to Sisterland."

"She didn't see it that way, mother."

"Obviously. But, Constance, she had to be unhinged. You must accept that. All over Sisterland, women are struggling to become sources. Yet she babyfused, and rejected her sacred condition."

Constance stood up, moving out of the mother's reach, concentrating on controlling her thoughts. The mother's eyes became needlepoints as she attempted to enter Constance's consciousness, and was blocked.

Neutral, Constance met the mother's gaze.

"I understand you told the peers she didn't discuss her intentions with you," said the Shaper Mother. "Perhaps you were protecting your other. But you can tell me, in confidence. Was it a spur-of-the-moment decision? Or did she plot it in advance?"

Constance had been able to fend off the peers, and the listeners, but the Shaper Mother was in another league. She had no choice but to answer her – the best she could manage was to be discriminating in her choice of words. "After Silence babyfused, she changed. Often, I found her sitting by herself, lost in thought. She wondered why she couldn't raise her own child."

The mother's eyebrows shot up. "Leaving childcare to

sources is irresponsible. These women have no training. Children are our most precious asset – that's why we send them to girlplace for communal rearing. We do it to help our girls reach their potential."

"Silence's baby would have gone to boyplace. She'd never have seen him again."

The mother tapped her mouth, choosing her words. "But when she discontinued, she took away its chance of life. She could have waited till afterwards. But she chose not to."

"Yes."

The Shaper Mother cocked her head to one side, studying Constance. "So if Silence wasn't temporarily insane, she must have been wicked," she suggested.

Constance looked at the floor.

"I see you don't wish to condemn your other, sweet child. Your loyalty does you credit. But Silence was in error. It wouldn't be safe to leave a boy-baby with its source. A bond might develop."

Constance couldn't help herself. "Silence said it's not a baby's fault to be born a boy. Babies are the same, female and male. They don't deserve to be punished for being one or the other."

Incredulous, the mother stood up, grasping the arms of her seat. "Then perhaps it's as well she discontinued. She could have corrupted our sisters. But jumping off the Hope Bridge in broad daylight? Hurling herself over, when innocent sisters were going about their business below it? How excessive!" She toppled back, hand pressed to her chest.

So, thought Constance, the Shaper Mother is prone to shadow-moes, too.

"I am," said the mother. "Inevitably, when you learn to mindmap, you become susceptible. But I guard against moes. Your other's treachery towards Sisterland made one rise up in me. It has passed now, I am composed again."

The Shaper Mother struck Constance as agitated, despite

19

her claims. She had slid the earring out of her ear, and was rubbing furiously at the lobe.

"There is no violence in Sisterland," continued the mother. "That's why Silence's public discontinuation is so damaging. Bad enough that she ended her own life, and that of a child! But the way she went about it is causing anxiety and uncertainty. The shaper cohort is working flat out, reassuring sisters. A deliberate public discontinuation is unheard of!"

"Discontinuations like Silence's probably happen at home, though," said Constance. "They'd be hushed up, wouldn't they?"

A pause developed.

During it, Silence's face floated into Constance's mind. Once met, her other was not easily forgotten. The combination of pale angularity and a reserved manner had made her appear to be austere. But that had been her outer shell. Constance knew Silence had been warm – fully engaged with life. Her discontinuation had been out of character.

When the mother spoke again, her voice was wheedling. "I hope you don't share your other's prejudices. They can be contagious."

"I love Sisterland, mother."

"I'm delighted to hear it, sweet child. Of course, if you had any latent inclination towards unpredictability, you'd never have made it onto shaper training. Obviously, since Silence was accepted onto the signifier programme, its selection procedures must be less scrupulous. They'll need to be overhauled."

"Silence enjoyed installing sigs."

The mother made a dismissive gesture. "Job satisfaction is a given in Sisterland, in any field. It doesn't confer competence, however. Now, Constance, when the time comes for you to babyfuse for Sisterland, I take it you'll accept all of our policies? Without letting your other's exhibitionism corrupt you?"

"I'm not due to go forward as a source for several more years, mother. I'm still in training."

"Come and sit beside me again." The mother patted the stool at her feet, and Constance was obliged to accept the invitation. "Yes, the co-keeper training. That's why I asked to see you. We think it advisable to interrupt it."

"You mean I can leave the programme? I can start work as a thought-shaper?" Constance could hardly believe her luck.

"That would be a waste of your talents, sweet child. In time, we think you could become one of our most effective co-keepers. The work that's being entrusted to this new division matters enormously for Sisterland. As you know, only thirteen memory-keepers are left. A number of them will not see out the decade. Already, more than half of our dear ones are too frail to travel."

Constance nodded. Increasingly, long-distance memory-keeping was being used – she had sat in on some of the sessions. But research showed that everything, from shaping to memory-keeping, achieved better results in person. There was no substitute for Togethertime. The solution was for thirteen young shapers to be trained up as co-keepers, eventually replacing the original memory-keepers.

It was impressed on the co-keepers that theirs was an anointed position. When all of the keepers were gone, they would be responsible for feeding the flames of memory. With a key difference. Instead of simply passing on memories, as supplied by the keepers, they would construct memories. New data about the past, new insights, new interpretations. As supplied by the Nine.

Sometimes, keepers' memories differed. Now, they would be smoothed into consistency. Muddled memories would be eradicated. It was this aspect of the strategy which troubled Constance.

"Memories are too important to allow random versions to confuse our sisters. We need uniformity of thinking." The

Shaper Mother had mindmapped her.

"But won't that create a uniform society, mother?"

"You might imagine so. But what it actually fosters is a calm society founded on agreement. Serenity allows us to flourish. It ensures our natural diligence is not disrupted, or diverted into counter-productive goals. Conflicting memories cause tangled thoughts, and those are as damaging as unregulated moes. You do see that, don't you, Constance?"

"Of course, mother. Forgive me, I'm just a little edgy. Since Silence."

"It's natural. I dare say we all need a few sharp edges. Without them, there'd be no stars. But you must strive for composure, as I do."

"I will, mother. I do."

"I had a look at your moe chart – you absorbed a U yesterday. Admirable choice. But you're strikingly liable to shadow-moe. Taking moes increases that tendency."

Constance felt rebuked, at which the mother patted her shoulder.

"Each one of our co-keeper trainees has this predisposition: it's why you were selected. But none, I think, with the charge you possess." Just then, a bell pinged. "Covenant Time already." The mother stood up.

Modesty entered, and took the mother's hand. Both extended a hand to Constance, and the three formed a circle. The mother's grip was strong, the skin dry. Her rings chafed at Constance, whose hand felt subsumed by the mother's. She looked away, to Modesty's child-sized hand, noticing the intricate henna patterns stencilled on its back. In unison, they chanted, "*Not the self but the State, not me but US. To the greater good: to universal sisterhood.*"

The mother cleared her throat. "See to that temporary permit we discussed, Modesty. She's a suitable candidate."

Modesty threw Constance a glance bubbling with curiosity, before withdrawing.

Alone again with Constance, the mother retrieved the threads of their conversation.

"Shadow-moe ability is essential to your work. A co-keeper must empathise on a profoundly intimate level with the keeper she's destined to replace. Moe acts as a bridge between minds. But you've been left vulnerable by the Silence situation. You need to take a step back. We intend you to become a co-keeper, but not yet. I know it's disappointing, but think of it as a pause, not a cessation. We need to be certain you've recovered from your other's contamination. And taking you off the programme will give you time to concentrate on curbing your shadow-moe tendencies. You must learn to access them only when needed for co-keeping."

"I try not to give way to them, mother."

"Periods of stress can trigger moes. This has been a challenging time for you, sweet child. Nobody is blaming you."

The Shaper Mother's kindness triggered a confession from Constance. "These shadow-moes make me unhappy."

"I should think so. That's why a previous Nine took control of them. I suppose moes provided solutions to problems facing our ancestors: they were gut reactions which allowed them to process information quickly, and respond. Fear, for example, was appropriate when confronted by a predator. But how necessary is it today, in a world without crime or violence? Many of these moes are obsolete now. Feelings cannot be allowed to dictate behaviour. You must continue to guard against shadow-moeing. Except when you need it for your work."

"I will, mother. But what work am I to do, if I'm off the co-keeper programme?"

The Shaper Mother clasped her hands together, eyes sparkling. "How fortunate you are, Constance. There's something else you can do for Sisterland, and yourself. Something that will distance you from Silence's taint.

Babyfusion! It's time to offer yourself as a source." As an afterthought, she tacked on, "If you're willing."

Constance was surprised. "I'm two years below the minimum age to apply for a licence. Wouldn't it be against the rules?"

"Rules can be suspended." The mother's tone was careless. "In exceptional circumstances, I mean."

Beloved's Pearls taught that everyone was subject to the same set of rules – even the Nine.

Forgetting herself, Constance raised her eyes to stare.

The winning smile sprang open. "Our plan has symmetry, you see. Your baby will replace the life your other was carrying."

"Yes, mother."

"Splendid. Your mating licence will be fast-tracked."

Fast-tracking: another suspension of the rules. The mother gave a tiny shrug.

Constance bowed, preparing to withdraw.

The Shaper Mother held up a hand, palm outward. "Coincidentally, sweet child, I can tell you're ovulating. Go to matingplace tonight."

"But the licence won't be through by then, surely? Even if it's speeded up?"

"I have discretion to award a temporary permit – Modesty should have uploaded it to your sig by now. See? There it is already."

Constance's gaze flew to her sig. The pinkification of the φ symbol had happened already, changing from black to a disturbingly insistent shade of pink. It was official. She was licensed to attempt babyfusion. But she wasn't ready! "I haven't been briefed on mating, mother. I'm not sure what to do."

"The Mating Board runs regular seminars. Ask Modesty for a list of them."

"But you said to go tonight. There won't be time. Shouldn't

I wait until after my briefing?"

The Shaper Mother frowned. "Why delay? What happens during mating is somewhat humiliating, I admit. But the end is what counts. Not the process. The Mating Board has compiled a fact file – we'll have that sent through to your comtel. Modesty will take care of it. And if you're still unclear on anything, ask the Mating Mother. She'll answer any questions before you mate." The Shaper Mother stood. "Babyfuse quickly, if you can. It's the ultimate act of sisterdom." In benediction, she laid both hands on top of Constance's head. "Know that Sisterland cherishes you, Constance. Always, at all times, we want what's best for you."

The door curled open, and Constance stumbled towards it.

Modesty was waiting on the other side. "Your mating permit's been uploaded. Some people have all the luck."

"I don't suppose there's time for me to squeeze in one of those Mating Board seminars?"

"No, I checked already. There won't be another session till Friday. But I've sent you its handout. *Helpful Hints for Himtime*." Modesty winked. "Informative little guide."

Constance tapped her comtel, and a header with the Mating Board's sleeping baby logo appeared.

Congratulations, sister! she read.

She skimmed the screen on to the next page.

You've been selected to attempt babyfusion!

Sisterland is proud of you!

She flicked forward.

It requires Himtime duties.

Below, you'll find diagrams. These can be linked to your entscreen for moving pictures. First, a list of frequently asked questions.

Again, Constance moved the screen.

Will it hurt?

Some discomfort can be expected the first time, but you

will be given a medicinal drink to minimise it.

Will I bleed?

The drink prevents bleeding.

Constance kept scrolling.

Who chooses the man?

The Mating Mother.

Can a woman refuse a man?

Of course.

She looked up, to find Modesty watching her. "Himtime! It sounds so masculine!"

"Don't worry, Constance, the mating urge will take over."

"The mating urge?"

"It's all in there. Just keep reading."

"I still don't understand why the mother wants me to do this. I haven't been sent for vetting – either physical or psychological."

"I guess the rules don't apply to you."

"I never knew rules were so flexible, Modesty."

"Welcome to the real world, sister."

Chapter 4

Constance had never been inside matingplace. But she had a fair idea of what to expect. Even before reading the *Himtime* file. After Silence had gone forward for babyfusion, she had told Constance what happened during mating. It had sounded repellent, and Constance had said so. But Silence had disagreed: mating was forceful, she had said, but not in an unpleasant way. The act of creation took energy, that was all. A hint of a smile had played on her lips, and Constance had felt excluded. Quickly, Silence had reassured her that it wasn't real intimacy – just a bodily function. Still, Constance had puzzled over that ghost of a smile.

Thanks to Silence, Constance knew things not included in the *Himtime* guide. That she wouldn't be expected to hold hands with a man, as she did with Silence. Nor would she lay her head on his shoulder, as she did with Silence. There would be no whispered words of affection. No leaving one another small gifts to find. No putting their arms about each other, swapping secrets. No sharing a pop-up bed all night long, waking to the sound of one another's breathing.

In fact, she wouldn't share any real closeness with this man selected for her by the Mating Mother. But she was required to spend time alone, in private, with him. And this would be a first. Interfacing with men happened at a superficial level: watching from a distance as they laboured at jobs demanding mindless repetition – never more than three together because men were not allowed to congregate.

Silence had told her mating took place in near-darkness, and that the man sweated and grunted during it. Certainly, those noises were unpleasant, she said, but other aspects of the procedure were less so. For example, while their bodies were harder than a woman's, the sensation was not unattractive. Firm flesh felt agreeable against a woman's body, according to Silence. It provided a sense of safety, which was irrational, and must be a genetic reflex. She had stroked Constance's hair, describing the mating that had led to her babyfusion. Telling her she would understand when her time came.

But Constance's time was already there. And it was too soon.

As she returned to the special projects floor, the progress-monitor beckoned to her.

Tone clipped, Patience said, "The Shaper Mother has sent instructions to take you off the co-keeper programme temporarily."

"Yes, sister."

"Such a waste of a place. There'll only be twelve co-keepers now, when we planned for thirteen. Speaking of waste, your records show you haven't vacated the unit you shared with your other. Is there any reason for the delay?"

"I haven't been allocated anywhere else to live." It was impossible to find accommodation in Harmony except through official channels.

Patience tutted. "How remiss of the unit-allocators. It's inefficient to have one person living in a twoser. Contact them before you leave, and make sure they understand yours is ready to be reassigned."

"Yes, sister."

Patience gave her a narrow look. "The mother has requested a oneser for you in the same zone. I see you live by the riverfront, in Oblong. Onesers are rarer than rainbows in that part of Harmony. I must say, the mother is taking a remarkable interest in your welfare. Run along, Constance. *Don't delay, obey!*"

It was a line from the obedience song all Sisterlanders learned at girlplace.

Don't fight, do right!
Don't wallow, follow!
Don't delay, obey!

Constance made contact with the unit-allocators at once, and was told she'd be moved out within the week. Then she left Shaperhaus, and stood for a few moments in Eternity Square, wondering where to go. A packing session at home didn't appeal. Knowing she had to move out of her twoser left an aftertaste in her mouth. The twoser connected her to Silence, who was present in every corner. Still, maybe it was for the best. There were days when she didn't want to think about Silence.

It was a boon to be allowed to stay by the riverfront, she reminded herself. Constance found it therapeutic to stare into that unhurried mass of water, or pace the riverbank, alert for the swivel of fish. Beloved had urged Sisterlanders to model themselves on the river's harmonious interaction with the urban environment. "The river doesn't go through obstacles, it goes round them. It doesn't crash through barriers, it smooths them away," she had said, in a landmark speech learned off by heart by every young Sisterlander.

Once, stately herons were common among the reeds, but no herons had been spotted by the river for decades. It was rare to see any wild birds in Harmony. Sometimes, flocks were sighted in the sky, migrating across Sisterland, and people rushed outside to marvel at them. Nobody knew where they originated, or where they were destined. They never seemed inclined to land. Some sisters kept caged birds, but they didn't last long – and they never sang.

Constance stuck her hands in her pockets, resentful at being confronted by two disagreeable prospects at once: moving and mating. She wished she had asked Silence more about mating. Like whether it would make her feel physically sick. That question wasn't included in the Mating Board's frequently-asked list. The authorities seemed not to realise that Constance had no-one to discuss this with. Maybe they didn't care.

With time on her hands before going to matingplace that night, she decided to pay a visit to her source. She had mated with a man – Constance was the result – and must have some guidance to offer.

Constance found Devotion 2723 perched on a ladder, attending to her window boxes. They were planted with heathers in muted tones of lavender and coral – she never varied what she grew, and was scrupulous about keeping the soil acidic and taking regular pH readings. Once, Devotion had made a brush from her heather, sweeping out the twoser with it. When Constance had asked why, she had said she had taken an N and a nostalgic memory had been restored to her: her own source sweeping with a heather brush. "Sometimes we don't know why we do things, but we feel compelled to do them anyway," Devotion had said.

Constance remembered those words as she watched Devotion three floors above. She wore a tool-belt round her front, its pockets full of gardening equipment. Constance noticed the innate grace with which her source worked – fingers floating through the air, the way underwater plants waved through the river.

"Shouldn't someone hold that ladder?" Constance called out.

Devotion peered down. "Constance! What a pleasant surprise. I've wedged a couple of rocks against the legs – I couldn't wait for Goodwill to come home."

Constance held the ends of the ladder anyway, while Devotion descended.

"Making time for Togethertime, ladybird?" There was a hint of reproof – Constance's visits were sporadic.

Constance ignored it. In greeting, she raised both hands, palms outwards, and Devotion responded by pressing hers against her daughter's.

"Shall I help you put away the ladder?"

"Leave it for now, I've more to do later. Come inside for some of my setting-sun wine."

Devotion dropped the weeds in her pocket into a mulch bin, and led the way upstairs. Once indoors, both women removed their skins, and siphoned off the moisture on their clothes with a vac-pump. Devotion looked askance at the careless way Constance set aside her skin.

"Don't leave your skin on the window-seat, ladybird. You might sit on it. I'll find a spare container." She left the room.

Constance picked up her skin which was made from plant extracts. She knew she was lucky to have it, rather than one of the cheaper, non-organic versions where the weave was visible. But sometimes it felt like a burden because it would take her years to work off the debt.

Devotion returned with a shell-holder lined in silk, and Constance placed her skin inside it.

"I wish I had your curls, Devotion."

"I wish I had your cheekbones."

"You always say that." Constance smiled. "Your source had curls, didn't she?"

"You know she did. You used to call her the Curly Lady when you were small."

"So I suppose my bony face –"

"More than compensates for any lack of curls."

"Must be down to my father."

Devotion poured honeyed wine into two liqueur glasses. "You know we don't have fathers. Only the source matters."

"Half of me comes from him."

"Just the biological matter."

"Do I look like him?"

"I never saw his entire face. I was only with him five times, over the course of a month. I babyfused, and there was no need to be with him again."

Constance digested this. "Was it horrible?"

"How could anything leading to you be horrible?"

"You were lucky to babyfuse in your first month. That's rare – and becoming more unusual by the year. Speaking of which, I've been –"

"Never mind all that, ladybird." Devotion pushed a glass into Constance's hand, and clinked another against it. "To universal sisterhood!"

"Universal sisterhood," agreed Constance. She finished the wine in one swallow, ready to persist with her questions. Devotion always changed the subject when mating was mentioned.

"Steady on, ladybird."

"These glasses are the size of egg-cups."

"My wine's potent."

"I need it. It's been a weird day already, and it's still got a long, long way to go."

"A top-up, and that's your lot. I don't have any food to offset it, apart from cosmos bites, and I know you don't like them. Quite right, too. Zero fat or not, I don't approve. But Goodwill has a weakness for them." She glooped another dollop into Constance's glass.

Devotion was a thought-hatcher, a responsible job but restful, in its way. Unruffled sisters were suited to it. Hatchers were required to bring batches of approved thoughts to fruition. But it was thought-crafters who devised the thoughts, and theirs was the more gruelling task. Devotion's other, Goodwill 824, was a thought-crafter.

Goodwill wasn't Constance's favourite person: she always

gave the impression of wanting more from Constance than she was prepared to give. Constance's behaviour towards Goodwill was sometimes studded with instances of low-level antipathy, because Devotion and Goodwill's affection for each another made her feel as if they were a self-contained unit. Meanwhile, she was an outsider with her nose pressed to the window of their life. The companionship she had experienced with Silence, with all its mutual regard, couldn't compare to the warmth of the bond between Devotion and Goodwill.

However, Constance accepted Goodwill was a relative, of sorts, in a world where they were not commonplace. A woman became a source only once, unless her child was a boy-man – in which case she was permitted to try again. No woman could keep her son. Sons couldn't be held, even for an instant, before being taken away, although some sources did manage to see their faces.

"Would you have liked another child?" Constance asked.

"Nobody has sisters unless they're a twin. But we're all sisters in Sisterland."

Constance noticed how Devotion presumed she meant another girl-baby, because who would want a boy?

Constance stood and prowled about. "How much did it hurt?"

"What?"

"Mating."

"It was unpleasant rather than painful. But I knew Goodwill was waiting here at home for me, and she'd understand exactly what I'd gone through. She'd done it already, without managing to babyfuse – a sacrifice in vain. Poor Goodwill. But I ended up with you for my trouble. So it was worth it all."

"Was it really a lot of trouble, Devotion? Would you have preferred not to mate? Or weren't you a little curious, maybe, about what it would be like?"

"All these questions! It's so long ago, I can hardly

remember. I do know I was relieved at achieving babyfusion so quickly. Now, let's have no more about mating. It's a distasteful subject, and you won't have to bother with it for a few years yet."

"Well, as a matter of fact –"

But Devotion wasn't listening. "Did I tell you we have a new Hatcher Mother? The previous one retired. She was worn out, bless her heart."

Constance picked up her glass, twirling the fragile stem between her fingers.

"You look as if the weight of the world is resting on your shoulders, ladybird."

Constance shook herself. "Just work problems."

"How's life on this top-secret course at Shaperhaus?"

"Top-secret. How's hatching?"

"I've been hatching some thoughts about civic duty for girlplace. I finished up yesterday – I'm quite pleased with the results. I concentrated on making them elevating but not priggish. It's a balancing act."

"Are they being transferred to the students now?"

"I expect so. Not my responsibility any more. I must say, I'm a little weary. Still, I have today and tomorrow off to look after my herbs and heathers, and play music. That should reboot me. Then it's back to the hatchery."

"For more civic duty thoughts?"

"I could be assigned to anything. Now, never mind me, you look peaky. Stay and eat with us? I'd like to make sure you have a nourishing meal. I know you mostly go to eat-easies."

"Eat-easy food is just as nutritious as a dine-all's. After all, the menus in both are monitored."

"Quite right, too. But it's always spicy dishes in eat-easies. Too much spice can't be healthy. Come on, Constance, I'm not asking for the moon. Just lunch with my daughter."

"All right. There's something I must do later, though. I'm under instructions to –"

Devotion was at the contact console, however, pressing the icon which connected her twoser to the dine-all in the complex. "This is Yellow B. We'll be three for lunch instead of two. My daughter's joining us. What's on the menu? Delicious. See you at the usual time." She turned back to Constance. "They have twiced-up pie – that was always your favourite as a little girl. Goodwill should be back from work soon. You don't mind waiting?"

Constance made a non-committal gesture.

"She's always asking for news of you."

"I do have some news, as it happens. I've been fast-tracked for babyfusion."

"Well, that certainly explains all the questions. But I must admit, I'm surprised." Devotion pushed her hair back from her face. "Why would they do such a thing? And what about your top-secret course? You're still in the middle of it."

"I'm off the course. Temporarily, anyway. Sisterland's decided my mission is to babyfuse. Or try to."

"How very curious. Still, I'm sure your mother has her reasons." Devotion brightened. "It's news that'll please Goodwill. She likes babies. Of course, there are no guarantees."

"How about you? Are you pleased?"

"You're a little young, but you may as well get it over with. Your mother wouldn't have licensed you if you weren't ready for the responsibility. Maybe it's just what you need."

A sour taste gushed up to coat Constance's tongue. "Maybe the mothers only care about what Sisterland needs."

Devotion frowned. When she spoke again, her tone was brisk. "I wonder where Goodwill can have got to? She's too committed to that job for her own good."

"But commitment to our work is Sisterland dogma."

"Stop it, ladybird."

Constance sighed, and offered an olive branch. "She's lucky to have you, Devotion. You take wonderful care of her."

"We're lucky to have one another. Lately, you seem to make a point of visiting when she isn't here. Don't think she hasn't noticed."

"I like to talk to you alone sometimes. Goodwill never lets anyone else get a word in edgeways."

"That's not fair."

Constance fidgeted with the crescent-moon charm on a chain round her neck. It was Silence's – she had been wearing it when she discontinued. A peer returned it to Constance afterwards. There had been an intensity to Silence which Constance valued. She should remember how people were drawn to complementary traits in one another, and accept that Goodwill possessed qualities which appealed to Devotion – even if they bypassed Constance.

Unexpectedly, a question bubbled up in her mind. Had she loved Silence? Honesty forced her to admit the truth. Not the way Devotion and Goodwill loved one another. The love Constance felt for Silence had been the moe a student felt for a teacher who took pains with her. She had been flattered when Silence had indicated a desire to other with her. There had been respect. And affection. But what had been between them didn't match what Devotion and Goodwill felt for one another. They were two halves of a whole.

Constance had only to look around Harmony to see that different types of love existed between others: for some there was passion, while for some there was companionship. She would have liked to experience the sort of ardour she observed elsewhere with Silence, but it had never kindled. There had been no clamour inside her at Silence's presence. Wanting to love someone wasn't enough. Love could not be summoned at will. Even Sisterland's scientists had stopped trying to manipulate it.

"Goodwill is fond of you, Constance," said Devotion. "Because of me. But for your own sake, as well. Try to appreciate her." She squeezed in beside her daughter on the window seat. "She's known you all your life,. She takes such trouble over those handmade birthday cards she paints for you every year."

"I like them," Constance conceded.

"She was offered the opportunity to switch to thought-mending recently. It would have been a sensible move – it's less pressurised. But she said she had no appetite for it."

"I don't blame her." Constance shuddered.

"It's necessary work. Someone has to fix all those wrong or broken thoughts – they're like a disease, they hurt the thinker. Repairing cracked thoughts is a humane act."

"But what if they're just different thoughts, not damaged ones? What if this is about control rather than compassion? Besides, if everyone sticks to safe, authorised thoughts, we might never get exciting, break-through thoughts to help us make progress."

"What progress? Sisterland is a paradise."

"A paradise? When we're told what to work at. Where to live. What to eat. We're even told when to mate."

"You're fault-finding for the sake of it. All of us love our work. And there's always a choice of menu in the dine-all."

"Yes, and it's always wholesome. Haven't you ever wanted to cook your own meal?"

"Certainly not! It's time-consuming drudge work. Constance, I'm concerned by your attitude. You must watch out for negativity. If you're not careful, you'll tip over into a downward spiral. You have a responsibility to think positive thoughts – we all do."

"But positivity can be monotonous and monochrome, Devotion."

"Stop this at once, ladybird! I won't listen to another word. Oh dear, I blame myself. I shouldn't have given you that second glass of wine." Devotion knotted her hands. "I wish Goodwill was here, she'd know what to say. This is about Silence, isn't it? What happened was ghastly. I know you looked up to her – she had so many gifts. Even if she had trouble coping. It's too bad that wasn't spotted sooner. The thought-menders could have recalibrated her mind. It would have been better for Silence, and better for you. It was a mistake to let you have such a young other. Best practice calls for at least a twenty-year age-gap."

"There was more than a decade between us. She had experience I could draw on. Besides, we wanted to be others. It was our choice."

"It can't be all about compatibility. It has to be about suitability, too. The senior other has duties towards the younger one: she's meant to guide her, and help her grow. How is throwing yourself off a bridge the act of a responsible mentor?"

Suppressed moe quivered between them, threatening to break through.

A door opened. Two heads swivelled towards Goodwill 524.

"Why, Constance, how lovely to see you!" She crossed the room and pressed her palms against the younger woman's, before tugging off her skin.

"Don't throw your skin on the chair, Goodwill, it'll get knocked. Here." Devotion held out a lacquer container.

Goodwill dropped in her skin, and Devotion rearranged it.

Goodwill started chattering, unconscious of the brittle atmosphere. Despite being a thought-crafter, she was devoid of any capacity to pick up on tension. Her skills were saved for the workplace. "I'm starving. I don't suppose you know what's on the menu, Devotion?"

"Twiced-up pie."

"Yummy. Devotion always lets me have some of hers, Constance. No wonder I'm so well-upholstered." Her laugh boomed. "I must have a cosmos bite to keep me going." She disappeared round the corner, towards the food box, returning with a bulky bag. "Think I'll have a triangular-shaped one – I always feel fuller after the triangles. No point in asking either of you to join me, I suppose. You gals don't have my sweet tooth. Though you could use a few cosmos bites, Constance – you're a bag of bones. And my gorgeous Devotion isn't much better." She squeezed her other's shoulder, and Devotion laid a hand on top of hers. "A bird flew into a window in the laundry block," Goodwill continued. "There's a dreadful mess outside."

Caged birds which managed to escape were invariably confused by the mirrored walls on buildings, and crashed almost as soon as they took to the air. Their taste of freedom was short. Yet life in a cage was brief, too. Constance had never been able to bring herself to own a bird. Once, Devotion had tried to buy a pair of doves as a gift for Goodwill, but she had refused point blank to accept them. At least she had that in common with Constance.

"Blood and feathers all over the ground," Goodwill was saying.

Constance thought about what must have happened to Silence when she hit the ground. She never saw her other's remains. The peers wouldn't let her. But it didn't stop her imagining how she looked. Constance swallowed. Goodwill and Devotion were swapping news, their words sounding fuzzy in her ears.

Constance stood up. "I need to go home."

"What about lunch?" asked Devotion.

"Not hungry."

"You have to eat, Constance."

"I'll pick up something later at an easy."

Constance's legs were heavy, carrying her downstairs. Skirting round the side of the laundry block, she saw a man clearing up the debris. Out of the corner of his eye, he noticed her looking at him, and his posture became deferential while his movements speeded up. She averted her gaze, reluctant to see bloodstains.

Near the Buzz station, Goodwill caught up with her.

"Devotion's just told me. And you have no other to talk it over with. I know I'm a poor substitute for Silence. But if you have any questions, I'd be glad to answer them, Constance."

"It's OK. The Mating Board's compiled a guide. I know what to expect. Everything you never knew you wanted to know about Himtime is in there. But thanks."

"Is it still the rule you go to the nearest matingplace in your area? To avoid cherrypicking?"

Constance nodded. "I'm due at the Tower."

"I know the Mating Mother there. She's well regarded. She'll look after you. Are you certain there's nothing you'd like to ask me?"

Constance shook her head, unwilling to admit that what really troubled her about trying for babyfusion was the aftermath – how she might react. Imagine if she responded like Silence. What if she, too, felt compelled to climb up a Buzz viaduct and fling herself off?

"Good luck, my dear," said Goodwill.

She hugged Constance and, for once, Constance didn't pull away.

Chapter 5

On the Buzz home, Constance decided to buy an ovu-pen. Silence had used one, so Constance was familiar with the device. She hoped she might not be ovulating yet – maybe she had wriggle-room to wait a night or two. It didn't seem too extravagant a wish. There was a medshop near her stop – she'd go there.

The medshop had a queue but Constance didn't mind waiting. Through the window, she watched a sister in Harmony Parks' livery polish the stones marking out the contours of a flowerbed.

After a few moments, a girl came to stand behind her.

"Excuse me, sister, is this where I can get an ovu-pen?"

"I hope so. That's what I'm waiting for."

"I've never used one. This is my first time at matingplace."

"Me too," said Constance.

The girl stepped closer. "If only we didn't have to do it this way. I wish we could go back to artificial insemination."

"It wasn't working. Babyfusion figures were falling too fast."

"So my other keeps reminding me. We have to think about the greater good. She says a woman and a meet actually doing it in real time doubles the success rates." She swallowed.

"And if that's not bad enough, I heard they'd prefer us to have boy-babies rather than girls. Something to do with their stupid stats. Still, *Mustn't Grumble*." She quoted from *Beloved's Pearls*.

"Can I help you, sister?" asked the medshop server.

Constance smiled at the girl, and turned away. "An ovu-pen, please."

"Scan in your sig."

Constance held up the back of her wrist to the console, and the pinkified φ symbol began to tremble. "A three-month permit has been uploaded to your account. You'll need to apply for a full licence if you continue to seek babyfusion after the period elapses. User instructions are inside the ovu-pen." She dropped one into a bag. "A temporary permit is extremely rare. You're fortunate."

Constance didn't feel fortunate. "How many els, please?"

"No charge. You're doing this for Sisterland."

Back in her twoser, the ovu-pen confirmed that Constance was ovulating. Just as the Shaper Mother had said. No help for it but to present herself at matingplace. She could always treat it as a trial run, and bail out if she couldn't go through with it tonight. Some women balked at the first attempt, according to the *Himtime* handout. It was forgivable, if a little weak-willed.

She remembered the girl in the medshop. She'd been right – boy-babies were preferable currently. Silence had told her so. Male numbers were dropping year on year, with the ratio 80:20 in women's favour. To turn the tide, studies into interventions to stimulate male births were being carried out. But their results had not been made public.

The extent of the population imbalance would not have been known generally, except for a comtel malfunction which transmitted it to everyone in the second city, Righteous, Sisterland's most southerly metropolis, in Grey Disjoint. In turn, they told their Harmony sisters, in the middle of Sisterland, in Green Hyperreal. Who told their sisters in the northern city of Steadfast, in Brown Convolution. And so on. For damage limitation, the Nine sent out shapers, whose silkenspeak patter focused on roosters and broods of hens. "Look at the animal kingdom. The most economically efficient communities have a large number of females and a few males," they said. "This is an evolutionary stable strategy." In the meantime, sperm was frozen. Yet despite the man shortage, and despite being told it was a selfless act to give birth to a boy-man, Sisterlanders continued to prefer daughters.

Constance showered, and patted transcendent gel over her face to protect it from drying out under her skin. Otherwise, there was a risk of faces becoming spongy. You saw it occasionally in forgetful sisters, but they only had themselves to blame. Next, she fell to considering which set of tunic and leggings to wear. Dresses were worn for ceremonial occasions, but she didn't put mating in that bracket. She supposed her outfit ought to be something that wouldn't get spoiled. At the thought of how it might get stained, she felt damp and overheated. But the obedience habit asserted itself, and she dressed quickly, pulling on her favourite boots – a long pair in stretchy mesh. Without stopping to check her appearance, she caught up her skin and left the twoser.

As she walked along, she stroked Silence's moon charm for luck. It kept her company on the pavement decorated with seahorses and other fish that led to the Tower. And here she was already. A metal arm extended from the building, from which dangled a sign shaped like a castle. She supposed it was intended to appear inviting. The dome-shaped door opened, side-to-side in the old-fashioned way, and a woman drifted out into the night air. She looked dazed. An older woman stepped out from the doorway opposite, where she had been waiting, and led her away.

The door was still swinging on its hinges when Constance entered. Inside stood a young woman in the domino-checked tabard and tights of a medieval page.

"Good evening, sister. Welcome to the Tower. I'm Unity, your greeter. Identify yourself, please."

"Constance 500."

She consulted a screen. "We've been expecting you. Please sig in."

Constance raised her hand, and the pinkified symbol on her inner wrist throbbed and became lambent. The greeter swiped an icon on the screen, and another woman approached, also in that anachronistic black-and-white uniform.

"This is our sister's first time – make sure the Mating Mother knows," said Unity. She turned back to Constance. "Be fertile, sister."

The second woman led her along a hallway, as far as an imposing double staircase. Flurries of chatter and laughter gusted out from the right. Taken aback by the noise, uncharacteristic in Sisterland, Constance looked left – an inviting area of quiet.

But the attendant shook her head. "You don't go there till later."

"Is that where it happens?" asked Constance.

"Wait and see." She pushed a button on the wall by the stairs, and a drawer slid out. It was blocked off into compartments, most of them containing a skin. "Check in your skin, please." Constance unclasped it. "You'll need to collect the skin again when you proceed to the mating floor. This way, sister. Here's the readying room."

She pointed right, and Constance found herself on the threshold of an ornate reception room. What she saw dazzled her. It resembled the interior of a castle, in so far as she could judge by pictures in books. Ahead of her was a sunken room, three steps leading down into a dramatic space. Candles glowed from sconces set high on walls made from slabs of stone, while gargoyles in alcoves grimaced, leered and licked their lips. Tapestries depicted flower-strewn meadows and lush orchards, some with unicorns, others with lions or stags. In paintings with gilded frames there were maidens in rooms similar to the one where Constance stood, open-mouthed. They wore flowing gowns and had blossoms threaded through their hair. Some strummed musical instruments, while others were dancing, or playing games. Pewter statues of mythical beasts reared up around the room, and earthenware pots held a profusion of tall flowers she couldn't identify. Their scent was intoxicating – perhaps they were a newly manufactured species. From the ceiling was suspended a blazing candelabra and, against one wall, a fire roared in a massive fireplace.

It was the fire which restored Constance to her senses. She knew it could not possibly be authentic, because fire had been designated unsafe and banned.

Down the centre of the room stretched a dining table laden with food to suit all palates. There were nasturtium pasties, spring quiches, hyacinth flans and full moon rolls, with fruit, cheese and nuts for anyone preferring to nibble. Women were gathered by the table, grazing and chattering. Many held heavy glass goblets, and pages moved about replenishing them.

But what caught Constance's attention was the magnificent dresses of the women, similar to those in the paintings: sleeves falling to a point below their knees and hems dragging on the rushes covering the floor.

There were other women in leggings, like Constance, and they were clustered round a wooden chest, out of which spilled an array of gowns in jewel shades. She drew closer, watching while each woman made her choice, fondling the luxurious materials. One passed nearby holding a moss-green length of cloth, and Constance couldn't help herself touching its sleeve. The woman smiled at her, glittering with excitement. Why, it really was velvet! Constance had expected some synthetic alternative. Her eyes flicked back to the chest. Then those glorious sweeps of material must really be satin, silk and brocade, rather than a wipe-clean facsimile. She tracked the woman with the velvet dress over her arm. Half a floor above, a minstrels' gallery ran the length of the room. It had a series of wood-panelled alcoves. She saw the woman enter one, and emerge a few minutes later in the gown.

"Welcome. I'm the Tower's Mating Mother." A diminutive woman, hips almost as narrow as her waist, appeared in front of Constance. Her voice reminded Constance of reeds sighing – she had to bend forward to hear above the hubbub.

Like her staff, the Mating Mother wore black and white, but it wasn't a uniform. Or maybe it was, in its way. She had on a gown similar to those in the chest, edged in white fur, with a train that fell from her shoulders and rippled on the ground behind her. Constance had never seen anything so sumptuous. Most astonishing of all, however, was her waist-length black hair. Constance couldn't take her eyes off it. Hadn't Beloved urged short hair, for practical reasons? Somehow, over time, it had become mandatory. She supposed it must be a wig, a perk restricted to high-ranking sisters. The Mating Mother ran a hand over her waterfall of hair, smoothing it. Constance was fascinated: how genuine it looked.

The Mating Mother beckoned to draw her apart from the women noisily handling gowns. As she moved, a ring of keys at her waist chimed. They caught Constance's attention: keys were a relic of the PS era, and only seen in museum display cases. Come to think of it, being in matingplace was almost like walking about in a museum.

"It's more like being in the theatre," the Mating Mother corrected her.

Constance jumped. She should remember she wasn't just

dealing with a petite woman in elaborate costume, but a mother, who must therefore be skilled at mindmapping. She ought to be careful about the direction of her thoughts.

"No need," said the Mating Mother. "You're among friends. The Sisterland cherishes you, Constance, and never more so than at this special time."

"Thank you, mother. What did you mean by 'like being in the theatre'?"

"I've been told you didn't have a chance to go to a mating seminar. It's explained there. You see, mating happens within a context which transcends normal life. It's like a performance, and the pageantry of the readying room helps to prepare you for that. That's why we chose this setting: because we know our sisters are drawn to these obsolete trappings, even though they have no place in their daily lives. We provide them to allow you to enjoy the fantasy, but also to see it for what it is."

"You said a performance, mother. Will I be watched?"

"Great Beloved, no! It's a performance in so far as it's not reality. In the sense of a mental wall between you and the meet. Even though both of you engage in the mating, it won't be an authentic encounter. There's no meaningful communication between you. He's just another part of the ritual. A prop, if you like. You do see that, don't you?"

"Yes, mother."

"Excellent. The setting is undeniably extravagant," the Mating Mother allowed her eyes to roam about her kingdom, an amused look on her face, "but it serves an additional function. It helps to rouse certain atavistic urges necessary to enable mating. Speaking of which, you must have some of our mead."

She clapped her hands. At once, a page carrying a tray approached, and proffered a baroque chalice with two handles to Constance.

"Drink," commanded the tiny woman.

The chalice hung heavy between her hands. "I'm not thirsty."

47

"Drink. It's to help with what comes later."

She sipped. The liquid stroked her throat, and she felt its warmth trickle through her body.

"Drink it all." The mother was observing her.

Costance emptied the chalice. It was as if liquid velvet was slipping along her insides. The mead seemed to pool in the area above her thighs, causing her muscles to relax. How soothing it was. But the sensation intensified, and released something else in her. A craving – for what, she didn't know.

"Divine, isn't it? The first time is always the best."

Constance ran her forefinger inside the chalice, and licked a drop of liquid from it. "I don't mean to be greedy. But do you suppose I could have some more?"

The Mating Mother giggled, a high-pitched sound. "One helping is all it takes to prepare you for mating. You can have wine now, if you wish, while the mating urge swells."

She clapped her hands again, and another attendant advanced with a glass goblet, taking away the chalice. Constance was reluctant to see it go.

"And now, relax. Mingle if you wish, have something to eat."

As she spoke, the Mating Mother was steering Constance towards the table. Someone put an empty plate in her hand, but she was too distracted by the sights and sounds to eat.

"Not hungry? Choose a gown instead," suggested the Mating Mother.

"May I ask you a question, mother?"

"I'm sure you have all sorts of questions, since it's your first time."

"It's about the keys you carry. Why?"

She jangled the ring at her waist. "All part of the Gothic castle fantasy."

"Whose fantasy?"

"Why, yours. You sisters deemed suitable for mating. We researched your daydreams – a sizeable proportion of you have a fancy for castle life. You young sisters latched onto it during an entscreen series about architecture through the ages, repeated for several seasons due to popular demand. Ridiculously impractical, of course. But we thought, why not? It's our way of thanking you for playing your part in populating Sisterland. These keys are inefficient compared with the modern alternative. Still, they do what's intended: they keep the meets where we want them till needed for mating. Excuse me now, I must run through my list. I need to pick out a suitable specimen for you. Don't forget to exchange your leggings for a dress. It helps to get you in the mood. And a dress is easier – when you're on the mating floor."

Constance expected to shudder, but nothing happened. Instead, she realised that the warmth between her legs had spread to the pit of her stomach. She joined the queue for clothes, and examined the room while she waited. There was something that troubled her about her surroundings, although she couldn't identify it. Perhaps it was the excess. So much abundance was beyond her experience.

When her turn came, the attendant at the chest ran a practised eye over her.

"Either of these should be the right length." In one hand, the page held out a dress with a stand-up collar. Its raw silk khaki skirt split to reveal a bronze underskirt, which echoed the bronze on the sleeves. In her other hand, she had a cobalt-blue gown overlaid with silver netting. "But feel free to rummage about, if you prefer. The dresses have side lacings, so they can be tightened or loosened. You'll find most sizes fit you. Quite practical, for such impractical things."

Constance took the dress with a bronze underskirt, and laid it against her body, utterly beguiled.

The attendant put a hand on her hip, and studied Constance. "Nice. Now try this one."

"Aren't there any mirrors?"

"Upstairs, where you try them on. But if you ask me, the blue looks best."

"All right, I'll take it."

"Come back if you don't like what you see in the mirror," said the attendant. "Oh, and you'll find more suitable footwear upstairs."

In the minstrels' gallery, Constance made her way to an empty alcove, and slipped off her clothes. She stepped into the dress, and tugged at the lacings. When she stood back and checked her reflection in the looking glass, the transformation startled her. How elated she looked! Her cheeks were flushed, her eyes sparkled.

A glance round the alcove, and she spied several pairs of soft-soled pumps. Off came her boots and socks, and she tried on a shoe. Too tight. She tried another. That would do.

Outside, in the gallery, a page was playing a strange string instrument. Constance didn't know its name, but the music was haunting. She leaned over the balustrade to watch four other pages dance a stately gavotte. Skimming the room for somewhere to be inconspicuous, she spotted a bench piled with cushions in a relatively deserted area. She made her way there, almost tripping on the hem of her gown, and sank down on the seat. She closed her eyes, a sensation of wellbeing building inside her as she listened to the music.

"I'm glad to see you looking so relaxed. That's the purpose of the readying room."

Constance opened her eyes. It was the Mating Mother.

"So, can I have my girls fetch you anything else? Or –" she paused, delicate – "are you ready to mate?"

"Right now, mother?"

"Do you need more time to collect yourself?"

"No, time won't change anything. I'm ready now." The sooner she did this, the sooner it would be over.

"Top girl! Let's go. I'll escort you to the mating floor." The Mating Mother caught Constance by both hands, and pulled her to her feet.

Her grip was inexorable.

Chapter 6

Holding her by one hand, the Mating Mother led Constance out of the readying room. At the doorway, Constance looked back, and realised what was odd about it. There were no windows. In fact, she had yet to see a window in the Tower. It delivered privacy: nobody could see in. But nobody could see out, either. This was a self-contained world – not just a castle in Oblong, but a castle in the air.

By the staircase, the Mating Mother pointed to the doorway on the far side of the banisters – the quiet area to which Constance had been drawn on arrival. "That's the respite room. You rest there when it's all over. Though don't worry, it's not really an ordeal. The meets are trained to make themselves agreeable. Which is yours?"

"Sorry?"

"Which skin?"

Constance realised the Mating Mother had opened the drawer by the stairs in which skins had been left.

"You don't want to show your naked face to a man, do you?" The mother tapped her own light-brown cheek.

"Of course not, mother." Constance found her skin and attached it.

"Follow me."

Constance swallowed.

They mounted the stairs, as far as the second floor. Constance copied the way the Mating Mother hitched up the trailing gown with one hand, bunching it to one side. The mother left her train to fend for itself. It rustled, thought Constance, as if it had secrets to share. They went along a wide corridor lit by subdued beams, the walls bare except for a coat of paint. The only echo of the luxury below was a thick-pile carpet which muffled their footsteps, but the pared-back effect was soothing after the tumult of the readying room. It allowed for a transitional stage.

As they passed between lines of wooden doors, Constance said, "It's so quiet. I thought there'd be some noise from behind them."

"Every mating cube is sound-proofed. We like to give our sisters privacy. We also believe in protecting them, of course. Each sister is alone with a meet, but help is always close by."

"How can help be close by if nobody can hear what goes on inside? Could you hear if someone screamed?"

"No, sound doesn't travel out from the cubes. But we wouldn't dream of sending in sisters without protection. I'll let Charity explain. She runs the mating floor."

Halfway along the corridor a door lay ajar. "That's the control hub. It's run by Charity 8521. We lured her here from the biggest matingplace in Righteous."

Constance blinked. People working in Righteous rarely had a chance to transfer to Harmony or Steadfast, or vice versa. "You must have had to pull strings with the Mating Board," she said.

"I did what I had to do. I saw Charity in action and knew she was exactly what the Tower needed." She raised her whispery voice. "Charity, incoming business."

A woman with an unfriendly expression was silhouetted in the doorway. She wore black tights, like the other Tower attendants but, instead of a tabard, her top half was covered with fake chainmail, with a belt crisscrossing her body from shoulder to waist. Against one hip dangled a strap, ending in a metal box about the size of her hand.

"Charity, this is Constance 500."

Shrewd eyes measured Constance. She noticed Constance staring at the piece of equipment, and stroked it. "You like my stifstat?'

"I don't know what it is."

"A necessary precaution is what it is. Shoots an electric shot into the brain, causing temporary paralysis."

Constance stiffened. She was about to register a protest when the Mating Mother intervened.

"History tells us men don't share our views on non-violence. Charity only uses it in exceptional circumstances. All well on the mating floor, Charity?'

While they spoke, Constance managed a glance into the control hub, where a large screen was broken into boxes, showing all the doors along the corridor. In the corner of each box was a purple timer ticking down minutes, while a green light glowed in the middle of the boxes. She was recalled to business at the mention of her name.

"Constance is a first-timer. I'm putting her in Dawn Cube."

"New meet in there," said Charity. "We just took delivery of him. Extremely fit specimen. Outdoors type."

"I know he's a first-timer – that's why I've earmarked him for Constance."

"Isn't that the blind leading the blind?"

"Constance is younger than most of our sisters. I believe they'll be a good match."

"What are those monitors for? To see inside the mating cube?" asked Constance. She still thought she might be watched – no matter what the Mating Mother said.

"Nope. Not allowed. If I had my way, I'd see and hear everything. But the Mating Board won't allow it." Charity's scowl showed her low opinion of that directive. "Ridiculously lenient. Just as silly as parties in readying rooms, if you ask me."

"Our guests need to be spoiled, Charity." Playful, the Mating Mother wagged a finger. "Now, Constance is concerned about her safety. I told her you'd put her mind at rest."

From a pocket, Charity produced a crystal ball with indentations on its surface. "Keep this near you at all times. See the button on this end? It sets off an alarm on the monitor I'll be watching." She pointed towards the boxes inside the control hub. "Those green lights turn orange and start flashing if there's a problem at your end. I'll be at your side in seconds if you need me. If things develop in a way where your control's lost."

"Charity practises how quickly she can get from the hub to a mating cube. She's always trying to beat her own record," said the mother.

"If the meet tries to take away this ball, I'll know at once. I'm going to set it now to memorise your handprint. Here, hold it." Charity passed the ball to Constance, and at her touch it glimmered green for a moment. "Squeeze this ball, and I'll be inside your cube so fast the meet won't have time to lay a finger on you." She caressed her stifstat. "They know what to expect. They've been warned. Remember, you're in charge at all times. Never surrender that, never allow it to be taken from you. Repeat, never allow it to be taken from you. The meet is here to do exactly what you require of him."

"Don't go giving her the heebie-jeebies, Charity. Constance's new to this, remember."

"I'm just preparing her, is all." Charity tapped her comtel. "You want me to message one of my people to come up and take her in?"

"I'll do it. One of your team can collect her afterwards. Follow me, Constance."

Retracing their steps along the corridor, the Mating

Mother said, "It'll be over before you know it. But, after mating, you must lie still for a time to increase its effectiveness."

"Do I send him away while I'm doing that?"

"Great Beloved, no! We can't have unsupervised meets let loose in matingplace. This is a controlled environment. We need oversight to keep our records accurate. He'll stay in the cube – he knows to wait till he's collected."

"Sorry, it's all new to me. I don't want to do the wrong thing."

"Top girl, you're the only person who matters here. Everyone's on your side. Now, when you're through, one of Charity's team will take you back downstairs. She has four girls, Sincerity, Humility, Verity and Purity. They're probably doing drop-offs or I'd introduce you. They bring sisters down to the respite room, leave meets back in their quarters, and so on." The mating mother stopped by a door.

"How will they know I'm through? What if I take longer than the other sisters? Or finish up quicker?"

"Oh – Charity should have said. Show me the alarm ball. Don't touch the button. Unless you need help, of course. If you give the ball a squeeze, it signals that you're ready to leave. You'll be collected, and escorted back to the respite room."

Constance rolled the crystal ball around the palm of her hand. Immediately, a bulky presence emerged from the control hub.

"Everything all right?" called Charity.

"Constance's just testing the ball. She's about to go in now."

Charity disappeared.

"So, Constance, I think that's everything. I'll see you in the respite room afterwards."

"What happens there?"

"You rest. It has hot showers, food and drink. We'll help

you to destress before you go home. Or you can spend the night in the Tower if you choose. Not in a mating cube. No-one ever spends the entire night in one. But the respite room has pop-ups, for those who'd like to sleep among friends. The first time can be an adjustment. We find the more facilities we offer, the higher our babyfusion rates. There's nothing like some old-fashioned tender loving care. Now, one final check." The Mating Mother curled her thumb into the palm, and tapped a sequence of digits onto her comtel. "Yes, Dawn's where you should be. Everything's ready. He's inside, waiting for you."

"One last question, please. How did you choose him for me?"

"I'm not supposed to answer questions about the meets. Naturally, he's in his prime: a healthy specimen, tested and disease-free. You go to him each month, for six months, while you're ovulating. If babyfusion doesn't happen by then, we select a different meet." She selected a key from the ring at her belt, unlocked the door, and pushed it ajar.

Constance looked towards the space. Inside it was dim. Was that the sound of someone breathing?

The Mating Mother extended the hand holding the key towards the gap, indicating that Constance should advance.

"You're not going to lock me in with him?"

"I'm afraid we must. It's to keep him in. Don't worry, you'll be perfectly safe – all our meets are trained, and help is never far away. Charity and her helpers are extremely capable. There's no situation in a mating cube they haven't had to deal with, at one time or another. Remember, you're free to go whenever you like. Otherwise, we'll leave you here with the meet for two hours. That's easily long enough. Oh, one final instruction. Under no circumstances must you ever remove your skin."

"Why not?"

"It's for your own protection: it helps you retain control.

56

Now, the hopes of Sisterland go with you. Be fertile."

Under the implacable sweetness of her smile, Constance entered the room. The door was pulled shut behind her, and she heard metal grind on metal as the key turned in the lock.

Chapter 7

A nightlight drilled into the wall just inside the door kept the room from darkness. Constance could discern the outline of another human standing in a corner. Her eyes flicked round the cube. She was expecting it to be compact, as suggested by its name. It was also utilitarian, its only furniture a standard-issue pop-up bed. She was relieved to notice it was temperature-controlled – otherwise, such a confined space would be claustrophobic. Predictably, it was windowless. A check back towards the door reassured Constance that there was no peephole – at least, not one she could make out.

Her gaze returned to the figure diagonally opposite. Its shape was neither particularly tall nor broad. The posture suggested tension. When her eyes grew accustomed to the gloom, she realised the meet had his hands crossed in front of his chest, and his back pressed into the corner where two walls intersected. Boxed in.

She moved a few paces closer. He cocked his head, listening. She noticed he wasn't wearing a hood, which meant his hair was visible. This was the first unhooded man she'd seen. More of his face was exposed than she was accustomed to, yet there was something hidden about it. Oh, he was wearing a blindfold.

No wonder his position was so defensive. Still, it allowed her to study him openly. Now she stood in front of him. Why, he was naked to the waist, his chest hairless like a woman's. He breathed in – was he smelling her? The movement caused a minor tremble through her flesh. Unexpectedly, a desire to reach out her hand and touch that skin shivered through her. This must be what was meant by the mating urge.

His unsure air gave her confidence. She slipped the alarm into her pocket, and reached up towards the blindfold. He flinched.

"I'm not going to hurt you. I just want to take this off. It doesn't seem right that I can see you and you can't see me." She pulled, but the strip of material didn't budge. "Turn round."

A momentary hesitation before he obeyed her. She tugged at the knot, but could make no headway with it. As she pulled, her fingers brushed against his hair, and she noticed its texture was sleek. The nerve endings on her fingers liked how it felt, but he didn't seem to enjoy her touch. There was an infinitesimal resistance.

His hair was paler than she had supposed was possible. It appeared to be blond. She was taught the colour had all but vanished from the gene pool. A man wouldn't have access to hair technicians – it had to be natural. Longer than hers, it parted in the middle and fell in two waves along his cheeks as far as his collarbone.

He must think she was pawing at him. Her hand fell away from the blindfold.

"Do you always wear your hair down?" she asked.

Nothing.

"Maybe all men wear their hair like that? The hood covers it, so I wouldn't know."

Still nothing. She wondered if he was tongue-tied, or deliberately dumb.

"Why won't you answer me?"

She heard him swallow, a painful sound.

"It's tied back when I work."

"I'm glad you don't think of this as work," she said.

He didn't answer.

"Or maybe you do?"

"When they made me ready for you, they told me to leave it down. They said it was more becoming." His voice was deep and low.

"Who are they?" asked Constance. He shrugged. "I suppose," she answered her own question, "the sisters who pick the men who'll be meets and the women who'll be sources. I don't suppose they asked if you wanted to be a meet, any more than I was consulted." He tensed. "Don't worry, I'm not testing you." She tried his blindfold once more, before conceding defeat.

"Can I turn round again?" he asked. "Or do you prefer me to stand with my back to you?"

"Turn, of course. I was only trying to take off your blindfold."

"It's forbidden for us to look upon one another."

How strange that he was reminding her of the rules – she was meant to be the one in charge.

She studied him. His face had symmetry, which pleased the eye. Even blindfolded and in semi-light, he was handsome. She wasn't supposed to find him so. But beauty formed its own rules. She noticed that his complexion looked surprisingly smooth. Any men she had seen in Harmony had sandpaper flesh, because they didn't wear a skin – none of them earned a wage, to pay for it.

There was something about the way he held his head on one side, in a listening attitude, that moved her. Here was somebody less sure than herself.

"Oh, your feet are bare," she said. He didn't respond. "Did they take away your shoes?"

A slight nod.

She opened her mouth to ask why, and stopped in time. To

make it harder for him to run away, of course. He was here for her convenience. A shadow-moe stirred: something that chimed with shame.

On impulse, she bent down and peeled off her pumps. "There now, my feet are bare, too. Don't you believe me? Feel." He stayed where he was. "Feel."

He knelt. Moving back her heavy skirt, he spread one hand on each foot. A sensation of comfort travelled up Constance's body. She closed her eyes, luxuriating.

After a few moments, he asked, "Do you wish me to continue holding your feet?"

As if caught doing something amiss, her eyes snapped open. "I – no – as you choose. I just wanted you to understand that we're the same."

"But we're not. You're a woman and I'm a man."

"Yes, of course." What was wrong with her? She was behaving in a ridiculous fashion. Perhaps even dangerously. Where was the alarm? She put a hand in the pocket in her dress, and wrapped her fingers about the ball.

"Does this give you pleasure? I've been instructed to do what satisfies you."

"Who said that?"

"The woman they call the Mating Mother."

"Did you meet any of the others? Charity, and her team?"

"I don't know them by name."

"Can't you read it from the sig? Or are you always kept blindfolded?"

"The blindfold is only put on before we're taken to the mating cube. But I can't read sigs – we aren't taught to read."

"You don't learn how to read and write in boyplace?"

"No."

"How about counting? Can you add and subtract?"

"I can count to twenty. More is pointless, they say."

Constance paused. She knew it was superfluous to educate men to the same standard as women, but she had presumed they were taught the basics. Maybe it was only the policy at this man's boyplace. "Can other men read and write?"

"None of the men here can. They come from all over Sisterland."

She hunkered down beside him. "What was it like at boyplace?"

"We were taught useful work."

"Nothing else?"

"That we were savages with violent instincts, and Sisterland needed to regulate us for our own good. We were shown images of war and death caused by men. They told us men are destroyers. We can never be trusted."

"But at least you had fresh air and plenty of food," said Constance. "You weren't ill-treated. If you were sick, you were given medicine."

"It's efficient to raise healthy specimens. Here in matingplace, they talk a lot about healthy specimens. The woman they call the Mating Mother says it feeds into success rates. She gave us instructions about touching a woman. She did not . . ." He broke off.

"Tell me. Help me to understand."

"She did not teach us how to speak to one. She said talk was unnecessary, and not talking was better. We were to remember we had a job to do, and anyone who gave satisfaction could expect extra rations and free time. Already, I've broken her rules."

Constance was pulled up short. The *Himtime* handout had said men couldn't help themselves mating at every opportunity. But this man had to be bribed with food and time off from the mating cube. Without incentives, was it possible some men might decline the honour?

"I've offended you," he said. "It wasn't my intention."

"I'm not offended. I just didn't realise mating was such a chore for men, too. Tell me, what did you do, before you became a meet?"

"I'm a forester. My home is seven days' journey from here by transer."

Seven days in a transer meant he had seen more of Sisterland than her, even if he'd been heavily sedated, a standard precaution as men were moved round.

"You were living in the Brown Convolution belt?" It was composed of farmland and forests, where men laboured under the supervision of female agronomists.

He nodded.

"I've heard about forests."

"You've never been in one?"

"No, only to some woods at the end of the Buzz line here in Green Hyperreal. What's it like, living in a forest?"

"The air is sweet and pure, and I can hear the birds sing. There's no birdsong in this place." He had been on his knees until then, but now he sat back on his heels. "Do you require me to start?"

"Can't we talk some more first?"

"As you choose."

"What kind of trees grow in the forest where you lived?"

"All the trees are the same, because they were planted to serve Sisterland's needs. We grow jack pines. Their branches are thick, and warblers build their nests on the ground under them. We have to burn down trees to keep the forest alive. Jack pines don't grow in the shade – fire clears a space for them. After a fire, we plant new jack-pine seeds. They spout quickly."

"It seems wasteful to burn trees."

"It keeps the forest alive. The earth is only scorched for a short time. Soon, it's green with new growth."

"This is your first time in matingplace, isn't it? Me too. I wasn't supposed to be a source yet. But something happened, and it's been decided I should babyfuse. If I can."

"Men are lucky to be a link in the chain. That's what the Mating Mother says."

"Do you feel lucky?"

He turned his head away. "I don't understand."

"Don't understand what?"

"Why you're doing this. Trying to know me. Why should you care?"

Constance had no answer. Except that he was another living being – a man, granted, not as evolved as a woman – not as clever, or as reliable, or as certain of the difference between right and wrong. But not radically different, either. He seemed able to experience moes all on his own. That was more than many women could manage, thanks to a century of having them suppressed. Even her shadow-moes didn't compare with the intensity of his, judging by his demeanour.

"Are all men like you? You're not what I expected."

"I was supposed to take something. To make me the way you wanted. I didn't."

"How did you avoid it?"

"Before they brought us upstairs, they handed out pills. But someone slipped, and water was spilled. In the confusion, I put my pill under my tongue. One of the older men told me about mating pills. They make us more eager to perform, but the men who keep taking them never reach old age. One day, the man's heart stops beating."

Constance told herself a man's life was of less significance than a woman's. Still, it seemed wrong to use them in this way. And there it was again. Another indicator that men weren't clamouring to mate.

"Don't you want to do your duty to Sisterland?" she asked.

"How is it my duty to mate with you? I don't know you. I ought to have a choice about doing it." He spoke in a matter-of-fact way, but his words made her defensive.

"I don't have a choice, either. You were assigned to me, just as I was to you."

"You have some choice. You could change your mind, and leave without mating. Or you could say I displeased you, and ask for a different man. I have no rights. I'm treated like an animal. Though that's nothing new – it happened from boyplace onwards. That's when you had us chipped as if we were beasts!"

"It's so your movements can be tracked. But I wear a comtel – I'm tracked, too." She reached out a hand to touch him, but let it fall. "I won't make you go through with mating. We can just talk till time's up. I won't breathe a word to the Mating Mother – nobody needs to know."

He inclined his head, as though accepting the bare minimum of what was due to him. It forced Constance to press on.

"I know you're not an animal. I'm sorry you feel –" She stumbled to a halt.

What did it matter how he felt? Feelings were a barrier to progress. Besides, men had sacrificed their humanity by incessant warmongering, and by their addiction to capitalism which had made one per cent of the population not just rich but indifferent to the remaining ninety-nine per cent struggling. That's what she'd learned in girlplace.

"I know you think we're beneath you," he said. "All women do. But you can't have men without women, or women without men. We're interdependent."

"Only for babyfusion. Women don't need men for anything else."

"And what if men said no? Where would Sisterland be then?"

"It would be difficult," admitted Constance. "But it's a meet's duty to attempt babyfusion with a woman licensed to become a source."

"Back to duty again. How can you talk to me about duty when only women are citizens of Sisterland? You use our labour. And give us nothing in return. We're invisible to you. But we exist. We think. And we feel!"

Constance's certainties began to crack. Her silkenspeak

training had taught her to mould information according to the message the Nine chose to convey. But he stripped down facts with no attempt to rearrange them. And while he was intense, there was none of the aggressive behaviour she had heard men engaged in. Indignation, yes, and conviction. But she would feel the same way in his position. If she could feel moes as freely as him.

"How is it you have so many moes?"

He considered. "I don't remember much in the way of moes in boyplace. But when I went to work in the forest, they began to grow. In the fresh air, where there were no walls to fence me in, it was natural to feel. I try to curb my moes here in Harmony. I don't want to draw attention to myself." His nostrils flared. "I hope I don't have to spend long in matingplace. A man and woman should mate outdoors, with the smells and sounds of the land about them. Not in these cubes. Where's the joy or beauty in that?"

"It's not about joy or beauty. It's about results."

"Joy and beauty matter. They can't be set aside. Nature makes space for them – people should learn from that."

Such fire! It was unsettling. Constance retreated to the pop-up.

"Have I displeased you?" he asked.

"On the contrary, I'm impressed. But I'm not used to so much passion – it causes turbulence. We strive to be composed here in Sisterland. I haven't encountered a moe outburst like yours before. Perhaps it's because you're closer to nature, as you say. I rarely go into the countryside. We have everything we need here in Harmony." Then, unable to help herself, she asked, "Is nature really such an extraordinary force?"

"Yes. But nature's been stripped out of the tamed patches of land near Harmony. I saw those timid spaces as we approached the city. Nature is gone from this place, too, with its squashed buildings, and low skies, and those buzzing trains no man is allowed on. If you could only stand under a high blue sky, looking towards a horizon with no beginning and no end, then you'd be conscious of something so powerful that nothing else would matter. You might feel insignificant. But you'd also know happiness."

Constance's pulse raced. She struggled for self-control. "Harmony's an aesthetically designed city. Our buildings and streets are pleasing to the eye."

He made a gesture of impatience. "No building can match a forest with treetops that pierce the clouds."

"We have clouds in Harmony."

"Nothing but clouds! Is the sky never blue?"

"Not really. But cloud patterns can be fascinating. I love to watch banks of them form into shapes."

The man's teeth showed: the suspicion of a smile, gone before it was fully formed. "If clouds move you, then my forest will grip you by the heart, and never let go." He started towards her, unsteady because of his blindfold, and she stretched out a hand to guide him. Sitting beside her on the pop-up, he spoke of his home, and the words tumbling from his mouth captivated her. She curved her mind towards his description of the sudden drama of shooting stars, and the tranquillity of moonlight reflected on glass sheets of water. Of the rapture let loose by spongy turf underfoot, and footsteps crunching over virgin snow. Of the sense of responsibility he felt for a line of saplings stretching their branches towards the light. Of the protective swell that overcame him at the brittleness of their bark beneath his hand – which she imagined, with an itching in her palm, that she could feel. As he spoke, and she listened, their heartbeats synchronised to the same pace.

A bell rang inside the cube. "*Your two hours are up,*" said an automated voice.

It was more than an interruption. It was an intrusion.

Rapidly, she pulled on her pumps. "I have to leave," she

whispered. "I don't even know your name."

"I don't know yours, either."

A clatter at the door told them it was being unlocked.

"It seems wrong not to know," said Constance.

He put his mouth to her ear. "I'm Harper."

"I'm Constance. I can return tomorrow . . . if you like."

He nodded.

Chapter 8

In the respite room, the surfeit of images shared by Harper left Constance breathless. His forest world had been summoned to life with a vibrancy lacking in Harmony. A pulse of longing stirred in her for a kinship as intense as his relationship with the earth. Cocooned in the city, Constance never thought about the land, and what grew in it, or lived on it, or hovered above it. The land seemed an irrelevance: society was what mattered. Yet societies were artificial, after all. The history she'd learned told her they rose and fell, whereas the land continued.

The Mating Mother took her by the elbows and scrutinised her, eyelids twitching as she circumnavigated the outer reaches of Constance's mind. Constance managed to keep her from encroaching any closer.

"You're changed. You must have mated well, top girl! Shower, relax. You're free to stay tonight in the Tower, or go home if you prefer."

Constance thought about Harper upstairs, or wherever he was now in matingplace. He must be somewhere under this roof. Some quality in this man made her receptive to him. It mystified her, but she acknowledged that it was so. "I'd like to stay."

"Then stay you shall. We have cubicles attached to the respite room. Give your skin to one of my girls to store until you mate again. We want you to feel completely at home here."

Constance slid her fingers under her throat and unhooked it. Balancing it in her hand, she considered how its warmth lacked the heat of life. Did Harper brush against it when he whispered his name? It must have felt false to him.

"What happens to men after they mate, mother? Do they mate again the same night with a different woman?"

"Let me take that skin, you're squeezing it hard enough to damage it. No, they only mate with one woman a night. Multiple mating isn't considered sound practice. Some meets would be able for it, but we like to ensure a meet is at his peak for each mating. We owe due diligence to the women seeking babyfusion. After they perform, meets are taken to a compound at the back of the Tower to eat, and sleep. Meets assigned to my matingplace want for nothing."

Constance doubted if Harper would agree that he wanted for nothing here. "I've never been alone with a man before. It wasn't what I expected. There was nothing threatening about him."

"Now, now, men would try to overthrow Sisterland if we relaxed our vigilance. The desire to dominate is latent in them, and always ready to rise to the surface. Tonight must have been a pleasurable experience. Well, no harm, we encourage pleasure. It sweetens the pill. But don't be fooled by your meet – men are riddled with belligerence and greed. Sometimes, they have disarming ways. But they're tools, nothing more. You must think of them as the spoon bringing food to your mouth, or the tap carrying water to your shower. Speaking of which, I'll have one of my girls show you to a bathroom. You'll want to wash the male odour off your body."

Next morning, as soon as Constance stirred, she was brought

breakfast in bed. The matingplace stewards were treating her like an invalid in recovery. She pecked at fruit, trying to envisage the landscape described by Harper. The trees in Harmony were pruned, while the countryside of Green Hyperreal, just beyond the city, was tamed and tidied. She almost laughed to think what he'd make of their grass, treated so that it never grew more than an inch high and was a consistent colour.

She fell to wondering if he had any curiosity about her appearance. Probably not, since he only touched her when he thought he was under orders to do it. She ought to go home, she supposed. But how self-indulgent it would be to idle away the day here in the Tower! Why not take the chance when it was offered?

She looked for her leggings and tunic, and found they hadn't been brought to her cubicle. Missing, too, were last night's clothes, although the pumps were there. Instead, another long gown was laid out, and her fingers couldn't help but stroke the saffron ribbons on its sleeves. She dressed, and swished through the deserted respite room. In the readying room, Tower stewards were clearing away the detritus of the previous night. It was less opulent by day, with food trodden through the rushes. But new rushes were being laid to replace the old. Constance recognised Unity, the greeter from the previous night, who was supervising the work. She looked a little discontented, until she saw Constance and forced her face into a smile.

"Excuse me, sister. Where are my clothes?"

"They're safe. When you leave, they'll be returned to you. In the meantime, you'll be supplied with a new gown each morning. I hope you like today's?"

"It's lovely. Does this mean I'm allowed to stay here all day?"

"Of course, sister."

"And tomorrow?"

"That depends. How many days into ovulation are you?"

"This is day two."

"Then you may stay for five nights. Or you can leave and return, as you choose."

"Always mating with the same partner as before?"

"Yes – you've been allocated that particular meet."

"Thank you, sister. One more question. How long is a man kept here?"

"You mean a meet," Unity corrected her.

"They're men, too."

"But these men are more valuable than most. There's no higher calling, for a man."

"How long do they stay in matingplace?"

"Depends on how well they score. If a meet is particularly virile, he may keep going for twenty years. Every year, he's rotated between different establishments."

Twenty years! Poor Harper. "Why move the men about so much?"

"What a lot of questions, sister. Your curiosity is highly unusual."

"I'm floundering, just a little. I didn't manage to attend a Mating Board seminar, you see." Constance tried another tack, remembering that discontented expression. "Sister, it seems a waste of your talents to have you superintending pages cleaning up the readying room. Don't you have admin to do? Or aren't there opportunities to upskill?"

"Too right it's a waste of my talents," muttered Unity. "Thank you for noticing." She looked over her shoulder, before lowering her voice. "Meets are rotated in case bonds develop between them and matingplace staff. It's rare. And unnatural. But it has to be guarded against." She cleared her throat, checking back over her shoulder again.

"What happens after twenty rotations? Does he go home then?" asked Constance.

"By that stage, a meet is judged to be past his peak."

"And he goes back to where he came from?"

"Few last that long. Most are spent before then."

"Spent?"

"They discontinue."

"What a life!"

Unity raised her eyebrows. "It is an honour."

Constance collected herself. "Of course. They must be proud to serve Sisterland."

"Being selected for matingplace is a plum position. They do no manual work, and their health is constantly checked. They eat the finest quality supplies, and have exercise and recreation opportunities."

Before Constance could ask any more questions, a bell pinged.

"Covenant time," said Unity. She held out a hand to Constance, and they formed a circle with the pages. "*Not the self but the State, not me but US. To the greater good: to universal sisterhood.*"

As soon as they were finished, Unity said she was needed elsewhere. Constance decided to take another shower, since there seemed to be no shortage of hot water in the Tower – unlike in her twoser, rationed to thirty-five minutes a week per head. Users could eke it out over seven days, or save it up, as they chose.

She luxuriated under the hot stream of water, giving herself permission not to think, or fret, or plan. Just to bask. Afterwards, stretched out on a pop-up, on top of a counterpane of quilted taffeta, she decided to treat this as a holiday – something she had read about, but never experienced. There were snacks in the cubicle if she felt hungry, an entscreen for programmes of Nine-approved educational value, and a dial for Sisterland's music-only radio channels. Speech radio had been withdrawn some decades earlier.

She leaned out of the pop-up and opened the door of a

locker. Books – what a treat! Books were restricted because the Nine said there were too many unhealthy messages in them. Fiction was no longer published. However, edited histories showing the PS Era to be harmful were allowed – although Constance suspected they were sanitised accounts. Philosophy books were permitted, along with approved biographies and self-help manuals. And, of course, *Beloved's Pearls* had never gone out of print. Collections of verse were virtually uncensored, as Silence had discovered – the red-pens hadn't realised how poetry could be home to anarchic ideas. However, hardly any sisters understood how to read poetry. The few who picked up a collection were bewildered by it, because they read it only with their eyes.

Constance lifted out a volume to browse through. It was a book of photographs without captions. She became engrossed in the black-and-white images of ruined properties, ranging from thatched cottages to stately homes. Even a crofter's cabin acquired a majestic quality in its dilapidated state. She turned the pages. What kind of people had lived in them? There was nobody in any of the photographs. Yet these buildings were put up for people, by people. A radical thought came to her. They might have been put up for women and men to live in. Together.

A gong boomed. She checked the time on her comtel. Unexpectedly, the day had fast-forwarded.

This time, she needed no guide to direct her to the readying room, where food covered the table and fresh candles burned in all the sconces. The Mating Mother glided here, there and everywhere, keeping a close watch on the proceedings. With a mead-server in tow, she advanced towards Constance, oozing welcome, and a chalice was placed in her hand. Constance sipped, and sank into the same unwinding experience as before.

She saw the Mating Mother wag a finger at the mead-server who was moving away.

"You must do better, Amity. Our guests don't deserve that face. *Smile All The While*." She redirected her attention to Constance. "I trust you enjoyed your day, top girl?"

"It's heavenly here, mother. I wallowed in it."

"That's as it should be. The usual rules are suspended in matingplace. Now, finish your mead, and then have something to eat. Yesterday, you only picked at food. You need to build up your strength for the task ahead."

Constance filled her plate.

A woman beside her reached for the cheese, and Constance jogged her elbow by accident. "Sorry, I've spilled your wine."

"No harm done. They'll give me more. As much as I like. Unlike that delicious mead, which they hoard like misers."

"I'm not usually so clumsy. It's all this excess – it makes me reel," said Constance.

"The wine went on the floor, not over me. Besides, the rushes catch the drips. Glad I don't have the job of changing them every day."

"If I worked in matingplace, I'd volunteer to be a mead-server."

"If I was in charge of the mead, I might forget about the guests and serve myself instead!" The stranger laughed, and Constance joined in.

They looked one another over, discovering compatibility. Constance glanced at the sig on her wrist. Benevolence 101. Oh, she was a thought-cruncher. She didn't look the type.

"This is my first time here," said Benevolence. Around her narrow neck, below a fine-boned face, multiple strings of amber were wrapped, and she plucked at them constantly with her free hand. The other held tight to her wine goblet. "I used to go to the Polygon zone matingplace. Do you know it?"

"Just by name. Firstfoot, is that the one?"

"That's right."

"How does the Tower compare with Firstfoot?"

"Different décor, same aim. They have a fantasy shoe

theme there. Its readying room has floor-to-ceiling shelves holding nothing but shoes. And such shoes! High heels, kitten heels, Cuban heels . . . so many kinds. I felt a throb of desire just looking at them – we all did. Though it defies logic. They were from PS Era. Trying them on helped me to understand our PS sisters. Their shoes led to corns and bunions. But you forgot about crooked toes when you wore them."

Benevolence waved her empty goblet, and it was replaced by a full one. Constance was also handed a goblet.

Benevolence took a long swallow. "I couldn't help myself choosing a pair. I went for polka dots and crossover ankle-straps. And it was a transformation. A sensation of empowerment grew inside me. All at once, I knew I could mate. Still wearing them, I went straight to a mating cube, and did it. That's why they pander to our make-believe dreams in matingplace. They've researched all our yearnings. Every matingplace offers a different fiction. It's a diversionary tactic from what's about to happen, of course. Funny, how they encourage escapism in matingplace, but nowhere else." Her lip curled as her glance swept the readying room. "This place takes 'let's pretend' to the outer limits."

"I didn't know you could switch from one matingplace to another," said Constance.

"I wasn't having much success. In fact, I wasn't having any. So I thought, change of venue, change of luck. I had to apply to the Mating Board, of course. They decided to give me another chance."

Constance examined Benevolence. Something feverish was imparted by her – perhaps she shadow-moed, too.

Benevolence emptied her goblet. "This wine is nearly impossible to buy now. They hive off most of the supplies for the matingplace circuit. Alcohol's always been part of the mating ritual, even back in PS days. I'll have yours if you don't want it." She swapped her empty goblet for Constance's full one, and took another gulp. "I'm starting to think I might be a dud."

"It's not given to every sister to reproduce."

"Don't chant the pearly book at me." Benevolence steered Constance towards a corner, from which a griffin glared. "Ugly brute. We all know the ones who babyfuse are given more respect. It's just how it is. Even in PS days, women were desperate to become sources. Not so different to us, then, for all the girlplace stories about having it so much better now. They used to perform all sorts of rituals to improve their chances. They had fertility dolls, fertility baths, fertility dances, fertility moons, fertility massages, fertility drinks . . . you name it."

"Did they work?"

"Maybe. Could be your chances improved if you believed they were going to improve. As a fallback, there were various goddesses they petitioned. Some of their goddesses were virgins who were also mothers. Points the way towards the Sisterland model, don't you think?"

"Benevolence, why don't we get you something to eat? I don't like the way the Mating Mother is looking at us."

"Later. Now, where was I? Oh yes, our PS sisters and their charms and amulets to bring about babyfusion. Ribbons tied onto hawthorns, and statues they rubbed, and something called a miraculous medal worn for luck. Sounds primitive – desperate, even." Her voice cracked. "And yet, it must have been reassuring to think there was someone you could turn to, who might wave a magic wand and grant your heart's desire."

"You'll feel better with something solid inside you," said Constance.

"I'd try some of that voodoo myself, if I knew how to go about it."

"I tasted the hyacinth flan. I can recommend it."

"Don't worry, I'm not going to have a meltdown." Benevolence managed a smile that almost convinced. "I suppose I don't have anybody to talk to about this. I'm not othered, you see. Too choosy. Or maybe just unchosen."

"How do you know so much about PS fertility?"

"I'm a thought-cruncher. You come across all sorts in that line of work." A shadow crossed her face. "Even if I fail to babyfuse, it's not as if I'll get sent to an outer belt. Nothing changes. Not really. Not ever."

Constance touched Benevolence's arm. "How long have you been trying?"

"Five years."

"Lots of women don't babyfuse. My source's other spent eight years trying, and never managed it."

"Bet she has a big job, though."

"Thought-crafter."

"I knew it. Crème de la crème. Women like her are given a free pass through life because their skills are needed."

"All work has equal value in Sisterland, Benevolence."

"Don't be such a pearl. It's a convenient fable – doesn't bear scrutiny. Look round the Tower. Who scrapes up the wax from those candles? Dusts those repulsive gargoyles? Sanitises the mating cubes? It's not men, that's for sure. The meets are needed for mating. And non-meets wouldn't be let anywhere near matingplace for fear of unauthorised mating. No, all those menial tasks are carried out by women. Don't tell me their work is treated on the same level as a thought-crafter's."

Constance eyed Benevolence's sig again: was she really a thought-cruncher? It was a respected job – crunchers were trained to dispose of thoughts judged to be unsuitable. But it probably didn't offer much scope for individuality. Crunchers didn't select the thoughts, or replace them with different ones. They just discarded. "Aren't you fulfilled by your work, Benevolence?"

"It was chosen for me in my last year at girlplace, the same as shaping was chosen for you. They mindmapped me, and decided creativity shouldn't be encouraged. Said it posed certain risks, in my case – whatever that means." She waved at an attendant for more wine.

"The ideal job doesn't exist."

"At least you get to interface," said Benevolence. "My job is solitary."

"I haven't been out in the field yet."

Benevolence squinted at her, malice gleaming in her eyes. "So, let's see if I have this straight. Shapers circulate new policies, encouraging sisters to welcome them. But sisters can object, and reservations are reported back to the Shaper Mother, who conveys them to the Nine. Leading to tweaks in policy, right?"

"We're told the Nine is always willing to consider improvements. Provided objections are constructive and mannerly." Constance's tone conveyed some doubt, however.

Lately, it had struck Constance that it took a particular type of Sisterlander to spot problems in strategy. An individual. Yet individualism was discouraged. During shaper training, it was explained that individualism was, of course, welcome in principle. But not individualism which promoted uncertainty. Or led to friction. So individuals who refused to compromise had to be sacrificed, occasionally. It was regrettable, but unavoidable. To this end, shapers were also schooled in how to identify potential dissenters, and report back on them to Shaperhaus. What happened subsequently was not a shaper's concern. The presumption was that they were sent for thought-mending. But no-one knew for sure.

Constance tried to psyche herself back into good Sisterlander mode. "There's always the comfort of knowing your work contributes to universal sisterhood."

"The best thing about being a shaper must be the chance to travel. There has to be more to life than Harmony."

"Don't crunchers travel?"

"Not a chance. We're stuck in an office. I don't actually do any crunching. I spend all my time in front of a screen, checking endless forms to make sure thoughts are crunched according to procedure. And I'm starting to realise why procedures are so rigidly imposed. Shall I tell you why? It's all about conformity and submission."

"On the contrary." The Mating Mother materialised beside them. "It's about consistency and order. Now, Benevolence, I believe you're over-tired – time for you to go to the respite room, and take a nap."

"I'm not sleepy. I want to go to a mating cube. It's show time, isn't it?"

"Not tonight, Benevolence." The Mating Mother clapped her hands together, and Tower staff stopped what they were doing and began to approach.

"I want to babyfuse!"

Six pages circled Benevolence. One of them removed the goblet to which she was clinging. They steered her towards the door, dealing with her as firmly as a fractious toddler.

"Bullies!" she roared, writhing in their arms, and the strings on her amber snapped, beads hopping on the floor.

The Mating Mother looked on, enigmatic.

"Why do we need licences for babyfusion anyway?" shrieked Benevolence.

"Manners, dear," said one of the stewards. "Yelling is simply not acceptable. *It's Nice To Be Nice*."

Constance wished she had the courage to speak up in Benevolence's defence. Benevolence seemed not to expect any help but, just for a moment, their eyes locked. And in them, Constance saw a glimmer. Not an appeal. Closer to a challenge.

"Don't be fooled!" Benevolence cried. "This is a fantasy world, but it's just as controlled as the one outside!"

A hand covered her mouth, and Benevolence was led from the room.

Constance bent to retrieve the amber, but the beads had scattered in every direction. She cupped a few in one hand, covering them with the other.

"Dear me, what a state she managed to work herself into.

Such unrestricted moes." The Mating Mother was thoughtful as she adjusted her fur-trimmed sleeves. "See how unhappy they makes the poor thing. The Nine is wise to insist on moe regulation. I haven't availed of my quota for almost a decade. I don't miss it."

The incident changed the atmosphere in the readying room. The air was ruffled, sisters staring in their direction. The Mating Mother clapped her hands, and a band of minstrels began to play, while more wine was distributed. The tiny woman assessed the scene, eyes darting from face to face.

By and by, her demeanour relaxed. She turned back to Constance. "Are you ready?"

Constance hesitated. She wasn't unwilling to see Harper again – on the contrary, she was looking forward to it – but the scene she'd just witnessed needed to be processed.

"Reluctance becomes you," said the Mating Mother. "Some of our sisters have to be reminded it's procreational rather than recreational. Still, you won't babyfuse standing here."

"Ready," said Constance.

"Excellent. I'll take those." She nodded towards the spheres of amber.

Handing them over, Constance felt a flicker of reluctance. She wanted to keep them for Benevolence.

"I'll send someone with you to the mating cube."

"I know the way now."

"We can't have people wandering round matingplace unsupervised. Anything might happen."

"Women and men might mate," suggested Constance.

The Mating Mother's eyes flattened.

Constance sensed she was sailing close to the wind. "I feel fertile," she said quickly.

"Top girl! Let's have you act on it."

Chapter 9

Harper was waiting for her. She knew it by the two quick paces he advanced, as soon as she entered the mating cube. It gave her pleasure to realise it. She waited while the key was turned in the door behind her, before pulling off her pumps so they were both barefoot.

"You came back," he said.

"Did you think I wouldn't?"

"I didn't do what I'm supposed to. You could be dissatisfied with me."

"Because we didn't mate? Only two people know that: you and me."

"You could have told someone."

How vulnerable he must feel. An unfamiliar moe welled up: not a shadow-moe, but a blast of the genuine article. Constance recognised it, having felt a scaled-down version once before, when she was a small girl and found an injured frog. She had made a pet of the creature, but one day it had hopped away. The moe inflating through her was protectiveness.

"I didn't tell anybody," she said. "You must trust me."

"Must?"

"I mean I want you to trust me." A beat. "Please." This

was extraordinary, from a woman to a man. Surely he'd appreciate that?

"What choice do I have?"

How prickly he was being. The ease she had felt with him the previous night seemed elusive, and its absence disappointed her. She tried to reach him. "We didn't do anything wrong. Mating isn't mandatory."

"It is for me. I'm not free to refuse. If I do, I'll be punished."

"You mustn't tell untruths. We don't punish in Sisterland: we send misguided people to the listeners. After a few sessions, they see sense."

"Is that what they tell you? Nobody's punished? Surely you don't believe that!"

Constance bit the soft flesh on her thumb pad. "I know men aren't sent for listening," she admitted. "I suppose I've never given much thought to what happens to them."

"That's obvious. Men are packed off to the outer belts. To Grey Disjoint, with mosquitos biting all year round. Or Black Particle, where there's only an hour of daylight."

"We have limited resources to reclaim people who go astray. Women must take precedence."

Below the blindfold, a nerve twitched on Harper's cheek. "Even women are punished in Sisterland. They're sent to Black Particle – to Safe Space."

Safe Space. The name caused Constance's heartbeat to skip.

"I suppose you're going to tell me Safe Space is just a scare-story?" he challenged.

By the nightlight's glow, Constance began to run her hands over the walls of the mating cube, trying to find an eavesdropping device. Over and over, she'd been told the cube was private. But would Sisterland really honour that principle?

When she was through, she whispered, "What do you know about Safe Space?"

"I heard about it here in the compound. It's how the Nine deals with opposition."

"I've never heard of any opposition. But I suppose . . ."

"They'd hush it up," he finished her sentence for her.

"There's nothing beyond Black Particle. It's where everything ends. That's why Safe Space is there. But we shouldn't talk about it. Nobody's meant to know it exists. We could get in trouble just for speaking its name."

"I'm going to stay out of trouble." There was a catch in his voice. "They'll let me go home once I've given them what they want. A year, I've been told. A year is manageable. I just have to put in the time. Inside my head, I stored an image of the last sunset I saw in my forest. I take it out and look at it when I need to – a ball of colour, bursting through the treetops. It helps to think about my forest waiting for me. The time will pass. A year is a blink of an eye to a tree."

Constance wondered if she should warn him that the year only referred to the Tower. After it, he'd spend another year in a different matingplace, and then another: twenty years, in total. If he survived that long. Yet how could she shatter his hopes?

"I'm lucky I wasn't sent to matingplace before now," Harper went on. "My forest is remote. But a shaper came, and noted down all the suitable men. And so here I am. Shaved, scented, stripped. Semi-stripped – they let me keep my leggings. At your service."

"Don't." Impulsively, she caught him by the upper arms. Unexpectedly, she became aware of a pleasurable sensation: the curve of biceps. She dropped her hands, but not before he noticed her altered demeanour.

"Do you require me to mate with you now?"

"I don't require anything of you. I'm not here to make demands."

He began to say something, but thought better of it. Sighing, he pressed the heel of each palm against the blindfold.

"Does it bother you that I can see you when you can't see me?"

"But I can see you."

"Is the blindfold loose? Or transparent?"

"I see you in my mind's eye."

"What do you see?"

"I see a troubled woman. I see a lonely woman."

"You see all that with your eyes covered?"

"I see all that with my heart."

"What else do you see with your heart, Harper?"

"I see sunlight through branches, making patterns on the earth below. I see the leaves uncurl and spread out to take shape. I see the knots on the trunk of my favourite tree, where I lean my face for comfort."

"Help me to see your forest."

As before, they sat on the pop-up while he talked, and she listened. Once, she rested her palm against his chest, testing its warmth. Needing to touch him, although she didn't understand why. Harper stopped speaking, and she could feel his muscles flex under her hand. When she took it away, he resumed his storytelling as if nothing had happened.

Later, she said, "Your body is smooth. I thought men were hairier than women."

"I've never seen a woman's body. Nor a woman's face, either. Why do you wear your skin to a mating cube?"

"The Mating Mother says we mustn't show our faces."

"But I'm wearing a blindfold."

"I know. It's just one of the rules."

"Does the skin itch?"

"I can't remember a time when I didn't wear it. You hardly notice it's on."

"It's to protect you from pollutants, isn't it?"

"Yes."

"Aren't men at risk from these pollutants?"

"Skins are expensive. Women have to save up for them,

and get loans." A shadow-moe of guilt strummed. She changed the subject. "Did they give you one of those pills? To make you mating-ready?"

"They're handed out every night. But I hid it under my tongue again. They didn't bother checking if I swallowed. They think we don't notice what happens to men who take their pills year after year. They think we're not capable of working it out."

"Don't be cross. I don't distribute those pills."

He didn't reply.

"Ask me a question. I seem to do all the asking," she went on.

"Why do you call us meets? Why not men?"

"It's just a word. It doesn't mean anything."

"Doesn't it? We have a name for you, too."

"What is it?"

"I'll tell you another time."

"Tell me now."

"Is that an order?"

"I'm not ordering you to do anything, Harper. I couldn't."

"Machines. As in time to oil the machines. It's what we say when mating time approaches."

Constance felt demeaned: an all-out moe. She'd had enough – she was going to leave right now. She stepped into her pumps, fingers sliding round the backs of her heels. "Do you call me that in front of the others?"

"I wouldn't do that. You must trust me." Deliberately, he batted back the words she'd used earlier.

Rubbing her thumb against the crystal ball in her hand, she wondered about activating it so that she could leave. But she didn't. Slowly, she sat back down. This man had a knack for stinging her. Yet she still wanted to talk with him. Quietly, she said, "We were interrupted last night. You were just about to tell me about the waterfall in your forest. I'd like to hear about it now, if you'd like to tell me."

He waited for a few beats, and she thought he might not cooperate. But then he began to describe the frothing torrent and the awe it inspired, and companionship took the place of tension.

Until a bell rang inside the cube. And he stopped in mid-sentence.

Their time was up too soon. Constance looked at Harper. He had a mole on his left cheek, which she felt an impulse to touch. Did he want to touch her, too? She couldn't tell.

"*Your two hours are up,*" said the automated voice.

"Till tomorrow, Constance?" he mouthed.

It was the first time he'd used her name. She realised she'd been wanting to hear it in his mouth.

And that question in his voice. Maybe he wanted her to come again. As the door creaked open, she sent a smile sailing towards him. Even if he couldn't see it, she hoped he could sense it.

In the respite room, Constance looked for Benevolence. A page told her she was in a cubicle. When Constance tried to get in, she found the way barred by Humility, one of Charity's helpers.

"Please," she said, "I won't tire her out. I just want to check she's all right."

"You can only have a minute," said Humility.

Benevolence looked wan, but she seemed calm as she sat on a pop-up with her back to the wall, drinking tea from a pottery cup. Constance sat beside her, and accepted a cup. She couldn't identify the flavour. Wood bark, perhaps? It tasted gritty.

"Before you ask, it's evening-primrose tea," said Benevolence. "Supposed to help boost fertility. And it has soothing properties. Apparently, wine overstimulates me. Who knew tea could deliver so much?"

"It doesn't taste of any kind of flower, especially not primrose."

"It tastes of pee. But the Mating Mother thinks I ought to drink it, and who am I to argue?" She rolled the pottery container between her hands. "So, mission accomplished in the mating cube?"

Constance lowered her eyes. Twice in a mating cube, and twice she had sat talking with the man instead of attempting to babyfuse. It wasn't as if the idea revolted her – in fact, she'd like to feel Harper's hands on her. But she wanted him to do it willingly, not because he was compelled. "I should go for a wash." She remembered she was supposed to feel sticky and nauseated.

"You enjoy mating," said Benevolence. "I can see it in your face."

I enjoy being with Harper, thought Constance. I go to him voluntarily. But he has to be blindfolded and led to me.

"You know," Benevolence went on, "women used to pick out meets, the way animals do. Several meets would compete for a female. But the Nine stopped that, in case the act of choosing gave us an attachment to the man. It might lead to intimacy, which couldn't be tolerated. Imagine if a woman thought she was in a relationship with a meet, and prioritised their bond above loyalty to Sisterland!"

Humility cleared her throat, one hand on her stifstat. "Constance should leave you now. You're overtired."

"Just a few more minutes. Please. Could you ask a page for some hot water for my tea? It's gone cold. The Mating Mother said I was to drink as much as I could manage."

With some reluctance, Humility left the cubicle.

Benevolence went on, "In my line of work, I come across all sorts of unacceptable thoughts that have to be crunched. Here's something I discovered: in PS days, women used something called contraception. It was a way of stopping babyfusion."

Constance recoiled. "Why would a woman want to stop it? Surely that's the whole point of mating?"

"Babyfusion wasn't the only reason for them to mate. They did it for pleasure. Think about it – women and men mating for pleasure, not purpose. We're more like men than we like to admit."

Benevolence's hands began to shake, spilling tea. Constance reached out and took the cup. "Constance, they give us mead here to help us feel the mating urge. When we leave, they give us something else to bank it down again. They say it's impossible to feel the mating urge naturally. They tell us we've lost it. But it hasn't been lost."

"Enough!" cried Humility, who had just stepped back in.

Words tumbled from Benevolence, faster and faster. "It's been taken away from us. For their convenience. By our skins. That's what stops us feeling the mating urge."

"This conversation is terminated!" cried Humility. "Leave us, Constance." She started pushing Constance through the door.

Benevolence was yelling now. "Skins stop us feeling all sorts of moes. That's why they order us to wear our skins in the mating cube. They're afraid we'll feel too much, and become disruptive. What if –"

Humility sprang forward and placed a hand on Benevolence's mouth. "You need sedation!"

As Constance stood outside the cubicle, Verity and Purity came tearing past from the mating floor, brushing her aside.

When Constance went in search of Benevolence the following morning, she could find her nowhere. In the readying room, staff were scattering dried lavender on the floor, where it pooled in fragrant bundles. She saw Unity giving instructions to one of the lavender-sowers, and approached her.

"Unity, do you know where I could find Benevolence?"

"The Mating Mother had to send her away."

"Why? When?"

"In the night. She became volatile, moe-unhinged, and

lashed out. Charity almost had to use the stifstat on her. But the Mating Mother stepped in."

"No! She can't have done anything to deserve the stifstat! Poor Benevolence."

"She'll be well taken care of, sister. Don't let it concern you." Unity moved off.

But Constance followed. "Spirited away in the night. It sounds heavy-handed."

"Serenity is crucial. Above all, in matingplace. We can't afford any disturbance."

"Forgive me if I spoke out of turn. Where was Benevolence taken? I'd like to visit her."

"She's in good hands. But right now, she's overstimulated. She needs isolation from outside influences. It wouldn't be appropriate to pay a visit."

"But where is she?" Constance persisted.

Unity's eyes darted left and right. She ran her tongue over her lips, and said under her breath, "She's on her way to Safe Space."

"That's a bit extreme, surely!"

"Shh! You'll get us both in trouble!"

Constance kept her voice low. "Something must have happened to provoke her."

"Watch what you're saying! We don't provoke our guests."

"Sorry. But could something have sparked this . . . episode?"

"The Mating Mother paid her a visit. She told Benevolence she wasn't allowed to proceed with mating at the Tower, and a report recommending withdrawal of her permit would be sent to the Mating Board. Benevolence reacted in an unfortunate manner."

"No wonder – she desperately wants to be a source."

"Wanting isn't good enough. You have to be approved."

"Approved for what?" It was the Mating Mother. She looked from Constance to Unity. Her little foot tapped.

"To be a source, mother," said Unity.

"Indeed. Being a source is the ultimate act of sisterdom. Sources must be vetted – rigorously – to make sure the best candidates are selected. Do you really have time to stand about gossiping, Unity?"

Unity melted away.

"But Benevolence must have been vetted if she had a licence," said Constance.

"Sadly, Benevolence is not what I'd call a top girl. This is her fifth season. A lot can happen in that time. A woman's mental state may deteriorate. Potential sources must be supervised closely."

Constance warned herself not to say something she'd regret. Don't even think it, she told herself

"Your own certificate is only for three months," continued the Mating Mother. "I understand it's a temporary accreditation. So you'll have to go for a full round of testing if you haven't babyfused by then. Of course, there's no reason why you shouldn't get the nod. Somebody obviously believes you have special talents to offer Sisterland, or you wouldn't be here." She gave Constance a cool appraisal. "I hope you live up to expectations."

Chapter 10

On their third night together, Harper and Constance fell to considering how names were allocated. He told her he had no registration number by way of a surname, as she did: his trade and location identified him. He was Harper the Forester, from the Brown Convolution middle belt, which meant he was inventoried as Harper FOR-BC. He held up his wrist to show her his sig.

"What's that?" Constance pointed to a bow-shaped character.

"It's the symbol for a meet. Now I'm Harper FOR-BC ∞ ."

"It's pretty."

He shrugged. "It's for record-keeping. At least my first name was chosen for me."

"Who by?"

"My source. That's more than some sons get."

"She must have been a prominent Sisterlander."

"Why do you say that?"

"A source has to make a case for being allowed to name her boy-man before he's taken away. Often, it's a reward for services to the State. It means she had status."

"Which is more than me. I'm just a meet."

"Not in my eyes. You're Harper the Forester to me. Whose name was chosen by his source. Who wanted to name him."

"Yes, I try to remember that when I think about her giving me away to strangers."

"She had no choice. Perhaps the name Harper meant something to her. It suits you."

"Sometimes, I wonder if I look like her."

"Sometimes, I wonder if I look like the man who mated with my source."

"Do you know anything about him?

"Nothing. My source changes the subject any time I raise it. She mated, babyfused, and blanked everything else out. Exactly as a good Sisterlander should."

He turned away.

There now, she'd offended him. He hadn't realised she was being ironic. Quasi-ironic, anyway. She couldn't rise to total irony. She kept forgetting how readily moe flared up in him. "Harper, I didn't invent the system." Her tone was conciliatory. "I'm a prisoner of it as much as you."

"No, you have more choices."

"Only while I cooperate. Deviate, and there are consequences. You were right about punishment." Benevolence sprang to mind, and she shivered.

At once, Harper turned back. "You're cold. Here, let me warm you."

He put an arm around her and she leaned against him, sharing his body heat – which shot a current through her. But he betrayed no response. Constance supposed the attraction must be one-sided. How potent this mating urge was! She could use it now to attempt babyfusion. Yet she didn't feel able to ask Harper to perform. He was proud and independent – he'd be belittled by taking orders from her. And she'd be degraded by giving them.

They began trading experiences, and Constance was surprised to discover that men had memory-keepers, too. It wasn't a formal arrangement – they didn't go by the same name, and could not travel about sharing their memories. But there were a few elderly men with a dim memory of PS days, or who remembered what others had remembered. They whispered about it to their younger comrades. To talk openly about a time when men were equal to women would be unwise.

"I met a fisherman who told us about a time when women, men and children lived together," said Harper. "They were a family. They shared a home. With a garden – space was set aside for gardens, then. And a woman and a man decided how to raise their children, not Sisterland. The fisherman said life was different then – noisier, with many people travelling through the air."

"Speed is reckless," she said. "We've slowed everything right down."

"The Nine travels by air," he observed.

"It's done for Sisterland. This is a vast land, you know. Didn't you say it took seven days to carry you here by road?"

He nodded. "I came with a group from my belt. All the young men were taken. There was nobody left to help the older men with the work. They'll struggle. Some will discontinue."

Constance brushed that aside. She couldn't afford to let him keep making her feel guilty. Each time, the shadow-moe would magnify. "The Nine's time is precious. These sisters can't spend weeks on the road. They fly only when they must, for the sake of universal sisterhood."

"The fisherman told us something else, too. He said PS women shared power with men. We were fellow citizens."

Constance realised Harper was unaware that men had been the dominant sex once, and women had seized power from them. Such information could be inflammatory. If men knew they had been in the ascendant previously, they might try for supremacy again.

"But now you use us like tools," he went on. "We might be made of wood, or metal, for all you care."

"We've freed ourselves from any reliance on men, apart from mating." She parroted *Beloved's Pearls*.

"You look to us to do your grunt work."

"Everyone must work, male and female."

"Our work is always physical. We mustn't use our brains. We're not allowed to choose what we do."

"Nor are we. Our roles are selected for us, based on ability and where Sisterland needs us."

"You claim to be free. But that doesn't sound like freedom to me."

Constance was stung. What right had a blindfolded Harper to tell her she wasn't free? "Who raised you?" she asked.

"The women who ran boyplace."

"I was raised by the women who ran girlplace. Not so different, you see?"

"You weren't sent to girlplace the same day you were born."

"No, when I was a year old."

"You still saw your source there, I think?"

"Yes, after the first month passed – the settling-in period – my source was allowed to visit often. But she couldn't make any decisions about me. What I studied, who I played with, what I ate or when I went to bed. Girlplace took care of all that."

"At least you could learn at girlplace. At boyplace, we were trained for work."

"I was prepared for work, too."

"Not at once. First, you were educated, and taught to think, even if you don't know how to think for yourself."

"I think! How dare you say I don't!"

"If you really thought – independently – you wouldn't be satisfied with the way half the people in Sisterland are treated. You'd be furious."

"Anger's a deselected moe," said Constance.

"How about a sense of right and wrong? Is that deselected, too?"

"I know you explained how working on the land helps you stay in touch with your feelings. But it's different for women. Moes held us back for centuries. So the Nine compiled a list of moes for certification, and purged the unhealthy ones. Some moes are simply too disturbing. We have to learn from history."

"Even disturbing moes are better than none."

Troubled, Constance scrambled to her feet to escape from this uncomfortable claim.

"It's not just working on the land that gives me moes," he added. "It's because I drink water from streams there, too. Tap water's different. Our old men tell us your Nine puts moe suppressant in the water supply. We think your skins bank down your moe capacity, too."

Benevolence had said the same! Constance searched his face, beneath the blindfold. Did this man have any idea how much disturbance he was causing her? "How well you argue," she marvelled.

"Ah, that's what the Nine didn't bank on. Men continue to think, even if we can't read or write, or count beyond ten fingers and ten toes. Perhaps they thought treating us like beasts would turn us into beasts. But we still dream."

"Do you dream, Harper?"

"I dream. But I wonder if you do. If you know how to any more."

Constance bowed her head, conscious of something lacking in her. Conscious, too, of a gap between them which she wanted to bridge.

"Why don't we try to take off your blindfold? Perhaps it's not knotted as tightly tonight. Come and stand by the nightlight."

He followed her, seeming reluctant.

She plucked at the blindfold, and her fingers snagged on something attached to the material. "Kneel down, Harper, there's something here."

It was a seal on the blindfold's loop. If she opened it, the wax would break and the Mating Mother would know he'd seen her. She could plead accident, but he'd suffer for it.

Something jolted inside her chest cavity. It was followed by a surge, too strong to be a shadow-moe. She had feelings for him! The intensity of the moe bewildered her. After all, Harper was a man.

"Am I allowed to stand up again, or do you require me to continue kneeling?"

Harper's quesion acted as a rebuke – as a reminder, too, of the impossibility of tenderness between them. She reined herself in. Moes could be stifled. She owed it to herself to curb this one.

"Why must you insist on treating me like an oppressor? Of course you can get up. Please yourself."

"I can't."

"That's hardly my fault – why blame me?"

"Sisterland treats me like an animal. You allow it to happen by accepting it. I must kneel when I'm told, stand up when I'm told, go to a mating cube when I'm told, mate when I'm told. Whether you admit it or not, you're one of my jailers."

Fury was not possible. But something lower down the scale rumbled within Constance. Resentment, with an undertow of defensiveness. She almost blurted out that he should get used to prison because he'd be stuck in matingplace for the next twenty years. But she managed to hold back.

Instead, she reached into her pocket for the alarm ball, and squeezed it to indicate she was ready to leave. Footwear on, she waited for the key to turn in the door.

Chapter 11

Throughout the fourth day, Constance fluctuated about whether or not to go to the mating cube. She meandered through the Tower, sometimes tripping over her skirts, and in the readying room she watched staff arrange catkins on elongated stalks in urns. Passing a display, she stroked one of the furry pellets. It disintegrated.

"Best not to touch," warned a page.

"Are catkins being manufactured now, too?" asked Constance. The page nodded.

As the hours ticked by, she wrestled with whether or not to see Harper again. Honesty overcame indignation. Harper was right: he had no freedom. Hers was limited, but at least she had some. She could, for example, choose never to see him again. But he had to wait in a mating cube whether he wanted to be there or not. She could opt for a different meet. But he had to take whoever was sent to him. He wasn't even trusted to look at the woman while they mated.

She considered why she was drawn to Harper. Was it because of losing Silence? Because he smacked of forbidden fruit? Because of the mating urge?

Encountering Unity as she prowled about, Constance asked, "Do meets ever refuse to perform?"

"I've never known it to happen. It wouldn't be logical. Men would mate every day, if they could."

"Would they do it even if they didn't like a woman?"

"Liking has nothing to do with it. They're genetically conditioned to mate as often as possible, with as many women as possible. That's just how it is."

Constance ruminated on this. Harper wasn't leaping on her. He preferred to talk – or to scold her for keeping him in subjugation. Was it possible some of the stories she'd been told about men were just that – stories?

And Harper was a word-weaver. His storytelling formed pictures in her mind. How did that tally with her lessons about all men being warmongers? Women and men weren't a different species – they'd simply developed along different paths. No boy-man ever made war. Yet he was viewed as a potential risk from birth.

Constance's head ached from all the questions ricocheting inside it. She wondered if she ought to cut her losses and go to the Mating Mother, telling her she'd like to postpone any further babyfusion attempts until next month. The Mating Mother would think she had mated with Harper on three occasions: it was advisable, but not obligatory, to stay for five couplings. All that day, she tossed round the pros and cons of bailing out. There were many sound reasons for leaving the Tower. And only one argument for staying: to be with Harper. Even when he unsettled her. Twice more – then she wouldn't be allowed to see him for another month. And if she achieved babyfusion, she'd never see him again. Not that there was any chance of babyfusion yet. But sooner or later they'd do what matingplace was designed for. And in their beginning would lie their ending.

"I was afraid you wouldn't come back," said Harper, as soon as the door was locked behind them on the fourth night. "I'm sorry, Constance." He reached out and laced his fingers through hers.

She looked down at their interlocked hands, admiring the herringbone pattern. Having her hand held made her feel safe. Not that a man could keep her safe from anything. It must be a reverberation from PS days.

"What are you sorry for?"

"For taking out my frustration on you. You're the first woman who's treated me like a person."

"I know so little about your life. I suppose I never gave it much thought. We don't pay you for any of the work you do, and that doesn't seem right. But you get everything you need, right? Food and shelter?"

"Food and shelter's supplied. But you don't really believe that's all someone needs, do you?"

"Harper, you have to be patient with me. I'm trying to look at things from your perspective."

"I know you are. You're not what I expected. I never thought I'd say this about a woman, but you're really quite open."

Open. As compliments went, it wasn't the most flattering she'd ever received. However, he seemed to mean it as praise. "I do my best. I can appreciate why you'd feel cooped up here, after your forest."

"I love the forest – I'm happy there. Is happiness something you can feel? Or is that deselected, too?"

"It's restricted. But we feel contentment at will." He laughed. Defensive, she said, "Rationing makes it all the more meaningful when a happiness quota is distributed. Last Sisterday, a H was piped into the atmosphere. It's the most magical sensation to be filled with happiness at the same time as everyone around you."

He said nothing, and Constance had an uneasy feeling she hadn't made the case for happiness regulation. Then again, why should she want to? He was right to be dubious. She was becoming increasingly sceptical herself.

"I feel complete in my forest," he said. "I don't need to go to Moe Express to feel glad when I see the sun rise, or sympathy for an injured animal. We passed some branches of Moe Express on our way to matingplace. It was the saddest sight. Women paying to have feelings, when all they need to do is walk about in the countryside, and moes will rise up inside them. How can anyone crunch over autumn leaves and not feel happy?"

"We treat leaves here so they don't fall off trees. It's tidier."

He shook his head, long, fair hair stirring. She found herself admiring the way it fell across his face.

"I pity you," he said.

She scrambled to her feet, heart pumping. A man couldn't pity a woman!

"I've offended you. I didn't mean to," he said.

"Not offended. Startled. We're the ones who pity you, for being less evolved than us."

He reflected. "Feeling pity for one another is better than feeling threatened by one another." He held up his hands in surrender. "Let's not argue tonight. Big, bad Charity will be clanking at the door shortly."

"How do you know she's big and bad, with your blindfold on?"

"From the way space settles round her."

"Does she scare you?"

"I wouldn't like to get on the wrong side of her. Let me guess. She carries a stifstat she's just itching to use."

Constance thought about Benevolence, and shivered. "She does wear one. Harper, tell me about the memories your keepers shared with you. Memories ours may have held back."

He tapped his mouth with a forefinger, and she noticed the sharply defined hollow in the middle of his upper lip. She'd like to touch the groove. She supposed she could, if she wanted. Better not.

"There was a piece of machinery that made information freely available. Everywhere. Anyone could use it. It was called the Internet. The fisherman I told you about spoke of it. He said it was the most important tool ever invented. But it was dangerous, too. Because of what it shared."

"A sharing tool?" asked Constance.

"Sharing and spreading."

"The same as a shaper – only a machine, not a woman."

"Shapers reshape the truth. The Internet just distributed it, for people to make up their own minds."

"Hey! I trained as a shaper."

"Look, it's how we see it."

Constance expelled a noisy breath. "Never mind. Tell me more about the Internet. Was it used for education or recreation?"

"Both. It had moving images on it. And voices. And books – if you could read."

"It sounds like the comtel. Who controlled it?"

"No-one."

"How was that possible?"

He spread wide his hands. "It just – was."

"If nobody controlled it, then nobody was able to limit the information people could access. So it was monitored less than the comtel. This was radical!"

"The fisherman said there were attempts to block it, because of its power. But it was like water – it kept trickling out. There now, I've shared all my treasures with you. I've nothing left to offer. And we still have what's left of tonight, and tomorrow." A hint of mischief danced beneath his words.

"Then we won't be able to see one another for nearly a month," Constance tested for a reaction.

"Meanwhile, I'll be expected to mate with a different woman each week."

"Don't you like the idea of mating?"

"Why should I want to do it with a stranger? Even animals choose their mates."

"I didn't choose you either, you know." She took a deep breath, and made a conscious decision to say what was on her mind. "But I would, now."

102

He approached, until he was standing so close that the warmth of his breath feathered against her face. Her heart gave an unsteady skip. He reached out the tips of his fingers and stroked the slope of her neck. She could sense the blood surge in her face at his touch.

It reminded her she was wearing a skin which acted as a barrier between them. But if the sensations he produced were so powerful through a mask, they'd swamp her without one. The Mating Mother's warning rang in her ears: under no circumstances must she remove her skin with a man. It was for her own safety, she'd been told.

But maybe it was really for Sisterland's benefit.

His fingertips travelled along her face, until they found her mouth. Gently, he rubbed the ball of his thumb against her lower lip. How close he was – she could smell his breath now: it reminded her of pears. She lifted up her hand, and traced his jawline with the back of her forefinger. She could feel him waiting. Her finger moved higher until it reached his mouth, where she rested the tip of it against his lips. They felt softer than hers must, through her skin. His mouth closed against her fingertip in a butterfly kiss. She reached behind her ear and tore off her skin, dropping it carelessly to the floor. Then she took his hand and cupped it to her cheek, so that he could feel her face was naked before him. Even if he couldn't see it. For a moment, he tested the contours of her face, confirming the skin's absence. Moved by the pressure of his touch, she closed her eyes. He gathered her into his arms, bent his head and pressed his cheek against hers. Bare flesh against bare flesh.

They stayed like that, at one in their desire to prolong the encounter. Constance was afraid to speak in case it brought this intimacy to an end. Finally, he stirred and drifted his lips down her face and along her throat, feeling her pulse beat there. He raised his head, and mouth touched mouth. He tasted vulnerable. He tasted hopeful. He tasted of life.

The impact of the kiss was volcanic. Overwhelmed, she

pulled away. Kissing was rare in Sisterland, because of skins. Even in the home, where they were removed, the habit had been replaced by pressing palms together. Just as personal, in its way, Constance would have said. Until that moment.

No sooner had she separated from him than she regretted it. Instinctively, she leaned back into him, her arms circled his neck, pulling him close, and she kissed him again. When finally they paused to draw breath, she sank her face into the side of his neck. Her legs were buckling under the force of the moe which convulsed her body. Only his arms kept her upright. Desire was making her feel less substantial – she felt herself dissolve with it. Melting into him. She could hear his heart pounding against her chest, as accelerated as her own. It could almost be drumming inside her body.

The bell rang. They were supposed to be finished. The voice told them time was up. They kissed again.

The door rattled, and Constance wrenched herself out of his arms, groping for her skin. As he reached for her again, she pushed him away, and dragged on her footwear. By luck more than design, she was a short distance away from Harper when the door opened. But the imprint of their shared moe trembled in the ether. Charity registered it, and scowled.

In the doorway, Constance looked back at Harper. The light from the corridor shone on his face, revealing its symmetry more clearly than she had seen it before. How dear to her he was becoming.

"Soon, you'll be leaving us," The Mating Mother told Constance, in the respite room. "Still, perhaps you'll be back next month. Instant babyfusion is rare."

"Will I be allowed to stay in the Tower at night when I return next month, mother?"

"It all depends."

"On what?"

"On me."

"Have I done something wrong?" Constance's fear of being spied on in the mating cube resurfaced.

"Not that I know of." The Mating Mother's hand travelled along the hair streaming over one of her shoulders, making sure it was sleek.

Constance hesitated. Could the Mating Mother have any inkling of what was developing between her and Harper? It wasn't impossible, in view of a mother's mindmap powers. She watched the small hand continue its grooming.

"Your hair is magnificent, mother."

"This is a wig – part of my costume. You didn't realise that? I'm flattered." The Mating Mother stood on tiptoes and waggled a finger under Constance's nose. "But how suspicious you are! You can't imagine a Mating Mother has perks denied to others? That's not how Sisterland works."

Constance hung her head. She couldn't contradict her, but she knew it was untrue.

The Mating Mother studied her. "My helpers tell me you seem to find mating congenial."

"Anything done for Sisterland is satisfying to me."

"Commendable. But Charity says you have to be prised out of the mating cube."

"I like to lie down for as long as possible – you advised it."

"The mating urge makes Himtime more enjoyable for some than others. Meets are trained to gratify physical desires, after all. But remember, this is a means to an end. " She tweaked Constance under the chin. "A word from the wise, top girl: a meet is a utensil, not a person. Don't mistake him for one."

Chapter 12

"Last night," said Charity, as Constance stood outside the control hub. "Most women are relieved to go home and put all this behind them." She snaked a glance at Constance, indicating knowledge: Constance didn't fall into that category.

Constance felt a compulsion to tell her she wanted to mate with a man, not to achieve babyfusion, but to be close to him. Imagine Charity's face if she did! But she had to be careful – her moe urges were becoming more intoxicating.

"I'll take you to him in a minute," said Charity, when Constance didn't rise to the bait. "The clock for one of the cubes is on the blink. Need to check my records."

Charity fussed with her comtel, comparing times on it against those on-screen, but Constance wasn't impatient – she knew Harper was waiting for her. She wondered how long he had been in situ, ready for her arrival, and whether time lay heavy on his hands. He was right; their relationship were unequal. But there was nothing she could do about it, except give him the freedom to say yes or no to her.

Perhaps he'd find another sister he preferred to her. After all, she was his first. He might only like her because he had nothing to compare her against.

"Let's go," said Charity. "Mustn't keep your succulent slice of meet waiting."

"Why do you speak of him like that?"

"They're all tasty, aren't they? It's their job to look mating fit."

The door was locked behind her.

"Constance," said Harper, arms held out, and she flew into them. When they drew apart, she said, "You know this is our last night?"

"I know."

She took off her skin and knelt on the pop-up, sliding the skin under the pillow to protect it. He followed, kneeling beside her. They began kissing, his tongue against her lips, and she fell back beneath the pressure of his body. He collapsed with her, half-lying on top.

His hands grappled with her dress. "I can't open it." His laughter was low in his throat. "You'll have to help me."

She guided his hand inside the material, and he stroked the curve of her shoulder, then swept his palm down across her belly.

"Stop, Harper, wait. There's something I need from you."

He bit lightly on her earlobe, still caressing her, and she pushed him away, and sat up.

"I know you can't see me through the blindfold. But I want to know you realise this is Constance with you. Constance, who chooses Harper."

"Who chooses her."

He understood. She was relieved.

He reached into the waistband of his leggings, and produced a nail. "We can use this."

"To do what?"

"To remove the blindfold. It's what you want, isn't it?"

"Harper! You'll get in trouble!"

"I found it in the shower. I think another man smuggled it in, but lost his nerve and tried to get rid of it."

107

"He was right to be afraid. I'll take it with me when I leave, and throw it away."

"Cut off my blindfold first."

"I can't."

"Why not?"

"You'll be punished."

"I want to do this for you."

"It's too dangerous."

"I know you need me to see you."

"If we see one another, it makes us more equal."

"So use the nail."

"But later, there'll be trouble."

"Now is what matters – we can control now. We can't control later."

He stroked the underside of her breast, but she wriggled out from under his hand. "Stop trying to distract me."

"Stop wasting time. Cut off my blindfold."

"No."

"It's for me, too, Constance. So I can see you wanting me. And you can see me wanting you."

She was persuaded by that, and sliced at the seal, trying not to tear the material beneath so it could be tied back on. The blindfold fell away. She waited – anxiety mounting. How would he react to his first sight of her?

His eyes were pale grey – almost silver: they flew towards her and locked onto hers, looking at her for the longest time. Finally, she lowered her head.

"Why won't you look at me?" he said.

"Because of the way you're staring at me. It makes me nervous. See how you cause moes to break through?"

"You're nervous of me?"

She looked up, to see astonishment, followed by hurt, drive out the silver in his eyes.

"I'm nervous of disappointing you."

"Constance, I'm memorising you. Every line, every curve,

every nook and cranny of you."

Moisture gathered behind her eyelids. They couldn't be tears because tears were impossible. Nobody wept in Sisterland – not even when they lost their other. Her fingers reached for the corners of her eyes to check if they were damp. Dry. Perhaps it was the ghost of tears which tickled at her lashes.

He leaned forward and kissed her eyelids, and she forgot about being misty-eyed, or imagining she was. Her breath quickened, and she kissed him back. He ran his hands over her, his touch causing a tingle in her flesh that penetrated from skin to sinew and bone.

And then they were naked.

They paused to look at one another, and a shiver of desire crackled between them.

He entered her.

She winced, and only just stopped herself from crying out. The surprise of it! It hurt! The *Himtime* question-and-answer file had only warned her to expect discomfort. He stopped at once, and withdrew. But Constance didn't want him to pull out.

Putting a hand on the nape of his neck and another on his hips, she eased him in. At first, his movements were tentative, and he watched for a sign that he was causing her pain. But already her body seemed to be adjusting. The entry pangs were less sore this time. Besides, see how his body fitted into hers. His thrusts gathered in speed. She made herself relax and keep breathing, as *Himtime* advised. But she did not follow its instructions to remove her thoughts to another place – she wanted to feel this sensation, to watch this man.

To her surprise, she found herself begin to move beneath him, joining in his rhythm, hooking her limbs around his. Why, it was almost like dancing. But almost at once he stiffened, groaned, and squeezed his eyes shut. Wetness flooded from him. The plunging came to a shuddering halt.

She could feel his chest heaving against her breasts, the insistence of his heartbeat. After a moment, he opened his eyes, and smiled into hers.

It seemed to be over.

She was puzzled. Himtime hadn't taken long. He had seemed to feel pleasure, yet she had only begun to share it towards the end. But she had wanted him inside her, she couldn't deny it. Her hands had taken hold of his body, and guided him into hers.

She became conscious that he was still inside her, and it pleased her to realise they hadn't yet separated. To accommodate his weight, she shifted slightly. But she must have made a sound, because he rolled off. A sense of loss fluttered but, before it took hold, he curled towards her. She felt his breath on her cheek, his fingers in her hair.

They lay there, at peace. A stirring beneath her breast-bone, and she was aware of some element quitting her body and hovering overhead. She watched the two of them beneath her: she was on her back, he was on his side, an arm across her waist, one leg crooked over hers. How interdependent they looked. Already, they seemed to be growing round one another – tethered, each to each. A pull of the invisible string attached to her breastbone, a falling sensation, and the overview was gone.

He lifted his head.

"Still memorising me?" she asked.

"Just checking you haven't changed, Constance."

"Could you really see nothing through the blindfold?"

"Outlines – not details, or colours. I'd never have known you have one green eye, and one blue."

"My eyes are strange." She was apologetic.

"They're extraordinary. In a good way."

"Harper, what will they do to you when they find the seal broken?"

He didn't answer.

"They'll punish you, won't they?"

"Maybe I'll be denied exercise. Don't worry about me."

"But I do worry."

"Then stop." One by one, he kissed her fingers.

It's his gift to me, she thought. He understands why I needed it.

She lay back, looking at the ceiling. She could feel him against her, and knew he was almost ready to couple again. So some of the stories about men were true. She longed for more time with him. To watch him walk, sleep, eat, bathe, laugh, think, work. To become familiar with his voice, his body, his likes, his dislikes. His life. To let him take her by the hand through his forest, and point out the rabbit holes, the animal tracks, the places where male deer rubbed their antlers to mark out territory.

Time lost all meaning.

Until the bell.

They clung to one another.

"They'll unlock the door and find us like this," he whispered when the automated voice intoned, as usual.

"Aren't we supposed to be like this?"

Their smiles were complicit. His gaze was loving on her face.

His eyes! He wasn't supposed to see her. Constance uncoiled herself from Harper. "Your blindfold!" She lifted the strip of material, working at speed to retie it. It passed muster – at a distance.

The key turned in the lock.

She threw the pillow on the floor, snatching up her skin, and jammed it on her face.

The door swung open.

But where was the nail? She was sure she'd set it under the pillow after removing his blindfold. It was nowhere to be seen. She had to take it with her – she couldn't leave Harper to deal with the repercussions.

111

Charity loomed in the doorway.

"I'm not dressed," said Constance. "I fell asleep while I was resting afterwards." She pulled on her clothes beneath Charity's glare.

The nail! Where was the nail?

"Almost ready, sister. I'm still dozy."

"You sound agitated." Charity's suspicions were aroused.

"It's because I fell asleep with a meet watching me." Out of the corner of her eye, Constance saw Harper had one of his hands behind his back. She stood with her back to Charity. 'Give it to me,' she mouthed. He blanked her.

"Let's go," said Charity.

Constance looked from Charity to Harper. Deliberately, she stood on tiptoe, put her left hand on the back of his head, and pulled his lips down to hers.

"Stop that!" bawled Charity.

Constance's right arm slid round Harper's waist towards his back, her hand burrowing into his.

"Break it up! Now!"

Constance's questing fingers found the nail, and she snatched it off Harper.

Trying to stop her, he jumped backwards. "No!"

"Don't you dare say no, meet!" The stifstat was in Charity's hand.

Constance had the nail, and he could not give her away. She tucked it up her sleeve, and walked past Charity.

Charity forged towards Harper, stifstat extended. "What makes you think you can say no, meet? Were you saying no to me?"

"He was saying no to me," said Constance. "No to the kiss. Weren't you?"

Harper's head turned to track her voice.

"Answer her," commanded Charity.

"You were saying no to the kiss," repeated Constance. "You knew it was wrong. Didn't you?"

112

"Yes." The word was pushed out between his teeth.

"He didn't like being kissed, Charity. You saw that. He tried to step away."

"Can't say I blame him. Although it's not up to him to like or dislike anything. I'm reporting that disgusting mouth-sucking to the Mating Mother."

"As you like. I want to leave, now. This room stinks of man."

A few minutes after Constance was back in the respite room, the Mating Mother marched up. "I understand you behaved inappropriately after mating." Behind her was Sincerity, one of Charity's helpers, who had escorted Constance away from the mating floor, and then reported her.

"What counts as inappropriate?"

"You kissed the meet."

"I wasn't aware kissing was forbidden."

"We didn't realise it had to be banned. Any right-minded Sisterlander would understand it's unnecessary. Unhygienic, degrading, vile!"

Constance knew she had to defuse the situation. Benevolence was proof of the Mating Mother's far-reaching powers. She assumed a horrified expression.

"Of course it's horrible. All that drool! I found it revolting. My stomach turns somersaults just thinking about it. But someone told me babyfusion was guaranteed if you kissed. We hadn't kissed once, over the five nights. As I was leaving, it occurred to me to give it a try. I did it for Sisterland."

"That's a lie about kissing. Who told you?"

"Benevolence 101." Since Benevolence was already in Safe Space, the betrayal couldn't hurt her. "The meet was unwilling," she added. "I caught him by surprise."

The Mating Mother beckoned to Sincerity who was listening unashamedly. "Fetch Charity."

"She was doing a check on the mating cube. She said she'd

113

be with you as soon as she was through."

"Very well, tell her to come the instant she's satisfied with her inspection."

"I'm sorry Charity had to witness such a nauseating act," said Constance. "But I believed Benevolence. She's mated many times before."

"Although with no success," the Mating Mother snapped. "It seems strange you should regard her as an authority on the subject."

Constance swallowed. "True, but I heard it from another sister, too. That's why I believed it."

"Who else?"

The Mating Mother was shaken by the kiss. It was clear, from the way she was conducting the interrogation in full view of everyone in the respite room.

"From my other. Silence 1999."

The name shivered through the room.

Constance pressed home her advantage. "And Silence achieved babyfusion."

Charity pushed her way through the huddle of women, planting herself in front of Constance. "We got a problem, mother," said Charity.

"Indeed we do. Charity, did you observe this deplorable kiss?"

"Yes. Obnoxious. But there's worse to come. The meet's blindfold –"

Constance jumped in ahead of her. "I might have damaged it when I kissed him. He was alarmed, and broke away. I think maybe the seal might have snapped under my fingers."

"No maybes about it," said Charity.

The Mating Mother let out a gasp. "So he saw her face?"

Constance looked the Mating Mother straight in the eye. "No. The blindfold didn't fall off. He didn't see me."

"Charity?" The Mating Mother turned to her.

"The seal was broken. That's what I came here to report.

The meet was wearing his blindfold when I unloc̲
But it looked tampered with to me. I don't b̲
woman. It's in her interests to lie."

"This is intolerable, Constance 500!" cried the M̲
Mother.

"I did it for Sisterland – that's why I kissed him,"
Constance stammered. "I only wanted to achieve babyfusion.
But I didn't take off his bindfold. I'd never do that!"

"Spare me your excuses. The Shaper Mother will be
hearing about this. Your friends in high places won't be so
indulgent towards you when they read my report." She
clapped her hands, and a page scurried up. "Bring this
woman's clothes to her. And the mating-urge decompressant
drink." She glared at Constance. "As soon as you've taken it,
you're to leave. Charity, can you spare someone to stay by her
side until she's safely off the premises?"

"I'll do it myself," said Charity.

The Mating Mother turned back to Constance, whipping
her train out from under her feet with a crack that cut through
the air. "You're barred from the Tower. I won't have you
under my roof ever again. You should never have been
licensed to mate. You, Constance 500, are a wicked, corrupt,
depraved young woman!"

Chapter 13

Constance followed the river home through the moonless night, the salty taste of the decompressant drink on her tongue. She had considered refusing to swallow it, but Charity had stood so close that she could smell garlic on her breath and threatened force-feeding if she didn't take it voluntarily. Constance had decided it wasn't worth arguing.

As she walked, Constance was aware of her body in a new way. She was tender, still, but her flesh hummed from being with Harper. She was glad there had been no time to wash because she wanted his scent to cling to her for as long as possible. Even now, she could feel the pressure of his mouth against hers, the imprint of his fingers on her flesh. She imagined light and warmth must radiate from her. Surely, if she met someone, they would see the glow she imparted?

It couldn't be like this for everyone, because her source shuddered at the memory of mating. But some other women must feel this way, too. Silence hadn't been repulsed – she had said nothing negative about her time in matingplace. Indeed, she had smiled more than usual afterwards. Constance had thought it was because of babyfusion. But perhaps her other had experienced this mating pleasure-pain, too.

Remembering Harper's nail, she transferred it from her

sleeve to a pocket. At least she had spirited that away. But would they punish him for the broken seal on the blindfold? Probably. No, definitely. She cringed for him, in the Mating Mother's power. Charity's, too. But she couldn't help him. Next time, she'd make sure to –

What next time? She was banned from ever seeing him again. Aftershock juddered through her. How could she bear it? A crushing sense of desolation was bearing down on her – an eddy so powerful that her breath came in tearing gulps. A vein popped up on her temple and throbbed there.

All at once, it occurred to Constance that she was in the grip of a barrage of full-scale moes. Primal, insistent ones. Mating seemed to have released them in her. Mid-step, she froze. Harper had taken a risk to give her the kind of Himtime experience she wanted. He had been willing to accept punishment so that she could have what she desired. Nobody had ever cared for her so deeply. Not even Silence. She grappled with the implications. At girlplace, Constance had been taught that self-sacrifice was a female characteristic. Not common, but the potential was present in all of them. Yet here was a man demonstrating it for her benefit.

Amid the turmoil, recognition sank in. Love was meant to be something only sisters could feel for their others, and even then it was not guaranteed.

Yet Constance knew she was in love with a man.

Before Harper, love was a safe harbour. But this love was the storm itself. An excess of moes – ones no Sisterlander could supposedly access without chemical assistance – jostled for position: among them, exhilaration at having mated with him, along with delight at loving him. He must love her back! Even if he hadn't used the words. This moe bombardment released in her by Harper was awe-inspiring. Wonderful, too.

But it marked her out from her sisters. Trepidation tiptoed in.

Constance rounded the corner, and saw the outline of the

unit where she lived. If the mating was successful, she'd have to leave it. All babyfused women were moved into communityplace to allow Sisterland to care for them during the danger period, when babydefusion was most likely. The babydefusion rate was running at fifty per cent during the first three weeks. And even women whose babies survived that critical phase had only a one in two chance of carrying their precious cargo to term. But at that moment, she didn't care if mating would lead to babyfusion or not. All she cared about was Harper.

In the courtyard, a shape moved. Constance could distinguish a woman holding an egglight which illuminated a strip of chiffon round her neck. The red cloth stood out vividly, as a fresh scar shows against flesh.

At Constance's footsteps, the stranger called out, "I know you! You're her other! Silence's other!"

"Who are you?"

"You're Constance. I recognise you. You're the one remaining link to Silence."

She slid two fingers into her mouth and let out a whistle. An answering whistle bounced back. Two figures sprinted into view, panting from exertion through the clammy air. They, too, wore lengths of a sheer, red material at their necks and carried egglights.

"Is it her?" called one.

"Yes," said the first. "It's Silence's other."

Reverent, their attention converged on her.

One of them found her voice. "Tell us about Silence. You must have learned so much from her."

"Silence has gone," said Constance.

"Sister, she's here."

"No, she discontinued."

"She hasn't discontinued. She'll go on forever."

"Who are you?"

"We're the Silenced. We live to honour her."

Questions began to rain down on Constance.

"Why did she do it?"

"Did her babyfusion cause her pain?"

"What was her message for us?"

Bewildered, she made no effort to answer them. Until a question shook her.

"Is it true she turned against Sisterland?"

"Silence loved Sisterland," Constance protested.

"But she chose nothingness above Sisterland. Why?"

Constance pushed past them, towards the communal front door. On the step lay a pile of red flowers, all shades of the colour, from flame through to a burgundy-black. Some were withered, but the flowers on top were fresh blooms. She raised her comtel for admission, braced to press the alarm button if the women followed. But they stayed put. Watching.

Inside her twoser, she went to the window to check on them. The three were directly below, watching for her. She activated the blankout on both windows. Rattled, she turned on her entscreen, flicking through the menu selection. She had a choice between two worthy options: the Steadfast City Orchestra performing works by a selection of Sisterland's composers, or a documentary about Beloved's tour of all the belts. She plumped for the tour. It was relentlessly uplifting, even in Black Particle, home to Safe Space and little else. Sisterland consisted of many territories, from snow-capped peaks to valleys with lakes, yet Constance's knowledge of them was theoretical. In Steadfast, the climate was cooler, and people could run without breaking into an immediate sweat. Righteous had hot springs, where sisters could bathe outdoors all year round. She knew this from the entscreen. She would like to know it from experience.

Constance switched off halfway through Beloved's grand tour.

She woke late, and for a few moments of drowsy joy imagined

herself still in matingplace, due to see Harper later that day. But her surroundings revealed themselves, and disappointment replaced anticipation.

Remembering the Silenced, she levered herself out of her pop-up and steered for the window, raising the blankout. They were multiplying. Below stood a group of six women, each wearing a scarlet scarf. They gestured when they saw her. Constance closed the blankout, and pressed the icon on the contact console that connected her with the unit-minder.

"Greetings, sister. Those women outside. How long have they been waiting?"

"Greetings, sister. Last night made five nights. They're obsessed with your other. I told 'em she was ordinary. But they won't believe me. They pounce on any snippet about her."

"Do the peers know?"

"Sure do. Been here checking. But as long as they don't make a nuisance of themselves, nothing to be done. They ain't breaking any directives."

"Aren't they causing a disturbance?"

"By talking about Silence? By leaving flowers on the doorstep? Mind you, some of the residents are unhappy about the flowers. They say it's disrespectful. Smacks of the flowers left at Beloved's feet. They drop 'em off at the Hope Bridge, too. Always red. Like their bows."

"What's behind those red scarves?"

"Something to do with remembering Silence. They've decided to turn her into something she wasn't, and there ain't a thing to be done about it. Ignore 'em, and they'll find something else to fix on. That's what I'd do in your shoes, Constance."

There was no food in the twoser, and she had missed breakfast at the dine-all attached to the unit. She'd have to go to an eat-easy. Constance didn't want to pass the Silenced, but there was no way to avoid them. She washed, dressed, attached her skin, and stepped outside, past a leaning pyramid of flowers. They were multiplying, too. Conversation among the Silenced ceased. She lowered her head and advanced towards them, through air with the consistency of yoghurt.

The questions began again.

"Did she have a favourite scent?"

"Is it true she read poetry?"

"Had she chosen a name for her child?"

Blocked by a tall woman, Constance stopped. "Why are you here?" she asked.

The woman put her hand on Constance's shoulder. "We're here because we love her, sister. We're ready to do whatever she'd want."

Constance shook her off and pushed past, perspiration making her neck itch. Already, she was longing to be indoors to remove her skin. They followed her to the courtyard perimeter, and stopped. She hardly dared to believe they wouldn't pursue her, but nobody went as far as the eat-easy. At least she could breakfast in peace. They'd have been within their rights to sit at the next table and continue peppering her with questions. The Silenced must want to stay by the twoser. Perhaps they fancied themselves closer to Silence there. We love her, the tall sister had said. Constance gave a loud sniff. How could they love Silence when they had never met her?

From her seat in the easy, watching the cloud banks swim apart and reform above the river, Constance considered love. Once, she'd have said she loved Silence. But the clamour that Harper raised in her – now that was love. It was inconvenient. A love without hope. But there it was. Love couldn't be corralled or directed or suffocated. It blossomed in spite of everything. What an astonishing, liberating, intoxicating moe it was.

Even when she knew it was a transgressive love.

She had reacted to losing Silence with puzzlement, regret and something chiming with loss. But losing Harper was a physical pain. Was it possible there were sisters who felt the same about men, and hid it, as she was obliged to do?

A few more days, to know him better – she'd have liked that. Imagine being with him in his forest. Trees as far as the eye could see, with Harper as their caretaker. Nobody truly owned them, he said. No matter how many decrees the Nine issued about forest maintenance.

His descriptions filled her mind. The tame warbler with white eye-rings and a bobbing tail, which snatched crumbs from his hand. The family of foxes he watched at night, emerging from their lairs to forage. The baby fawn he'd chanced across, dappled coat camouflaging it from predators – the doe had left it behind while she hunted for food. Cool air scented by nature, not artifice – air which didn't claw at the throat, or clog the nostrils.

Constance shook her head to clear it. Ten hours, they had spent together. Ten hours to last a lifetime.

She left the eat-easy and dawdled back to her twoser. Once inside the courtyard, she had to pick up her pace to run the gauntlet of the Silenced, now swollen to fourteen. The stack of red flowers by the door was waist-high.

One of the Silenced tailed her to the door. "Is it true Silence chose the Hope Bridge for a reason?"

"I don't know why she did it there. I don't know anything. Please go away."

"It's the highest bridge in Harmony. She wanted to be seen. That's why she jumped from it. She did it for us – to tell us something."

"What was she telling you?"

The woman whispered, "Some of us have doubts about Sisterland. But nobody dares to speak them. We were alone with our fears. Till Silence brought us together. Her doubt allows us to doubt."

Constance hurried indoors. But the woman's words pursued her. She felt herself pulled to the window to see what the Silenced were doing. A young woman wearing a flimsy strip of red was approaching the entrance with a bunch of tulips, a serrated strain. She laid them on top of the pile and stood with her head bowed.

On impulse, Constance went along the corridor to the communal door.

"I'll take those inside, if you like," she said. "I can put them in water. For Silence."

For a moment, the girl was too tongue-tied to respond. Then the words came galloping. "Yes, please. I pray to her. To Silence. Instead of Beloved."

Constance looked at the tulips. Already, their heads were open and they were starting to bend at the waist. They wouldn't last. Even so, their scent filled her nostrils. Gently, she said, "She can't answer your prayers, sister. She was only a woman."

"Silence?"

Constance was about to agree. But a shocking thought fountained through her mind, causing her to drop the flowers.

Not only Silence, but Beloved. Both just women.

It was the seventh day after mating and time for Constance to be tested for babyfusion. It could be detected at this stage, and Sisterland needed to know immediately so that precautions could be attempted against babydefusion.

Constance keyed into her comtel for instructions, and read that she was expected at a clinic close to the Tower. No appointment necessary. She might as well go straight over. Babyfusion was unlikely, after a single mating, but the test was mandatory.

She thought about lobbing some information at the Silenced as she passed by. "She never ate breakfast." Or "Pale blue was her favourite colour." But she shouldn't encourage them. Instead, she waved, as though they were work colleagues she hadn't time to chat with, and kept moving.

There were at least twenty outside her twoser now, never without their gauzy red scarves and egglights. Keeping vigil.

There was no need to pass the Tower to reach the clinic. But Constance did it anyway, impelled by a need to be where Harper was, even if she couldn't see him. She fixed her attention on the door for a few moments, motivated by the same hunger with which the Silenced watched her window. Had they docked his food rations? Put him in solitary confinement? Surely Charity and her stifstat wouldn't have been let loose on him! She willed loving thoughts through the walls, to wherever he was in the building. *I'm thinking of you, Harper. Are you thinking of me?* Nobody went in or out. By and by, she turned her steps towards the clinic.

There were six women ahead of her. None of them had babyfused. Each one tried to remain detached, but was clearly disappointed. When her turn came, the medico was chilly as she accepted Constance's urine sample. But, after testing it, her demeanour became animated.

"Congratulations, Constance 500. Sisterland is proud of you. I'm gratified to report babyfusion. All being well, you'll be a source in three months."

Wide-eyed, Constance gasped, "Babyfused? Already? Are you sure?"

"We don't make mistakes about babyfusion." Seamlessly, she corrected herself. "We don't make mistakes about anything in Sisterland. Now, here's a pill to override the old nine-month timetable. It might leave you a little nauseous for a week. If that happens, switch to high-calorie liquids. There's a special range for babyfused sisters, available free as soon as I send through notification. I'll do it at once. Your new status will be registered on your sig later today."

"But what if it doesn't . . . I mean, what if I defuse?"

"Statistically, the odds are against you becoming a source, unfortunately. But let's cross that bridge when we come to it. For now, you're babyfused. Well done."

"I only mated once," Constance blurted out.

"Really? You must be exceptionally fertile. Lucky, too, to get a result so quickly. You ought to swallow that pill right away. It has to be taken as soon as babyfusion is confirmed. Your body needs to begin the fast-forward. You don't want to drag round in a babyfused condition for nine months!"

While the medico stood over her, Constance chewed the fuchsia-pink pill. It tasted bitter.

"There now, you're on the way. Your system will need eight hours to process that." While she was speaking, the medico delved into a box, and lifted out some tubes. "There's a little turbulence initially, while the pill adjusts your body's rhythms, but you'll be glad of it only lasting thirteen weeks, I promise you. Hard to believe PS women used to have forty-week gestations. What were their scientists thinking of? I could see it being kept if success rates were higher, but it just seemed to allow more time for things to go wrong." She set the tubes in front of Constance. "From tonight, you should start taking these protein poppers twice a day. You're going to be ravenous – the poppers will help to fill you. It's essential you remember to take them. I always advise sources to set an alert on their comtels. Just till they get the habit. I must warn you: if you miss a couple of days, your motor skills will begin to shut down. Fast-forward babyfusion is a wonderful advance – but it can take a toll on women's bodies." She smiled. "Congratulations again, sister. I haven't had a babyfusion for months – I was starting to think I was jinxed."

"When do I move into communityplace, sister?"

The medico's face tightened – even the skin couldn't disguise it. "That may not be happening, sister."

Constance was bewildered. "But don't all babyfused women spend their first weeks in one? I thought it helped to prevent babydefusion."

"I'm not at liberty to discuss this, sister. Be patient. Information will be sent thorough to your comtel as soon as you need to know it. Rest assured, Sisterland has your best interests at heart."

In a dream state, Constance made her way home. Still dazed, she passed through a throng of the Silenced, impervious to their clamour. Inside her twoser, she operated the blankouts on the windows, and collapsed into the pop-up. But she lay awake on it, staring at the ceiling. Loss kept reconfiguring her life. First she had lost Silence. Then Harper. And now she was carrying a child she was destined to lose. Even if she didn't babydefuse, her child would be taken from her. After a year with her, the baby would go to girlplace.

How did Sisterlanders live with the loss? Why did nobody talk about it?

Chapter 14

Staccato pips from her comtel woke Constance. A message, coded urgent, was flashing. **SM wishes to see you.** SM was the Shaper Mother. Could she know about the babyfusion already? Constance had hoped to hug it to herself for a little while. But she supposed the medicos must report every successful mating. They were rare enough to attract attention – babyfusion wasn't a secret she could be allowed to keep.

Constance splashed water on her face, and sailed out past the Silenced. Wanting to share her good luck, she called as she passed, "Silence hiccupped when she laughed. She had freckles on her hands. She liked to daydream – she said it wasn't time wasted, but time invested."

Waiting for a Buzz, her sig caught her attention. Pinkification had vanished – she was no longer licensed for Himtime. Instead, a dark-blue circle had been added. It represented babyfusion. Constance laid her fingertip on the new symbol, wondering what Harper was doing right then. Wishing she could share the news with him. What a persistent presence he was, even though she had to accept him as absent from her life. Still, she liked to think of Harper living under the same sky above her.

Please don't let him be blamed for the blindfold, she

thought. And if he has to be punished, let it be over now.

She boarded a Buzz, and looked at the women seated nearby. Some were with their others. Everyone knew the other system was more sophisticated than inter-gender pairing, and relationships were on a higher plane now. Yet Harper was the one she'd choose to have sitting here beside her on the Buzz. Except, as he had reminded her in matingplace, men weren't allowed on the Buzz.

To distract herself from anti-Sisterland thoughts, Constance looked out of the window. All about her, the city unfolded. Viewed from the Buzz that morning, it sparkled with promise. Buildings reared up like icebergs, their mirrored glass frontages shivering with pale colours. Sisterland was a place of beauty, she reminded herself.

Quick as lightning came another thought. Harper would call it a false beauty.

A few stops away from the Eternity Square station, a stitch in her side transfixed Constance, the physical pain jolting her system. Hunger pangs, but on a scale she had never experienced before. Belatedly, she realised she hadn't taken her protein popper the night before, or this morning. She scrabbled in a pocket for the packet, pressed the seal, and an orange pill tipped into her hand. Its outer coating was powdery, yet it didn't dissolve, and she found she couldn't swallow it.

"Sister, you'll never manage that without water," said the passenger opposite. "I remember those pills – don't miss having to take them."

"I don't have any." Constance doubled up, another hunger spasm overtaking her.

The woman produced a water tube. "Have this. You can't afford to miss those poppers. Your body isn't your own for thirteen weeks. Babyfusion gobbles you up."

Constance swallowed a pill. It took effect quickly and, as soon as she was able, she tapped in a twice-daily reminder on her comtel. She'd have to be vigilant about those poppers.

By the time she reached her stop, she was capable of disembarking. She rested on a bench, before joining the flow of foot traffic into Eternity Square. Yet more beauty, she thought, at the spectacle of splintering light beams from the mirrored wings above Shaperhaus. But could it truly be beauty if it was sterile? It surprised her to realise just two weeks had passed since she was last at Shaperhaus. So much had happened. Back then, she lived in the same world as Harper – but their lives hadn't touched. Now, they were connected forever.

Constance reported directly to her progress-monitor. "The Shaper Mother has sent for me."

A speculative expression flitted across Patience's face. It was clear she wanted to ask Constance what it was about, but couldn't presume – not when it concerned the Shaper Mother.

"You're popular upstairs, aren't you? Well, go on up, if she's expecting you."

In the Shaper Mother's outer office, her assistant Modesty was studying rotas. "You'd need eyes in the back of your head to keep track of the shapers on location," she said. "Her majesty awaits you."

As before, the Shaper Mother was seated on her ersatz throne. This time, however, her customary composure was absent. Her fingers tugged at a bead on her shawl, and Constance had the impression her analytical mind was unpicking a problem.

"Sweet child, how rested you look. More peaceful, I think. Sit." She turned her hand palm outward, and indicated a footstool. "You mated successfully, I believe?"

So, the medico had passed along her results. Constance took the seat, but pulled it back as far as she dared. The Shaper Mother's lemongrass scent was making her nauseous. "Yes, I'm babyfused, mother."

"Splendid. Time will tell if it leads to a baby. We must hope

129

for the best. Have you taken your pills yet?"

"I took one yesterday to speed up babyfusion. And now I'm on the protein poppers."

Fingers heavy with rings propped up the Shaper Mother's chin. "I had a report from the Mating Mother in the Tower. She levels a serious accusation against you."

Constance moistened her lips, her defence rehearsed already in her mind. "I admit it, I kissed a meet. I heard it improved success rates."

"That's not all you did."

"It was an accident. The Mating Mother is mistaken if she thinks I did it deliberately. There was another incident at the Tower – a guest became hysterical and caused a disturbance. She had to be removed. Naturally, the Mating Mother was out of sorts about this episode. But it may have caused her to jump to the wrong conclusions in my case."

"She didn't mention an overexcited guest. You could be right about it colouring her view of what happened. I wonder . . ." Tap-tap, went the Shaper Mother at Constance's mind.

Constance had a wall erected round it.

The mother sat back, and adjusted her rings. "You've babyfused – you won't be going back to matingplace. I think we can afford to take a lenient view of this."

"Mother, may I ask a question?"

"Certainly."

"At the clinic, I was expecting to be given details about moving into communityplace. But the medico suggested there may be a change of policy."

"That's right, sweet child. Studies show the communityplace system doesn't affect babydefusion rates, after all. It turns out that babyfused women are just as safe in their own homes, provided they're sensible. You see? The Nine listens to sisters. Especially to sisters engaged in such a patriotic enterprise. They never took to communal living, and their voices have been heard."

"All the women I met in matingplace expected to be sent to communityplace."

"They'll be pleasantly surprised. Are you questioning the Nine's decisions?"

"Of course not, mother." In fact, it was a reprieve.

"I should hope not. Now, I have a mission for you: you're needed to interchange a memory-keeper's memories."

"I understood I was off the co-keeping programme, mother. You said I had to concentrate on babyfusing, and moe-suppression."

"This is a one-off assignment. The memory-keeper is extremely old and in poor health. Medicos are keeping her pain-free. But they don't expect her to continue much longer. She has one last nook of memory to release before she discontinues. We know it's there, stored in her memory banks, but we haven't been able to persuade her to share it. Until now."

"Which one is she?"

"She's our oldest keeper, Honour 1020. She visited Shaperhaus shortly after you were admitted as a trainee shaper, and gave a talk to your class. Afterwards, you spoke to her about a PS poet called" – the mother consulted her comtel – "Emily Dickinson. That's why she's latched on to you. Odd, of course, but we must indulge her. She deserves our kindness and respect."

Constance recalled a memory-keeper's visit in her second week at Shaperhaus. She had no recollection of talking to her about Emily Dickinson, yet it sounded plausible. Silence had enjoyed Dickinson's work, and sometimes she'd share her observations.

"Watch those facial expressions, sweet child. You'll pucker," the Shaper Mother reproved.

Automatically, Constance relaxed her muscles, but an impassive face left her no less puzzled. Even if they had discussed a poet, why would the keeper ask for her? She had been unexceptional: one among many students.

"Mother, I haven't interchanged a keeper's memory on my own. I've only done it under observation in class. What if I mess up?"

"Just remember the Triple E methodology you were taught: empathise, extract and exude. You become the memory. Immerse yourself in detail. Nothing is too trivial: details combine to form a mosaic. Live the experience along with her. And take possession of it when she finishes. You're a quick learner: I have every confidence in you."

"I'll do my best, mother. Should I go to her now?"

"Do, indeed, there's no time to be lost. It's peculiar, Constance – all her life, Honour was a model sister, but on this matter she never budged. She refused to describe what it was like growing up in a cake shop. It's my belief some residual loyalty to her early years prevented her from discussing it. Because of Sisterland's view on cakes, you see. We'd sooner license euthanasia shops than cake shops. But now, with the medicos telling her it's only a matter of days, she has conceded. It's heartening to see her deep-rooted loyalty to Sisterland assert itself: even at the end, still keen to be of assistance. With her final breath, you might say."

Constance had never eaten cake, and its absence was no hardship.

The Shaper Mother's voice bisected her thoughts. "Honour will be a loss to Sisterland. But her memories will be preserved and studied."

"But why should we want to preserve her memory of something as harmful as a cake shop, mother? Wasn't sugar added to cakes? Surely these cakes would have made people obese?"

"Cake was embedded with complex symbols for our ancestors. We'd like to try and understand its allure. There's an element of sensuality in baking, we concede that. But it mystifies us why Pre-Sisterland women were once negligent enough to feed cake to their children, knowing sugar rotted the teeth. The keeper's memories may help to unlock the secret. We're relying on you, Constance. The porthole through which to retrieve this information is narrow. Can you take on the interchange, and unravel the moes inspired by cake?"

"I'll do my best."

The Shaper Mother's thoughts turned inward. "Clearly, there's some fetish attached to baking. Perhaps it's about power: the knowledge the cake will give pleasure. Even though pleasure is such a transitory state of affairs." She became intent on Constance again. "Hurry to her side, sweet child. Regrettably, our keeper is on borrowed time. Modesty has forwarded her address to your comtel."

"With your permission, I have a question, Shaper Mother." The mother's expression of polite inquiry had an edge to it, but Constance persevered. "When I returned home from matingplace, I found some women outside my twoser. They're still there. Paying homage to my other. They call themselves the Silenced."

A tremor rippled through the Shaper Mother, and her voice shook. "Those poor creatures are under a delusion. We've been indulgent towards them. But they try our goodwill."

"They aren't annoying me. I just wondered about them."

"I'm not surprised. The Nine wonders about them, too. About the effect such extravagant behaviour may have on sisters elsewhere. Extravagance is unacceptable. It's immoderate – it smacks of moe."

"They don't make any noise. They just wave their egglights about."

"They also gather in the Octagon zone, holding hands and singing by the bridge where it happened. Unfortunately, there's a public square there, they have space to congregate. None of this is helpful. These women are becoming a curiosity. A focal point. An eyesore. Tell me, Constance, have you spoken with them?"

"Just in passing."

"Do you find them persuasive?"

"I haven't given it any thought. I just wish they weren't there. But their numbers are growing."

The Shaper Mother shuddered, the whites of her eyes showing. "If they approach you, urge them to disband. Perhaps you could tell them it's what your other would want. Say she'd dislike the attention. Could you do that?"

Constance didn't believe she could speak with authority about Silence's preferences. She hadn't known Silence wanted discontinuation, after all.

'You'd have dissuaded her if you knew what she meant to do," said the mother.

Belatedly, Constance tried to close off the mindmapping. "The Silenced are only leaving flowers, mother."

"One thing leads to another. Red flowers have an air of violence about them. I don't care for them. But how did these deluded sisters find you? Does this mean you haven't moved out yet?"

Constance was confused. "You said babyfused women are no longer required to spend time in communityplace."

"Yes, yes. But are you still in the twoser you shared with your other?"

"I've reported my willingness to go. But the unit allocators have no vacant onesers. They say I must wait."

"Wasteful." The Shaper Mother tsked her tongue against the roof of her mouth. "Tell Modesty to follow it up. We can't condone waste in Sisterland. Resources are precious, and must be safeguarded."

"You did kindly say I could stay in Oblong, mother."

"Indeed I did, Constance. I know you're a loyal Sisterlander, with much to offer. *Sisterland Prizes . . . ?*"

"*Obedience.*" Constance finished Beloved's quote.

"Quite so. And we believe in rewarding service." She

tapped her hands together, rings clanking. "I need your memory-keeper interchange by tomorrow morning. The Nine is anxious to know its contents."

Constance was dismissed.

Chapter 15

The memory-keeper's frame barely disturbed the patchwork quilt covering the pop-up in which she lay. Constance recognised Honour 19 as soon as she saw her again in mindedplace, although what lay before her was a shrunken version. She remembered her because of the keeper's hair. It had surprised her then, and still made an impact. Her hair was grey – a pewter shade from crown to tip. An antidote to grey had been discovered, and a monthly shot could hold it at bay. Nobody's hair needed to change colour as they aged, unless they were willing for it to happen. Few were.

Honour was propped against pillows, eyes closed and breathing laboured. The quilt was tucked under her armpits, and she gripped a corner between her fingers. It seemed to comfort her to have something to hold. Lines from *Beloved's Pearls* were sewn into the quilt squares. *Mustn't Grumble* lay close to the shrivelled hand that curled on top.

The medico who brought Constance to her bedside leaned close to the keeper. "This is Constance 500. She's from Shaperhaus. You asked for her."

Honour opened eyes with lashes sticky from sleep. "Tired," she croaked.

"I can come back another time," Constance offered, at a

louder pitch than normal, taking her cue from the medico.

"Time. No. Not much left." Honour sifted a breath through her lips.

The medico gave a nod to Constance, and left the room.

Her skin lay on the bedside table, reminding Constance to remove hers. She laid it beside Honour's. An old face and a young face. They didn't look much different.

Honour's gaze drifted towards the skins. "I remember when sisters didn't wear skins. That's how old I am." Her laugh was dusty.

"I expect their faces were in a terrible state."

"They had lines. That's all." Honour wet her lips and her voice gained in strength. "Their faces were moe thermometers, showing how they felt. Some said it was ugly. All those moes left tidemarks. But I never minded them. For every groove from grief, there was a laughter line from happiness. You the Emily Dickinson girl?"

Constance touched her bare face, which felt tight after the skin. "I am. You came to Shaperhaus when I was a trainee. You told us why the PS world had to be overturned. And about Beloved, who wanted to safeguard the Sisterland way of life."

"Didn't I tell you any fun stuff?"

"When you were leaving, you looked at us all lined up in our uniforms, and said something about the tyranny of good taste. Nobody remembered how liberating tastelessness could be, you said. The progress-monitor looked scandalised, and you said to pay no heed to you – it was just an old woman's crankiness breaking through."

Honour hacked out a laugh. "They've got you on this new co-keeper programme?"

"Yes."

Her neck creaked as she moved her head against the pillows. "Co-keepers. Like to see how they expect that to work. A person either has memories, or she doesn't. Can't go

137

round taking possession of somebody else's."

"Hardly anyone's left who remembers the PS days, sister. You're one of the last."

The ancient face grew wistful. "Last of the summer wine. I was born in summer time. Won't see another summer. That's all right – I'm ready to let go." Her hands fluttered. "So you're the Emily Dickinson girl. You told me she used to lower a basket of cakes out of her bedroom window on a rope, to children waiting below. I liked that."

"My other said so. A recipe for coconut cake was found among the poet's papers."

"Come closer. Yes, you're the girl. I remember those eyes. One among so many memories. Sometimes, I think memory-keepers are nothing but curiosities. Like museum pieces." Her fingers fidgeted against the quilt. "It's stuffy in here. I miss the wind."

"You remember the wind?"

"There were winds when I was a girl. Playful winds and bossy winds and refreshing winds. You never knew what the wind might throw in your path."

The medico padded back into the room, and adjusted some dials attached to the foot of the pop-up. "Honour, if you feel the slightest twinge, send your visitor to fetch me. I'll be right outside. We don't want you to suffer. Not for a minute."

"All right."

"You'll call me if you're concerned about her?" The medico addressed Constance. "Honour dislikes making a fuss. But pain relief is a right at her age. There's nothing to be gained by suffering when we can take away the pain."

When it was just Constance and the memory-keeper again, Honour pulled a face. "That medico talks about pain relief every time she walks into this room. When I feel a creak in my bones, I know I'm still alive."

"Are you in pain now, Honour?"

"Girl, I have a pain in my heart, if that counts. A dread I

might not get a chance to share my secret. With someone who'll understand it. Been fretting about it for weeks, till you came to me. I knew you were the one. Now, no more chit-chat. We need to press on."

"Anything you want is fine by me, sister."

The keeper's eyelids floated downwards. "What I want is to slip away. Here too long. Living gets tiring, when you been doing it as long as me." The eyelids were forced open again, and bleached eyes fastened on Constance's. "I'm ready for the share now."

Constance tapped a code into the sig on her wrist. Next, she took Honour's blue-veined hands in hers, guiding the keeper's fingers to tap the same series of codes onto her own sig. She touched her sig to Honour's, where they flashed and locked onto one another. Constance rested the papery arm gently on the quilt, her own alongside it.

It meant that when she shared the memory, Constance would relive it: not just the words, but what underpinned them. The smells, tastes, sights and sounds colouring the memory. To all intents and purposes, it would become her memory. When she repeated it, she'd convey every nuance. Exactly as if the experience had been hers.

"Do you need a drink of water, before we start?"

Honour shook her head. "I was seven the year World War III broke out. My parents owned a bakery, and I used to help out after school. That was a kind of girlplace, but we lived at home while we went there. Even during the war, my parents managed to keep the bakery going."

"Did you live in Harmony?"

"There was no Harmony then. No Sisterland, either. It went by another name. Only the keepers remember it, but we're not allowed to use the name any more."

"What do you remember about that time?"

"Everything. Our bakery was always busy. Customers travelled from a long way away. We sold only cakes – no bread – and our cakes sang of pleasure and indulgence and celebration. They gladdened the dullest day and the saddest face. But I took that time for granted – I never knew happiness would come to be rationed."

Constance stroked the hand moored to hers, and Honour returned to her story.

"We piled them high on cake-stands. Jam tarts with their lids cut into shapes, and cup cakes in every shade and flavour you could imagine. Millionaire's shortbread and iced fancies, fruit muffins, and pies sprinkled with sugar crystals. Yes, sugar crystals! And the sky didn't fall in! There was angel cake, lemon drizzle cake and chocolate biscuit cake, all baked to an old family recipe. There were gingerbread women, men too, and we decorated them in line with the season. In springtime, our gingerbread figures held a bunch of flowers, in summer they wore sunglasses and hats. It was scarves and mittens in autumn, and snow boots in winter. At Christmas – that used to be a holiday, like Sisterday – we made kissing pairs, under a sprig of a plant called mistletoe. They were always my favourite. There's no mistletoe left any more. Such a pity. No kissing, either."

Constance thought of Harper, and a smile slipped across her face. The interlocked sigs flashed, reeling her back in.

Absorbed in the past, Honour kept talking. "My parents worked side by side. They were a team. My mom – I know we're meant to call them sources now but that's what she was to me – she took care of the shop and the business end. My father was the creative one – his cakes were works of art. Everything was baked by hand. It was labour-intensive. Old-fashioned, I suppose. But he insisted cakes knew the difference, and tasted better with the personal touch. My father told me stories as he measured and stirred, sprinkled and trickled. He spoke of his father, and his father before him, all bakers. I was their only child. People had brothers and sisters back then. But not me. I never wanted any, because I had my father all to myself. He saved his lightest cakes for me – they floated onto my tongue. For my birthday, I had cakes decorated with jungle animals, or the solar system, or a carousel – the year I learned to swim, he showed me doing the backstroke, wearing my candy-striped bikini. Each year, he surpassed himself."

Constance swayed, her balance affected by all the sensory imagery interchanged into her mind.

"They say people who work in kitchens can be crotchety, with the heat and the pressure, but my parents never exchanged a cross word. He baked, and she sold his cakes, and they were happy together. Our customers were happy, too. They always left happier than when they came in."

Honour took on a radiance as she reminisced, the years peeling away. For a few moments, she was lost in thought. Constance knew she should move her along – it was a co-keeper's job to keep the memories flowing, but she left Honour alone. Not all memories were meant to be shared.

When she was ready, the keeper retrieved the threads of her story. "Baking cakes was gratifying, my father told me. You knew you were doing something that would give a stranger pleasure. He called his cakes a gateway to goodwill. He taught me how to bake, and my cakes tasted finer than fine. Oh, they did!" She kissed her fingertips, and blew them out. "But they never achieved his heights. I took over the gingerbread people, and they always sold out, no matter how many I baked. That was my special skill. But my father had a gift. He told me his secret: he whispered to his cakes as he put them in the oven. Told them they'd bring joy to the person who ate them. You see, not everything in the PS world was wicked. Our cake-shop gave the neighbourhood something it valued. It was loved." She sighed, her eyes clouding over. "Women thought we could make a better world. Learn from men's mistakes. But we made a fundamental mistake of our own: we never forgave men. Got off on the wrong foot, and been wrong-footed ever since. The experiment has failed. Sisterland will never be a success till we forgive men. And even if we do, will they forgive us?"

Constance recoiled. Her moe response was picked up by the interlocked sigs, and they juddered, giving her a mild electric shock. A momentary gap would show up later in the memory interchange at that point, but no sister could listen unmoved to Sisterland being labelled a failure. Constance's doubts had never pushed her to such a damning conclusion.

Yet Honour's words had the ring of truth.

Honour gave no sign of noticing her distress, but she began to slow, gaps creaking between each sentence. "We didn't try to reason with men. Didn't try re-educating them. Didn't try to ban the belligerent ones from mating. We didn't try anything. Just washed our hands of them. Every last one." Her fingers worried at the quilt. "I grew up in a family. It worked. The Nine won't welcome these memories. Could be, I'm the last keeper with them. But they're true. And I've done wrong by my father, staying silent."

An attack of coughing racked the narrow frame, and Constance held a tube of water to Honour's mouth. Some drops dribbled on her chin, and Constance lifted a cloth from the bedside table to wipe them away. Her brain was teeming from the memory-keeper's incendiary words. The coughing fit continued, and Honour pointed at their sigs, as though the interchange was contributing to her discomfort. Constance paused the connection.

At once, Honour leaned forward and whispered a few words in her ear.

Constance recoiled.

"That's for the Nine's ears only," said Honour. "If I put it on the memory record, the Nine will never go public with it. And I want sisters to hear about my father." Her breath began to rattle in her chest. "You don't have to tell it if you're afraid. But maybe one of them could profit from the truth."

Wheezing, Honour slid down her pillows.

To Constance's alarm, an ashen pallor crept across her face. "Help!" she called. She looked over her shoulder, towards the door. "Help!" she cried, at full throttle. Nobody was coming. But she couldn't move – their wrists were still attached at the sig. She bit her lip. Ought she to wait, in case there was more?

Honour's hand clutched at Constance's front. "There were good men. My father was one. He baked cakes. Magical cakes."

The eyes blazed, and Constance marvelled that she had ever thought them faded. Even as she watched, the light in them was doused, the fingers loosening.

Constance unclicked sigs, and sprinted for the door. "Help!"

"Is there any hope of saving her?" Constance asked the medico escorting her to the exit.

"Honour is in a fragile state," said the medico.

"I don't know if she was finished saying everything she needed to – maybe I could come back tomorrow?"

"Interchanging exhausted her – she has so little strength left. But I know the Nine wants her to share as much as she can." The medico hesitated. "Let's wait and see if she rallies. You never can tell. She's all willpower, that one."

"I'd like to call by again, if I may. I don't care about interchanging. I could just sit with her, and hold her hand. I wouldn't get in the way, I promise."

"I suppose she did take quite a shine to you. Tell you what. I'm on night duty. Here's my comtel code: message me in the morning, and I'll let you know how she is. Perhaps it's not the end yet. I'm sorry you didn't get everything you wanted from Honour."

Constance reflected. "You know, I believe I did."

But whether it would be what the Nine wanted was another matter.

Chapter 16

Constance made her way to the Buzz station, hoping the memory-keeper would pull through. And then she realised the hope was for her own sake and not Honour's. The keeper was ready to let go. She checked her comtel: no messages from Shaperhaus, which meant she was free to go home. The interchange could be run there, and delivered to the Shaper Mother the following morning.

On the Buzz, her mind was surfeited on father imagery. All her conditioning was that a man's Himtime role was his only part in the babyfusion process. But Honour's father had nurtured her as well as any woman. Constance rested her hand on the sig containing Honour's memory. A revolutionary idea was stored on her wrist.

Stepping off at the Oblong stop, she became aware of an unfamiliar sensation. It stirred her hair and flapped her clothes. Why, the air was breezy! It had been years since Harmony's soupy air had been agitated. What a coincidence, on the same day as Honour 19 reminisced about the winds of her girlhood.

Constance stood still, feeling the wind tease her. How liberating it would be to pull off her skin and let the air tiptoe across her face. She put her hand to the fastening, but allowed it to fall away. Pollutants could be carried on the breeze. Still, as she turned for home, she was able to pick up her step along the riverbank, without feeling as if she was wading through the atmosphere. Another eddy, and her tunic ballooned. She wondered that there were no alerts on the comtel advising of the change in the weather. She checked the sky but, instead of scudding clouds, it was packed with the usual low-hanging cotton wool.

As she walked, Constance watched the river whipped into ridges that collapsed and reformed. How strong the wind was, controlling the water. A gust blew an object into her face, and Constance jerked to avoid the missile. Only a twig. That was the downside to wind. Already, her eyes felt itchy. All the same, she hoped Honour was able to hear this wind rattle against her window. Maybe someone would open it so that she could feel the refreshed air.

A chugging sound was followed by a human voice. A salmon-pink vehicle, diagonal black stripe running from wheel-arch to roof, rolled past. It was the peers. From inside, a voicebox issued a warning. "*Attention, all sisters. Freak weather conditions have blown up. You are advised to go indoors and stay there until further notice. Repeat: go indoors and stay there until further notice.*"

Constance picked up her step. At the courtyard outside her unit, she was surprised to see the Silenced were still there, despite the wind. She counted some two dozen women, the tails of their scarves tossed about by the wind, looking as if they were attacking one another. She should take them out some ocean tea. Their clothes had that damp sheen from being too long outdoors. But wouldn't drinks encourage them to stay? The Shaper Mother had asked her to persuade them to disperse.

"Constance!" called out a member of the group, "Stay awhile and talk to us about Silence. We want to understand her better."

Constance kept walking. "I don't understand her myself. Which of us does truly know anyone else?"

Several of the group fell into step beside her. "Tell us something. Anything," begged one.

"You know so much about her already," said Constance. "Though I can't imagine how you do."

"What did she work at?" asked another woman. "Someone told me she was a thought-crafter. Someone else that she worked in Sistercentral."

In the face of misinformation, Constance relented. "She was a sig-tagger."

"Oh . . ." The group expelled a mass breath.

"I wonder if Silence installed my baby's sig?" said one.

"Imagine if she held my Diligence!" cried another.

Peers rolled by, the voicebox still playing. "*Calling all sisters. Unusual weather conditions have blown up. You are advised to go indoors.*"

"Shouldn't you think about leaving? It might be unsafe to stay outside," said Constance.

"The peers want us gone," said a voice from the outer fringes of the group. "This wind is meant to 'coax' us."

Constance misstepped, turning over on her ankle, and a hand caught her by the elbow.

"You believe the peers control the wind?" she asked.

"No, but the Nine might be able to – just for a short time."

"A short time can be long enough," said the first woman. "But the courtyard is sheltered. We'll be all right."

"I'd just as soon go home," said another.

"Go, if you like, Comfort. But I'm staying."

"Me, too," chorused a number of voices.

Comfort stayed where she was.

"Talk to us about Silence," pleaded the group.

Perhaps it was the unsettling effect of the wind. Or it might have been down to her memory-interchange with Honour. But Constance was unable to resist.

"Silence had no interest in material possessions. She used to leave a trail behind her, wherever she went. Scarves, hats, necklaces, poetry books – although she missed the books when they were lost. If you admired anything of hers, she'd give it to you at once. Even if she was wearing it."

Several of the Silenced wore replete expressions, as though they had drunk deep on insights. Constance edged round a mound of carnations, snapdragons and hibiscus blooms, and her comtel chirped admission to the unit. She left her companions outside, and climbed the stairs to her twoser, raising her comtel to beep in again. But the door wouldn't open. She waved her hand about, but the light on the lock didn't change. Back downstairs she went, in search of the unit-minder. No sign of her. She tried outside.

"Have you seen the minder?" she asked the Silenced.

"She had her coat on. Said she was due a plate of sea-stew." Comfort jerked her thumb downstream.

"Thanks. She must be at the easy on the riverbank."

Constance turned up her collar as she followed the directions. She was walking against the wind, which no longer felt like a friendly arm nudging her along. This time, it was a barrier, and she had to battle against it. Irritation broke through. She'd prefer to be indoors among her ferns, working on Honour's interchange, not hunting for someone to let her into her twoser. But it couldn't be helped.

The unit-minder sat with her back to the water, concentrating on a plate of food. She looked up when she heard the door open. "Come about your twoser, I suppose. Been reassigned. You're in the only oneser we have – it's on the ground floor. Reed D. Your comtel's activated for it." She nodded towards Constance's thumb.

"But what about my things?"

"Already moved in there. Unit-allocation people did it this afternoon."

"They went into my twoser and handled everything I

147

own?" Constance's voice grew louder, and people at other tables looked up. "They lifted it all out and carried it away, and put it somewhere else?"

Indifferent, the minder scooped some stew onto her spoon.

"How do I even know they took everything? They might have forgotten something."

"Looked empty to me. Lot of room for one woman on her own. You were lucky to have it as long as you did. Lucky to stay in the same unit, too – they could've moved you clear across town."

"Why wasn't I told? Somebody could have left a message on my comtel. Was that too much to ask?"

This time, the minder didn't answer. She spooned the stew into her mouth, and began chewing.

"I should have been told," repeated Constance.

A bell pinged. "Covenant Time," said the eat-easy manager. Everyone stood up, and formed a ring. The manager held out her hand to Constance. "Sister?"

Constance kicked over a chair, and left the easy.

"*Not the self but the State, not me but US. To the greater good: to universal sisterhood.*" The chant drifted after her.

So this was what anger felt like. She had never experienced its raw compulsion before. There was satisfaction in venting this moe.

Returning to the unit block, she was still obliged to push against the wind. Even though she was now walking in the opposite direction. Back in the courtyard, she brushed off the Silenced, and went directly to Reed D. Her comtel beeped admission, and she pulled off her boots. Her toe-treat slippers were in the cupboard just inside the living area, exactly as in the twoser. Her vac-pump for removing moisture from her clothes was beside them, along with her skin box. Just as they were in the twoser. She had to hand it to the units' team: their attention to detail was excellent. Her angled lamp was in the corner, the birds-in-flight cushion was on the armchair, and on the wall behind it was the image of her and Silence taken at last year's Sister's Day parade. They were laughing from the piped happiness pumped out for the national holiday. Silence's head was thrown back.

There were no bookshelves in the oneser, however, and Constance's books had been stacked on the floor. They were lined up neatly, spines outward.

Constance stood in the centre of the room and did a slow, 360-degrees spin on her heels, absorbing this new space. It was a replica of the twoser upstairs, except almost half the size. A sense of invasion simmered. Strangers had handled her stuff. All of it. From her underwear to her toiletries to her plants. Probably, the ferns would melt away now – they went into a decline if they were touched by anyone else. Everything she owned had been examined. They knew what brand of shampoo she used, how much of Devotion's setting-sun wine was in her fridge, whether her laundry basket was full or empty, the outline left by her body on the pop-up.

The trappings of her life might not amount to much, but they were hers. And for the second time, they had been violated. Peers had crawled all over her twoser after Silence had been found, looking for clues as to why she did it. Constance had hunted for clues, too – a note, perhaps. A reason. But there had been nothing. Apart from that final message on her comtel from Silence, which Constance couldn't bring herself to delete. Now, she touched the gadget on her thumb, but resisted the temptation to read the message again. She didn't feel strong enough.

Today's violation was different to the last one. Silence's discontinuation had been shocking. It had to be investigated. But this was a way of controlling Constance. Picking her up from one space and setting her down in another, like a chess piece. Or a doll. Tears pricked, but she refused to surrender to them. She dug her nails into the soft flesh in her palms, willing herself to resist. She was becoming more moe-susceptible by the day. That was anger in the easy. This was outrage. Her moe-controls were malfunctioning.

She paced through her new home, trying to remind herself it was small because space was at a premium in Harmony. That's the price she paid for living in the capital city. But Silence's possessions were crowding the rooms. A dash of resentment floated up. She managed to suffocate it: of course she couldn't throw them out. They were loved by her other.

Now, Constance was overcome with nostalgia for her time with Silence. She dropped her face into her hands, and realised she hadn't taken off her skin. Unclipping it, she examined the transparent oval. No traces of those racing moes were left on the skin. Naturally not. The Nine was insistent on the need to wear them. But could the rumours be true? Could it be about moe-control rather than air pollution?

To escape the see-sawing moes, Constance explored the oneser. The living area had a window – all homes in Sisterland were equipped with at least one. She inspected her view: it pointed in a different direction to the twoser. At least the Silenced weren't outside her window any more. Turning back to the room, she saw a cupboard just inside the front door, inside which was the usual glass cone for boiling water and hotbox for a snack. The bathroom was blind, however, with just enough space for a shower, sink and toilet. At least the tiny bedroom also had a window – she should be thankful for any mercies that were going.

All at once, a wave of exhaustion hit her, and she had to sit down: babyfusion's way of reminding her she needed to take more rest. She was nauseous again, too. The medico had warned her about sickness in the first week, from the babyfusion speed-up pill. She must remember to pick up some of the recommended protein liquids. In the meantime, she should take a popper. She staggered out to the living area, poured water, and swallowed an orange pill.

As soon as she was able, Constance settled down to deal

with the interchange of Honour's final memory. Her range of expressions became the memory-keeper's. Her connections. Her sympathies. Her tone of voice. And yes, her moes – that was it. That explained why she was fizzing with moe, tossing over chairs and verging on tears.

Moe and memory couldn't be separated. Memory was sparked by moe and moe by memory. Interchanging Honour's memories left her open to the moes once felt – perhaps still felt – by the memory-keeper. Hopefully, when the interchange transaction was complete, she'd regain her equilibrium. Constance didn't care for this whirligig. A moe every now and then was agreeable, but one crashing in on top of the next was draining. Especially in the early stages of babyfusion.

Constance worked on, reliving Honour's final memory. She concentrated on interchanging the moes that accompanied the memory, while trying to sidestep sharing them, despite their tendency to seep in. When she was finished, her mind continued to race. On impulse, she decided to visit her source.

She hurried past the knot of needy Silenced followers, ignoring their calls, and caught a Buzz to the Circle zone.

Devotion twanged the door-lock mechanism and Constance was admitted. While Goodwill frothed up herbs to make ocean tea, Devotion chattered about a thought consignment she had just finished hatching: patriotic ones, bulky with unquestioning pride in Sisterland.

"Do you ever hatch any of Goodwill's thoughts?" Constance asked.

"Not knowingly. We're never told who's crafted them. But sometimes I've sensed her mind-print on a batch." She sent an affectionate look towards her other. "My Goodwill has a rare mind. Such clarity and precision." She returned her attention to Constance. "You're quite the regular here these days."

"I'm Making Time for Togethertime. I'm babyfused, remember? I messaged you on your comtel about it."

"Oh yes, good job. Universal sisterhood is proud of you." Devotion patted Constance's shoulder.

Goodwill bounced over and hugged Constance. "What happy news! You should have told me, Devotion."

Constance threw a surprised glance at Devotion. Why hadn't she told Goodwill?

"It slipped my mind," said Devotion.

"I remember when you were a baby," Goodwill went on. "You were such a solemn wee creature. Wasn't she, Devotion?"

"She hardly ever cried."

"Let's all toast Constance's babyfusion. Never mind ocean tea. Devotion, break out your top-of-the-range sunset wine."

"It's all top-of-the-range. But Constance can't drink alcohol if she's babyfused. I suppose we could have some, to wish her luck. I do hope you don't defuse, ladybird, and have to go through all that messy mating again."

Constance rolled her eyes at Goodwill, who pulled a sympathetic face.

After Devotion and Goodwill had clinked glasses, Constance said, "Babyfusion seems to make me want to be around my family. It must be a biological reflex."

"Sisterland is one large family, Constance," said Devotion.

"I hope I'm allowed a special bond with my source, all the same. Surely Sisterland isn't threatened by that?"

"Sisterland isn't threatened by anything. Really, Constance, you need to practise self-control. Doesn't she, Goodwill?"

"Constance is a little out of her groove, dear. We should offer her something to eat. You were ravenous when you were babyfused. Are you hungry, Constance?"

"I do feel empty."

"Why didn't you say so?" Devotion tutted. "You have to learn to ask for what you want."

"All right, Devotion – what I want is to know why you never mention my father. Why do you have no stories about him?"

"He was just a meet."

"I wouldn't be me without him."

"Stop being awkward."

Goodwill spoke up for Constance. "I'm glad she thinks about him, Devotion. Perhaps you should remember him, too. He gave you a precious gift."

"What's got into you, Goodwill? Don't encourage her. Sisterland has no use for fathers."

"I met a memory-keeper who thought they mattered," said Constance.

"Really, Constance, babyfusion is making you imagine things." Devotion looked concerned. "You're overtired. I think you should go straight home to bed as soon as you've had something to eat. Goodwill will find you a snack. But I don't want to hear any more of this ridiculous talk about fathers. You'll only land yourself in trouble, ladybird."

Chapter 17

The sound of fast-moving traffic woke Constance early. It couldn't be the peers back again – their vehicles had a distinctive chug, and didn't achieve high speeds. Neither could it be transers moving men about. They went at an even slower pace, and were restricted to certain roads. It must be the Nine. No-one else was licensed to travel at speed in personal carriers. They had been on circuit in Righteous, and were not due back for several more days. Something must be brewing.

She shrugged, propped her pillow against the wall, and sat up to message the medico's comtel with an inquiry about Honour. While she waited for a response, she washed and dressed, but the medico didn't reply. Maybe she was busy. She'd try again later.

Constance set off for Shaperhaus to report on the memory interchange. Outside her unit, half a dozen members of the Silenced dozed in sleeping pouches in a corner of the courtyard. They looked chilled to the bone, and no wonder. Surely their eccentric discipleship would wither away soon? Yet last night's wind hadn't deterred them. Which reminded Constance. She sniffed: the wind was gone. Once more, the air was dense.

She picked up an ocean tea at the Buzz station, and sipped

it on the journey. Something was definitely afoot in Harmony today. Peers patrolled the streets – she could see them from the train.

At Shaperhaus she met a trainee co-keeper in the foyer.

"Curious wind last night, wasn't there?" said Constance.

"Don't know what you mean."

"It was windy last night."

"I wish."

"Of course it was. The peers drove round, telling everyone to stay indoors."

"Not where I live, they didn't. Where was this?"

"Oblong."

"I'm in Cone. Deliverance here's in Polygon, aren't you?" She addressed a shaper walking by. "Any wind out your way yesterday, Deliverance?"

"You kidding? Since when do we get wind?"

"Must just have been an Oblong wind, Constance. Unless you dreamed it."

"Harmony's not that big. There aren't different weather conditions all over the city."

The co-keeper shrugged, losing interest. "Is it true you're off the co-keeper programme?"

"Temporarily."

"That's tough."

Constance made her way to the stairs, past the

SMILE ALL THE WHILE

lettering, an uneasy feeling taking hold. She met her progress-monitor coming from the opposite direction.

"The Shaper Mother's been asking for your report," said Patience.

"I have it here."

"You can pass it to me."

"The mother said it was for her ears only."

"She isn't here – she's at Sistercentral. The Nine has convened."

So that explained the traffic. "In that case, perhaps I might be allowed to return to the memory-keeper today," said Constance.

"I'm afraid that's impossible."

"Honour has more to contribute, I'm sure of it."

"No doubt. But she discontinued last night. She left it absurdly late to share her final memory. Still, better late than never. Now, no time to dawdle. I'll take care of the memory interchange. I'll make sure the mother gets it as soon as she returns to Shaperhaus."

Constance was deflated. Honour had changed before her eyes, from an elderly woman into a small girl at her father's elbow. But that metamorphosis had been her swan song. She braced herself to do what she knew she must.

"In that case, I need to go directly to Sistercentral. The information I carry should be placed by me personally in the Shaper Mother's hands as soon as possible."

Patience folded her arms. "She left no instructions to that effect."

"The memory-keeper's discontinuation makes it essential. It's in Sisterland's best interests."

Patience looked irritated at being obstructed. "You presume too much, Constance. But go, since you're so insistent."

"I'll need Sistercentral admission uploaded to my comtel at once." Trusting to a show of confidence to win the day, Constance pivoted on her heel.

In the square outside, a giant screen showed images of Honour 19, while a voicebox gave news of her discontinuation, along with a précis of her life. Constance stopped to watch a clip of the memory-keeper speaking at a Sisterday celebration sixty years earlier. How certain she sounded. But her absolutes had undergone a sea-change. And Constance had the evidence.

There was no more magnificent building in Harmony than Sistercentral, which had been designed with panache. It was shaped like a horseshoe, with columns of half-moon windows, and nine steps leading up to a curved entrance doorway. On either side of the front door, brackets held torches in which perpetual flames burned. The façade was constructed of golden sandstone which glimmered constantly, day and night, giving the impression of tiny diamonds embedded in its surface. Even on days when the air was particularly moist, they retained vestiges of sparkle. It was the only building in Harmony constructed from golden stone, and it lent Sistercentral a totemic quality.

An ugly building had been flattened to make way for it. There were no unattractive buildings left – an aesthetics committee had put them to the vote, and all were now eradicated. Phallic symbols had been toppled, too – freestanding spires, for example. Some people believed the committee should have been more willing to take public soundings before sending in the bulldozers, because what one Sisterlander regarded as unsightly, another interpreted as idiosyncratic. However, the result was a harmonious city, even if closer study revealed something anodyne in its totality.

Sistercentral stood on a hill overlooking the city. By a quirk of design, it was visible to Harmony but Harmony was not visible to it. Scientists had worked with architects to position massive optical crystals at either end of Sistercentral's perimeters – bending the light, so that the city vanished from view. This illusion allowed the building's occupants to believe Sistercentral stood independent of the urban sprawl surrounding it. And nobody seemed to think that odd.

Constance walked up a sloping path, through grounds decorated with statues. Her favourite was a tightrope walker, except beneath the woman's feet lay nothing. The tightrope existed only in her mind. Belief allowed her to walk in mid-air.

Constance tried not to feel intimidated as she walked through the entrance, beneath lettering chiselled into stone:

SISTERLAND

PRIZES

OBEDIENCE

Scrutineers in Sistercentral livery, a tortoiseshell-patterned one-piece, stopped her in the doorway. She explained that she had urgent business with the Shaper Mother, who was meeting the Nine. Inscrutable, they told her she was not listed on their scanner, and could not be admitted.

"My permission was only just uploaded from Shaperhaus – perhaps it isn't showing yet," she said.

Courteous, they agreed this was a possibility, but she was obliged to wait while they investigated. Voice recognition compared her voice with a sample on record, and they allowed her into the foyer. Constance sat on a marble bench, breathing in the twilight scent of foxgloves, and observed the arrivals and departures. People looked important, or abstracted, or solemn. Nobody, however, looked happy.

Fifteen minutes passed, and Constance was beginning to think her bluff had been called by Patience. She was no pushover. But it had been important to Constance to try. She wanted to be there in person, explaining Honour's words on her behalf – it was essential that the memory-keeper's final message for Sisterland was understood.

"Those torches are something else," a passing comment sang out.

Overhearing it, Constance grasped why she felt so strongly about Honour's interchange. The memory-keeper had passed the torch to her.

Unable to settle, she walked about the circular foyer. As her heels tapped over the tiles, she realised they were shaped into the image of a gigantic, babyfused woman – hands resting on the orb of her belly. The child inside was also depicted, not side-on, but facing out: eyes open, challenging.

"You like our mosaic?" A scrutineer had noticed Constance studying it.

"It's striking. I was in Sistercentral once before, but never noticed it."

"You don't, when there's a lot of footfall. Its proper title is *The Coming*. But we call it *Lemme Out*. Impatient-looking gal, if you ask me."

"Is the baby meant to be anyone in particular?"

"Beloved, of course. She's the baby."

Constance looked again. Of course – her identity was signalled by a pearlised coating overlaying the mosaic.

"She commissioned it before she discontinued," the scrutineer went on. "Approved the design, but didn't live to see it carried out."

"Your authorisation has come through, sister." Another scrutineer broke in on their conversation.

"Thank you," said Constance, relieved. "Where can I find the Shaper Mother?"

"Eighth floor, turn right, then it's first on the left. Running Woman conference room."

"Running woman?"

The scrutineer mimed slow-motion running.

No wiser, Constance set off. Everything was built deliberately on a mammoth scale. The steps were high, straining her hams to climb them, and the corridors stretched apparently endlessly into the distance, echoing to the sound of purposeful footsteps. This was not a building designed to encourage loitering. Every door was marked with a stick woman, the sort Constance used to draw in girlplace. Each was engaged in a different activity: sleeping, kneeling, digging, dancing, sleeping. Constance kept walking until she found herself outside a door on which a stick woman was running.

She rapped, and out peeked Modesty's head with its shiny black ponytail stub.

"Patience messaged to say you were on your way," said Modesty. "Come in, the mother's waiting for your interchange."

The Shaper Mother sat beside a rotund metal object from which heat was emanating. The room looked like somebody's parlour from PS times. A hand-knotted striped rug lay on the floor, while the mother sat in a floral-printed armchair with a high back and a matching footstool, on which she rested feet shod in midnight-blue velvet shoes with silver stitching. A midnight shawl, also edged in silver, was draped round her shoulders, covering her tunic. Armchairs were distributed about the room, each with its accompanying footstool.

Constance was nonplussed by the surroundings – there wasn't even a table at which delegates could sit to conduct discussions.

"Welcome, sweet child. How do you like our pot-bellied stove? There's one in every conference room. Lends snugness. Come and enjoy the comfort for yourself."

Constance approached, the mother's scent enveloping her. She must dose herself in it at regular intervals.

"You don't like my perfume? Never mind. Though how anyone could object to bergamot and lemongrass is beyond me. Now, put your hand on the stove – careful, mind. See how cosy it feels? Wouldn't it be wonderful if every oneser and twoser in Sisterland had one? But they take up space, unfortunately."

"I have my report ready for you, mother."

"I commend your initiative. Such a shame about Honour discontinuing last night. But at least she interchanged with you first. I hope she didn't waste time talking about that poet she associated you with. I've never understood poets. Such impractical creatures." The Shaper Mother flexed her long fingers. Hers were graceful hands, but no longer young, and

160

the fingers cracked in the stretch. "So, was Honour still lucid?"

"Her memory was clear. She spoke with love, and in detail, about her childhood. The bakery wasn't just a business to her, but a home. She talked about her parents, too – especially her father. I believe they had a particular bond."

The mother's tawny eyes flared. "Upload your interchange." She extended an arm displaying the sig on her inner wrist.

Constance tapped a code onto her own sig, before repeating the sequence of numbers on the mother's. She touched her sig to the mother's, they flashed and locked together.

During the transfer, Constance could feel Honour's essence in the room with them. The memory-keeper's image shimmered before her.

"You may wait outside."

At the sound of the voice, Constance's chin jolted off her chest – she must have nodded off. How unlike herself the Shaper Mother sounded. There was an odd note in her voice – you might almost call it wounded. She was cradling her head in her hands, face hidden.

Outside in the corridor, Constance walked up and down, looking at the pictograms, until Modesty summoned her inside.

"You've certainly rattled the mother." She waved her sig. "Your interchange is in here. I'm taking it to the Nine."

"You can do an interchange?"

"Not exactly. This is a carrier interchange – I'm not allowed to absorb it. Just a vehicle, me. Feels like a sizzler, though."

This time, there was no magnanimous offer to sit by the stove. "Your report has implications. I can only presume that winding down towards discontinuation clouded Honour's memory, and cluttered her thought processes. Presumably, you arrived at the same conclusion."

"No, mother."

Perspiration glistened on the mother's face. "Do you know what you're saying?"

"Yes, mother."

"You don't believe this to be a faulty memory?"

"I believe it to be one of the truest memories ever shared by a memory-keeper."

The Shaper Mother slid a narrow look over Constance. When she spoke again, her earlier friendliness was back. "You're babyfused. Sometimes, it can lead to realities becoming scrambled. Let me put my hands on you, sweet child, and see what I can sense."

Constance did not want this intuitive woman raking over her being, although she could not prevent her if she insisted. "Forgive me, mother, but I'm anxious about any outside disturbance affecting my babyfusion. The defusion risk is particularly high in the early weeks."

"Very well. We mustn't count our chickens before they're hatched. Yours is the most challenging role in Sisterland, but also the most gratifying. Sources bear not just children, but responsibility for the State's continuation." The mother's expression grew remote. "And speaking of the State, memory-keepers serve Sisterland in a particularly important way. You're privileged to be one of the last people to talk to Honour 19. Let me share a secret with you, Constance. I idolised her as a girl. Her dedication to the cause was inspirational. We're determined to hold a public memorial service for her. Such women don't pass this way often. Perhaps the synchronised release of a general moe to mark the occasion will be approved. An N might be appropriate. Nostalgia isn't as appreciated as it ought to be – sales are low, I'm told. Now, where were we?"

"With Honour, mother."

"A memory-keeper who always put Sisterland first. She met our founder, you know: that far-sighted woman who devised the Nine principle of consensual government. When she was a young girl, Honour was taken to hear the great Beloved speak in public. It was the Midsummer Address – I expect you learned it off by heart in girlplace. Yes? Me too. Those words give me goose bumps, still. '*Our hands will shape Sisterland. Our vision, our will. Destiny is ours to create.*' Afterwards, Beloved walked among the crowd. She stopped by Honour and spoke directly to her. 'Will you play your part, little sister?' she asked. 'Can Sisterland count on you?' It changed Honour's life. She devoted herself entirely to Sisterland."

"Honour said Sisterland had gone terribly wrong. She said we needed to forgive men. And hope that men might forgive us, in their turn."

"Constance, in fairness to Honour, we ought to set aside one throwaway remark from a sister on the verge of discontinuing. A sister who could have been misunderstood by a trainee co-keeper. She'd never do anything to unravel Sisterland's legacy. I expect she was a little muddled."

Constance broke free of those persuasive eyes. She owed it to Honour to stand her ground. The truth might not be the most solid piece of earth under her feet, but it was the position she chose.

"Truth is never absolute," said the Shaper Mother, reading her resistance. "You could call it a question of perspective."

Modesty interrupted – a welcome respite for Constance. "Greetings from the Nine. They request a meeting with the Shaper Mother and her trainee co-keeper. Didn't sound much like a request to me."

Instantly, the mother was businesslike. "When?"

"At once."

Constance gulped. Sisterland's executive elite – a group she had only glimpsed in the distance at public events – wanted to meet her.

The Shaper Mother unhooked her skin. Her face seemed

naked to Constance without its high-gloss coating. "Leave your skin here, Constance. It's disrespectful to wear it before the Nine." She pointed to a wooden bowl.

Constance fumbled to unlatch it, all fingers and thumbs. "Why should they want to see me?"

"About Honour 19, I suppose. They won't like what they learned."

"That's hardly my fault!"

The Shaper Mother pursed her lips. "You interchanged that corrosive memory, Constance. It's yours now. Have you any idea how that contaminates you? The problem is, it contaminates Sisterland, too." With a sweep of her arm, she threw aside her shawl. Now she stood before Constance and Modesty, her uniform matching theirs. "Let's see what the Nine says about it."

Chapter 18

The Shaper Mother sailed from the room, with Modesty jogging along in her slipstream. On her short legs, Modesty always appeared to move at a trot, her ponytail bouncing. Constance, stunned at being defined as contaminated, brought up the rear. She was led up two levels, into a cavernous space. Even the Tower's readying room was pokey by comparison. A sunburst chandelier was suspended from the ceiling, rainbows dancing from the tips of its lustres. Constance was dazzled by the glittering ball, and it took her eyes a few moments to adjust.

When they did, she saw white marble everywhere, on the walls as well as the floor. A series of niches were carved into the walls, in each of which stood an icon. Some were painted, some plain. There were statues of the Greek goddess Hera, the Roman goddess Venus, the Hindu goddess Shakti, and more whom Constance didn't recognise. A rough-hewn, goggle-eyed wooden shape with an exaggerated vulva, to which the figure pointed, caught her attention.

"That's a Sheela-na-gig," said Modesty. "Celtic goddess of fertility. She's several thousand years old. Not a thing of beauty. But a compelling sister, you have to admit."

The Shaper Mother put her finger to her lips. Relenting,

she murmured, "These figures are conduits: agents for dynamic creative power. They are metaphors for womanhood."

Sisterhaus attendants, hands folded in front, stood against the walls. At the far corner of the room, a stand held a profusion of lilies.

Modesty nodded towards it. "They sprayed the wrong scent on those flowers: it smells of the seaside."

As Constance inhaled the salt-spray tang, there came a sound like cymbals shaking, and an attendant opened the door to the left of the floral arrangement. Nine women in ankle-length white robes filed in: Sisterland's ruling elite.

They were an eclectic assortment, with flesh colour from vanilla through to liquorice. Three features they shared in common, however. Each sister had her eyebrows shaved off. Each wore a curved headdress in looped semi-circles – first rose-gold, then copper, and finally bronze, from which was suspended a diaphanous veil that floated onto the floor. And each had a glow about her, a strangely youthful radiance. It was as if a nimbus surrounded every one of the Nine.

"Nine sisters working in unison. Three times three: a potent combination," murmured Modesty to Constance.

The Shaper Mother took two paces forward, and bowed from the waist. In unison, they inclined their heads. Constance noticed that all of them wore their skins, although no-one else did.

An attendant indicated to Modesty that she should leave.

"The mother's banking on one of those fancy metal crowns," whispered Modesty again. "Biding her time."

The attendant beckoned more insistently. Modesty backed away.

The Nine formed a horseshoe round the Shaper Mother and Constance. Attendants darted forward with marbled white stools, their legs ending in birds' feet, and each of the Nine sat, arranging their gossamer veils with care. Lower stools without the ornamental legs were also provided for the Shaper Mother and Constance. When everyone was settled, one of the Nine stood up, an arresting sister with multiple plaits. Constance supposed they must be a wig, remembering the Mating Mother. Despite Beloved's advice on short crops, wig use showed how some women remained drawn to long hair.

"The universal sisterhood welcomes you," said the Plaits Sister. She unleashed a smile entirely lacking in friendliness. "First, let us pay tribute to our sister, Honour 19, and celebrate the riches of her long life."

She crossed her hands over her breast, one on each shoulder, and bent her head, causing the metal discs of her headdress to clink. Everyone stood and followed suit, giving themselves over to meditation. When she dropped her hands, everyone sat while she remained standing, and waited for the rustling to stop.

"Next, we must consider her legacy," she continued. "We have studied the interchange of Honour's final memory. It bewilders us. And causes us pain. This is an undisciplined memory – utterly contrary to the Sisterland ethos." She looked left and right along the semi-circle, and everybody assented. "The memory-keeper suggests there was a time when the two sexes co-existed compatibly. Yet this is untrue: the man-made world was always hostile to women. Men could not evolve sufficiently to value the female contribution, and so we were obliged to impose a woman-made world on them. Shaper Mother, introduce the young sister to us."

"Greetings, sisters. May I present Constance 500? She's a promising recruit to our new co-keeper programme. Honour asked for her specifically. But the interchange poses challenges."

The Nine focused the searchlight of its gaze on Constance.

"We'd like to hear from you, Constance," said the Plaits Sister. "Was Honour in her right mind, in your view? Could she have had some score to settle? As life ebbs away, queer obsessions can seize sisters."

Constance straightened her posture. Her heart was thundering, but she tried to appear composed.

"Greetings to the Nine. I don't believe Honour had a grievance – only a desire to put her talents at her sisters' disposal. It was a privilege to meet her. Her discontinuation fills me with a sense of loss."

"That goes without saying," said the Plaits Sister. Her tone smacked of reprimand. "But we need to analyse her message, and what lies behind it. You did the interchange. Honour made many preposterous claims. But perhaps the most regrettable was that Sisterland is a failed experiment. That wounded all of us here when we heard it. It's incomprehensible. But we want to give her the benefit of the doubt. Did she truly believe it? And if so, why?"

"I'm afraid she did believe it," began Constance.

Tumult erupted.

"Sisterland is a society on the highest plane of human existence!" protested one sister.

"Imagined and brought into being by an inspirational woman – our dear Beloved," cried another.

"Agreed," said the Plaits Sister. "But we said all that already, after listening to the interchange. Now let's hear from Constance. She may be able to throw further light on this disruptive missive from Honour."

Constance groped for words. "I think Honour was ill at ease about that last memory. That's why she kept it to herself for so long. She was afraid of what it meant. But more afraid of discontinuing without passing it on." She broke off, her mouth dry.

Intent, the Nine waited. Constance found it disconcerting to be the convergence point for those eyes.

She tried again. "Honour realised the interchange would cause upset. But she was one of the last people who remembered a time when women and men lived together with their children. Her memory told her it had worked. She said it was a mistake not to have fathers play a part in child-rearing – that we'd forgotten how fathers had skills to teach their children."

"Nonsense! Their tricks are no match for a woman's talents," exclaimed a sister with cropped platinum hair tipped with black, her veil fluttering under the force of her protest. "Men knew it, and from the dawn of time they kept us subjugated."

Agreement whirred from one end of the horseshoe to the other.

"Honour's final memory is a rogue memory," said another sister. The diamond stud in the crease of her nose flickered an icicle sparkle. "It's damaging, disruptive and dangerous."

"My young sister meant no offence," intervened the mother. "This was her first interchange. No doubt inexperience has led her to misinterpret it."

"Is that possible, Constance?" asked the Plaits Sister.

Constance was quailing before the Nine's annoyance. She had known there would be fallout from the interchange but hadn't expected to be present for it – to witness this clamorous vexation. She closed her eyes, and saw Honour's hand curled on top of quilt squares embroidered with messages from Beloved. Messages could be misconstrued. Was she jumbling Honour's? All she really knew for certain was that Honour had loved her father.

She opened her eyes and looked at the Nine. "Honour believed Sisterland to be a failure. Her PS memories of her father were used in evidence."

A hissing sound ensued – a group intake of breath. The Shaper Mother swooped a warning flash of the eye. But what was said couldn't be unsaid.

One of the Nine raised a hand to head height. "We must be willing to give Constance a hearing. Even if we dislike her message." She was among the more mature sisters, her golden hair curling soft as a baby's under the diadem.

Even as Constance mentally positioned her among the oldest present, she realised it was an incongruous word to use about any of the Nine. Once again, she was struck by the youthful flush which created a halo effect round each of them.

The Baby-Hair Sister continued, "Understanding Honour's memory interchange is crucial. Our repugnance at the contents shouldn't blind us to that. Remember, she met our dearest Beloved, and laboured in the early years as Sisterland was built. But the Honour I knew saw sharing government with men as an unworkable idea. It's always been too risky. Inevitably, they'd try to snatch power."

A shudder quivered from sister to sister.

A sister with long, curling fingernails spoke up. "Men have a primitive animal drive which can be useful, but it must be controlled and directed. We can't leave them to their own devices. It's not safe."

"Honour's father may well have been a sympathetic person," said the Baby-Hair Sister. "We don't dispute that certain individuals had potential as human beings. But men abused their powers. Their bestial sides got the better of them. It's unfortunate that Honour should have set aside this essential truth."

An approving buzz followed, broken by the Baby-Hair Sister.

"She made one point that interests me. About forgiving men. I wonder if we shouldn't consider it."

Mouths were puckered round the semi-circle.

"They're cunning enough to try to profit from any softening on our part, Gracious," said a sister.

Constance looked at the Baby-Hair Sister with renewed interest. Gracious was the senior sister among the Nine, with a casting vote in split decisions. Only the Nine had names without numbers after them.

"Poor, dear Honour must have slipped into dotage," put in another sister.

"Why do you suppose she wanted us to forgive them, Constance?" asked Gracious.

"She didn't say."

"But what was your impression? Didn't you sense anything from the interchange? Go on, I see you did pick up on something. Speak freely."

Constance took a deep breath. "Her mindmap held some residues: a suggestion that failure to forgive stunted our development. That Sisterland was the loser by it. As you heard on the interchange, she believed it was unfair to write off all men. She thought we could have tried to phase out destructive male characteristics to improve the gender, over time. If aggressive males were forbidden from Himtime, eventually the problem would vanish."

This provoked merriment.

When it died down, the Nose-Stud Sister spoke. "Too simplistic. Hyper-male tendencies can skip generations, and crop up again. Isn't that so, Temperance?"

The Platinum Sister answered. "Indeed. Of course, castration has been proven to have a pacifying effect. But we are not that cruel."

"Not that stupid," the Nose-Stud Sister corrected her. "Castration limits the mating pool."

"And the most hostile males are often the most effective meets," put in Gracious.

The Fingernails Sister spoke up. "When Sisterland was established, we realised we were dealing with inbuilt male limitations. We came to the conclusion it would be impossible to change them. You're correct, Constance – or Honour is correct, I should say. Once, the two sexes must have co-existed and cooperated. But men went horribly wrong – wedded to selfishness, greed, and above all war, endless war."

Now the Plaits Sister spoke. "As soon as men were set aside, a visible improvement in the world took place. There was no alternative. Was there, sisters?"

"None, Innocence," rippled back.

"But look at the world we've created," said Innocence. "It's safe, nurturing, and fair. Every girl is encouraged to achieve her full potential. We've eradicated poverty and crime. Sisterland knows only peace. Armies have been disbanded. The only war we waged was against social evils, which are eliminated. Sisterland is a utopia!"

A round of applause greeted her pronouncement. And Constance understood that Honour's message had made no more impact on the Nine than on the tightrope-walker statue outside.

Innocence continued, "The rules were man-made, now they're woman-made. And the result? Collective serenity and well-being. Universal sisterhood."

Nine hands reached out to their neighbours. "A universal sisterhood!" they chorused. The Shaper Mother and Sistercentral attendants joined in the chant.

After the echo died away, Gracious leaned forward, her gaze intent. "Constance, did you intuit anything about the Nine from Honour? She said nothing outright, but I sensed something."

Constance's forehead furrowed.

"Go on," urged Gracious.

Surfacing in Constance's mind were Honour's whispered words when the connection between their sigs had been paused. But they couldn't be spoken aloud. Shouldn't be spoken aloud.

"The co-keeper must speak," commanded Innocence. "She shirks her duty."

"Don't be nervous. Tell us," said Gracious. Her smile was beguiling, but her willpower was the persuader, and it began to lap against Constance's reservations.

Constance felt its heat melt her resistance. The memory-keeper's words about the Nine had scared her then, and frightened her even more in their presence. She did not dare to repeat them. Still, Gracious's willpower stroked hers.

"It wasn't in the interchange," she gasped. "It was just something she said. Right at the end."

The air changed, and grew dense. Nine sets of willpower merged and advanced on hers. Her breathing grew ragged, dizziness took hold. She wasn't being mindmapped – she was being suffocated.

The words were torn from her. Panting, she said, "It's not consent but command the Nine wants. The Nine is a failed experiment, too. That's what Honour said."

The release was a blessing. But its grace was temporary.

From all sides, a series of shocked looks crashed down on her. The words were met with a stillness that was absolute. Trembling, Constance covered her face with her hands.

Slowly, Innocence rose, and adjusted her veil. Constance parted her fingers and watched her through them. Innocence went from sister to sister, bending over their ears. Constance strained to hear but could pick up nothing, until Innocence had navigated the end of the half-circle and spoke aloud to the group.

"So, we have consensus? Good. Unity of purpose is always more seemly."

Her gaze landed on Constance like a scalpel. Constance let her hands fall. A sense of dread hovered.

Innocence said, "Honour 19's memory, along with that supplementary sting in its tail, undermines Sisterland. Sisters would be distressed by its contents – their wellbeing compromised. Our only concern is for their welfare. This memory must be erased permanently for the higher good. Constance 500, our judgment is that you be sent to MUM.

Chapter 19

Constance unwound her feet from around the legs of the stool where she sat, needing to plant them firmly on the ground. Judgment? The Nine had sat in judgment on her, without indicating she was on trial? And then her mind skipped forward, to lock on the verdict – she was ordered to MUM. The Memory Unmapping Manufactory.

She stared at the semi-circle. How benign the Sisters looked. Perhaps she had misunderstood. But Innocence's words rang in her ears. *Our judgment is that you be sent to MUM.* She tried to bring to mind what she'd heard about memory-unmapping. It was said to cause a drastic change in anyone who underwent it.

Into the stillness, the Shaper Mother cleared her throat: a sound like cloth tearing. "Is it possible the Nine might consider deletion rather than unmapping?"

"Indeed, Shaper Mother," said Innocence, "as you remind us, we have the expertise to isolate a set of memories and detach them. But why take the risk? Memories are leaky: they colour each other, one memory tipping over into another. Deletion isn't foolproof. Unmapping is the prudent course. Especially in circumstances so keenly related to Sisterland's best interests."

"Naturally, Sisterland should be the primary consideration," said the Shaper Mother. "However, there's a fact I ought to alert the Nine to: you should know that Constance 500 is in a sacred state. She is babyfused."

Every head swivelled to regard her, while Constance's alarm ratcheted up. If the Shaper Mother was using babyfusion to argue against unmapping, did that mean it could hurt her baby?

"Her condition makes the need for memory-unmapping still more regrettable," said Innocence. "But this interchange is explosive. If made public, it could have undesirable consequences. Social cohesion can never be compromised. Not even for babyfusion. Isn't that so, Sisters?" The insistence of her gaze swept the horseshoe of seated sisters.

This time, the murmurs were troubled. Gracious made a bridge with her hands to rest her chin. Constance trained her eyes on her, in a concentration of appeal.

The Shaper Mother persisted. "Naturally I appreciate the Nine's position. But before you authorise unmapping, there's another fact I ought to draw to your attention."

"The Shaper Mother tries our patience," said Innocence.

"Let her speak, Innocence," said Gracious.

"Thank you, sister. Perhaps I should have made this known to you earlier, but I was concerned it might influence your response to the memory interchange. Constance 500's other died in unusual circumstances – at the Hope Bridge."

The Platinum Sister tensed. "She was other to the sister called Silence 1999?"

"She was."

The room was transformed into a beehive.

"Do I have the Nine's permission to give a briefing?" asked the Shaper Mother.

"Proceed, please," said Gracious.

"As no doubt you know, Silence's action has generated a chain reaction. A group of supporters has sprung up calling themselves the Silenced. It's my understanding they regard her as a martyr. Clearly –"

"We've been monitoring the Silenced," interrupted the Platinum Sister. "They exhibit hysterical tendencies. As my sisters know, I believe we're showing them too much tolerance."

"Temperance, allow the Shaper Mother to continue," said Gracious.

Constance scanned the semi-circle. Her babyfusion had diluted some of the antagonism caused by Honour's criticism of the Nine. How many of the sisters could be swayed to show mercy? Not Temperance or Innocence. But some of the others, perhaps?

"Clearly, sisters, this is an extremely delicate situation," said the Shaper Mother. "The Silenced might presume unmapping was ordered because of Constance's connection with her other. An unmapping could be interpreted as a way of suppressing information about Silence."

The warning registered with the Nine. Significant looks went winging round the horseshoe.

"You do well to alert us, Shaper Mother," said Gracious. "We'll give it careful consideration. Sisters, I believe we ought to retire to reflect on this matter."

They bowed and withdrew, veils floating behind them – as elegant in their departure as in their arrival.

When they were gone, Constance leaned towards the mother. "I don't know anyone who's gone to MUM. Could it hurt my baby?"

The Shaper Mother avoided her eye. "Unmapping is rare."

"But what would it do to my baby?"

"We'll talk about that later, if it comes to it. Pleading the belly should have been enough. But it wasn't. The Nine has grown –" The mother pressed her hands into prayer peaks, and laid them against her mouth. A pause followed, during which she regained her composure. "Still, Silence may tip the

Nine in your favour. I made the best case I could. Now, we have to wait."

Constance burst out, "How can I just sit here and wait?"

"You can because you must. I'll wait with you. You're not alone."

"This isn't fair! I was sent to Honour – I didn't ask to go. I did the interchange, just as I was taught. How is it my fault if her memory is unwelcome? Co-keepers can't be held responsible."

The mother sighed. "It's not just the interchange. It's what Honour said about the Nine. It wasn't prudent of you to share that."

"What choice did I have? They dragged it from me!"

"Constance, I'm sorry you've been put in this position. Especially in view of your babyfusion. We must hope for the best now."

"Mother, please tell me. Now. Not later. If I'm sent for unmapping, will my baby discontinue?"

The Shaper Mother's eyes were unfocused. She didn't answer.

Constance's throat tightened. "Mother? I have a right to know."

"No unborn child can survive MUM."

Constance half-stood but her legs gave way beneath her. She crashed back down, skidding the stool backwards.

A Sistercentral attendant approached them, and the mother waved her away. Under her breath, she said, "You must steady yourself, Constance. Remember where you are."

Constance saw anxiety pooling in her eyes. And something else, too. Guilt, perhaps?

"If the worst comes to the worst, wouldn't they wait until after my baby is born?"

"I'm afraid not. Once a memory-unmapping sentence is passed, it's carried out immediately. Within 24 hours."

"Monsters!" Face crumpling, Constance jumped up and

177

walked to the furthest point of the room – burrowing into the only corner without one of those serene-faced goddesses standing sentinel. Didn't people pray to goddesses in PS days? None of them looked as if they'd listen to her prayers. They were indifferent to her fate. Just like the Nine. Constance rocked on her haunches, her back buffeting the wall.

The mother hunkered down in front of her. She took Constance's head between her hands, holding it with a steady pressure. "Sweet child, you must practise restraint. There might be a reprieve. The Nine is not without compassion."

"The Nine is scared stiff of Honour's memory. And even more petrified by her criticism," Constance ground out.

"You must understand, Constance. It's not about what we want, it's about Sisterland. Sometimes, sacrifices have to be made for the common good. Sisterland is a community: the group matters more than any individual. We learn that from the earliest age: *Not the self but the State, not me but Us. To the greater good: to universal sisterhood.*"

"Why must I understand? I won't understand! I refuse to!"

"Constance, Constance, collect yourself! Moe is unbalancing you. The Nine is wise, it knows what's best for all of us. You must have faith."

"Faith in a group of women who'll gladly murder my baby, and justify it on the grounds of protecting Sisterland? They're not wise, they're unnatural!"

Scorched, the Shaper Mother dropped her hands. "Stop that! You're giving way to moes!"

"Yes! Because I'm human first, and a Sisterlander second! The same as you. The same as all of us. Only we're taught to deny it." Constance hunched over, cradling her stomach, her head almost touching the floor. "I need air," she moaned.

"I'll send for water."

"I have to get outside. I can't breathe!"

"Constance, you must be calm, I beg you. You can't leave – you need to be here when the Nine returns."

"Am I a prisoner?"

"Of course not. But we don't know how long the Nine will be at its deliberations. You must be waiting when it comes back."

"Why should I wait for a group of talking statues to troop back in and tell me my fate?"

"Stop questioning everything, Constance."

"Mother, I'm babyfused. Have you ever been babyfused? Wouldn't you want to protect your baby? Wouldn't you resist having it discontinued?"

"All this moe pouring out of you! It's uncivilised!"

Constance went still. Through clenched teeth, she spat, "I'm the uncivilised one here? Me?" A flash of unease crossed the Shaper Mother's features, and Constance seized her chance. "Let me go outside. Just for a few minutes. Please. I'm not hard to find, with a sig on my right hand and a comtel on the left. I'm not going to run away – how far would I get?" She raised her voice. "I just want some air!"

The Shaper Mother knelt forward and gathered her into her arms, speaking into her ear. "Do you want the Sistercentral scrutineers to use a stifstat on you? That's the way you're heading. And it won't help your baby, either. You must control yourself. Do you hear me? Do you?"

"Yes," Constance gasped.

"All right, go outside, but Modesty stays with you. I'll let go of you when I count to three. Can I trust you not to make a scene? Can I? You're sure? *One . . . two . . . three.*" Gingerly, she disengaged.

Constance panted, reining back the moes.

The Shaper Mother examined her, before straightening and tapping an instruction on her comtel.

Modesty bounced through the door.

"Modesty, take Constance out for a quick walk. Don't leave the grounds of Sistercentral. And don't let her out of your sight."

Chapter 20

"I brought your skin." By the Sistercentral entrance, Modesty handed Constance her mask. She looked at it blankly.

"Better not go bare-faced," Modesty added.

"I can think of riskier things. Don't you ever wonder about skins, Modesty?"

"I wonder about a lot of things. But unlike you, I keep my head down. And my skin on."

Constance clipped it on.

She and Modesty passed between the eternal flames, emerging into the terraced grounds. Constance rested a protective hand on her stomach. Already, her clothes felt tight across it. Her body was changing shape. Today, for the first time since learning she was babyfused, the baby felt real to her. Did she feel real to her child? Could the warmth of her palm be felt through her body, to where the cells were growing?

Modesty watched Constance, but held her peace.

The air was clammy without Sistercentral's temperature controls. Even so, Constance was able to breathe more easily. By and by, she spoke. "Do you know anyone who's been sent to MUM, Modesty?"

"Not personally. Just on the grapevine."

180

"It doesn't happen often?"

"No, you really have to get up someone's nose." She chewed the ball of her thumb. "I hear the Nine intends sending you there, Constance."

"News travels fast."

"My job is to know what's going on. I know you're babyfused, too – any data the mother sees, I see. Look, I don't mean to butt in, but someone ought to tell you this. Just so you know where you stand. Of course you're worried about the baby. But unmapping doesn't only lead to babydefusion. It changes everything about the person they unmap. Every last memory is snuffed out. You forget anything you ever knew: from your name, to how to do your job, to the way you take your ocean tea. Today could be your last day as Constance 500. Tomorrow, if the Nine gives the word, you'll become a version of her nobody recognises. Not even yourself."

Constance stood still. A premonition of emptiness hurtled towards her. She wouldn't remember how to read, or count, or talk. She'd no longer recognise people she once knew. And how could she earn a living if she recalled nothing about her shaper training or her co-keeper lessons? But these skills could be regained. What troubled her most were the important memories that could never be retrieved: her childhood, the year with Silence, those five nights with Harper. What if she didn't even know she had once babyfused?

"The Nine would do this to me?"

"You better believe it."

"I don't care what happens to me. But I want this baby. Whatever the cost. If I'm allowed to have my baby, I'll go to MUM afterwards. No fuss."

"Babyfusion must turn a woman's brain to ocean tea. It's not a case of either-or. The Nine makes the rules – you don't get to negotiate." Modesty looked Constance over, head on one side. "You didn't take long to babyfuse. Risky business, since they jizzed it up to three months. Everything puffs up:

body parts you'd never expect to bloat – throats, hands, you name it. I knew a progress-monitor whose eardrums swelled. She was tormented with ear bleeds."

Constance walked away from her chatter. She had nothing against Modesty, but if these were her final hours as herself, she didn't want to spend them hearing about the downside to babyfusion. Concentrating, she conjured up Harper's face. The sound of his voice. The smell of pears on his breath. The touch of his hands. His passion for his forest. Soon, she might no longer be able to call him up. Would her mind even realise something was missing? She could hear the blood thundering through her ears. Wrapping her arms about her body, she stifled a sob.

Dimly, she became conscious of Modesty rubbing her between the shoulder blades. She seemed to be apologising for blurting out the truth about MUM. When Constance was in command of herself, she said, "The mother thinks she's talked them round. But the Nine won't take a chance on me. I make those big, important sisters nervous. I tried to keep them back, but I guess my doubts about Sisterland showed through."

"Have you any idea what you're saying?"

"Sorry, Modesty, I suppose I've alarmed you."

"But I agree with you. Lots of us have to hide our true thoughts."

"Really? You, too? You question the way Sisterland is run?"

"Some things could be done differently."

The admission was unexpected. Modesty gave the appearance of being the ultimate insider. Granted, she had a cheeky side, but she wouldn't last long as the mother's assistant unless she was trusted.

Modesty caught her by the elbow. "Come over to the waterfall. I want to show you something." They reached a miniature waterfall tumbling over a rockery. "Acid yellow.

Who in their right minds would turn water that colour? Stand closer, Constance. Makes it harder for eavesdroppers."

"Are they listening in?" asked Constance.

"Maybe. They tend to be. It's a habit that stuck. From the early days of Sisterland, when they kept expecting men to mount a coup against them. After four years in Shaperhaus, I do my fair share of it. Strictly unofficially, mind you. Just for my own purposes. To keep up." She turned her hands over, studying the henna swirls on them. "The Nine wants women and men kept apart, but we have to connect for mating. And some sisters discover they like it. They like their meets, too. It's true. And that threatens the Nine. Inter-gender relationships would destabilise Sisterland. So the Nine vetoes Himtime except for babyfusion, and justifies it by saying the sex instinct has withered away. Except it hasn't. Some sisters would mate with men outside ovulation, if they were allowed. Some sisters would do it as an end in itself. For pleasure." Modesty tilted her head to one side, and a knowing tone entered her voice. "I see you understand what I'm talking about."

"Why don't you put in for a babyfusion permit, Modesty? Won't the mother part with you?"

"They turned me down. I can't reproduce – my internal plumbing's defective. So I'll never be allowed to mate."

Even with MUM hanging over her, Constance felt for Modesty. "Poor you." She touched Modesty's hand lightly.

"No, poor you. What they're doing to you isn't fair. Not that 'fair' matters to the Nine. Especially not to Innocence – she's a joyless one. Has her eye on Gracious's seat as the number one sister, too. Ambition's supposed to be a restricted moe. But she has an ambitious streak wider than the wings above Shaperhaus. The Nine isn't really interested in other Sisterlanders. It's what's best for the Nine – that's what counts. Power is everything. Dried-up old crones."

"Except they're not, are they, Modesty? I've never seen them in the flesh before. I was surprised. They looked – not

183

young exactly – but new-minted."

Modesty watched the waterfall tangle through tastefully selected pebbles. Constance thought she looked nervous.

"What is it, Modesty?"

"You're right. A sister starts getting fresher-looking as soon as she joins the Nine. I don't know why. Nobody ever mentions it. It's as if we're not even supposed to notice." The look she gave Constance brimmed with foreboding.

There was a chirrup on her comtel, and Modesty checked the screen. "The mother wants you back indoors."

A Sistercentral aide was waiting with the Shaper Mother. The Nine had decided to sleep on its decision: Constance should present herself at Sistercentral at eight the following morning.

"I'll meet you in the foyer," the mother told Constance.

"Pardon me, mother, you aren't required," said the aide.

"I wouldn't dream of letting her go through this alone. She's under my supervision."

"The Nine's instructions were that no-one is to accompany her."

"They can't have meant to exclude me, surely."

"No-one is an explicit term, mother."

"I see. Come with me, Constance."

Outside the chamber, she halted and beckoned to Constance.

"An overnight delay is highly unusual," she said. "It means they can't agree on your case. They must be almost evenly divided, five Sisters to four. All that's needed for unmapping is a two-thirds majority."

"So I might be off the hook?"

The mother ran a hand across the top of her skull. "You might be." Her smile was an instant torn from tension.

A spring uncoiled inside Constance. "Honour is protecting me," she said.

"Perhaps. Let's see what tomorrow brings."

As they walked to the Sistercentral exit, Modesty fell into step beside them. In the courtyard, the mother stood, watching a woman spray a row of ornamental trees to stop the leaves falling. A gentle whoosh came from her equipment. When leaves needed to be replaced they were detached by vacuum suction.

"The mother's shaken – she never loiters," hissed Modesty. "What's the Nine's verdict?"

"No decision yet. I'm to return to Sistercentral tomorrow."

Collecting herself, the Shaper Mother began marching towards the Buzz. Her strides made no allowances for the thundery atmosphere, and Constance and Modesty grew sticky keeping up. At the entrance to the Sistercentral station, she drew to a halt. "Which direction do you go in, Constance?"

"The Oblong zone, mother."

"I'll say goodbye here, then. Don't be tempted to stay away from Sistercentral tomorrow. Otherwise, peers will arrive on your doorstep. Cooperation is always the best policy. Modesty, why don't you keep Constance company? Take her to Moe Express – my treat. Choose something . . . something to help her look on the bright side."

"There's a bright side to any of this?" asked Constance.

The mother didn't respond. Turning, she marched away.

Modesty tugged Constance by the elbow, steering her towards the train platforms. "No point in falling out with the only champion you have."

Constance relented, looking down at Modesty, whose head didn't quite reach her earlobe. "You make me feel tall."

"I make everybody feel tall. It's my gift to the sisterhood. But what I'd like to make you feel right now is grateful to the mother. She's on your side."

"She's not the decision-maker."

A train approached.

"I'd just as soon be on my own, if you don't mind,"

185

Constance said. "Don't worry, I'll go straight home like a good Sisterlander."

"You're not shaking me off till you juice up. We'll find a Moe Express near your unit, then I'll leave you alone. The mother's suggestions aren't suggestions, in case you hadn't noticed." Modesty's voice softened. "We'll get you something to help you make it through till tomorrow. We can't have you sitting up all night fretting."

Once seated on the Buzz, Modesty produced a vac-pump and set about removing the faint mould left on her clothes by the air. Constance watched the brown hand busy with its task. Modesty kept up a running commentary. Words were flooding from her, threatening to drown Constance.

She turned her face towards the passing cityscape and fixed on the child inside her: part Harper, part Constance, part itself. If she believed it would live, with every atom of her being, then the power of belief would protect it. It must.

The Buzz cornered towards Octagon station, and against the skyline the curve of the Hope Bridge could just be glimpsed beyond the stop. And a piece of jigsaw puzzle slotted into place for Constance. The Buzz stopped, its doors opening. Constance watched for her chance and, as the carriage doors began shutting, she darted through.

"Hey!" Modesty's arms flailed, but the doors closed before she could follow.

Constance didn't look back. She jumped over the exit barrier and, running as though her life depended on it, made straight for the bridge where Silence had discontinued.

Chapter 21

At the Hope Bridge, a configuration of women with red scarves milled about. Constance slowed to a halt, lungs gasping for air. She pushed through the crowd until she reached one of the bridge's supports, so close she could smell the metal. Laying her hand on it, she tipped back her head. Above the viaduct the clouds were torrid – a mirror for the turbulence she was feeling – and for the commotion on the ground, she realised, as the numbers congregated there registered with her. What were so many people doing at the bridge? And why were they all staring in the same direction? Something on one of the bridge's series of arches had snared their attention. Constance followed their line of vision, but could distinguish nothing out of the ordinary. The flowery scent she associated with the Silenced, underscored by the cloying tang of decay, attacked her nostrils, and she started coughing.

A hand thumped her back. "The red scarf is distinctive," said a familiar voice.

It was Goodwill. By this stage, surprise was beyond Constance.

"It gives them an identity," continued Goodwill. "I heard they wear it because Silence had one on when she discontinued."

"She was wearing a red scarf when she jumped," said Constance. "But it wasn't tied securely, and blew off halfway down. A peer told me. She said eye-witnesses claimed it flew through the sky. Escaping. Like Silence, in a way." Exhaustion pummelled her. "I think I'll go home now. I needed to be here, to see where it happened. I never came before. But it's too crowded."

"You can't leave without seeing her," said Goodwill.

"Who?"

"Silence."

Goodwill pointed towards a central section of the bridge, around which the knot of Silenced was thickest.

Constance began to elbow her way through the throng. "Out of the way. Let me pass." In a society where politeness was prized, her behaviour was unusual, and sisters stared as they backed away.

She stopped by a ridged metal trunk, the thickness of four women, holding up the bridge. Silence had climbed this support, according to observers. Constance wished she didn't know this piece of information, but it had been passed on to her by a peer. It was clear why Silence had chosen it: the centre upright was the only one with convenient edges offering toeholds. This pilgrimage ought to have been made when there was nobody about. Not when she was surrounded by a carnival of sightseers. But she had come too far to turn back. Constance craned her head towards the point creating the stir. A pale oval was pinned against the top of the support.

It was Silence's skin.

Constance flinched, and would have stumbled if Goodwill hadn't caught her.

"Lean on me," urged Goodwill. "I'll get you out of here."

"I just need a minute." Constance was slick with sweat, her hair clumping. "I never expected to see that again. Silence took it off before she jumped. She left it at the side of the bridge. The peers impounded it afterwards. When they returned

188

her possessions, it wasn't among them. I asked for it, but they said it had been destroyed. State policy in the case of unnatural discontinuations."

"So why is it here?" asked Goodwill.

One of the Silenced nearby answered. "It's a message from Silence. To show she's still here." She raised her voice. "*Silence is with us!*"

"*With us*," chanted the crowd.

"*Silence is watching over us*," said the woman.

"*Watching over us*," they repeated.

"*Silence will show us what to do.*"

"*Show us what to do.*"

"Speak to us. Speak on behalf of Silence," the woman urged Constance.

"I've nothing to say."

"Speak," said the woman.

The refrain was taken up by those around her. "*Speak*," they cried.

"Why not give them what they want?" said Goodwill.

"I don't know what they want."

"Nor do they. Whatever you give them will be what they want."

"*Speak*," said the women in red scarves.

The chant passed from one to another, until it was in every mouth.

"They aren't going to stop," said Goodwill. "Not until you address them."

Tomorrow she was probably going to forget Silence ever existed, thought Constance. Today, while she could, she ought to remember her. She'd honour her memory. She turned back to stare at the skin. It was Silence – and yet not Silence. Still, it retained enough of her other for inspiration.

Words began to form in her mind, and take shape on her tongue. They were halting at first, but gained in fluency.

"Silence loved Sisterland." The crowd was mesmerised.

"She loved the baby she was fused with. She loved life. But she discontinued herself and her child."

A moan drifted from the audience.

"She sacrificed herself," someone called out.

Pitching her voice to the outer fringes of the gathering, Constance said, "Yes, Silence sacrificed herself, but she did it for a reason. To teach us something." She wasn't sure if her voice was carrying. In her ears, it sounded reedy. She looked about. The central pillar, the one Silence had climbed up, had a metal rim two feet off the ground. She jumped onto the ledge, and leaned back against the pillar.

"Silence died because she was carrying a boy-baby. She didn't want to hand him over, to be raised in some distant belt of Sisterland – never to set eyes on him again. Boy-babies are precious, just as girl-babies are." She rested a hand on her stomach.

Some of the Silenced looked at one another, struggling to reconcile what she said. But they remained attentive.

"Who here has given birth to a boy-baby?" Constance called out.

An arm was raised, then another, followed by several more.

"Did you want to hand over your baby?"

"It was our duty," muttered one.

"Duty," said other voices, although not everyone spoke with certainty.

"Did you believe it was right?"

"They told us to do it," said a woman. "They made us believe."

"And now? Do you still believe? Do you?"

"Peers!"

The crowd scattered as the peers chugged up in their carriers, each with its distinctive black stripe against the pink background. Peers in salmon-pink leather one-pieces poured out, the colour intended to make them look non-threatening. The peer emblem was embroidered in gold thread on the left breast pocket: an O nestling inside a C, for 'Compliance Overseer'.

One of them had a voicebox, and spoke into it. "*Sisterland is disappointed in you. We expect more from our sisters. There will be sanctions unless you leave immediately.*" It was like being ticked off by a bossy head teacher.

Peers moved through the group, clapping their hands. "Go on home now. Everybody, home." They were polite but insistent.

One of the peers motioned to Constance to dismount. She started to scold Constance but, buffeted by the crowd, they were separated. Somebody – Constance couldn't see who – pushed her under one of the arches, where she was less likely to get knocked. Several of the Silenced were huddled there, trying to keep out of the way.

"What will happen to us?" asked one.

"A demerit," another answered.

"What if we're sent for listening?"

"What's wrong with that? It's just counselling."

"Don't be such a pearl!"

"They can't send all of us for listening," said a third sister. "There are hundreds of sisters here."

"But they might pick out some at random. As a lesson."

One of the peers loomed over them. "Signifier inspection."

"*Smile All The While*," said Constance.

The peer's expression grew stern. She clicked the comtel on her thumb over a line of wrists, registering their details. Logging Constance's sig alerted her to Constance's babyfusion. "Someone in your condition ought to know better. Babyfused sisters need their rest."

"What harm were we doing?" asked Constance.

"Don't answer back. Use your head and don't come here again. Now, straight home. Same goes for all of you."

One of the Silenced spoke out. "You can't choke Silence's message – you'll only make it stronger."

The peer tapped her sig. "This is going on all your records. You can expect repercussions." She moved on.

The Silenced swapped anxious glances.

Constance ducked out from under the bridge, wondering about Goodwill's whereabouts. The peer with the voicebox was still ordering women to disperse, although most had left the Hope Bridge area already. A light glowed on a camera mounted on a pulley, recording the women as they scattered. Still thudding with adrenalin, Constance walked directly towards the camera.

"I spoke here to pay tribute to Silence," she told it. "While I still remember her."

A woman with a torn, cherry-red scarf between her hands approached. In her eyes was a sense of loss that could almost be touched.

"I had a boy-baby," she said. "I saw his face for a few seconds. Not a day passes but his face enters my mind. It comes to me whether I want it there or not. It's twelve years since I gave him up. I'll carry that face with me till the day I discontinue."

Chapter 22

Back in her oneser, the hairs on the back of Constance's neck prickled. Someone had been there. She could sense it. She walked from room to room, and found the feeling strongest in the bedroom. She opened the wardrobe built into the wall. Nothing unusual there. She moved her attention to the only free-standing piece of furniture, a chest of drawers. One by one, she opened the drawers, fingers dredging the contents. Nothing. Next, she took them out, and laid them on the floor. Her hand groped inside the frame. Still nothing. She slotted them back in.

On a hunch, she tapped a series of digits into the console which protruded from the wall. A gap opened in the floor, through which a pop-up was propelled upwards. There, on top of the pillow was a copy of *Beloved's Pearls*.

Constance picked it up. It was Silence's. It had gone missing when the peers had rummaged through their home. There could be no mistake. Here was Silence's name embossed on the cover, and inside was her handwriting: the twoser's address. It must have been the peers who put the book on the pillow. Which meant they had been back checking through her belongings again. And they wanted her to know what they'd done.

A shiver threaded along Constance's spine.

She turned towards the blank pages at the back of the book, on which sisters were supposed to write their own uplifting thoughts, inspired by Beloved. Everybody tended to copy down clichés, however. Perhaps Silence had written something original there. Or maybe she had left a message only Constance could decipher. But the pages were blank.

Constance laid her lips against Silence's name on the pearlised cover, and placed it on top of the chest of drawers. Instead of undressing and getting into the pop-up, she went back to the living room and curled herself into a ball on the couch. She was conscious of two hearts beating inside her body. The next day's judgment might put an end to that – she wouldn't waste the night in sleep.

Her thoughts turned to Harper, who didn't know he was going to be a father. Imagine a world in which she could turn to him and say, "Guess what? We babyfused!" and have him share the excitement. If she had a daughter who looked like Harper, something of him would remain with her – provided the Nine allowed her to continue with her babyfusion.

And what if it was a boy? Restless, she changed her position, remembering the woman with the torn scarf at the bridge.

Moments later, or so it appeared, morning announced itself, along with a crick in her neck. At once, she remembered she was due at Sistercentral. She checked her comtel: almost seven o'clock. Not much more than an hour left.

Passing over the Hope Bridge on her way to Shaperhaus, Constance looked down from the arched metal structure. She expected to see the square beneath it deserted, but sisters with red scarves were congregating there once more. Yesterday's visit by the peers hadn't deterred them. Passengers on the Buzz stretched their necks to see what was happening under the bridge.

The Buzz stopped at the next station. Someone boarded

and sat beside her. Quietly, she addressed Constance.

"Heard the latest about the bridge?"

Constance shook her head.

"There's an image on it. They say it represents an ancient goddess."

"I wonder what it means." Constance was curious to hear the passenger's theory.

"Change, I expect."

"What sort of change?"

The passenger shrugged.

"What would you like to see changed?" Constance pressed her.

The woman withdrew a little, and Constance realised she thought she was a peer. Casually, she rolled up her sleeves, as though too warm, allowing the woman to see her shaper identity on the sig. "I'd certainly welcome some changes," said Constance.

"I guess maybe I'd like ..." The passenger tailed off.

"Yes?"

"Maybe access to a few more moes. I seem to use up my rations real quick. Some of the lower-grade ones could be easier to come by. Nothing fancy. But a burst of U every now and then would perk up my day. How about you? Miss any of them?"

"I wouldn't say no to a U. If I ruled the world, everyone on this Buzz would have an upbeat pep right now this minute."

"Wouldn't that be something!"

"Except the Nine decides everything for us. Everything." Constance's words were delivered without emphasis, but the woman stiffened.

The Buzz pulled into a stop, and the woman disembarked, waiting on the platform for the Buzz following behind.

However, a nearby passenger slid into the seat beside Constance. She nodded towards her pocket, from which the tip of a red scarf protruded.

Stealthily, she tipped her words into the hubbub of boarding passengers. "I was there yesterday. I heard you."

"Did the peers scan your sig? So you have a black mark?" asked Constance.

The stranger waited for noise levels to rise. "Yes. But I'm going back. They won't keep me away."

Constance turned in the seat to study her. The woman's skin was cracked, and in need of repair. Her eyes burned through it. "What are you looking for?"

"A reason."

"For what?"

Once more, the woman waited. A girlplace party boarded, causing a distraction, and she took advantage of it. "The point to Sisterland."

"Sisterland *is* the point. That's what we're taught."

"Do you believe that?"

The compulsion to be honest swept through Constance. "I don't know. Sisterland is choked full of rules I don't understand. My other told me something once. She said any price was worth paying in return for knowledge. But Sisterland is run by women who believe in anti-knowledge."

Constance's stop was next. The Buzz was already slowing. The woman stared at her, neck mottled from a flush, and Constance half-expected her to shout for the peers.

Instead, she said, "Come to the bridge again. We need you."

Constance paused at the automatic doors. "But what can I do?"

"You can find it for us. The reason."

Constance sat in Sistercentral's foyer waiting to be called before the Nine. Walking up the avenue, tipping a nod to the tightrope statue, she had felt sure that all would be well – but now her confidence was dented. This building was frosty, with its marbles and mosaics. The Nine shared that chill. She stretched out her legs, kicking her heels against the tiled floor. The bench was cold, and she pulled off her jacket, folded it up, and sat on it. A uniformed woman began to perfume the air with a cinnamon fragrance, and Constance watched her work. She smiled as she sprayed, enjoying her task, but to Constance the scent was overpowering. Was she the only one who objected to it? She searched the surrounding faces, looking for resistance to this tyranny of smell, but everyone appeared oblivious.

She thought about Silence's copy of *Beloved's Pearls*, and why she had left no message inside it for Constance before throwing herself off the Hope Bridge. It was a pointed place to discontinue – there could be no doubting her intention to make a public statement. Silence would have realised a written message could be destroyed by the Nine. They wouldn't hesitate to order it. But a symbolic act was more difficult to eradicate. Gestures could outlive the people behind them.

"Constance 500?" An attendant appeared. "Please come with me."

Run! screamed a voice inside her. *Obey!* urged another, more insistent one.

She followed the attendant.

Instead of being brought to the conference room with its line-up of goddesses, Constance was led down a back staircase, and along an underground passageway towards the rear of Sistercentral. Artificially lit, it appeared to be composed of endless corners, some of them doubling back on themselves. They passed no-one.

Apprehension built inside Constance. "Where are we going?"

"Nearly there."

"I thought I was being taken to the Nine."

The attendant didn't answer.

Constance's mind raced. Something out of the ordinary

197

was happening. Elsewhere, Sistercentral was an anthill of industry, but this maze of corridors was deserted and dim, windows reduced to horizontal slits at the top of the walls. Another right-angle turn, and a mesh screen blocked their progress. A scrutineer emerged from behind it.

"This is a restricted access area. Are you approved to pass?"

For answer, the attendant held up her wrist, sig side out, and the scrutineer scanned it against a hand-held screen.

Constance's trepidation turned to a drumbeat of fear. Perhaps the Memory Unmapping Manufactory was right here, in Sistercentral. Her breathing became shallow, perspiration spotted her hairline.

The scrutineer looked Constance over. "Something wrong, sister?"

Constance was convinced her air supply had been stoppered. She yanked at her skin, dropping it. Legs buckling, she felt herself being sucked into a long tunnel.

The scrutineer pushed Constance's head between her knees. "Breathe. Keep breathing."

Something acrid was waved under her nostrils, and consciousness returned with a start.

"Eau de nitar. Works every time." The scrutineer replaced the seal on a mustard-yellow tube, and slid it back in her pocket.

"Do you feel well enough to continue?" The Sistercentral attendant bent to pick up her skin.

Constance knew she ought to snatch at any excuse to go back upstairs. But she was numb – no resistance was left in her. She nodded and allowed herself to be taken down corridors which grew narrower, sloping further underground. Dully, she berated herself for a fool. She should never have shown up at Sistercentral to accept whatever sentence the Nine decreed. She ought to have packed up and fled. But instead of making a flight plan, she had indulged in grandstanding at the Hope Bridge.

The attendant stopped outside a brushed metal door, and rang a buzzer. The door wheezed and separated.

"Go through – you're expected."

Constance fastened her eyes on the open door. Behind another door on a windowless corridor, she had met Harper. They had made a baby. If only she could save it. But she couldn't save herself let alone their child. Why hadn't she tried? Why was she handing herself over like this?

"You should go in," said the attendant.

Constance knew she was beaten. She stepped through the door.

Innocence was inside. Her headdress lay on the table beside her, the veil puddling beside it, her plaits coming apart. Her features were blurry with tiredness. Yet through it all, her youthfulness glittered: a gloss that conveyed beauty but nothing of charm besides.

Barely glancing at Constance, she said, "Constance 500, the Nine has decided not to send you to MUM. Sisterland has something else in mind for you. For your sake, I hope you deliver what's required. The Shaper Mother insists you will. We'll see. You'll be given no further chances. Meanwhile, the Shaper Mother has accepted responsibility on your behalf. And extremely fortunate you are, too. You may leave."

At the reprieve, Constance sagged against the wall. Something flashing on-screen snagged Innocence's attention, and she paused to read it, letting out an exclamation of dismay. When she looked up, she frowned to see Constance still waiting.

"Yes?"

Constance tried to speak, and found her tongue glued to the roof of her mouth. "Where shall I go?" she croaked.

"Back to Shaperhaus, of course."

"On the keeper programme?"

"Don't be naive. You're unreliable. I told you, the

Sisterland has something else in mind for you. The Shaper Mother will explain."

Innocence turned back to the screen. Constance caught sight of a map. She tried to read the name. OUTSIDE was all she could decipher.

The attendant was still in the corridor, and guided Constance back through the maze to the foyer.

Relief coursed through Constance as she arrived at the front door and passed under the sign chiselled into stone.

SISTERLAND

PRIZES

OBEDIENCE

"Hey! Come back!" called the attendant.

Constance froze.

"Don't forget your skin." She held it out, and Constance attached it. "Lucky it didn't crack," said her guide.

Outside, winded by the aftershock, Constance sat on the bottom of the granite steps leading to the entrance. While she rested, she noticed an unusual number of peers milling about in the grounds, flamingo bright in their leathers.

A familiar figure approached along the avenue. When she was close enough to hear, Constance called out, "Hello there! What are you doing here?"

"Don't you dare to speak to me, Constance. You landed me in it, disappearing off the Buzz like that. I doubled back at the next stop, but couldn't find you. And then the peers showed up and scanned my sig. They refused to believe I wasn't one of the Silenced."

"Sorry, Modesty, I wasn't thinking straight."

Modesty began to climb the steps, intending to sweep past, but Constance's hand on her arm detained her. "I didn't mean to get you in trouble. What are you doing here? Is it because of me?"

"It's not all about you, you know. There are developments. Not that it's any of your business."

200

"Modesty, I'm truly sorry for leaving you high and dry on the Buzz. I'll do a report for the Shaper Mother taking all the blame."

"The Shaper Mother isn't too concerned about you right now. Events have overtaken you."

"What events?"

"Wouldn't you like to know?" Modesty's dark eyes had a secretive glint. "Anyhow, I can't stand about letting my tongue do all the work. I've another carrier interchange on my sig. It's from the mother – I'm to deliver it personally to the Nine. It's too sensitive to be sent over the comtel."

"Sounds serious."

"It is." Modesty adjusted her ponytail, preening.

"Except I suppose if it's a carrier interchange, you don't actually know what it's about."

"I know who it concerns, though. And that's enough for starters."

"Modesty, what's happening? I've just been inside, and there's something odd in the air. And the grounds are crawling with peers. Won't you tell me? By the way, they let me off."

"Off what?"

"Unmapping. I've been given a reprieve."

"Oh, good. Sorry, I should have asked."

How quickly people forget your problems, thought Constance. She scrutinised Modesty. The Shaper Mother's assistant was bursting with knowledge. "Come on, Modesty, what's going on? You know everything. Shaperhaus would fall apart without you. I always thought you were never given enough credit."

Susceptible to flattery, and a shade remorseful that she hadn't inquired about Constance's unmapping, Modesty wrestled with herself. But the information was too confidential. "Can't say."

Constance wasn't ready to give up. If she dangled some information as bait, she might pick up a titbit in return. "It was weird inside Sistercentral just now, Modesty. I was brought to a basement, a restricted area. Innocence couldn't take her eyes off a map. And it was nothing like any map of Sisterland I've ever seen."

Modesty was galvanised. "I know what she was looking at."

"What?"

She shook her head.

"Whatever's happening, it kept her up all night," said Constance. "She was wearing the same clothes she had on yesterday."

"The mother was up all night, too."

"I saw writing on the map. Just one word. OUTSIDE."

"You saw that?"

Constance nodded.

"Do you know what it means?"

"No."

Modesty whispered, "OK, I'll tell you what's going on, but not here. Not with wall-to-wall scrutineers and peers. You're never going to believe this, Constance. I can hardly believe it myself."

Modesty wheeled about, and Constance followed her halfway along the avenue, as far as the woman-on-a-tightrope statue. Modesty checked there was nobody nearby. Even so, she shielded her mouth with one hand.

"An intruder's been captured. From Outsideland. Innocence must have been looking at a map of Outsideland."

"Outsideland? What do you mean Outsideland? Is that in one of the outer belts?"

"Shush, not so loud. No, it's beyond Sisterland."

"Beyond?" said Constance. "What beyond? There's nothing outside Sisterland, except sea and empty desert."

"That's what I used to believe, too. But there are other countries beyond Sisterland. With people living in them."

"More than one? Many Outsidelands?"

"I don't know. Keep your voice down. Look, I know it's a lot to take in. I didn't know they existed either. But some people knew. Like the Shaper Mother – she wasn't surprised. She explained it to me. She says Outsideland is full of perils, and our way of life is threatened by it. The Nine doesn't want sisters knowing in case fear takes hold."

"How does anyone know it's dangerous if no-one's been there? They haven't, have they?"

"Don't know. Who'd want to go, anyway? They might never get back to Sisterland."

"But, Modesty, how do we know it's dangerous?"

"You don't have to touch hot metal to know it burns. Outsideland is full of risks because there's no universal sisterhood there."

Constance assessed this unexpected information. There was a place beyond Sisterland where the Nine held no sway: it meant the world had more possibilities than she was taught to believe.

"Why has the Shaper Mother told you this, Modesty?"

"Because she has to trust someone to report to the Nine for her – this information can't go over the comtel. Unauthorised eyes might see it. She's been mindmapping the intruder. Outsideland is where men live who survived World War III."

"But they all live here."

"Not all of them. That's only what we've been told. Some of them formed their own societies. Men from before."

"Outside the Nine's control."

"Exactly."

"So the interchange you're carrying is what the mother's learned from her."

This was Modesty's trump card. "Not her. *Him!*"

"A man? The intruder's a man from Outsideland?"

Round-eyed, Modesty nodded. "He calls himself an explorer, whatever that means. It could be another name for a spy, or a criminal, or a lunatic. He was held last night at

Compliance Space – this morning, he's being brought before the Nine. I can't wait to see what he looks like. The only thing the mother said is that he's different." Modesty shuddered, but excitement gleamed in her eyes. "Between you and me, she's quite shaken by him. Not her usual self at all."

"I expect the Nine wants to question him."

"You bet. Who sent him, why, and whether he's alone."

"Surely the mother's mindmapping has given us those answers? Hasn't she found everything we need to know?"

"Not everything. She finds it draining, because the information stored in his mind is so repellent. She can only work on him for short bursts."

"Can't someone help her?"

"She has a sister from the Nine's staff assisting her. My security rating doesn't stretch that far. Anyhow, better get inside and upload the interchange."

Constance watched her retreating back, mesmerised by the notion of Outsideland. What kind of life would a child born there have? She stroked her belly. Looking down at her thickening waist, she realised she wasn't wearing her jacket. Where had she left it? Not in Innocence's bunker, hopefully. Wait, she had made a cushion of it in the foyer. She must have left it on the bench near the mosaic of the babyfused woman. She started back in through the double doors.

"Where are you going?" A scrutineer challenged her.

"I've permission." Constance held up her comtel for scanning.

"You were scanned through already today."

"I left my jacket behind. I see it over there, on the bench."

"OK, but straight in and out."

No sooner had Constance retrieved it, than a door opened off the foyer, and a phalanx of peers whisked through. In the middle of them was a man. He was unlike any man in Sisterland – even Harper. His clothing had no hood at the collar, leaving his head and face visible. The face was shadowed with stubble, while his body was flabby, unaccustomed to labour. But the real difference lay in his stance: he wasn't cowed. When he met her glance, he looked back, instead of dropping his eyes as Sisterland men were trained to do.

As these impressions formed, the Outsidelander continued walking, three columns of peers on either side. No, he wasn't walking, he was strolling, as though admiring the sights. A half-smile was fixed on his face while his eyes flicked about. The row of peers behind bumped against him, and several attempted to hustle him on.

"Hey, no need to crowd me. You girls are like a bunch of turbo-charged nannies," he complained.

The intonation was foreign, but what struck Constance most was his lack of fear.

The desk scrutineer hurried over to Constance. "Why are you still here? You must leave at once."

"Who's that man? Why is he here?" asked Constance.

"Move, I said. We don't have time for idle gossip." The scrutineer made a sweeping motion with both hands.

Constance did as she was told. This was no time to push against boundaries.

Walking through the Sistercentral grounds, the notion of an Outsideland perplexed her. It meant the geography she was taught at girlplace gave an incomplete picture. How many outsidelands were not pictured on maps? And if the geography they learned was a qualified version, what about subjects such as history and politics? If the Nine lied about the world outside Sisterland, what else was it dishonest about?

Preoccupied, Constance passed the gardener from the previous day, still spraying leaves on ornamental trees. She almost missed her, but a blast of air from the gadget she was using caught Constance on the right flank. It occurred to her that Sisterland must be home to sisters with monotonous jobs bringing scant satisfaction. Apart from serving Sisterland, of course. Such sisters were inconspicuous and sometimes heard things.

Constance pulled off the jacket she had returned to Sistercentral to fetch, and offered it to the woman. "Swap?"

The woman's mouth fell open. "For what?"

"The chance to pick your brains."

Hurriedly, the gardener sister took it, stuffing it into a pannier on her wheeler.

"So," said Constance, reminding her there was no such thing as a free coat. "Have you heard anything about a stranger being held?"

The woman nodded, cautious.

"A man?"

"Yes."

"What do you know about him?"

"He comes from a place called Outsideland."

"I know that already, sister. What else?"

"He had a map of Sisterland with him."

Constance stared. That meant someone had left Sisterland and told Outsidelanders about where they came from. "How did he get in?"

"At Brown Convolution, they think. A strange vessel was found near the shoreline."

"Has anyone from Outsideland been here before?"

"Two men were found three or four years ago."

"What happened? Were they expelled?"

The gardener shook her head. "Strangers can never leave. They'd speak about Sisterland and more men would arrive." She began to back away.

"Wait! What did we do with them?"

"Discontinued." The gardener was gone.

Instead of going east to Shaperhaus, Constance took a westbound Buzz swooping towards Octagon. In the carriage, she rehearsed a story in which Sistercentral staff kept her kicking her heels for hours, in a flap about some sort of emergency. It was only a stretched version of the truth. The progress-monitor could track her on her comtel, if she was concerned about her movements, but she was gambling on people being too busy to notice her absence.

Constance was drawn back to the Hope Bridge. She wasn't going because disobedience was addictive, although she was starting to realise that Sisterland operated largely on the basis of compliance. She was going to test whether there was any truth in her theory about Silence's choice of venue to discontinue. She would never know for sure. But if she stood there and listened, with her nerve endings instead of her ears, maybe the answer might reveal itself.

At the bridge, Silence's face was again visible, on the same spot as her skin had hung. It wasn't the skin this time, but a stylised rendition of it, scratched onto metal. It could not convey her essence. Yet it was recognisably Silence. Constance stood below the image, taking in the elongated face, chin and neck. She wanted to touch the face, but it was too high off the ground.

"The Nine won't let you stay there, Silence," she said aloud. "Before long, you'll be painted over." But Silence would always be part of the Hope Bridge, whether her image was superimposed on it or not.

Constance remembered Silence's excitement at the prospect of becoming a source. Weighing up possible names. Debating what she would look like, which skills she would possess, what work might be chosen for her when she grew up. She didn't remember Silence worrying about the baby being a boy-man, and how she would react at handing it over. Always, the hope was that it would be a girl.

A hope shared by every babyfused Sisterlander.

But in the final days, Silence had become convinced it was a boy. Their last conversation had been about that.

"My scan's this morning," Silence had said.

"Why bother with a scan? You've waited almost three months. What difference can another day make?"

"I have to be sure. But I know already in my heart. It's a boy."

Constance had hugged Silence. "Sisterland needs boys, too."

"Not mine. I'm not letting them have my boy-baby."

Constance wished she had insisted on going to the scan with Silence. She had offered, but Silence had said it was something she wanted to do alone. And then the comtel message had arrived.

A son.

Nothing more.

Poor Silence, Constance had thought. She should have realised the word 'son' was deliberate. It took ownership of the baby.

For Sisterland she had messaged back. No response.

The first Constance had known of her other's discontinuation had been a news bulletin on the screen in Eternity Square. She had read it leaving work that evening. *A babyfused woman has fallen from the Hope Bridge. All Buzz services travelling east and west have been suspended.*

No suggestion of deliberate discontinuation had been indicated in those first reports. The presumption had been an accident. But Silence left the Buzz at Octagon station, walked to the Hope Bridge, climbed the central upright to the top, and flung herself off. Every bystander corroborated the account. She climbed with determination, steadied herself at the top, spread her arms wide – and leaped. No indecision.

And she did it immediately after a scan, carried out the day before she was scheduled to give birth, confirmed her child was a boy.

Some interpreted this as loyalty to Sisterland taken to extremes: the desperate cry of a woman devastated not to be carrying a daughter. But Constance understood differently. A drop of moisture interrupted her reverie. Then another. The sultry air was squeezing out a few drops of rain. Several landed on Silence's face.

"It looks as if she's weeping," said a voice from behind.

It was one of the regulars. Constance was starting to recognise some of them.

"Silence never cried," said Constance.

"How could she? Sorrow is no longer available. But I've heard it was part and parcel of life in PS days," said the woman.

"De-listing sorrow isn't much of a hardship."

"Sorrow is the flipside of joy. Maybe you can't have one without its opposite."

Constance considered this. Tranquillity was the norm in Sisterland, but was it too high a price to pay for experiencing neither joy nor sorrow?

The woman went on, "Silence is teaching us something right here, right now. She's showing us we should make time for tears."

"Silence isn't doing that. It's the rain."

"You see what you see and I see what I see. For me, it's a teachable image. But of course, as her other, your insights are meaningful."

Constance knew most of what she said about Silence was guesswork. Nobody else realised it, however. Which could be an opportunity. She tested the ground.

"Silence did believe moes were too restricted in Sisterland. She said women had grown wary of them. But not all moe-responses were negative. To her, they could be faster than logic, and just as effective. Not always, of course. But she called moe-reaction a useful tool – one we were foolish to abandon."

Silence had said nothing of the sort. But the follower was rapt.

"What else did Silence believe?"

"Yes, what else?" Voices were raised.

Constance hadn't noticed them draw near.

"Let me ask you a question. How many of you have babyfused?"

A number of hands were raised.

"Do you ever wonder about the men you babyfused with?"

"You mean the meets," said a voice.

"No, I mean the *men*. When you look at your children, do you ever ask yourself, are those his eyes? Does that talent for music come from him? It's wrong to keep men away from their children."

She sensed resistance. Perhaps she was nudging them along too quickly. She could understand that. It bewildered Constance how quickly she was turning against Sisterland – a hairline crack in belief had turned into a ravine. For inspiration, she looked at the representation of Silence on the bridge, and tried another tack.

"Some of the things we do are unnatural. Like taking babies away from their sources at the age of one."

"Isn't girlplace more efficient?" somebody suggested.

"What do you think, sisters?" Constance appealed.

"I didn't want to be separated from my Honesty," said a woman. "It took me a long time to adjust. That first month she was in girlplace, when I wasn't allowed to see her, was really tough."

"I found that month hard, too," said another woman. "I understand girlplace is for the best. And a transitioning period helps them settle in. But I'd have liked to visit my little Chastity sooner. I thought she looked peaky when I was finally allowed in."

"I did, too!" said the first woman.

"So did I," said a third voice. "I complained to the girlplace overseers about my Prudence. I said she was rosy-cheeked when she went in to them, and now she was off-colour. They told me I was an over-protective source. But I knew she'd been unwell."

210

"Your daughters missed you, sisters. If you loved Honesty and Chastity and Prudence – as I can see you did – did you never think about their fathers?"

"Universal sisterhood can't get distracted by men!" called a voice from the back.

"Perhaps that's where universal sisterhood has gone wrong," said Constance.

Shockwaves from her audience travelled up to her. Yet they weren't turning away from her – they stayed to hear more.

A sense of power inflated Constance. Today, she had defied the rule about going to work. Perhaps tomorrow, or the next day, she could disobey a different rule.

Her heart gave an odd, skippety beat as a world of possibilities opened up.

And then she thought about Harper trapped in matingplace, punished because of the blindfold she'd wanted him to remove. And that world of possibilities closed in again.

Chapter 23

Constance expected to be reprimanded when she turned up at Shaperhaus, after going absent without leave for almost 24 hours. Idly, she wondered what her punishment would be. They'd already taken away her home, by transferring her to a oneser. Her job was gone, too. She had no other to be separated from. There was a black mark the size of a Buzz carriage on her record because of the memory interchange. What was left? Loss of els? Inconvenient. But not a real deterrent to independent thought.

It was almost with academic interest that she faced her progress-monitor the next day.

Patience simply told her she'd been reassigned. Her manner was crisp, but lacked any hint of censure. "Your co-keeper authorisation is now deleted permanently. You're to report to the Shaper Mother as her temporary assistant."

"She has an assistant."

"Modesty's been seconded to different duties. You were expected to take up the post yesterday. We tracked you, and saw you spent most of the day at the Hope Bridge. A note has gone on your record."

Victory! All they could do was note down her insubordination. "Is the bridge out of bounds?"

"Not so far. But you were required here. It was inappropriate to be elsewhere." Patience ended the conversation.

She won't miss being my progress-monitor, thought Constance, gathering her plant and spray, plus the box in which she kept her skin. She hoped she hadn't robbed Modesty of a job.

Modesty was in the Shaper Mother's outer office, compiling a list. Her ponytail quivered when she saw Constance. "The mother pulled strings to have you allocated to her."

"I didn't push for this, Modesty. I don't know why I've been given your job. I won't be able to do it half as well as you."

"You couldn't very well stay where you were, could you? The co-keeper with a rogue memory? They had to find something else for you to do."

"I suppose." Constance had wanted out from co-keeping, but her presumption was a return to shaping. She didn't know the first thing about assisting the Shaper Mother.

"You'll never be let anywhere near shaping, either. You can't be trusted – you're not on message. You're presenting quite a problem, Constance." She squinted at her. "What puzzles me is why you're still here."

"But I haven't done anything wrong!" wailed Constance. "I'm not a danger to Sisterland. I just asked some questions, that's all. You don't agree with everything one hundred per cent, either."

"I don't know what you mean."

"You told me –"

"I told you nothing." Noisily, Modesty pulled open all the drawers in her desk, one after another, checking they were empty. She took a container holding her skin from the bottom drawer, adding it to a transparent box in which her personal possessions were stacked.

"Where are you being assigned?" Constance asked.

"The Sistercentral staff."

"Plenty of opportunities there, I should think."

"Depends on where they put me. The Shaper Mother lets me do things my own way. I'd still be here if it wasn't for you."

"Things aren't exactly going my way, either."

"True. But you're the one making waves. I'm getting splashed by them."

"Why am I still in Shaperhaus, Modesty? Why am I not in MUM? Or Safe Space?"

"The mother fought to keep you. She has a soft spot for you. I heard her say she's intuited something about you – you have enormous potential. Gifts for Sisterland to harness." Modesty sniffed, to show what she thought of the prognosis.

Constance was bemused. She had no special qualities – these days, she was in a permanent state of confusion. The Shaper Mother must be mistaken. "I don't know how I'll ever be able to repay her, Modesty."

"I'm sure she'll think of something. Well, that's that. I'm off. I've messaged your comtel with a note of all the codes for the office." Modesty lifted her box, and slouched towards the door. "Try to stay out of mischief."

"Wait, Modesty! I don't know anything about this job."

"Not my problem. I have to learn how to do a new job, too."

"You'll be a terrific asset to Sistercentral. You could run it standing on your head. I'm sure you'll be promoted to some crucial position in no time."

Mollified, Modesty stopped and rested the container on her hip. "Look, here's what you need to know about the mother. She works all hours, and you'll be expected to match her. She takes naps on a pop-up in her office. She's hopeless with technology so you'll have to switch everything on and off for her. She claims anything she can't work is temperamental or broken. And she has exercise gadgets she sometimes likes to use. They're stored under the floor, beside the pop-up. She's rather proud of her arm strength. If you can keep on top of all that, you'll be fine."

"Thanks, Modesty. Good luck." Constance squared her shoulders. "Right, I expect the mother wants to see me straight away."

Modesty shifted her load. "She's at Sistercentral. She won't be in today."

"What am I supposed to do?"

"The job's mainly about using your commonsense. You'll be fine. At least until your baby arrives. I wouldn't count on anything after that."

When Constance arrived for work the following day, the Shaper Mother was in the outer office, some sheets of paper in her hand. When she saw Constance, she folded them over, and slid them into her pocket. Her head was minus its trademark high-gloss sheen, and the cream lace shawl she wore over her Shaperhaus uniform had a stain on it.

"Ah, Constance."

"Good morning, mother." A pause, during which Constance expected to be given some instructions. Finally, she said, "Would you like me to fetch you some ocean tea?"

"I don't care for ocean tea – too salty. Unfortunately, I have a sweet tooth. I try not to indulge it. Perhaps I could make allowances today. I've had a difficult night. A mindmap assignment. The subject was . . ." Uncharacteristically, her voice trickled away, uncertain.

"Resistant?" suggested Constance.

"No, the subject went over easily enough. But the information we interchanged was disconcerting. I encountered a marked hostility towards our way of life."

'The subject'. Clearly, the mother didn't want Constance to know she was intuiting from a man. And not a word about

215

him being from Outsideland.

"Can't we learn from criticism, mother?"

"Learning is one thing, contamination is another. We value our civilisation. It must be safeguarded against agents of pollution."

"Surely Sisterland's more resilient than that?"

"Naturally Sisterland has the utmost confidence in itself."

Constance decided to test her. "May I ask, mother, where the subject comes from?"

The Shaper Mother lied fluently. "From Black Particle. It's so far away, inhabitants can drift out of step with our ways here in Harmony. We're suspicious of this renegade's motives. We've worked too hard to construct our society – we can't allow it to be destabilised."

The mother walked across to the window to watch the street life below. Activity was disciplined, pedestrians all moving purposefully, although respectful of one another's personal space. It seemed to soothe her, and she nodded in approval.

"I've witnessed ugly sights, Constance. Sights that weigh heavily on me. They don't believe in cooperation, except when it suits them. Every decision is based on personal gain – community interests are sidelined. The individual always takes precedence. Such a selfish, driven way of life!" Wearied, the Shaper Mother leaned her forehead against the glass.

"You should rest, mother. Surely someone else can continue with the interchange?"

"Unfortunately not. I'm linked in to the subject now, I must see it through. That's the protocol. We have a system for dealing with renegades. Not that we encounter them often. The oceans protect our borders."

Why, she's forgotten herself, Constance realised. She's just admitted Sisterland has outer limits in need of guarding. Exhaustion must have caused the blunder. As the thought formed, she suppressed it, but the mother was flagging visibly and not sensing as she usually did.

"It might be a good idea to close your eyes for an hour, mother. Even if you don't sleep, the rest will help."

"Sometimes, I wonder if I'll ever sleep again. The cruelty of this person's world is seared on me. The violence! The tumult!" She was overtaken by a yawn. "By rights, I shouldn't have left Sistercentral, but the subject has been allowed a few hours' sleep, and I couldn't bear to be under the same roof any longer. I felt soiled."

As the Shaper Mother pulled her shawl tight, Constance experienced a beat of pity. She had never seen her so vulnerable.

The mother's head snapped back on her neck. "Incidentally, I presume you've been informed: the Nine has new plans for you."

"Innocence said I wasn't being sent to MUM. I know I owe it to you, mother. You spoke up for me, and I'll never forget it. But it's only a temporary reprieve, isn't it? The Nine is busy now. My case has been aside. But something will be done about me, maybe after I become a source."

"Constance, child, I really don't know what's to become of you. All I can tell you is this: have faith in the Nine. Believe me, I'll do my best for you. And now, I think I will lie down after all. Another long day stretches ahead."

She retreated to the inner office, Constance following to activate the pop-up.

"I'll make sure you aren't disturbed, mother."

"Call me at once if the Nine needs me."

"Of course. Shall I fetch you a container for your skin?"

"I'm still wearing it? I must be more tired than I realised." She reached up to unhook it. "There's a holder in the footstool beside my chair. Just lift the stool's lid."

Constance found a carved onyx box. "How dainty."

"It was a gift from my other."

"What exquisite taste, mother."

"Yes, she was rather amazing." A remnant of sorrow settled on the Shaper Mother's face, visible without the barrier of her mask.

It moved Constance. Despite the difference in their stations, she wanted to reach out to this woman who had championed her before the Nine. "Should I organise a moe? It might revive you."

The mother recoiled. "I hardly ever indulge."

"I'm sorry, I didn't mean to presume. But I don't fully understand how I'm supposed to assist you."

"It was a thoughtful suggestion. But the upper echelons in Sisterland rarely take moes. It's seen as a sign of weakness. On the odd occasion when I do, it's always an E."

"Nothing else?"

"Nothing. Empathy helps me to connect with my sisters. Moes have their place, but not in my life. I don't suppose you'd consider . . ." She paused, leaving the words dangling.

"I'm sure I'd consider doing anything you wanted of me, mother."

"Would you? Would you really?"

Constance gave a start at the urgency in her voice.

"That's good to know. I'll talk to you later, sweet child. Operate the blankout on your way out."

Back in the outer office, Constance found some folded sheets of paper on the floor, by the window. They must be what the mother had been studying. She picked them up and opened them out.

ACCOUNT BY OUTSIDELANDER OF SISTERLAND'S ORIGINS

Scribbled on the margin was an instruction.

Cross-reference with memory-keeper versions

Constance began reading the printed text.

Q. What's known about the birth of Sisterland?

A. It happened in response to World War III which broke out in the year 2035. The war lasted for two years and caused some 2.5 billion deaths. When peace was negotiated, the

world lay in rubble. A generation was annihilated – young men, for the most part, along with significant numbers of young women. Contrary to expectations, nuclear weaponry was not a factor, but sustained heavy artillery action severely compromised the planet's ecosystem. Species of wild animals became extinct. Priceless artworks were lost when museums and galleries were shelled, while iconic landmarks were destroyed beyond repair.

Q. Were women forced to join this war?

A. Fighting was conducted largely by men but with some female participation. For the most part, women were not regarded as useful in the field, and ran non-military operations in their home territories. They headed up government bodies concerned with healthcare and education, in addition to any multinational companies still able to function. For the first time in history women became accustomed to power. And when they saw what could be achieved with it – even during wartime – they decided to try to put a stop to warfare, once and for all.

Q. How?

A. An alignment of women known as the Nine, headed by a charismatic leader of obscure origins called Beloved, came together to develop a strategy. During the war's wind-down phase, the Nine arranged for giant screens to be erected at all of the main meeting points for homecoming troops in docks and airports. Exhausted combatants were warned that their military leaders were addicted to war, and would declare it again on another front. Exclusively female government was the only way to guarantee peace.

Q. And men saw sense?

A. Nobody likes to lose power. After peace terms were negotiated, there was an attempted male resumption which proved unsuccessful. This was largely due to the debilitating impact of a pathogenic strain of bacteria unleashed during the final phase of WWIII. It only attacked the XY chromosome combination – women's XX genetic composition meant they were immune. The scientists who developed the bacteria as a weapon of biological warfare believed they had an antidote to safeguard their own side. But while the counter-agent worked for a time, the bacteria mutated and overrode it. The men who survived the war were weakened, and their vulnerability allowed women to consolidate their position. The Nine took drastic steps to separate the genders – and to programme women to be suspicious of men.

A commentary was scribbled at this point.

And a new world order emerged! A nation ruled by women. It was a metamorphosis. A transfiguration. A perfection!

Q. How did other countries react to the Sisterland State?

A. At first, the rest of the world was busy licking its wounds. By the time it woke up to what had been established, Sisterland's borders were secure. Efforts to make contact through diplomatic channels were rebuffed, and

The office door opened. Constance shoved the pages into the drawer of the desk.

Modesty walked in, moulded to the one-piece garment worn by all Sistercentral staff.

"Modesty, back already! Don't you look smart!"

Modesty trailed a hand down her front. "This is self-cleaning. Dirt dissolves on contact, like foam on sand. Why are you looking so shifty?"

Constance took out the pages and handed them to Modesty whose eyebrows disappeared into her hairline as she read them.

"Where did you get these?"

"The mother dropped them."

"Must be notes from her sessions with the Outsidelander. Don't let her know you've found them. You'll catch it, if she does."

"What'll I do with the pages, Modesty?"

"Put them back where you found them."

Constance dropped the sheets of paper by the window.

"Did you find them like that? Or were they folded up?"

Constance picked up the papers, doubled them in half, and let them fall again.

"Too conspicuous," said Modesty. "Kick them out of sight. Over there. By those stupid scatter cushions. Glad to see them earn their keep at last. Now, I'm under instructions to fetch the mother back to the Sistercentral: the Nine needs her. She was sent a voice message on her comtel, but she always forgets to check it – I used to do it for her. You'll have to remember, in future."

"But she's only just left the Sistercentral. She's exhausted."

Modesty shrugged. "I'm to brief her en route."

"Is she needed right now?"

"Of course right now. Why? Has she something better to do than answer a Nine summons?"

"She's trying to sleep, that's all I meant. She worked all night on a mindmap subject. Modesty, why would the mother sleep in the office? Why wouldn't she go home?"

"She doesn't like going home."

"Why not?"

Modesty's face reflected her usual struggle between discretion and a desire to gossip. "Maybe she's afraid of its associations. Something unfortunate happened to the mother's other. She wound up with facial burns – utterly disfigured, the damage ate down to the bone. A chemical in her skin caused the accident."

"I thought she lost her other. She always mentions her in the past tense."

"Lost, in real terms. Her other is no longer a companion."

"Don't they share a home any longer?"

"Her other's in mindedplace. And the mother can't face her."

"Because of the scarring?"

"Because of the guilt. She bought her the skin, as a gift. It was made under a new procedure, not fully compliant with safety standards."

"That's hardly the mother's fault. She gave it to her in good faith."

"True. But the Nine persuaded her the story had to be suppressed in case it caused panic. Sisterlanders might throw away their skins, and that would lead to . . . complications."

Constance looked at her skin, in a box sitting on her desk. If it caught fire, it would stick to her face. She could never remove it in time to save herself.

"So does she see her other at all now?"

"She visits her now and again, but her other screams at the sight of her. At least the mother didn't choose a new other. That was loyal of her."

"But it would have been impossible. Sisters are only allowed one other in their lifetimes."

"What a pearl you are – even now. Don't believe everything you've been taught." Modesty gave a tiny nod towards the scatter cushions, and the Outsidelander's account.

Constance went to fetch the Shaper Mother.

She was instantly alert, rising and asking for water, before going through to the outer office.

"I hear you're on the Honour 19 team, Modesty."

"I do have that privilege."

"Good. I told Innocence you're a natural-born organiser." Turning to Constance, the Shaper Mother said, "The Nine's plans to commemorate Honour have been upgraded. A public holiday is to be announced. The date hasn't been fixed yet, but we're working towards this time next month. Right, Modesty?"

There was only one annual holiday a year – Sisterday, celebrated on August 24th – so the addition of a second holiday was momentous.

"Yes, there's going to be a yearly event, called

Memoryday," said Modesty. "June 29th is the date chosen."

"Memoryday – won't it be splendid!" said the mother. "This year, Honour will be the focus, but we'll extend it to cover all our memory-keepers. They've been pivotal in advancing the Sisterland ethos. How do you like that idea, Constance?"

"Honour deserves to have her contribution recognised, mother."

"Indeed, but it's not only about her. The individual, no matter how outstanding, is not what matters. It's the group. After all, memories are too important to be left to individuals – that's why central control had to be taken of them. So, Memoryday will celebrate Sisterland, and Sisterland will celebrate Memoryday. We need reminding of everything achieved, and everything yet to be achieved."

Constance's forehead wrinkled. "Forgive me, mother, but we're taught that Sisterland is already ideal. So what does the Nine believe is yet to be achieved?"

"What you were taught was correct at the time you were taught it. But perfection, it turns out, can be honed still further. Something of enormous significance is now under way. Something that takes women to a new level as life-givers."

This development sounded ominous to Constance, and a sidelong glance told her that Modesty's eyes were also boggling.

"Impatient." The Shaper Mother straightened her shawl, chuckling. "All will be revealed soon. When the Nine judges the time is right."

"Mother, what's that by the cushions?" asked Modesty.

"I don't see anything."

Constance approached the cushions. "Some papers." She bent and picked up the pages. Without opening them out, she handed them to the mother.

The mother stuffed them into her pocket, and looked

closely at Constance. Constance fought the mindmapping.

"You're putting on weight, child. Don't forget you're entitled to new clothes – Sisterland provides everything free to waiting sources."

"Yes, mother."

"Our sources are dear to us."

"Yes, mother."

"But Sisterland is dearer still."

Chapter 24

At home time, emerging into Eternity Square, Constance decided to go for a walk. She followed a pavement constructed from hexagonal slabs of mica, on which the outlines of musical instruments were imprinted. This would lead her to Courtesy Avenue, where she could pick up some source clothes – the Shaper Mother was right, everything she owned was now too tight. Somewhere along the way, however, her feet had different ideas, and she found herself outside the Tower. If only she could find out if Harper was all right. If only she could let him know about their baby.

Just then, Unity emerged. Even at a distance, Constance knew her by her stiff-bodied walk: as though her head was balanced insecurely on her neck, and might tumble off unless she proceeded with caution.

She set out after her. "Unity? I attended the Tower recently. Maybe you remember me?"

"Oh, I remember you, all right. We lost a top-grade meet because of you."

Dread prickled along Constance's scalp. "What do you mean? What happened to him?"

"He had to be taken off the job. Refused to mate with anyone after you."

Constance felt a thrill of pride at Harper's defiance, swamped at once by fear for the consequences. "What did they do to him?"

"Food deprivation, and when that didn't work, sleep deprivation."

"And then?"

Unity turned a suspicious glance on Constance. "You seem more worried about the meet than the havoc he created."

"Please tell me. I feel responsible."

Unity was walking at a cracking pace, and a stitch developed in Constance's side. In lockstep, they skirted round a wheeler belonging to a worker from the city's ambience division. The worker was twiddling the dials on a box set into a wall, and birdsong began to carol out.

"How do you like our new policy?" she called to them. "Sisters have been missing the sound of birds. Not their droppings, mind you. This is the best of both worlds."

A dawn chorus orbited around them.

"Perhaps you should know what you provoked," said Unity. "The Mating Mother was worried the meet's behaviour would be contagious. Imagine if other meets started refusing to take part in Himtime, too. She had to nip it in the bud. When food and sleep deprivation didn't work, she sent for him, and offered to improve his living conditions. His attitude showed the kind of throwback defiance we thought was bred out of men. He said slavery was slavery, no matter how the cage was prettied up, and demanded to be sent home. Can you believe it?"

Fear for Harper hollowed out Constance. When she tried to speak, she found her throat had seized up. Licking her lips, she tried again. What emerged was a croak. "Wouldn't that have solved the Mating Mother's problem?"

"Solved the problem? Created a nest of them, more like. Every meet in the Tower would've spun the same line. Besides, Sisterland can't reward disobedience. What kind of precedent would that set? No, The Mating Mother did the only thing possible. She couldn't cover up his disobedience. She went to the licensing authorities and admitted she had a meet she couldn't control. They took over the running of the Tower, and all the unpleasantness died down. Except the Mating Mother's been downgraded to greeter. Which was my job. So I've been downgraded to mead-server. And all because of a rebellious meet."

"Where's Harper now?"

"He was taken away."

Constance's flesh chilled. "Shipped off to an outer belt?"

"Should've been, for the trouble he caused. But I hear he's still in Harmony. There's a shortage of young men to do the grunt work in eat-easies. So he was sent to one. And that's where he'll stay, while he's able to work. Guess he must be living in Hutchtown."

Male labour lived in that zone, to the north-east of the city. It would be like hunting for a leaf on the floor of Harper's forest.

"Unity, could you find out which easy he's in?"

"What a strange question! Why in the name of Beloved would you want to know where he is?"

"I can't explain. But it's important. Can you find out?"

"You're as perverted as the mother said!"

"Please, Unity. I'll make it worth your while."

"Leave me alone! This meet cost me my job. Don't you realise the trouble I'd be in, just for talking to you about him?"

"I'd pay you for information. Nobody has enough els."

"Get away from me, or I'll tell the Mating Board you're looking for him."

"Name a price – anything you like. Anything at all." Unity did not speak, but Constance could tell she had her attention. "It must be hard work in matingplace. Creating all that fantasy, but never sharing in it. I saw how the Mating Mother

227

treated you – you were nothing but a pair of hands to her. And now she's pinched your job."

"She was a tyrant!" Unity burst out. "And being demoted has made her worse. She still acts as if she's in charge. I never wanted to work in matingplace. They pump us full of hot air about it being a patriotic job, but it's like being a servant. Waiting hand and foot on pampered women with a permit to babyfuse. I never get offered one of those licences. The Mating Mother kept promising to propose me for retraining if I stuck with the job, but every time I reminded her she said, 'Be patient'. She was stringing me along. And after mismanaging the Tower, she has no pull to recommend anyone now."

"So get even with her, and make some els for yourself into the bargain," said Constance.

"I don't want els, I want a chance. Can you vouch for me? You seem to have friends in high places."

"I could try. What is it you want me to do?"

"Put in a good word. Get me on a training programme. Anything. I don't care what – I just want out of matingplace."

Constance was in no position to recommend anyone. But Unity was unaware of that. She considered making the promise anyway, but couldn't deceive her.

"Unity, I don't have any influence. I've been transferred to the Shaper Mother's office on a temporary basis, though. I could mention you to her as somebody with potential. I can't do any more than that, I wish I could."

Unity stuck her hands in her pockets. "Better than nothing, I suppose. More than the Mating Mother ever did. All right, here's what I heard. He's in an easy in Octagon, near the Hope Bridge. Which one, I don't know. You'll have to do the legwork."

"The Hope Bridge. Odd how all roads lead there. Is there any chance they'll ever let him go home now? After he's done his penance?"

"No chance. He should be thankful he's not in a worse place. There was talk of Grey Disjoint for him. Conditions there would soon quench his fire."

"There's something else I need to ask you, Unity."

"Make it quick."

"Do you remember Benevolence? She was taken from the Tower to Safe Space?"

"What is it with you and defectives? She went on the blink – the Mating Mother had her licence revoked."

"That was unfair. She was a bit upset, granted, but since when is that a crime?"

"A bit? She's having aversion therapy."

"Aversion therapy to what?"

"Babies."

"How extreme! She just wanted to be a source."

"She needs aversion therapy. Otherwise she'll self-destruct, and that's a waste of Sisterland's investment in her. A thought-cruncher, right? Takes years to train up one of them. Aversion therapy's for her own good. Don't look so sorry for her. I know she wanted to be a source. But wanting's not enough. You have to be suitable, as well. You won't forget your promise, will you, Constance? I have to get out of the Tower."

"I won't forget."

Constance boarded a train for the Octagon zone. A leaflet lay on the seat – there was one on every seat. She picked it up.

She looked round, to see if there was any reaction. Most of the passengers were pretending they didn't see the leaflets, but one or two made eye contact. Tellingly, nobody was asking what the message meant. Either they knew already – or didn't want to know. Constance pocketed her leaflet as she disembarked.

She discovered three eat-easies within a stone's throw of the Buzz station, and a dozen more in the labyrinth of streets behind the bridge. The smell from the easies made her ravenous. By the fourth, she was bloated. Detective work would leave her as broad as Sistercentral if she wasn't careful. She switched to ocean tea for the next four easies. By the ninth, however, the smell of food weakened her resolve and she decided to try some cloud noodles. In this easy, as elsewhere, she positioned herself for a view through the hatch to the kitchen area. It gave her an occasional glimpse of the staff. Everywhere, the men were in late middle age. Naturally, they didn't emerge, not even to wipe down tables, as they weren't allowed to approach women.

"Don't you employ any young men? Who does the heavy work?" she asked the girl who brought down the cutlery she had forgotten to pick up.

"We could use a strong pair of hands for lifting. But it's hard to find young men for kitchen work. The Buzz network is being renovated – they all get diverted into that."

"That man I saw through the hatch seems to be lame. There must be a lot of labour to working in a kitchen."

"He has to work if he wants to eat."

Constance was troubled by the girl's shrug. It reminded her that she had noticed things once, too, and deliberately pushed them aside. How there were no old men in Harmony, for example. They disappeared from the workplace once their strength and fitness levels declined – vanished from sight, too. Old women were treated with deference. Their others took care of them for as long as possible, with free mindedplace accommodation for any who needed nursing. She had been told that men who were old, or unable to work, were cared for in Brown Convolution. But for the first time, she wondered if that was an untruth. Just one more, among many, as she was now aware.

Unsettled, she watched the hatch, behind which a man limped to and fro. The light went on for Constance to collect her order, but when she fetched it she didn't remove the heat-lid from the dish.

"Don't ya like the noodles?" The woman at the next table jerked her chin at the bowl.

"Lost my appetite. Are you from round here?"

"Live in the next street, eat here most nights. Ain't seen ya here before."

"I just happened to be in the neighbourhood."

"One of them Silenced gals?"

"No, I'm not one of the Silenced. Why, what have you got against them?"

"Nothing." A glug, and a forkful of noodles vanished. "Can't figure them out, is all. Dunno what their game is."

"Me neither," said Constance. "But they aren't doing any harm."

"Guess not. Don't let the food get cold."

Constance tasted some of the fluffy noodles, which melted as she swallowed them.

"Cloud noodles are good here." Bowl empty, the woman at the next table was watching her.

Constance forced herself to eat.

"But if ya don't mind me sticking my nose in," the woman went on, "a babyfused sister needs something more substantial. Next time, try the spinach dumplings. Plenty of iron in them."

"I suppose I'm showing now." It pleased Constance to think her babyfusion was visible.

"Can't rightly see your middle over the table but it's there in your eyes. Something changes 'bout the eyes when a sister's lining up to be a source. Been maybes thirty years since I babyfused, but I still got a nose for it. Don't stop eating on my account – ya gotta keep your strength up. Baby'll gobble y'up from the inside, otherwise."

Constance concentrated on the bowl in front of her. "Are there many eat-easies round here?"

"Plenty. It's a busy zone."

"Do you have a favourite?"

"Here suits me. Set in my ways, maybes. But if it's busy, I sometimes go to one off Gentle Street. Tucked in outta the way. Can always get a seat there. It's called Rice-Wise."

"I'll check it out."

"First right outta here, right again, and a sharp left brings you to it."

Constance finished her food, nodded at her neighbour, pushed back her chair, and left the eat-easy.

The directions brought her to Rice-Wise. It was closed. She tried to see through the shutters, in case someone might be clearing up in the kitchen, but no lights shone. She'd have to return tomorrow. If she was organised and persistent, maybe she'd have all the eat-easies in the area checked out within a week or so. Although it might take longer – she couldn't specifically ask in each one if they had a young, male worker. She'd have to sit there, and watch every time the hatch to the kitchen was lifted. The trouble was she needed to do this quickly while she had the stamina – Silence's energy levels had flagged during babyfusion. "On the fifth, sixth and seventh day she rested," she used to joke. Already, Constance was conscious of having to build in relaxation periods.

A twinge in the small of her back reminded her to make tracks for home. As she waited for a westbound Buzz for Oblong, she reassured herself that Harper was more accessible to her in an eat-easy – any eat-easy, provided she could locate it – than in matingplace. Security was naturally tight for Himtime, but a close watch over diners was unnecessary. A discreet way of making contact shouldn't be impossible. She couldn't approach him directly: a woman falling into conversation with a man would attract attention. But she could slip him a note, perhaps. No, wait, he was unable to read. It would have to be a verbal message.

Constance refused to dwell on the possibility that Harper might be swallowed up by Harmony, and beyond her reach. She was consumed by the need to find him. Into her comtel, she tapped the names of the eat-easies already checked out, and a reminder to upload a detailed street map of the Octagon zone.

Next day, the Shaper Mother's office was empty when Constance arrived. No matter, a list of duties had been sent through to her comtel. Star priority was given to compiling research notes for the mother to write a speech to be delivered on Memoryday. Its theme was the importance of authenticated memories: the State laboured on behalf of its sisters to sift out genuine memories from imposters which would confuse citizens. The irony of the subject matter wasn't lost on Constance. The Nine had the power to classify a true memory as a rogue one, as she knew to her cost.

Constance tackled her assignment standing up because the baby wouldn't allow her to sit down. She smiled, thinking how controlling it was. A future candidate to join the Nine. By and by, her mind wandered, and she fell to considering Honour. As her life receded, the memory-keeper had been preoccupied by her relationship with her father. Constance once again wondered about her own father, and what part he might have played in her upbringing, given the opportunity.

A catalogue of what-ifs circled in her mind.

Might she have developed different skills? Might she have a different perspective? Might she have become a different person?

"Constance, you look as if you have the weight of the world on your shoulders."

Constance jumped. She hadn't heard the Shaper Mother enter. Today, a shawl in a black-and-orange eye-print covered her tunic. The eyes were elongated, with a whorl of lash.

Constance felt an immediate antipathy to the print. Two side-on eyes dangled from her earlobes.

"Constance?" prompted the mother.

"Waiting for inspiration, mother."

"Inspiration never waits for us, why should we wait for it? I was watching you for a moment, sweet child. You looked unquiet. Is there anything you'd like to confide in me?"

"No, mother."

"Nothing at all?"

"No, mother."

A sigh. "I see." The Shaper Mother traced a hand along the top of her head. The maternal note was stripped from her voice when she spoke again. "Speaking of watching, we know where you've been and what you've been doing. Don't think your activities have escaped our notice."

Did she mean her encounters with the Silenced – or her search for Harper? Please let it be the former, the lesser of two evils. Constance reined in the thought as soon as it occurred to her. Fortunately, the mother was still speaking and didn't pick up on it.

"Someone in the sacred state of babyfusion should be more prudent. But your comtel records show a regrettable lack of discretion." She walked towards the inner office. "It's time we spoke about the Nine's plans for you. Follow me."

Chapter 25

The leopard-print door peeled away from the wall. Biting her lip, Constance followed the Shaper Mother through it. The mother began to fuss with her wrap, unwinding it from around her shoulders and folding it. Constance fetched the onyx box for her skin and waited. Working as an assistant was a bizarre combination of responsibility for menial jobs and access to confidential information.

"I only ask you to take care of work-related matters," said the Shaper Mother. "Never anything to do with my private life. You don't do my shopping, or deal with problems at my oneser."

Oops, she'd read her mind that time. She must be well rested.

The mother allowed herself a tight smile. "Comparatively," she said.

Settled on her throne-chair, she indicated to Constance to approach. Their positions had an air of choreographed formality. Constance concentrated on emptying her mind, feeling it clear, the way furniture is lifted from a room. She had to be the gatekeeper of her thoughts.

"We know you've been in regular communication with the Silenced," said the mother.

Constance blocked the relief that bubbled up. So they were unaware about Harper!

"You demonstrate a certain ambiguity towards these foolish women," continued the mother. "We've tolerated it – we see you occupy a unique position in their eyes. And it occurs to us that could be useful. As you know, you're off the co-keeper programme. That's a permanent decision. It won't be reversed. However, the Nine is offering you a second chance. Constance, a wonderful opportunity has come your way. You're invited to do something important for universal sisterhood." A current of attention flew from the mother to Constance. It was as if Constance had been caught by the chin, and held there by the Shaper Mother. "Sweet child, we'd like you to make contact with the Silenced leadership. This movement hasn't just sprung up. Some disaffected women are directing it. Women with a plan. The Nine needs to discover their intentions."

Unblinking, her tawny eyes bored into Constance's: she felt the Shaper Mother's willpower pouring through her. *Acquiesce*.

"Why would they pay attention to me?" said Constance.

The willpower stream stalled, before regrouping and flowing again. "Come, come, Constance, this is no time for modesty. We both know why you matter to the Silenced."

Constance owed a debt to the Shaper Mother. But what the mother was asking bothered her. Conflicted, she said, "I haven't a clue who's leading the Silenced. I wouldn't know how to get in touch with them."

"Ah, but *we* know. The Ess has compiled a dossier. Not as complete as we'd like it to be – we can't risk bugging her twoser. She's sharp enough to spot any device planted there, and then she'd know we were on to her. Still, a certain amount of information has been collected. Much of it's classified but I can give you access to some of the data. The sister leading the Silenced is a valued member of the community. Such a perversion of her talent pains us. You know this woman socially, but you must now form an ideological connection."

"If she's as clever as you say, she'll regard me as a risk. After all, she must know I work for you – it's not exactly a secret. Anyone in Shaperhaus could tell her."

"How humble you are, dear Constance. Having you on board will seem like a stroke of good fortune. Oh, you can be sure she's been watching you – I'm surprised she hasn't made an approach already." A weighted pause. "Has she?"

"No! I don't even know who you're talking about. I've spoken to the Silenced a few times, but all they want to know is what my other was like. Nobody's asked me to do anything."

"Believe me, this person will. You're too big a catch for them not to try and hook you. Agree to everything, but report back on their plans. It allows us to lull them into a false sense of security. And then . . ."

Constance looked at the mother as if she'd never seen her before. *And then you pounce,* she thought, deliberately allowing the thought to reach the mother.

She made a dismissive gesture. "No state allows itself to be undermined. Steps must be taken. There's no point in wounding the snake by a series of cuts – the head has to be struck off. With your help, we can remove all the Silenced leaders in one blow. Isolating one or two won't put an end to this when there are others who'll take their places. And believe me, an end will be made. This movement will never challenge the Nine."

Constance thought quickly. She was being asking to become a spy – here was the reason she'd been spared MUM. She kept her voice deliberately flat. "And if I supply you with information, my baby lives?"

"Of course. But don't look on it as a bargain. It's a once-in-a-lifetime opportunity to do something meaningful for Sisterland."

Constance couldn't help herself. "But to worm your way into someone's confidence, only to inform on them! It's horrible!"

"We must protect our way of life, Constance."

"Perhaps some of their ideas are worth looking into. You said it yourself: Sisterland is a work in progress."

"Sweet child, the wellbeing of our society depends upon harmony – that's why our capital city was named for this virtue. Each of us must pull together. We hoped the Silenced would fizzle out, but the movement is growing. We can't allow random elements to disrupt the whole. Group interests must take precedence over" – her mouth slitted – "individualism."

Sensing Constance's ambivalence, the Shaper Mother locked eyes with her. Tension quivered between them. Constance felt the mother's willpower press against her own.

"The Nine has decided," said the mother. "The Silenced must be neutralised. You're invited to help."

"And if I say no?"

"The Nine cannot envisage you refusing. It would be unnatural. Of course, there are other sisters we can turn to if you pass up this opportunity. But it would be unwise, Constance. So very unwise. I dislike being blunt, but I must remind you: you have a lot to lose."

Constance traced the lifeline on the palm of her hand. She was babyfused, and ought to take the path of least resistance. At least until she gave birth. This invitation from the Nine was one in name only. She was boxed in. Surely there could be no harm in meeting the head of the Silenced and hearing what she had to say, before making a decision.

"Do I really know this woman socially?"

"Trust me, you know her well."

That *trust me* singed Constance's mind. There was no-one she could trust, except herself. "All right, I'll take a look at the Ess report and arrange a meeting."

"Excellent, you justify my faith in you." The mother left her throne-chair, and laid a hand on Constance's shoulder. Her voice was soothing. "My child, you'll find life easier if you focus on what matters. Universal sisterhood. Everything else is white noise."

On her way home that evening, an excited babble from her fellow passengers penetrated Constance's reverie. She looked up, and saw the Buzz train was shunting towards the Octagon stop. A banner hung from the Hope Bridge. Five words.

The next morning, when she was at her desk in Shaperhaus, a vibration indicating a voice message thrummed on Constance's comtel. She activated it. *Security clearance received. Prepare to receive Ess data.* The name Ess filled her with foreboding: it was a dedicated intelligence section within the peers. But what choice did she have? She hit the transmit icon, and an image popped up. It was small but recognisable.

Goodwill.

Constance was transfixed by the image. A subversive! Goodwill! It was difficult to believe.

And yet, she had been at the Hope Bridge. She retraced their conversation.

"*Why not give them what they want?*" *said Goodwill.*

"*I don't know what they want.*"

"*Nor do they. Whatever you give them will be what they want.*"

Constance touched the comtel again, and the voice listed biographical bullet points about Goodwill. Words such as plausible and astute were used about her. So, too, were maverick and scheming.

Did this mean Devotion was also one of the Silenced? She struggled to envisage her source in any sort of movement, let alone a resistance. All Devotion cared about were her window boxes and brewing homemade wine. She replayed the message. There was nothing about Devotion but maybe she had a dossier of her own.

Constance brooded over bumping into Goodwill at the bridge. Goodwill had no way of knowing she'd encounter Constance there – her decision to jump off the Buzz was unpremeditated. She must have been there for her own reasons, perhaps to gauge support levels for the Silenced, or to see how the peers would handle the gathering. But Goodwill could have slipped away without Constance seeing her. And why had she encouraged Constance to speak when she had no control over what she would say? Did she make a snap decision to assess Constance, too?

She sent Goodwill a comtel message suggesting they needed to talk. "**Alone,**" she wrote. Such an approach from Constance was unprecedented – Goodwill's response would be telling. She replied at once, inviting Constance to the twoser. "**Devotion's just left for work.**" said the message. "**She'll be gone all day.**"

Constance's breath rattled in her chest. Before she could do this, she needed to juice up. She approached the Shaper Mother's office, and the door peeled open. One day, she thought, I really am going to applaud that door. The mother was standing at the window. She seemed to spend an increasing amount of time just looking out at the activity in Eternity Square.

"I'm going to pay a visit to this sister," said Constance. "The one the Ess says is a ringleader."

"Good."

"I'll need extra moe approval first."

"I'll sign off on one right away."

The mother could use some moes herself, thought

Constance – she could do with loosening up. That had been self-indulgent baloney about only needing to access empathy. Deliberately, Constance let the opinion spread through her mind, and watched with satisfaction as the Shaper Mother picked up on it.

The two women ahead of Constance in Moe Express dithered over their selection. One ordered a G, because gratitude had recently been made available at a knockdown price and she said feeling better about everything was worthwhile, while her companion vacillated between a Z and a U before coming down on the side of Z.

"Zest, last gift of the gods to humankind," murmured Constance, remembering Benevolence from matingplace. There had been traces of zest in her.

The customer blinked rapidly. "No such moe, surely? I wanted zeal. I'm hoping for promotion."

"You've chosen such a pushy moe, Reverence," said her friend. "Mine's a more female one."

"Why should any moe be masculine or feminine? Surely they're just moes: gender neutral," said Constance.

The two shoppers turned their backs decisively against her. My questions upset other sisters, thought Constance.

"What can I tempt you with today, sister?" asked the flicker, when her turn came. "Shall I list the offers?"

"No, thanks. I need something to stiffen my resolve – I have a difficult meeting ahead."

"And you'd like to tackle it in a diplomatic way, am I right? You might consider a hybrid moe. A double C blend, perhaps. Courage plus constructiveness."

Constance nodded, and watched as the flicker netted the moes and bagged them, fluttering, within the same container. She never tired of the spectacle. When she attempted to pay, she was told Shaperhaus was taking care of the bill.

The flicker's manner became confidential. "We have a

facility for special customers who wish to ingest on the premises. Allow me to escort you there."

Constance had never heard of such a perk. "Does every outlet provide this service?"

"Certainly. We appreciate time is more valuable for some sisters than others."

Constance didn't fancy wandering about searching for a public space to consume her moe. And that attitude, she realised, was how favouritism crept into a supposedly equal society. However, the high moral ground struck her as draughty right then.

"Thank you. I'd like to avail of it."

The flicker led her to a room equipped with nothing more than a white rug into which her feet sank up to the ankles, a plump plum of a sofa, and a tall vase on the floor from which emerged three gladioli. "You won't be disturbed here. Remember you're taking a blended moe. They pack a twister punch."

As soon as she was alone, Constance opened her cargo. She bent her face over it, tapped the seal, and the bag flew open. The impact made her totter back, her fall broken by the sofa. Her finances rarely ran to a blend, and this was a humdinger. As the moe swooshed through her bloodstream, a volley of self-assurance reached her: she was able for whatever was required. The blended moe in her bloodstream sang to her, its music drowning doubts.

But it didn't last. Not even a hybrid blend could hold her for long. The music screeched to a halt. She sat up.

Artificial moes were no longer effective on her. She supposed it must be because she could access genuine ones on her own. Dehydrated, Constance hauled herself out of the sofa's embrace. These moes were giving her a hangover, too – it had been weak of her to rely on one.

From now on, she must manage without Sisterland's crutches.

Chapter 26

Constance pulled off her skin, and propped it against a cushion. "I lost you at the bridge the other day. Did the peers log you?"

"No, I managed to melt away," said Goodwill. "How about you?"

"I'm not as experienced as you at giving peers the slip."

"That's too bad, dear. But you're young. They'll offset it against your age. The blood runs hotter in our youth." Her honking laugh filled the room.

Constance considered her. Goodwill was billowing out of her waistband, her face was blotchy, and a button was missing from her shirt. If the Ess said she was one of the ringleaders of a new resistance movement, it must be so. But a less prepossessing ringleader it was a struggle to imagine.

Of course, that was the beauty of it.

"An el for your thoughts," said Goodwill.

Goodwill couldn't mindmap, not even at an elemental level. Which explained why Constance had never felt Goodwill tiptoe through her mind.

"Have you ever seen an el? I haven't," said Constance.

"Back when I was a girl. People still dealt directly with money then. But a lot has changed."

"Except we're not supposed to call them changes, because that implies previous Nines were wrong on some issues," said Constance. "When I studied silkenspeak, I was taught nothing in Sisterland is ever altered: it's restructured to maximise benefits."

Goodwill's mouth twitched. "Of course. We don't change things, we refine them. Many refinements have happened since I was a girl."

"Were men kept apart from us then, too?"

"Yes, because it's safer. The fine-tuning is mainly cosmetic: we have less noise now, less ugliness, less conspicuous consumption – partly because of space pressure in homes."

"You know, I've never understood why we're squeezed into such tiny spaces. It's not as if the population is growing. On the contrary. There's no reason why bigger onesers and twosers couldn't be built."

"Uneconomical. It takes more energy to heat a larger property." Goodwill settled back, pleased to have Constance as her audience. "When women took over, we prioritised. Daft, futuristic trappings were discarded – in fact, one of the first decisions made by the original Nine was to axe the space programme. Better to focus on taking care of the world we have, rather than search for new worlds."

"Exploration isn't something we're keen on." Constance thought about Outsideland. What would it be like to explore that world? Or even – an idea flared, frightening her with its insidious appeal – to live there? She wrenched her attention away from Outsideland. "We're told Sisterland has reached the epitome. But it hasn't."

"There have been missteps."

Constance waited, but Goodwill was waiting, too.

Constance plunged in. "Does it never strike you, Goodwill, that Sisterland might have lost its way? I know I shouldn't even think this, let alone say it. But wouldn't it have been better to share?"

"We do share."

Constance took her courage in both hands. "Not with men."

"Men can't share. And women dare not. That's what we're taught."

"Do you believe it?"

Goodwill took so long to reply that Constance thought she must have miscalculated. There was no way to retrieve the situation – she ought simply to leave. It was only when she reached for her skin that Goodwill found her voice.

"Look outside, Constance. What do you see?"

"Devotion's window boxes."

"Do you know what she's growing?"

"Basil and dill."

"Herbs co-exist if the conditions are right. You couldn't plant mint in there – it would take over. The trick is finding the right combination of herbs that can flourish together, and isolating those which are still useful, but need specific growing conditions."

A smile etched itself on Constance's mouth. "Why do I get the impression you aren't talking about herbs?"

"I like mint tea, but I also like basil in my tomato salad. I'd never have both if basil and mint were put growing in the same window box. Mint would smother the basil. And that's the problem with the sexes: they don't seem able to co-exist unless one of them is on top. The trick is finding a way to keep them separate, but cooperating."

"Has that ever happened?"

"Not that I know. It's worth trying to bring about, though. Wait, I want to show you something." Goodwill disappeared into the bedroom, returning with a skin between her hands. It was Silence's – the one that had been pinned to the bridge.

"Where did you get that?"

"A friendly peer slipped it to me after the raid. Cooperation, you see? Our cause has wide-ranging support."

"Which cause is that?"

"I think you know, Constance."

"This belongs to me. I'm Silence's next-of-kin. The peers should have returned it to me."

"Won't you consider donating it to us? The Silenced will cherish this memento of her."

"Does that mean you speak on behalf of the Silenced?"

Her eyes probed Constance's. "I believe I do."

The hairs on the back of Constance's arms stirred. The Ess was right. "And what is it the Silenced want?"

"Our sisters are full of vague yearnings. Shape needs to be given to them."

Constance ran the ball of her thumb along the curve of Silence's skin. It wasn't like touching Silence: this was an inanimate object. She returned it to Goodwill. "Have it. I don't want it. Silence removed it before she jumped – there was a reason why she took it off."

Goodwill handled the skin with reverence. "To leave something of herself behind for us."

"I doubt that. I suspect she didn't want to hide behind her skin, the way the rest of us do. She knew they suppressed moes – turned us into sisters hatched from the same batch."

"I can't remember a time without skins. The memory-keepers have never spoken of it." Goodwill set the skin on a side-table. "It's like an icon. See how it turns the table into an altar. It makes me want to bow my head and pray."

"Except there isn't any formal prayer in Sisterland. We have no goddesses. Only one another."

Goodwill caught Constance by the wrist. "Some say our sisters in the Nine make living goddesses of themselves."

"They do."

"Goddesses can be arbitrary."

"They can."

"And merciless."

"They are."

"The Nine must be replaced. Soon. Before it's too late."

Constance wrenched herself free, rubbing at the marks left on her flesh from the pressure of Goodwill's fingers. "What do you mean, before it's too late?"

Goodwill lowered her voice. "The Nine has a plan. Scientists have been working on it for years. It's nearly ready to be rolled out. But it can't be allowed to go ahead. Someone has to stop it."

"What plan?"

"The Virgin Birth Project."

Constance's mouth flapped open. "The virgin birth was just a story!"

"But some stories are real. Not all of them are invented. Virgin births occur in the animal kingdom: they give some species a reproductive boost. Virgin birth is an evolutionary advantage – and the Nine is determined to harness it."

"How?"

"The Nine believes people possessed the ability, but lost it. Virgin birth is mentioned in the legends of many ancient cultures. Gods were always disguising themselves and mystically impregnating maidens."

"Those are just parables. They were used to suggest someone exceptional was born."

"But what if non-sexual procreation happened in our earliest years on Earth, and gods tricked out as showers of golden rain, or lotus plants, or swans, were a way of trying to understand it? Isn't it telling that when pagan myth coalesced with early Christianity, the virgin birth tradition survived? Christianity turned it into dogma, inventing a dove which pentrated the goddess they called the Virgin Mary. Babyfusion without men. It happened before – the Nine wants it to happen again."

"Slow down, Goodwill! I can't keep up!"

"OK, here's how it goes. Sisterland's scientists are studying parthenogenesis: a form of reproduction where embryos develop without fertilisation. It occurs naturally in many plants and in some invertebrate animal species – scorpions, bees, water fleas and aphids. And it's been induced artificially in a few species, such as fish and amphibians."

"The DNA differences between fish and people must be huge."

"True, but the principle's the same. Lately, their research's led to a breakthrough."

"It's actually working?"

"All I know is they've progressed to testing it on mice and monkeys. Their DNA is close to humans'. So it's only a matter of time before they start trials on women."

"You mean a new form of assisted reproduction?"

Goodwill's smile was crooked. "Oh, something far more radical than that, Constance. I mean artificially created embryos. And if embryos can be manufactured, then sex can be determined, too. I wouldn't bank on too many baby boys making the final cut."

"Wouldn't they be needed, still, for labour?"

"For a while. But I think the Nine would find a way round that. Why take the risk? Safer to use machinery, or women with lower IQs. For all their talk about universal sisterhood, it's still an unequal society. Ask the women who work in dine-alls and easies."

"Or matingplace." Constance thought of Unity.

"Exactly. No, gender selection can only mean one thing. Men will become obsolete."

Constance became aware of a succession of movements, low in her stomach: a light drumming from the inside. Could this be what they called the quickening? She slid both hands inside her clothing, trying to communicate with her baby. *I'll keep you safe.* Hoping it was a promise she could stand over. Goodwill was still speaking, her words rushing towards her, but darkness claimed Constance.

Chapter 27

Constance resurfaced to find herself on the floor of the twoser, Goodwill kneeling beside her. She held a water tube to Constance's lips, and Constance drank greedily. Drops of water left a series of stepping stones smudged on her tunic. She struggled to rise, but Goodwill pressed her down.

"You need to stay horizontal a little longer. You fainted – you're probably still woozy. I'm going to make you some ocean tea." Joints creaking, Goodwill huffed to her feet and bustled about.

When she was resting on a chair, nursing her drink, Constance said, "I'd like to hear some more about the Nine's plans. I promise not to faint. I don't know what came over me."

"It's your condition. Devotion used to take dizzy spells when she was babyfused. You need to be aware of the tendency over the coming weeks. It's not a good idea to live alone right now. I'm surprised you aren't in communityplace."

"That's been stopped."

"Really? How odd. I wonder what's behind that? Anyhow, we could make space for you here. I'm sure we could rearrange the furniture and fit in a pop-up."

"No." Constance was blunt. "Now I know about the

249

faintness, I'll keep something sugary close at hand."

"You'll need medical authorisation. Sugar substances are only allowed under licence."

"Of course, but I'll be able to cite health reasons. What else can you tell me about this Virgin Birth Project?"

"It makes you anxious, doesn't it? Your empathy is unusual. Can I ask, is it a spontaneous moe?"

Outed, thought Constance. She avoided the question. "At Shaperhaus, I've heard whispers about a science programme. They talked about the evolution of the female gender. I had no idea they meant a world without men. What if it weakens the stock?"

"True. Genetic diversity would be halved. Men have more physical strength, for example – that's important to the gene pool."

"How do we know something fundamental in what it means to be human wouldn't be lost?"

"We don't. But the Nine thinks its policies are not just beyond criticism, but beyond error. If Sisterland proceeds with the Virgin Birth Project, it can never be reversed. We'll have tampered with something intrinsic to the natural order."

Constance pulled her legs up to her chin, and rested one cheek on them. "I saw statues of goddesses at the Sistercentral."

"I've heard about them. I'm told there's something majestic and awe-inspiring about each one, no matter which obsolete religion she represented. You're fortunate to have seen them."

"They had a physical presence. I understood why people knelt before them. Goodwill, some of those statues probably came from outside Sisterland. I never realised Sisterland isn't worldwide till I saw an Outsidelander. He was in Sistercentral. He looked different to our men. Less tamed."

"You saw him?"

"Briefly."

"One of the Silenced told us about him. She works on the

Sistercentral staff. What was he like, this Outsidelander?"

"Alert. Inquisitive. Confident. He didn't know to be afraid of Sisterland. Yet." Constance subsided. Her last sight of the Outsidelander had been of someone striding towards an ambiguous fate. "I might try to stand now."

Goodwill helped her to her feet, and watched as she walked around the room. "Are you looking forward to being a source?"

Constance glanced up from her feet, smiling with more animation than she had shown so far. Goodwill's hands reached out, wanting to respond to it, but a wobble made Constance look back down at the floor. Goodwill let her hands drop.

"You're the first person to ask me that," said Constance. "I didn't think I'd be ready, but now I realise I am. The Shaper Mother was right, all along. She organised the permit for me. She said it was what I needed."

It occurred to Constance that at least her babyfusion licence had allowed her to know Harper. With mating-free reproduction, no woman would have a reason to be with a man again. And then men would be gone altogether. She swallowed, and felt her way towards a seat. If she had a boy-baby, his future would be bleak.

Which reminded her. She'd been sent to probe Goodwill. Otherwise, her own future was bleak, too. Here was an opportunity to earn credit. All she had to do was report back to the Shaper Mother that Goodwill had first-class contacts – in the peers, because a member gave her Silence's skin; in Sistercentral, because she knew about the Outsidelander; and in the laboratories, because she was well-informed on virgin-birth tests. This was valuable information.

Except Constance didn't want to betray Goodwill. Even if she had an agenda, as a leader of the Silenced.

"Why have you told me so much, Goodwill? You know I work for the Shaper Mother – what's to stop me denouncing you?"

251

"Nothing. My fate's in your hands."

"You're remarkably relaxed about it."

Goodwill hooted, the folds of flesh beneath her chin wobbling. "Do you think I'm worried about myself? My anxieties are for Sisterland. Constance, the facts of what lies ahead for Sisterland are nasty. But facts matter less than what people choose to believe in. And the Silenced are longing to believe in her."

"Do you believe in Silence?"

"I believe in turning situations to advantage. We don't have many cards to play compared with the Nine. We'd be foolish not to make something of Silence."

Constance gave a grudging nod. She knew Silence had wanted her gesture to mean something.

"Let me share a secret with you. If a sister can learn not to care about what happens to her, it's liberating. It frees her up to do anything."

"Don't you care what happens to you?" asked Constance.

"Not much."

"How do you reach that state?"

"By believing in something greater than myself. How about you, my dear? Could you believe in something bigger than Constance?"

"My baby. That's what I believe in."

"Your baby. Understandable." Goodwill's tone softened, becoming more playful. "You know, you get that gap in your teeth from the man Devotion mated with. It's something I've always noticed about you."

"You knew him?"

"I arranged for the mating."

Constance was astounded. "Why have you never said anything to me about this?"

"I knew Devotion wouldn't like it. She can't bear to think about mating. It makes her feel unclean. And there's a complication, something she doesn't know about." A beat.

"He was my brother."

Constance stared at Goodwill, hardly able to comprehend what she was hearing. "Your source was allowed a second babyfusion?" Her tongue fumbled the words.

"No, she only babyfused once. He was my twin. We shared a womb."

Turmoil swirled through Constance. Unexpectedly, she had been given the answer to a question nagging at her for some time. Now, she knew the identity of her father – Goodwill's twin brother. Her brain teemed with whys and hows, but she was unable to verbalise them.

Goodwill watched, sympathy in her eyes. She seemed to understand, and began answering the unasked questions. "My source told me about it shortly before she discontinued. She fretted about it, towards the end. Perhaps that's why she let me in on her secret. I almost wish she hadn't, because it preyed on my mind to think I had a brother who grew up without knowing about me, or vice versa. It took me years, and many false turns, but eventually I tracked him to matingplace. I made it my business to befriend the Mating Mother there. And then I began calling in favours. When Devotion was licensed to babyfuse, I arranged for it to happen at the matingplace where he was based. Next, I persuaded the Mating Mother to let me check their records – files are kept to prevent incest. I chose my brother for Devotion. The mother was surprised: she said he was no longer in his prime, and a younger meet would be more suitable. I used that as an excuse to look him over, and managed a brief conversation. He was blindfolded, of course. Still, we talked for maybe ten minutes. He had hands like my source, and some quality in his voice reminded me of her. I never truly knew my brother. I saw him only once, spoke to him only once. I didn't even dare to tell him I was his sister. But he babyfused with Devotion, and you were the result. Which makes me your –"

"Aunt. And you've known this all my life."

"It was my privilege to watch over you as you grew, Constance. And now, your babyfusion gives me a sense of continuity."

Constance looked at Goodwill as if for the first time, trying to recast her as a man. Trying to glimpse her father in Goodwill's face. Trying to catch a resemblance between herself and Goodwill. Were their noses similar? The way their hair grew back from their foreheads? "Is this why you oppose the Nine? Because of a brother you lost?"

"Maybe that's where it stems from. Once you question Sisterland's policies, the floodgates open. I never knew what to do about it till the Silenced began gathering. They're a resource. They can help us mount a challenge to the system."

"Us?"

"There are sisters who think as I do, Constance." Goodwill frowned. "They want to recruit you to our movement. You'd be an asset: you're a natural orator, and the Silenced are drawn to you. But I'm against it – I've told my sisters it's unfair. You're babyfused. It isn't right to ask you to take risks. Even for a cause as important as ours. I don't mind using Silence – it can't hurt her. But you have too much to lose. I blame myself for encouraging you to speak at the Hope Bridge. Curiosity overcame me: I wanted to see how an audience would react to you." Impulsively, Goodwill caught her by the hands and, for once, Constance didn't pull away. "My dear, stay away from the bridge. Stay away from the Silenced. And stay away from me. I don't trust myself. The day might come when I forget myself, and try to enlist you to our cause."

A moe that could no longer be suppressed hummed between them.

"Goodwill, the Nine knows about you," said Constance. "The Ess have a file on you. You need to tread carefully."

Goodwill squeezed Constance's hands. "I wondered about that. I've been checking the twoser for eavesdropping devices every day, but found nothing. Still, it seemed unlikely I could have escaped their surveillance."

Just then, the door of the twoser opened. A warning look passed from Goodwill to Constance, quick and then gone.

"Constance, what a pleasant surprise!" Devotion was unhooking her skin as she spoke. "But you look tired. I hope you're taking plenty of rest."

"I decided to come and eat with you, if you'll have me," said Constance. "I want to pump you about babyfusion. Is my backache normal, should I be eating anything in particular, why do my fingers tingle at night?"

"Of course we'd love you to join us for a meal, wouldn't we, Goodwill? As for babyfusion, I don't remember much. I seemed to want to eat pond chowder every day when I was carrying you – can't touch the stuff now. Can't even bear the smell of it. I hope you're remembering to take your protein poppers, ladybird. You need to be disciplined about them. Not having an other to remind you is a disadvantage."

Constance winced, but this was no time to take offence at Devotion's insensitivity. "I'm starving now, for what it's worth."

"In that case, we'll eat as soon as the dine-all can take us. I want to hear all your news. By the way, Goodwill, they have floating eggs on the menu. Nourishing, but non-fattening."

"I prefer my eggs submerged."

"I know you do, but floating is healthier. What have you and Constance been talking about?"

"She wants your help with baby names."

"Does she really?" Devotion was dubious. "I don't know how much use I can be. I had trouble enough deciding on Constance. I suppose you could always use my source's, if you were stuck."

"I hope my daughter inherits her curls," said Constance. She slid another glance at Goodwill. Would the baby inherit anything from her?

"That would be nice," said Devotion. "Naturally it's important to do this for Sisterland, but becoming a source is a nuisance. My feet swelled up two shoe sizes and never went down. And your life isn't your own for that mandatory year of breast-feeding."

"There were a few plusses, Devotion," said Goodwill.

"Well, it did lead to Constance. But you always had the best of the bargain, Goodwill: Constance in your life, without the trouble of babyfusion."

"If you say so, sweetheart."

Constance left as soon as she decently could after the meal. Her stomach was in knots over what she'd learned. Huge sailor's knots making a shipwreck of her digestive system. Tasting reflux from the meal, she rested against a building, willing the food to stay down.

When she felt able to walk again, thoughts of Goodwill filled Constance's mind – leaving a residue as acidic as the nausea. She was claiming to be Constance's aunt. A blood relative. Constance hardly knew how she should feel about having an aunt. The one-child policy meant they were as scarce as blue skies in Sisterland. But Goodwill's story could have been concocted as bait to hook her. She could see no obvious resemblance between the two of them. Which meant she had to make a choice about believing Goodwill – or not – and stand over it, because there was no way to verify her claim.

As for the Virgin Birth Project, it alarmed Constance. The Nine wanted sisters to believe the State was a female Eden. But if so, why was information about Outsideland suppressed? It mustn't trust its own people to stay put if they had alternatives. Sisters weren't being protected, they were barricaded in.

And what to do about the Shaper Mother's expectations of her? Constance racked her brain for a solution. Her mouth was parched. She tapped her pockets, but the water tube was missing. She must have left it in the dine-all. All at once, her legs folded up and she found herself sprawled on the pavement.

"Can we help you, sister?" Two girls materialised, and moved her into a sitting position on the edge of pavement.

"Water?" One of them handed her a tube.

Constance felt a little better after drinking from it. Her eye fell on the silver stars which decorated the pavement. There was so much kindness in Sisterland. So much beauty, too. And yet the more she discovered about the way it really worked, the more appalled she became.

"Would you like us to wait with you, sister?"

"No, thank you. I'll head for home in a minute. I just need to gather myself together."

After they left, she sat on, pondering what to do about the Shaper Mother. Could she string her along, feeding her a few titbits? Nothing to land the Silenced in trouble, just enough to keep Constance out of MUM – at least until her baby was born.

A peer tapped her shoulder from behind. "There are seats at the Buzz station, sister. This isn't an appropriate spot for resting."

"What's wrong with it? I'm not doing any harm."

"It's not a designated seating area. It's a pavement. They're for walking on." The peer's eyes fell on a splash across Constance's front. "Is that red paint on your clothes?"

"It's tomato sauce. I had spaghetti just now at a dine-all."

"Which one?"

Constance pointed down the road. "My source lives in that unit there. I ate with her and her other."

"Can they confirm that?"

Constance did a double-take. "Yes, she lives in Yellow B. Her name is Devotion 2723. What's this about, sister?"

"Incident in Sister Plaza. I'll need to note your sig." She

gestured towards Constance's wrist, and Constance held it up for scanning

"What happened?"

"Anti-Sisterland activity. Less said about it the better." The peer nodded, and walked off, towards Devotion and Goodwill's twoser.

The plaza was in front of the entrance to Sistercentral, so anti-Sisterland activity there would act as a direct challenge to the Nine.

On the Buzz, Constance asked the passenger opposite, "Did something happen in Sister Plaza, sister?"

"Not that I heard."

As she disembarked, another passenger fell into step beside her.

"Sister Plaza is cordoned off," whispered the stranger. "Rubbish scattered all over it."

"Seems a bit extreme to close it. Couldn't they just clean it up?"

"It was wall-to-wall rubbish. But that wasn't all." The stranger looked left and right. "Grafitti. Sprayed in red paint on Sistercentral's perimeter walls. In letters twenty feet high. Right under the Nine's nose, you might say."

"The usual? '*We will not be Silenced*'? I keep seeing that slogan."

"Not this time. This graffiti taunted them." She muttered something, making a chopping motion with her hands, before walking away rapidly. Her parting words vibrated in the air. "It said, '*The Nine will be broken*'."

Chapter 28

Next day, Constance reported to the Shaper Mother that she had no hopes of gaining Goodwill's trust. Her position within Shaperhaus linked her too closely to the Sisterland regime. The mother tilted her head to one side. Constance breathed evenly, willpower at full throttle, barriers in place.

"The Nine will be dissatisfied," said the mother. "They are sisters with high expectations. They take disappointment hard. Try another meeting. Persevere." The Shaper Mother plucked at her earrings, twitchy. It puzzled Constance – the mother was usually so contained.

"We discussed the Silenced. Goodwill criticised them," said Constance.

"She's testing you."

"She knows I work for you. Why would she open herself up to me? It's too risky."

"You could give her confidence in you."

"I can't."

"You know you can, Constance. She held you in your arms when you were minutes old – she's watched you grow. She loves you."

The idea of being loved by Goodwill smacked into Constance with a presence that was almost physical. It had never occurred to her. At that, she felt the mother gain entry to her consciousness.

"Why, your moe triggers are more sensitive than ever. And you have sympathy for the Silenced! Sweet child, resist their siren call."

With an effort of will, Constance erected a wall. "The moes are sparked by babyfusion. They'll fade afterwards."

"Like the Silenced, you're taken in by a symbol. I understand it. Symbols have potency. But they cannot be relied on. Just as Silence couldn't be relied on. She left you, Constance. Left you without a backward glance. That's the reality."

Constance gritted her teeth. "I know. I don't care about Silence any more."

"Symbols have their uses, of course. They can be shaped this way and that. You were Silence's other, you can have a hand in the moulding."

"I don't want to mould anyone. I just want to be left alone to live my life."

"Is that really enough for you? I suspect you want more, much more, than that." The tone hardened. "Support for the Silenced continues to grow. It must be checked. We know the leadership wants to recruit you – don't try to deny it, we have other conduits of information. I'm going to offer you one last chance to infiltrate the Silenced and report back to us. Go home, Constance, think it over. I should warn you, your usefulness to Sisterland hinges on your answer. And if you're not useful to Sisterland, what purpose do you have?"

After work, Constance found Modesty sitting on a bench in Shaper Square. She stood out in the Sistercentral livery.

"Were you waiting for me, Modesty?'

"Maybe."

Constance sat beside her, and together they watched the action on the giant screen. There was no volume, but it was easy to see what was happening from the images. Children in girlplace were reading aloud from *Beloved's Pearls*, their faces rapt.

"Remember memorising her words of wisdom?" said Constance.

"Who can forget?" Modesty slid a careful look at Constance. "Who's allowed to?" She adopted a sing-song tone. "*Numbers are an improvement on surnames. Surnames belong to an outdated idea called the family unit – but the State is our true family.*" Another veiled look. Then she said, "Of course, there are numbers and numbers. I wonder who your source bribed to get you a low, three-digit one?"

Once, Constance would have denied the possibility of corruption. Now, she knew better. "Someone in the registration division, I suppose. They'd be able to alert sisters to surrendered names."

"Surrender. It's required from all of us. The great and the lowly. Speaking of the great, how far do you trust the Shaper Mother?"

"Are you asking as a member of the Sistercentral staff?"

Modesty fingered one of the tortoiseshell buttons on the front of her fitted one-piece. "A uniform is only what's on the outside."

Constance studied her profile. She couldn't tell what lay inside Modesty – she was hard to read.

"I know you're unsure of me. I'm ambitious, I don't deny it," said Modesty. "So I'll set the ball rolling. I think the mother's changed. She's in a bit of a state. Before I left, she was finding it hard to deal with the Nine. For the first time, she let slip a few disapproving words. Some supplies those sisters rely on have dried up, or maybe it's not safe to access them right now. Anyhow, she suggested the Nine might be losing its grip. Mistakes were being made. If you want to know what I think, there'd have been a crackdown on the Silenced long before now but for this issue about the supplies."

"What kind of supplies, Modesty?"

"Some sort of miracle drug. Keeps them operating at peak levels, apparently."

"Can't the scientists rustle up another batch?"

"You'd imagine so. But it isn't happening. Meanwhile, the Nine isn't running on full power. Everyone says so in Sistercentral. Lucky for the Silenced."

"Why are you telling me this, Modesty?"

"You need tipping off. Maybe you think the mother's on your side. Especially if she doesn't see eye to eye with the Nine. But I know her. She'll always put Sisterland first. Always."

Constance left Shaper Square and headed for Gentle Street. She was on borrowed time – she knew that now, beyond a shadow of doubt. Whether it was losing its grip or not, the Nine was ruthless. And the Shaper Mother's protection would cave in before it. The next time she was asked for information, and failed to supply it, she was finished. Confronted by evidence of menace and manipulation, she grew desperate to see Harper, who represented something pure and true. At the Rice-Wise counter, she studied the electronic display for that day's choice of dishes, checked to see what her neighbours were eating, and ordered some toasted rice squares.

"Oh, and a bowl of calcium soup," she added. She should remember the baby's needs.

"Calcium soup? Don't know as we have any." Serenity 65438 was printed on the server's tag. "I'll check out back."

Constance watched her swing through the door into the kitchen. A rectangle of preparation area was visible, along with two backs. Both wore hoods. She kept her eyes trained on the door. When Serenity carried out Constance's tray and set it in the designated area for collection, she caught a side view of one of the men. Just a patch of face between mouth and eyebrows was visible, but she was fairly sure it wasn't Harper. She felt no instinctual pull towards this man. Besides, his nose wasn't the shape she remembered.

"No calcium soup, but we have dried calcium in the store cupboard," said Serenity. "Not as good as fresh, but better than nothing. You could sprinkle it over your rice squares. You want some? I brought it out, in case."

Constance nodded, and accepted the phial.

"Calcium soup has to be ordered in," continued the server. "No problem, but we need to know a day in advance. Will I put you down for it?"

"No, leave it. I'm not sure if I'll be back this way." She shook some flakes over her food. "Busy easy – you must catch a lot of passing trade, so close to the Hope Bridge."

Serenity shrugged. "Fits and starts."

"Is there just you out front?"

"Jus' me. I got two sets of hands out back dealing with the orders."

"Been doing it long?"

"Three years. I was in an easy on the end of the Buzz line before this."

"I meant the two sets of hands. Have they been doing it long?" Serenity looked askance, and Constance added, "It's well run. Experience shows. Last easy I ate in, it was new hands. Food was soggy, and they mixed up my order."

"Sloppy. Can't abide it. One set of hands was here before me. Second set's just arrived. But he's a quick learner, I'll grant him that. How can I help you, sister?"

Another customer was at the counter, and Constance carried her tray down to her table.

She ate languidly, watching and listening. Snippets of conversation drifted across the eat-easy.

"Plan your work and work your plan, I told her, but she wasn't listening. Can't put an old head on young shoulders."

Then two events happened simultaneously. There was a

lull, and Serenity swung open the hatch to the kitchen. A sentence floated out.

"Deer are colour-blind."

It was Harper's voice: no doubt about it.

Relief and joy surged through Constance, loosening her limbs and causing blood to rush to the surface of her skin. She had found him! Against the odds, luck had gone her way. She rolled her head back on its neck, savouring the release from tension. Just a few yards separated them.

Except now she had found him, how to make contact? She strained towards the closed hatch, willing it to fly open again, and for Harper to look at her. But it didn't happen.

Paying for her meal, she said to Serenity, "What time do you close tonight?"

"Another hour."

"I'm sure you're looking forward to going home and putting your feet up."

"Been a long day. But it's a privilege to feed my sisters."

"Does everyone finish then?"

"I didn't say I finished then. That's when the easy shuts. Takes us about a half-hour to clear up. I'm always the last out – can't leave men to lock up. They don't exactly have the reliability gene." She snuffled, and Constance joined in. "They collect empty plates, stack chairs, and so on. They're good for that."

Constance could find no pretext to prolong the conversation. Outside, she loitered along the street. As men weren't allowed on the Buzz, to reach Hutchtown they were obliged to walk, or be moved about in transers. That meant he could head off in any direction. She found a doorway to shelter in, and watched the easy.

The last customer left, Serenity locking the door after her. The outline of a man appeared, and the blankout was activated. It wasn't Harper: this man struggled to stretch his arm above his head to the controls. Soon after, she heard a door close, followed by footsteps, and a man emerged from behind the easy – there must be a staff entrance at the back. His build was too solid to be Harper.

She stayed waiting, and the sound of a door opening and shutting for a second time carried across the street. Nobody came into view. That had to mean a laneway behind. Perhaps Harper used it to cut along to the transer pick-up points. She sprang for the back lane. Ahead of her, footsteps tapped out the rhythm of someone in a hurry. She wished she could call out to the man to wait. But it might attract the wrong attention.

Another lane forked away from the first one, and the choice checked her. The footsteps had faded, there was nothing to guide her now. Staying on the right-hand track, she pelted along, trying to overtake him. The lane looped round towards the Buzz entrance. Not a man in sight.

Downcast, she did an about-turn and trudged back towards the easy. The opening times would be posted outside, and she could try to catch Harper the following morning before he started his shift. It would be daytime, and less private, but it was better than nothing.

Near the fork, the shadows crunched, separated, and a man stepped out.

It was Harper.

And yet not Harper.

Beneath the hood she had never seen him wear, his face had a forbidding cast. All the same, a feeling came over her, so suddenly she had no inkling of its approach.

She felt restored.

Constance reached out to touch him, but he read her intention and held up a hand to stop her, beckoning towards the side of the unlit building where he had been standing.

"Why didn't you wait for me, Harper?"

"All I knew was a woman was chasing me. I didn't know it was you. I still wasn't sure, even when I showed myself."

His voice was muffled because of the hood covering his mouth.

"But you did show yourself." She braided her fingers through his. "I've missed you. Have you missed me?" He nodded. "I babyfused, Harper. Part of you is inside me."

His eyes kindled, but he said nothing.

"I was expecting some kind of reaction," she said.

"Why? It's not as if I can be a father. I won't even be allowed to see the baby. I don't count."

"Still, it's something we made together. You and me. Us." He shrugged. She tried again. "Harper, you cared about me once, even if you've changed your mind. I know what happened: you refused Himtime with anyone else. I loved you before, Harper, but I loved you twice as much when I heard what you did. I still love you. Thanks partly to you, I have moes – spontaneous moes – that break through whether I want them to or not. And now I could never bear to go back to the way I was before."

When he still didn't respond, she released his hand. Arms hanging loosely by his sides, he stared at the ground.

"Say something, Harper. Anything. Tell me I've ruined your life, tell me you're trapped in the city because of me, tell me why you're behaving like this."

"It's not safe for us to be together. Someone might report us."

"I'm willing to chance it. I'll say I made you talk to me. If there's any fallout, I'll take it."

"You can't protect me, Constance."

He was right, and she knew it.

She cast round for a way to reach him. "I haven't forgotten what you told me about the creatures in your forest."

"What did I tell you?" It was a challenge rather than a question.

"You told me about the snowshoe hare. How its fur turns white for camouflage in winter, and rusty brown in summer.

How its ears are shorter than those of other hares, and ferns and grass don't seem to satisfy it because it steals meat from traps."

His lips twitched upwards. "I did tell you that."

A chirping came from her comtel, and Harper jumped.

"Nothing to worry about. It's just an alert, to remind me to take my pills."

"Why are you taking pills? Are you ill?"

"They're for babyfusion. I'd have to eat every half-hour if I didn't take them. They keep me going between meals."

"But you're OK otherwise?"

"I'm OK. Did they hurt you at the Tower?" She pushed back his hood, searching his face for signs of injury, and his hair gleamed silver in the moonlight.

"It's not important."

"It's important to me, Harper."

"The Mating Mother let the stifstatter loose on me."

"Charity."

"That's the one. She gave me a few jolts. Enjoyed herself doing it." Constance cringed, but he shrugged. "Women boast about their non-violent world. But they use force when it suits them. It made no difference. They couldn't make me mate. That's the weakness in their mating system: it only works if men go along with it. We could send it all crashing down."

"Harper, there's something I have to tell you. They'll never let you go back to your forest. They'll keep you here in Harmony forever."

"I know that now." His words came from a long way off.

"If there was a chance to escape, would you take it?"

"Escape from Harmony?"

"Escape from Sisterland."

"But Sisterland is everywhere."

"It's not. There's a place called Outsideland. I don't know where it is, except that it's far away. The men who live there don't wear hoods. They move about freely."

"How do you know?"

"An Outsidelander is being held in Sistercentral. If people can sneak in, then people can sneak out. I saw this man. He's different to ours. He's ..." She drew shapes in the air with one of her hands, searching for a way to explain him. "Independent."

"Is he much different to me?"

Harper sounded jealous! Constance liked how readily the moe surfaced in him. "Perhaps not so different. You have freedom of spirit, too – it's why you're working in an eat-easy instead of in matingplace."

"The easy is grim. Hutchtown is worse again. But I could never go back to matingplace. Though it's where I met you, so I should be grateful I spent time there."

"And there'll be a child of ours to show for it, if the babyfusion sticks."

"What do you mean 'if', Constance?" His voice splintered. "Are you afraid you might lose our baby?"

"There's always a chance. Babydefusion is common. But the baby feels strong inside me – it wants to live."

He relaxed. "I'd have liked to show our child the forest."

He curved his free hand round her cheek, stroking it with his thumb. She shivered at the ease with which her skin remembered his touch.

"Harper, you have to get away from here. Maybe you could find a forest in Outsideland. I know it wouldn't mean as much to you as your own one. But you'd be free."

He brought his face level with hers, holding her by the arms. Urgent, he demanded, "Did you mean what you said about escaping?"

"Of course I meant it."

"How?"

"There's a woman I know. She's in a movement. They want to challenge the way Sisterland is run."

"Why? Surely it suits women?"

"Not all women."

"Why should she risk herself to help me?"

"I think she'd do it for me. If she could."

"When?"

"Harper, your fingers are digging into me!"

"Sorry." He released her. "When could they get me away?"

"I haven't spoken to her yet. It's just an idea. I hate to think of you trapped in that easy."

"A lot of men are trapped in places they shouldn't be."

"And I wish I could free them all. But let's start with the one I might be able to do something for. Yes?"

"Yes."

In the office complex behind them, a whistle shrilled: on-off, on-off. It reminded Constance of the time.

"Is it all right for you to be out here, talking to me? Isn't there a curfew for men?" A nod. "So I've landed you in trouble again?"

"What can they do – send me to matingplace as punishment?"

"But they'll discipline you for breaking the curfew, won't they?"

"Suppose so. But they'll know I didn't leave the easy area – my chip tells them where I am. So they mightn't be too suspicious. I'll say I hurt my foot, and had to rest it before I could try to get back to Hutchtown."

"Will they believe you?"

"Maybe yes, maybe no. I'll live. Especially if I have hope."

"I won't let you down, Harper."

"When do you think you'll have news?"

"Soon. Tomorrow, I'll meet this woman – I'll put your case to her. If she won't help, I'll find a different way. I promise. You're not alone in Harmony, Harper. I'm with you."

"Except you're not."

"Part of you is always with me." She caught him by the wrists and laid his palms flat on her stomach. "I found you in

269

the eat-easy, didn't I? I didn't let you vanish from my life."

"That's true."

They gazed at one another.

When she spoke again, it was with reluctance. "They won't believe the foot-sprain story if you stay out much longer."

"No."

"Is it far?"

"I can pick up a ride near here. I know a spot where some late shiftworkers get collected."

"I'll see you soon, Harper. I promise."

"I'll watch for you."

"Harper, wait. Before you go, please let me know if you're glad to see me again. Please say it."

He turned back, the shadows making his face impenetrable to her. "Can't you tell?"

Constance shook her head.

"I'm so full of moes, I'm trembling from them."

"Positive moes?"

"Constance, I haven't felt free since I came to this city. There's been a weight sitting on my chest, pushing me to the ground. Just the sight of you lifts some of that load. I'm not on my knees any more."

"Harper, you were never on your knees. That's why I love you."

She was hoping to hear the words 'I love you back'. But Harper had dissolved into the darkness.

Chapter 29

There was no small talk when Constance met Goodwill the following morning.

"Goodwill, I need your help."

"I'll do anything I can for you."

Instead of going to work, Constance had made her way to the Circle zone, to Devotion and Goodwill's twoser. She had the perfect alibi for shirking her duties at Shaperhaus. If her comtel was checked, they'd think she was attempting to infiltrate the Silenced.

"The man I mated with – we talked during Himtime," said Constance. "And now, I'd like to do something for him." She took a deep breath. "I want to help him escape from Sisterland. I know it's a lot to ask. But please do this. Do it for me."

Goodwill's sympathetic expression faltered.

Constance pressed on. "Do it for the baby he fathered – it's your brother's grandchild."

"You're asking too much, Constance!"

"Hear me out. Symbols matter, you said so yourself. Like Silence, he could be a symbol. Free him, and make a public gesture of it: the Silenced refusing to collude with the Nine's policy of keeping men caged."

"Hold on there. 'Caged' is a strong term. Men aren't

271

captives – they have a reasonable life. Food, clothing, shelter."

"They aren't free."

"Not exactly, no."

"You're either free or you're not."

"Stop using silkenspeak on me."

"This isn't silkenspeak and you know it."

"All right, males aren't free. But maybe they don't want to be free. Maybe they're content as they are."

"Listen to yourself, Goodwill. We don't have zoos because we think it's wrong to keep wild animals in captivity. So how is it acceptable with people?"

"Males aren't people the way women are. I don't hold with downgrading all of them – some show promise. But trying to make a symbol of a man, on a par with Silence, is lunacy. Great Beloved, she was your other! Show some respect!"

"I am showing respect. That's why I want my man set free."

"*Your* man?"

"Yes, mine. Just as I'm his."

"Careful, my dear! You don't sound quite yourself. Have you been sleeping badly? Maybe the speed-up pills are disagreeing with you. Remember your babyfusion. Your responsibility is to your child now, not to some man."

"He's not 'some man' – his name is Harper. Together, we babyfused. If you care anything about me, Goodwill, show me. Otherwise, it's just empty words."

Goodwill scratched at her neck, mottling the flesh into angry stripes. "I need to discuss this with somebody else, Constance. It's not my decision."

"But will you back me? Say you will, please. You've known me all my life. Devotion's my source. You say your brother's my father. If that's the case, we're family. I know that's not supposed to have too much significance in Sisterland. But it ought to. Promise you'll do your best, Goodwill. I want this more than anything. Help me. I'm begging you."

It was an appeal Goodwill could not resist. "When you talk

about this – this Harper – escaping, where do you want him sent?"

"Outsideland."

"That's a tall order. For starters, we don't know exactly where it is. Or how to reach it. We have no escape network. And we don't have any spare capacity right now – important plans are being drawn up."

"Why not make Harper part of it all? A plan within a plan. I don't pretend it's going to be easy. But it's possible, surely. You have contacts everywhere, you told me so yourself. Steal him from Hutchtown, and spirit him away to the outer reaches of Sisterland. Then put him on a ship. The Outsidelander came here by sea. Why not do it in reverse?"

"The coast is a long way from Harmony. And the women who hid him on his journey would face consequences if caught. There could be no forgiveness for such a transgression. It flouts every principle of Sisterland."

"To help another human being flouts every principle of Sisterland? Doesn't that tell us something?"

Goodwill rubbed hard at a spot between her eyebrows. "Conditions for men will be improved, given time. Right now, we have other priorities."

"Think of it as challenging the Nine's authority. This man is a meet who refused to mate on demand – he mated with me, and then wouldn't do it again with another woman. He said even animals have a choice about whether or not to mate. They sent him to an eat-easy because they were short of labour. Otherwise, who knows how they might have punished him? Freeing him is a gesture that won't be lost on the Nine."

"I guess that makes him an unusual man."

"How many men do we know, to judge whether or not he's unusual? But this much I'm sure about. He's sensitive, independent and brave. He said no to the system. Isn't that what the Silenced is trying to do, too? Please, Goodwill. Let's help him."

"Your feeings for this man are dangerous, Constance."

"You must have had feelings for your brother or you wouldn't have chosen him to mate with Devotion. Feelings are natural. That's something else the Nine has done – made us nervous of feelings. They've convinced sisters they're wrong."

"Tread carefully, my dear. You're in a vulnerable condition, between babyfusion and losing your other. Love between a woman and a man is impossible."

"Wouldn't you have freed your brother, if you could?"

"Maybe. But he discontinued years ago. Not long after you were born." Goodwill's voice thickened. "Matingplace doesn't agree with men."

"How do you know he discontinued?"

"I tried to see him again." This was offered up as a shameful admission.

A spark of triumph ignited inside Constance. "Goodwill, did you have loving feelings for your brother?"

"Nothing as strong as that. Some traces of affection, I suppose."

"Affection's a start. If you had a son, wouldn't you love him?"

"I have no child. I was never fortunate enough to babyfuse. You're asking me to imagine how I might feel."

"So, imagine."

A beat. "Yes. I'd love my son."

"So will you help someone else's son to escape?"

Another beat, longer than the first. "I'll speak to my sisters in the movement. I can't make any promises. But we'll look into it."

Constance went close to Goodwill, taking her by the hand. "Your brother is gone, Goodwill. But something of him lives on in me. And in my child now, thanks to Harper."

"I'll do my best for your Harper."

"When?"

"Soon."

274

"How soon? Harper can't stay in Sisterland. He'll wither away here."

"It's not my decision."

"Aren't you the leader?"

"You flatter me, Constance. I'm not without influence. But there's a sister more senior than me who needs to be won over. Someone from our organisation will be in touch."

"How long do you expect it to take?"

"Why the rush?"

"Once I have my baby, I can't be sure of anything. Not even that I'll still be around."

The air shifted between them, solidifying. "My dear, are you at risk? Is there something you haven't told me?"

"The Nine didn't like a memory interchange I uploaded – its solution was to send me to MUM. Before that happened, the Outsidelander was caught, and acted as a distraction. And I suppose Silence, and my babyfusion, make me a special case. But the Nine will deal with me after I have the baby. I'm under no illusions about that."

Goodwill's eyes bulged. "This escape plan should be for you, not Harper!"

"I can't go anywhere – it wouldn't be safe for my baby."

"Constance, I'm afraid for you. Though . . . how can I be? Fear's a delisted moe."

"Moes can't be delisted. Not permanently. They can be discouraged. Suppressed. Denied. But they can't be deselected for good. Think how love wouldn't conform to rationing, despite the best efforts of earlier Nines. All moes are just as resistant. They're only buried, not abolished. I can feel fear, too – I may not like it, it's not a moe that brings me any comfort, but it pushes me to do something for Harper."

Goodwill pressed the heel of a hand against her sternum, trying to moderate her racing heartbeat. "We need to stay rational. There's a risk that moe could undo the two of us."

"And there's a risk that lack of moe could undo all of us."

Chapter 30

Constance ticked her way through a list left for her by the Shaper Mother, who did not appear. At times, she felt spasms in her lower back, and had to walk round the room to relieve the discomfort. They reminded her another babyfusion check-up was due, and she made a lunchtime appointment. Babyfusion cases were always prioritised, even if it meant other sisters were bounced down the list.

The medico ran some tests on Constance and, with brisk approval, told her she was a healthy sourcing sister. Walking back to work afterwards, Constance came upon a crowd gathered under the giant wings above Shaperhaus. They were staring at the screen on the far side of the square. Constance shielded her eyes with her hand to see the image more clearly. On continual loop, it showed three women in red scarves on a rope ladder scaling the Beloved statue in the park. At the top, they tied a red bow about her neck.

"Somebody says they belong to a group that has spontaneous moe eruptions," said one of the onlookers. "They can't restrain themselves – they're capable of anything!"

"Why is this being shown on a public screen?" demanded another.

Back in the office, the Shaper Mother was leaning against

Constance's desk. "Have you seen it?" she asked. Constance nodded. "Such a ridiculous gesture, but it drew a crowd to Beloved Park, and leaflets were distributed before the peers had the situation under control. These acts of civil disobedience are cropping up all over the city. But gaining access to the public entscreen system to upload that image is in another league. I suspect we may have underestimated this movement, Constance. Speaking of which, your comtel showed you in the Circle zone yesterday. I presume you saw sense, and were trying again with your Silenced contact. What news?"

"Nothing yet, mother. But I have hopes. Progress was made. If you could give me a little more time, I should have something for you."

The Shaper Mother tapped a reprimand on Constance's forearm. "You need to redouble your efforts."

"Yes, mother."

That evening after work, Constance stood on the street, considering what to do. With the Shaper Mother pushing hard, she knew she hadn't much time to persuade the Silenced leadership to spirit away Harper. But she couldn't force the pace with Goodwill. The desire to see Harper was keen in her, but it was risky to make contact. Time enough when she had an escape plan to share with him.

She needed to eat, but the bright lighting and noisy atmosphere of an eat-easy held no appeal this evening. There was still time to reach the dine-all attached to her unit. She didn't usually bother with it, finding the meals staid, but it was exactly the kind of wholesome food she ought to be eating now. She turned her hand thumb outwards, and on her comtel clicked through a request to hold a dinner.

As she made for home along the riverbank, a flash of green alerted her to a frog hopping into the water. Harper would feel less homesick for his forest if he could walk here and observe the city's wildlife. But the only men she saw in the river's vicinity were dredging it. Men's free time was spent resting before a return to work. That was another of those inconvenient facts which she had discounted, before knowing Harper.

In the unit, she noticed the absence of the Silenced for the first time. A patch of red by the main entrance showed that flowers continued to be left there, but the bouquets were few compared with earlier mounds.

"No Silenced?" she asked the unit-minder, who was helping herself to a rosebud.

"Vanished like melted snow. You don't mind, do you?" She held up the flower. "I'm going up to Beloved Park later. Always like to leave a token by her statue."

"I don't mind. You might have trouble reaching the statue, though. There was an incident earlier."

"Saw it on my entscreen. But the day a sister can't leave Beloved a little something is the day the world stops spinning."

"I wonder what Beloved would make of Sisterland now?"

"Take a tip from me, sister. Keep thoughts like that to yourself." The unit-minder walked away.

Constance headed into the dine-all, which was emptying out as she arrived. She was working her way through a dressed rock-nut casserole – a protein boost which her body craved – when a Buzz driver who lived two floors above joined her.

"Don't often see you eating in here, sister," said the driver, whose name was Justice.

"It was handy tonight."

"Guess you're eating for two, right?"

"Right." Hungry though she was, the next words made Constance set down her fork.

"A sister is interested in meeting you."

"Am I interested in meeting her?"

Justice held Constance's eyes. "Five o'clock tomorrow

morning, by the universal sisterhood memorial on Integrity Street." Without another word, she left.

Constance mopped up the last of her meal with a corner of spiral bread. Five a.m. was a time when few sisters would be going about their business. She couldn't presume the meeting had anything to do with her appeal to the Silenced leadership. It could just as easily be the Nine losing patience with her. Perhaps they intended removing her unobtrusively. If peers were sent into Shaperhaus for her, or if they turned up at her oneser, they'd be seen. It would cause speculation. Especially in view of Silence. She pushed away her empty bowl and went home, qualms spiking about who might be waiting for her tomorrow.

Indoors, she stood by the window. No Silenced beneath it. How quickly their focus shifted. No wonder they were easily manipulated. She activated the blankout, and settled down in front of the entscreen to a documentary on Sisterland's flowers and fauna. But doubts intruded, insistent as insect bites, over the next day's appointment. She abandoned the documentary, undressed, and set her comtel to wake her at four a.m. Despite the uncertainty, she couldn't afford to miss an opportunity to help Harper.

It was almost six the following morning when a noise in the communal area outside her door disturbed Constance's sleep. She'd slept through the alarm, missing the rendezvous. In a foggy state, she rang across to the dine-all to say she'd breakfast there – starving again – before washing and swallowing her popper.

When she arrived, the Buzz driver was sitting at a table, eyes trained on the door. Constance went to the counter to order.

"Good morning, Constance. Won't you join me?" called Justice.

Constance sat opposite Justice, who picked up her knife and started hitting it against the table by the handle. "I heard a catchy tune last night on my entscreen – it goes something like this. Do you know it?" She kept knocking with the knife. Under cover of its rhythm, she said quickly, "Lucky you didn't show up. Integrity Street was watched. We'll try again. On your way into work, stop at Beloved Park. You'll be met by the entrance."

Under a hazy sky, Constance walked up Virtue Boulevard, the clouds suspended so low it seemed as if they might sink to earth under their own weight. Her joints ached. Standing sentinel by the park gates was her progress-monitor. Patience called out her name, and Constance had little choice but to advance.

"I heard the giant sunflowers here have grown to the size of dinner plates, and decided to see for myself. Isn't nature wonderful? Considering we've had hardly a blink of sun in years? Walk with me." Patience linked arms with Constance.

She was not the sort of sister who touched others, and Constance was nonplussed. Still, she aimed for a show of nonchalance. "I wasn't expecting to see you here."

"Who doesn't like a stroll in the park?"

Constance felt trapped. Discreetly, she flicked her eyes round as they walked, wondering if the sister due to make contact with her was watching and waiting, or if she had backed away.

"Looking for someone, Constance?"

"You never know who you'll run into in Beloved Park."

"I thought you might be keeping an eye out for a friend of mine – Goodwill."

"You know Goodwill?"

"We share common interests." She turned her head and looked at Constance. An intent look.

Constance was astounded. The moe fizzed through her, unchecked. Patience was in the Silenced leadership!

"I am," said Patience. "And by the way, your moe

responses are exceptional. You'd have made an excellent co-keeper. Except it wasn't to be."

Constance marshalled her thoughts. She hadn't been aware that Patience could mindmap.

Patience was watching her. "Constance, we can do something for you, but will you do something for us in return? We'd like you to be part of our plans."

Constance considered lying. Just long enough to get Harper away. But she couldn't do it – lies would trip her up. "I'm not much of a joiner. Besides, I'm babyfused: my baby comes first."

She felt Patience tapping for admission as she tried to mindmap. She resisted. Patience's mouth turned down, and she tried to convert it into a smile.

"I'm running ahead of myself. Of course your baby has to be your priority. We can talk about this again. Now, we've considered your suggestion about helping this man to escape. But we can do better than that. How would you like to have him live with you here in Sisterland?"

Constance stopped walking. "Is that possible?"

Patience halted too. She stepped close to Constance, so close she could see where her skin was attached.

"The Nine wants us silenced. But why not silence the Nine? Why not replace it? Constance, we can have a Silent Revolution! And afterwards, we'll set up new structures." Her tone became confidential. "Some of us have been disappointed with the way our society has developed. It's too controlling. Too closed against new ideas. We'd like to see Sisterland progress along different lines."

"No more separating men and women?" A nod. "Would we be allowed to live together? In families?"

"I'm afraid that won't be possible for every sister. Not at first. But for some, yes. For exceptional sisters, like you."

"There's nothing exceptional about me."

"You stand for something. Silence isn't with us. But you are

– you're a link to her. You can be our figurehead. And in return, you'll find us willing to reward sisters loyal to our vision. We could arrange for you to share a twoser with this man you appear to have bonded with."

Constance was dumbstruck. The Silenced were offering her the chance to make a home with Harper. It was beyond anything she had dreamed was possible here in Sisterland. Delight surged. But even as it did, the terms being set snagged on her joy.

"A figurehead? I wouldn't know how."

"It'll be a walk in the park." Patience had an unconvincing laugh. It tinkled now. "Just be yourself."

"You wouldn't expect any more from me?"

"Some speeches, as well. You have talent. Your oratory will swing sisters all over Sisterland to our cause."

"I'm not interested in causes."

"You're interested in a different way of life, though. The benefits will be tangible. You'll have incentives, Constance. Sweeteners."

Temptation nibbled, and she struggled against it. "We're all meant to be equal in Sisterland. Privileges are wrong."

"They exist already. Some of the perks are hidden in plain sight, and some are hushed up. Let's see. The Shaper Mother has a private chef. The Peer Mother has a travel permit. Some of the mating mothers have the right to Himtime without a babyfusion licence. Mothers in all disciplines who reach certain targets are entitled to larger living spaces, and join a waiting list for threesers."

"I never even knew they existed!"

"You'd be surprised what's available to the top tier. This society needs to be reformed, Constance, and to do that we need talented sisters like you."

"But you're offering me perks! That flies in the face of reform."

"It's not ideal. But let's focus on the positives. In time, we'll extend as many privileges as possible to every sister. For now, we intend to start by offering them to those we consider friends."

Again, Constance felt Patience's willpower circle her mindmap, hunting for admission. She fended it off. "And when I have my child? Does she live with me, too?"

A ripple whisked across Patience's face, and she dropped Constance's arm. "We don't seek to sweep aside everything in Sisterland. That's wasteful. Girlplace works well. We'll maintain it. Your daughter stays with you for the first year, then she goes to girlplace. You can see her often there. Maybe we could bend the rules about no source visits during the first month."

"I want to keep my child. I don't want her sent away."

"But who'd look after her when you're carrying out your duties?"

"Harper."

"Is he the man you want us to help?"

Constance nodded. Patience beat her fingers against her mouth, considering the proposal. On tenterhooks, Constance watched her. What a gift, if she was allowed to keep both her baby and Harper beside her.

However, Patience shook her head. "You overestimate a man's capabilities. Your bond with him blinds you to his limitations. After the Nine is replaced, we can set up an education programme for men. In time, some will manage to accept certain responsibilities. But childcare is the highest calling – not even an outstanding man would be fit for it. We mustn't expect too much, or rush the pace. It's unfair to make them take on more than they're capable of."

"Harper knows how to love. That's all he'll need to care for our child. You're offering me a deal, Patience. Those are my conditions."

"This is a once-in-a-lifetime opportunity to be an agent for change. Yet you're half-hearted about it. Though you show a great deal of interest in how the Silent Revolution can improve your life."

"I have to look out for myself."

Eyes glittering, Patience scanned Constance. Without further speech, they reached the flower gardens. Patience stopped by a Harmony Parks worker combing the grass to make it grow in the same direction. "Where are the sunflowers, sister?"

"Gone. They've been vandalised. Someone hacked them down overnight. Such a sorry sight this morning. All those golden heads lying in the dirt."

"Why would they do that?" asked Constance.

"Your guess is as good as mine," said the gardener.

They moved on.

"It must have been your supporters," said Constance. "Attacking beauty isn't the way to challenge Sisterland."

"Some of them can be a little misguided."

"Perhaps it's because even flowers are controlled – their scent, their flowering seasons."

"Let's inspect the damage."

There was no sign of wreckage, however. Already, it had been cleared up, and anemones grew where the sunflowers had blossomed.

"Sisterland remains beautiful," said Constance.

Patience did not acknowledge the sarcasm. They continued on their circuit, and arrived at Beloved's statue.

"I saw the red scarf on Beloved yesterday," said Constance. "It was a declaration of war, wasn't it?"

"War? That's overstating the case. What's warlike, after all, about a red bow? But it made the case that Beloved doesn't belong to the Nine. She belongs to all of us."

They steered towards the Virtue Boulevard gates, Patience cloistered inside her thoughts, while Constance hoped against hope that Patience would give her what she wanted. She supposed asking for both Harper and her child was excessive

– it looked as if the gamble hadn't paid off. Constance longed to be indoors, and able to remove her skin. A rash was itching beneath it – either babyfusion didn't agree with her skin, or her skin didn't agree with it. Who was she to make conditions? This Silent Revolution was her best chance of survival. She considered telling Patience she'd changed her mind, that her child would go to girlplace like every other Sisterlander. But loath to look weak, she held off.

"Goodbye, sister," said Constance.

"Wait. You strike a hard bargain. But you have your deal."

Constance's spirits leapt. Here was the best of all possible worlds! "Thank you, Patience. I'm grateful. You've no idea how much this means to me."

"We'll expect a lot from you in return."

"I'll do my best for the Silent Revolution. Is there anything you want me to do now?"

"Not yet. You'll be told when the time comes. Wait here for five minutes. We shouldn't arrive at Shaperhaus together."

Constance watched the retreat of the straight spine and precise steps.

Unexpectedly, Patience doubled back.

"I presume you'll be at the Memoryday ceremony in three days' time? For Honour's sake?"

Constance nodded.

"Make sure your seat is near the steps to the stage. They have more space round them. It'll be full to capacity, and a babyfused sister shouldn't risk being caught in the crush."

So even Patience had a soft spot for babies! "I'd need a priority pass for one of those places."

"So ask the Shaper Mother. Do it for your baby. Public events can be unpredictable beasts."

Chapter 31

That night, Constance went to Harper's eat-easy. Graffiti that was now a familiar sight was printed on the wall outside.

Beside it, a removal spray in her hand, was Serenity. She pouted, as red as the paint.

"That slogan's springing up all over town, sister. I've tried scrubbing it with every cleaning product on the market, but it's impossible to budge. They even painted it on a wall in the Sistercentral grounds. Hard to believe, with all those scrutineers. But my other saw it with her own eyes. Back looking for calcium soup?"

"I didn't order it in advance."

"As it happens, I did. I knew you'd be back. Anyone who tastes our rice squares always comes back for more."

They went inside, where Constance hovered by the counter, trying to make conversation so that Harper would hear her, until Serenity said, "I'd take the weight off my feet, in your condition. Swollen ankles are no joke. I know all about them in my line of business."

Constance sat with a view of the kitchen hatch. She thought she could detect the back of Harper's head, but it was impossible to tell with a hood. How hot it must be for men in kitchens. Yet they weren't permitted to unhood. No allowances were made for working environments.

After eating, she lingered, until Serenity hinted about closing time. Outside, Constance waited at the back of the office building where she and Harper had spoken a few days previously. It was an uncomfortable wait, her tolerance levels compromised by babyfusion. Her feet were throbbing, her armpits itched and her hairline was slick with perspiration. By the time Harper arrived, she ached all over.

"I heard you talking in the easy."

"I hoped you would."

"You look different."

"Because I'm babyfused? I seem to be ballooning."

"No, because of the skin."

"You don't like me in it? I was wearing it the last time we met, but you didn't mention it."

"It makes you remote."

"I'm still me under it, Harper. You look different, too, in that hood. But I try to see past it."

"A skin masks a woman's face. It's a copy of what lies beneath, but it hides something essential."

"Fair point. But I wear it to guard against environmental damage and not to cover my face."

"Though it does."

"Though it does," she conceded. "Look, let's not waste time. Those women I mentioned. The ones who don't like the way Sisterland is run. They belong to a group called the Silenced. They're planning a Silent Revolution – for a different kind of Sisterland."

His eyes became twin torches. "They'll help me to escape?"

"Something better than that. At least, I think it's better.

You'll be able to stay in Sisterland, and live with me and our baby. If you want to, I mean. You can look after the baby while I work – they want me to play some kind of figurehead role. It's because of Silence, my other. Those details don't matter, though. What matters, Harper, is there's a movement to replace the Nine. And it wants change. Conditions will improve. For men. For everyone."

"The Nine won't go quietly."

"True. But there's a chance it will happen. We have to hope."

"What else will they change? Will they do away with hoods and skins? With matingplace and Hutchtown? Will they pay men for their work?"

"Maybe. I only know what I've been promised: that we can be together. That's how it used to be, in PS days. You didn't know, did you? Women have hidden that from men. We used to live together, and raise our children. Would you like that?"

"We'd live together in my forest?"

Her pleasure in the deal offered by Patience was checked. She hadn't factored in how attached he was to his forest. "We have to live in Harmony, Harper – your forest's a long way from here. You see, the new regime will expect speeches from me. I'll have to appear at rallies, and so on. That's the price we're obliged to pay. I know you love your forest – I know living away from it would be a sacrifice. But surely who we're with matters more than where we are. This allows us to be together. With our child. Wouldn't that be enough for you, Harper?"

At first, he said nothing. Then he pushed back his hood, and his eyes fastened on hers. "I've forgotten what a tree looks like." His voice was desolate.

"I don't understand."

"The Hutchtown Mother. To keep me under control, she's had things taken away from me."

"What things?"

"My mind picture of trees. I know the names, and I know they matter to me, but I can't call up the images any more. Constance, I'm a forester, and I don't know what a tree looks like. They say, 'It's dangerous to remember too much' but they're lying. It's dangerous to remember too little."

"You'll remember them again one day. The memory will break through. It won't stay smothered."

"The man I work with in the easy says there are trees in Harmony. But if I've seen them, I don't recognise them for what they are. I don't connect with them."

"We have some trees in the city, along boulevards and avenues. They're small – we use them for decoration. And there are beautiful trees in the grounds of Sistercentral – not that you can go in there, I'm afraid. When you see a forest again, you'll remember trees."

"I hope so."

"Concentrate on afterwards. When we're allowed to be together. I live near the riverbank, it has a few trees. Not many. But it's peaceful there. You can see frogs, and fish, and all sorts of insects. Well, maybe not all sorts – many are extinct. But some still survive. We could build a good life, Harper. If everything goes according to plan."

He took her hand between both of his. Turning it over, he kissed it on the inner wrist against the pulse point. "If, Constance, if. You're not free here, any more than I am. And how free will you be with this new group of women? Using you as a figurehead because of something your other did – that's another control. Another untruth. I don't like the sound of it."

"I know it's not ideal. They say I'll be part of an elite. That sets warning bells ringing for me, too. But what alternative do we have? Trying to escape is riskier. I can't go yet, I'm babyfused. Even if we wait till after the baby, Outsideland is a total unknown. At least Sisterland is knowable. And we can be together."

"We could be together in Outsideland."

"They're not offering to help you escape. This is the deal. I become some kind of figurehead, they let me be with you. And we raise our baby together. Think of it, Harper! That's an amazing prospect! You can teach our child about the forest, and the creatures living there. Perhaps the three of us might be able to visit there one day. How about it? Isn't it worth a try, at least?"

"I guess so." In a rush, he said, "Don't get in any deeper than you have to, Constance. Not for me, not for anybody. This is dangerous."

Constance filled her chest with oxygen. "I didn't want to tell you, but things are unsafe for me anyway. I don't fancy my chances after I become a source. The Shaper Mother's protecting me, but she won't be able to keep me out of harm's way for much longer. Not now, when I won't spy on the Silenced for them." She laid her hands on either side of his face. "The truth is, I don't have anything to lose by accepting this deal. But I have you to gain, Harper."

He tilted her chin, drawing her face closer, mouth fastening on mouth. And possibilities glimmered.

When they drew apart, he said, "All we do is talk about me. How are you feeling? How's our baby?"

"It wants me to eat all the time, and then it gives me heartburn."

He laughed, low in his throat, and the love she felt for him caught at her. She pressed herself close to him, feeling his body heat against her through the coarse material of his clothing. She longed to believe the Silenced would succeed against the Nine, and she could be with Harper. But she didn't know if she truly could believe it. It had to be an act of faith. For now, she'd have to make herself believe. It would keep her putting one foot in front of the other.

As they prepared to separate, he asked when they could be together again.

"Not till after Memoryday. Will you have the day off? Most of the easies are closing."

"I'll be in Hutchtown. Out of sight, out of mind. That's how your sisters like men."

"Not me. I'll be thinking about you. Always. I suppose the Silenced might try to make an impact at one or other of the events. It'll be too good an opportunity to pass up."

"Keep your head down, Constance. You don't owe them anything."

"But I do, Harper. I owe them for you – for what they're promising to do for you."

With an abruptness she wasn't expecting, he stepped back, pulling up his hood. She knew, without being told, that he resented his dependence on her to free him.

"If this revolution of theirs fails, there'll be discontinuations, Constance. Stay on the sidelines for as long as you can." He backed away, into the darkness.

"Wait! Harper! You're frightening me! I'm not one of the leaders."

His voice floated behind him. "You're a symbol. Nothing's more dangerous than that."

Chapter 32

On Memoryday, Constance was struck by an unusual ambience. Something had taken hold of Harmony and shaken it out of its customary detachment. Girlplace was closed, matingplace was closed, Shaperhaus was closed – everyone except essential workers had the day off. But that wasn't the reason. Nor was it the uplifting music and images coming from public entscreens. Nor even the promise of a general moe-release that evening. It was difficult to pinpoint its origins, but a live current was running through the city.

Constance walked about, observing the holiday atmosphere. Except it was more than that. It was febrile.

"Sister, you're advised to make your way indoors as soon as possible." A peer, holding a small mesh bowl over her lower face, spoke to Constance.

"Is something wrong?"

"A moe factory was infiltrated last night by subversives. A rash of moes was released any which way. A clean-up operation was activated at once, but traces of moe remain in the atmosphere. All sorts of moes, all mixed up. It's causing sisters to be excitable. Unpredictable."

"I don't feel as if I'm absorbing any moes." The hybrid blend had worn off quickly – here was further proof that she was growing immune to artificial moes.

"Maybe not. The unauthorised release was interrupted. But better safe than sorry."

"Has the rally been called off?"

"I don't have any information on that. It would certainly be a shame if the Silenced stopped the rally. It's the Memoryday highlight."

There was a burst of high-pitched laughter from a group of sisters further along the street. Another sister ran across the road to join them, darting in front of a peer vehicle which swerved to avoid her. Its horn blared.

The peer talking to Constance clicked her tongue against her teeth. "Jay-walking – how irresponsible!"

She started towards the group. Constance watched as they argued with the peer. Were they mocking her? She'd never seen a peer faced down before. A snatch of the obedience song drifted back.

Don't fight, do right!
Don't wallow, follow!
Don't delay, obey!

But it was being sung with derision.

The sound of rubber on concrete made her look in the other direction, as the peer vehicle reversed. Peers were emptying out, all holding white mesh receptacles over their noses, and the singing stopped. The women were persuaded to disperse.

Constance turned her steps towards the rally. Breaking into a moe factory was quite a coup for the Silenced. She wondered whether it had been Patience's idea, or Goodwill's, and if it was part of a plan to disrupt Memoryday. But her sandals pinched, distracting her. Her feet were spreading outwards under the weight of babyfusion. Soon, she'd be unable to fit into any of her footwear. Roll on the tenth week, when she'd be allowed time off on full pay, and could pad about barefoot in the oneser. Imagine if the Silent Revolution had the vision to allow space in the world for fathers to live with babyfused women, and help them through it.

En route, she tramped past a public art gallery and the civic offices, both floodlit pale blue because it was Honour's favourite colour. Already, she was developing a headache from the all-pervasive rose scent, also in Honour's memory. It was even wafting up from the paving cracks.

"If they really wanted to please Honour, they'd hand out gingerbread figures," she muttered.

But today was only about Honour in passing.

The pavement was decorated with insets of all the symbols representing Sisterland's professions. From habit, Constance searched until she found the φ for shaper. It was still listed after Constance 500 on her sig, although she didn't know how she ought to be classified any more. On the other hand, why should she be?

As she walked, she noticed knots of peers at regular intervals – more peers than was normal at a public event. Usually they looked relaxed, but today they were vigilant, and all of them wore stifstats. Their hands rested on them. Peer numbers increased the closer she approached to Sister Plaza. At the entrance they were conducting body searches. A peer examined Constance, smiling at her bump, but the shakedown was thorough. Constance looked about. Everyone was being patted down carefully. No doubt security had been stepped up because of the moe factory break-in.

After scanning her sig, the peer directed Constance towards a scrutineer who led her to a front-row seat at the side of the platform. Anxious not to compromise her babyfusion, Constance had taken Patience's advice, and had asked the Shaper Mother for the boon. "For Honour," the mother had said. "She'd want you there."

Constance skimmed the rows for the Shaper Mother, or anyone she might recognise. There was nobody. Some Sistercentral officials occupied seats near her, and she hunted in vain for Modesty among them. The Peer Mother made an entrance, festooned in loops of gold brocade over salmon-pink leather. Soon, all the seats were filled. But on the dais, nine azure chairs with backs shaped into butterfly wings remained vacant.

Constance's gaze travelled uphill, towards Sistercentral. It was early evening, and the setting sun turned its golden sandstone into a glimmering palace. Not floodlit blue, then. Even on days of national celebration, Sistercentral was a place apart. She wondered if the Outsidelander was still in Harmony, or if he had been moved elsewhere. Or if he was discontinued by now. They hadn't exchanged a word, but he had made a difference to her. Her forehead attempted to pleat, but was prevented by the skin. The Outsidelander would pay a high price for his adventurous spirit.

An elegy played by a string quartet billowed out from voiceboxes. It was the signal for a procession of nine young girls, arms bare, floral wreaths in their hair, to proceed down the centre aisle. They wore ankle-length, cobweb dresses in a pink so pale it was blush-white, and carried baskets from which they distributed posies of forget-me-nots to spectators.

Images of Honour 19 flashed onto giant entscreens around Sister Plaza. Similar screens throughout Harmony, and the rest of Sisterland, showed the memory-keeper. Not as she had been when Constance interchanged her final memory. But as a girl – at the age when she had met Beloved, dedicating her life to universal sisterhood – and later, in her prime, sometimes in the company of other memory-keepers.

To rapturous applause, the Nine filed onto the platform. Gracious led the way, as insubstantial as the veil trailing behind her. She was followed by the one Constance still thought of as the Plaits Sister, Innocence, and the remaining seven. Spotlights picked out the stage, dancing across their metal headdresses. Each Sister sat on a butterfly seat.

Except for Temperance, the sister with cropped platinum

hair tinged black at the tips, who advanced centre-stage to deliver an address. She was a dramatic figure in her triple-tier golden headdress with its veil floating to the floor. But her speech was peppered with the usual public holiday platitudes about how women had succeeded by unsexing themselves.

It struck Constance that the Nine had grown complacent – no longer making a genuine effort to engage sisters. Hers wasn't the only negative reaction. The crowd stirred, with some of the spectators muttering. That multiple-moe discharge from the factory break-in had left them less tolerant to waffle. Innocence made a signal, cutting short Temperance's oration.

Now, a trumpet call rang out, the prelude to an approved moe release. The Shaper Mother mounted the steps. She bowed as she passed the Nine, before turning to the front, where she held out her arms, curved upwards: a pose reminiscent of one of the goddesses in Sistercentral's inner chamber.

"My name is Honour 42."

Constance started. To her, she had always been the Shaper Mother.

"I was named for Honour 19. And in her memory, the Nine has decided –"

The mother's address was sabotaged by two concurrent actions. The sound was cut. And on cue, some hundreds of women stood up, silken scarves tied over their mouths. It was a silent protest, projected onto the entscreens in Sister Plaza, and every screen in Sisterland. A camera panned along the standing rows of Silenced, lingering on their bound mouths and on their hands, which held one another's in a human chain.

Visually it was eye-catching. Constance admired the spectacle. But she was surprised that more of the Silenced hadn't assembled. A sea of scarlet was needed. There were fewer here than at the Hope Bridge on the day when Silence's skin was suspended from it. Perhaps more had intended joining, but were deterred by the security cordon around Sister Plaza.

Still, for the first time, Sisterland in its entirety must be aware of the Silenced. Even if sisters didn't know what they represented, they must recognise that a challenge had been thrown down.

Next, a background commentary from someone unseen offstage replaced the Shaper Mother's tribute. The voice was Patience's, the effect bewitching – its honeyed quality making her demands sound mild.

"We are the Silenced. But we will not be silenced! We insist on change. Matingplace. Wrong! Boy-babies taken away. Wrong! Absolute control by the Nine. Wrong! Join with us, sisters. Together, we can build a New Sisterland. A better one. An emotional one. Yes! Moes! We're taught to fear them. But moes are natural. The Nine rations moes. Suppresses them. Demonises them. Sisters, moes are not evil!"

At that, the screens turned white. The ranks of the Silenced, red scarves across their mouths, could be seen no longer.

Undeterred, the voice continued, *"You may block out our faces but you can't stop our words. The Silenced refuse to be silent. The tide of history is propelling us forward. A Silent Revolution has begun!"*

The blare of high-pitched whistles drowned out Patience. At a comtel command from the Peer Mother, every peer in the square was blowing on the whistle she carried. Prominent in her gold braid, the Peer Mother was directing subordinates, and the pounding feet of peers accompanied the whistles. Each one took a Silenced protester by the arm. No scuffles broke out: the Silenced consented to be led away. Constance was puzzled at how uneventfully the demonstration was broken up. Some of the Silenced grinned as they went, exchanging meaningful looks with their fellows. Perhaps they were pleased to have made their point. Even so, their compliance made no sense. This was the same band of sisters that had scaled Beloved's statue, hacked down sunflowers and painted graffiti on the Sistercentral perimeter walls.

Constance's attention was caught by Gracious, whose head was shaking repeatedly. One of the Nine had left her seat and was bent over her, but Gracious was waving her away.

"If I may resume at the point where I was so rudely interrupted," boomed the Shaper Mother, restored once more to the airwaves. She received a scattering of applause, and some of the dignitaries at the front tried to turn it into a standing ovation, but the crowd wouldn't cooperate.

Order was not yet restored, however. The Silenced didn't only have members in the sound division – they had supporters in lighting. Now, the spotlights dimmed, and onto the stage a series of images was projected. Baby boys crying for their sources. Phantom baby boys crawled over the outlines of each of the Nine, and across the Shaper Mother, waving their arms, sucking their fists, and kicking their chubby legs. The audience gasped.

"Stop this! Get rid of these baby-men!" shrieked Innocence.

A wail went up from the crowd.

"He looks like my boy. My boy who was taken from me!" came a cry.

Once more, a voice was amplified over the hubbub. This time, it was Goodwill's. Its tinny sound suggested she was using a peer voicebox.

"*To Acceptance 77807 a son. To Clarity 3021 a son. To Consideration 4158. To Diligence 227 a son.*" Nobody tried to bring the litany to a halt. Its effect was hypnotic. "*To Gratitude 98 a son. To Integrity 84003 a son. To Justice 54395 a son. To Loyalty 22195 a son. To Moderation 127 a son.*" And still the images of baby boys drooling their flirtatious charm were superimposed across everybody onstage. "*To Punctuality 1507 a son. To Simplicity 4248 a son. To Thankful 97842 a son. To Verity 11113 a son.*"

Electrified, Constance felt herself fuse with every woman in the audience. They blended into a whole – moeing together, spontaneously, with the loss of those children. Babies taken, not from one woman, but from all of them.

As the roll-call drew near its conclusion, Patience materialised at the side of the stage, beckoning to Constance. Patience's voice entered her mind, urging her forward. *For Harper,* it said. The name propelled Constance from her seat. She passed a number of peers, but no-one stopped her. They were as mesmerised by the liturgy of the list as everybody else. In a trance, she advanced up the steps to where Patience stood.

Patience seized her by the hands, sizzling with conviction. "Our cause, like all causes, is collecting its legends. Constance, this is your time to shape one! Today, you shall be heard everywhere. Every entscreen in every city and town will beam you out. Your voice, your image, your message. You're about to become the new face of Sisterland!" She gave Constance a gentle push.

Constance found herself stranded at the front. The baby boys vanished. She was alone. A spotlight was trained on her face, another on her belly. Nobody could be in any doubt that she was babyfused.

"*This sister is Constance – Silence's other.*" From offstage, Patience's voice introduced her. "*She's babyfused. She carries the future inside her. All babies are precious. But this one is exceptional. Rejoice, sisters, because the sister before you is babyfused with the spirit of Silence!*"

Chapter 33

"Constance," the crowd murmured. From sister to sister, the name spread. "Constance." They laid the name before her in homage.

Blinded by the lights, she was at a loss.

What do they want from me, she thought.

They want to hear you speak. Patience was trespassing into her mindmap again.

For now, Constance raised no barriers. *What should I say?* she messaged back.

You'll know as soon as you begin. The words will flow – follow your instincts.

"Constance!" the crowd chanted.

The name rained down on her, and she gained substance. What was wanted from her became possible. Constance began filling out to transform into the sister they longed for her to be. Her eyes travelled across the rows of spectators, absorbing the love. Some of those calling out to her were peers. There were Sistercentral officials, too.

Turning her head to the right, she saw the Shaper Mother in the wings. Members of the Silenced surrounded her. Some of the Nine were there, blocked in place by sisters in crimson scarves. Constance looked to the left. Ranks of the Silenced

300

waited there, too. The three hundred or so marched away earlier was only a foretaste, a diversionary sample. Her gaze moved to the front again, and she saw that red scarves were omnipresent. Visible now was that cloudburst of scarlet whose absence she had regretted earlier.

Power tingled through Constance. She was ready to reach out to those who called her name. Their need for her was intoxicating. She could communicate with them on a deep-rooted level – without a shadow of doubt, she knew it. She had the ability to give them what they wanted. And she was willing to do it. She burned to do it. Words sped from her brain to her tongue.

But as she opened her mouth, Temperance eluded the Silenced and dashed onto the stage, pushing Constance aside. Unbalanced, Constance threw down her hands instinctively, breaking her fall to land on her hands and knees.

"Don't listen to these degenerate women!" Temperance reared up in the spotlight. "They seek to drag us backwards. To retreat to the warped days of two-gender society. It's a corruption of nature's law. We must never tolerate it, sisters. Never! Better a noble end to Sisterland than the ignobility of male domination!"

Constance pulled herself to her feet, arms wrapped round her stomach, wrists and knees aching. Outside the spotlight, she was invisible. She stared at Temperance, who was in an altered state. Her movements were jerky, fingers scissoring and elbows jabbing. But she was compelling.

"The sanctity of Sisterland must be preserved, whatever the cost. Sisters, I'd hold a pillow over my own child before I'd permit her to live in a manmade world! They are natural oppressors. They can't help themselves. We must never allow them to rise again. We should kill ourselves and every girl baby first!"

A posy of forget-me-nots flew through the air to land at Temperance's feet. She picked it up and waved it, interpreting the flowers as support. Another posy arrived. Then another. Thick and fast, they sailed through the air, thrown with intent. One struck her on the cheek, another on the forehead. She flinched. At first, the crowd was silent, purposeful as it took aim. Soon, it began to heckle and boo. Temperance was being pelted by flowers.

Two of the Silenced dodged out and caught Temperance by the elbows, leading her away. She did not resist. Constance slipped into the wings, too. Behind her, the giant entscreens flickered into life again, and a film was projected. The audience watched a re-enactment of the story of Silence, and her climactic refusal to part with her boy-baby.

As it played, the Shaper Mother snatched her opportunity. She made her way to where Constance stood, disorientated.

"Why are you allowing yourself to be used? Don't get sucked into this treacherous movement, Constance. It's bound to end badly. Can't you see they're using you?" She took Constance's hand, her tawny eyes limpid with affection. "They don't care about what happens to you."

Constance felt herself drawn into the embrace of those eyes. She shook off the hand. "And you do?"

"How can you doubt it? I've always tried to protect you. I spoke out against sending you to MUM. I vouched for you, and took you under my care."

Constance remembered her sense of isolation facing the Nine, and how the mother had been an anchor to which she could cling. But she also remembered the pressure to spy on the Silenced leadership. She wrestled with the conflict and, as she did, the Mating Mother was able to mindmap her.

"I did it for Sisterland, Constance. It was horrible for you, I understand that. But it was justifiable, sweet child. For the greater good – for universal sisterhood."

At that, Constance rebelled. "Mother, why can't sisters speak honestly to one another? Why are we stuck on this continual loop of the greater good? The Nine was willing to delete me and my baby in the name of universal sisterhood. Whatever I did or didn't do, sacrificing an innocent baby is barbaric. So let's not pretend the Nine cares that much" – she snapped her fingers under the mother's nose – "about me. Or about any of us. I'm finished with universal sisterhood. It's poisonous! I want what Sisterland should want. But doesn't. I want what's best for my baby." The mother opened her mouth to speak, but Constance held up her hand. "I don't want to hear it. I'm not interested in your explanations, your prevarications, your justifications. I did nothing wrong. But I was written off. And so was my unborn baby. Don't even try to rationalise that – it's beneath you. I know you pleaded to the Nine for me, mother. And I'm thankful. But once the decision was made, you couldn't have stood between me and MUM. I'm on borrowed time, and you know it. And that's the system you're defending here. I'm ashamed of you. I'm ashamed *for* you."

"Constance, Constance, you're overwrought. You weren't sent to MUM – you were given into my care. The Nine listened to me – they showed mercy. And now I'm watching over you, just as I've always done. I have your best interests at heart."

"You tried to pressurise me to spy for you. You threatened me when I said no."

Troubled, the mother pressed the heels of her palms against her eyes. Her breathing grew ragged, her body shuddered. When she took her hands away, she said, "Sometimes, mistakes are made. When they happen, it's always a matter for profound regret. But our intentions are always for the best. Truly, Constance. You must believe me."

"But I don't believe you, mother. I think you're too bound up in Sisterland to see its weaknesses. I feel sorry for you."

"Sweet child, you're in danger of making a grave error. You've become moe-ridden. For your own sake, you must control these impulses. You resent how the Nine is treating you, and your moes are making made you petty, self-centred, vengeful. I had such high hopes for you. I still do. Surely you understand. It's better to operate from within than without. To construct, not dismantle. To consent, not reject. Constance, I've watched your progress for years. I've guided you. Be guided by me again. Leave Sister Plaza. Do it now. Get away from these women who want to use you. While you still can. Later, we'll think of a way to deal with your concerns. On my honour as a mother, I guarantee it."

"You know as well as I do that my days are numbered under the Nine."

"No, Constance, I'll have you spared."

"I believe you want to. But I don't believe you can."

Patience spotted them talking. Speaking rapidly into her comtel, she sprinted to join them. "Whatever she's saying, don't listen to her, Constance," she panted. "This is the Shaper Mother: she's an expert at silkenspeak. When she sets out her stall, she's almost irresistible. Soon, the stage will be yours. Open up to our sisters. They're longing to hear from you. Tell them what's in your heart."

"It's immoral, the way you're using her!" hissed the Shaper Mother. "How could you tell our sisters she's carrying the spirit of Silence? That's hocus-pocus. Constance will be swallowed whole by your movement."

"We can protect her," said Patience.

"You can't. She'll be sucked dry by the Silenced. You're sacrificing her for your own selfish ends."

"And you aren't?"

At that, a group of the Silenced arrived, and began to hustle the Shaper Mother away.

They had only gone a few steps before her innate authority exerted itself. "Stop this! Take your hands off me!"

The Silenced fell back.

The mother turned to Constance, eyes blazing. "These women are dangerous. Don't promote their cause. They'll make a puppet of you. And what about your baby? The spirit of Silence? What a burden for any child to carry! They're trying to use her before she's even born!"

"The Shaper Mother is overtired. She needs to rest." Patience signalled to the Silenced to move her along.

But the mother hooked eyes with Constance. "Take my advice, Constance. Even if it's for the last time. Run away from here – run as far as your legs will carry you. While there's still time."

Constance began backing away.

"Stay out of this, Shaper Mother," said Patience. "We mean you no disrespect. We're prepared to work with you. But you'll go to Safe Space if you use your silkenspeak here."

The Shaper Mother trained her bright gaze on Patience. Her voice trickled syrup over her. "Dear sister, I can't deny Sisterland has lost its way. Some of our policies need to be reassessed. We need new blood. New ideas. The Nine is open to them. Let me act as a go-between. Let's all of us sit down together and talk."

"The Nine isn't open. It's threatened by questions. It shuts down opposition."

"We can address that. I'll speak to Gracious. She understands what needs to be done. She's willing to bend." Her tone became confidential. "I know we have weaknesses – I'd like to see changes just as much as you. But I believe in Sisterland. Flawed as it is. With every fibre of my being, I believe in it. Evolution, not revolution – that's the way forward. You can be part of that evolution, sisters. All of you can be part of it. Join with us, sisters. Come back to us. Believe in us."

A vein popped up on the side of Patience's neck as she fought against the mother's charisma. "We have a different vision for Sisterland. The Nine is a spent force. It must make way for a new order."

"A new order? I think not." Emphatic, the Shaper Mother

shook her head, earrings ricocheting. "No, there won't be any new order. Loyalty to Sisterland runs too deep with our sisters. You won't reach them with your talk of baby boys, and the spirit of Silence. Myth-making machinery, Patience. But it doesn't convince."

"You dare to accuse us of myth-making?" Goodwill joined them. "You – part of a caste which has blanked out history! Erased realities! And now seeks to control memories! Your hypocrisy is limitless!"

"Hypocrisy is a stern charge, Goodwill. I call it loyalty. Staying true to Sisterland. As for recasting history – it's always a story told by someone. Who knows what's true, really?" In an elegant gesture, she fluttered her hands, and her mouth stretched into a rueful half-smile.

Constance was shocked by the Shaper Mother's cynicism. "Why not trust people with the truth instead of myths, mother?" she intervened.

"Where a myth is more appealing than the truth, people will always choose the myth. Ah, I see Patience and Goodwill agree with me. We have more in common than divides us, sisters. Enough of this unpleasantness. Let me arrange a meeting between the Nine and representatives of the Silenced. Let's see what mutual aims can be agreed." She advanced towards Patience and Goodwill, and her voice descended into a husky murmur. "Incidentally, Patience, I won't be Shaper Mother forever and I'd be glad to recommend you for the position. And Goodwill, so devoted to Devotion. Think what pleasure a private garden would give her. I could organise that. She deserves it, doesn't she?"

Uncertain, Goodwill flicked a sidelong look at Patience. Both were tempted. Until a whirlwind landed among them. It was Temperance, rushing the group, shouting about universal sisterhood under siege. But it could never be routed, she screamed, because it had right on its side. In the heat of her advance, she knocked against the mother, her flailing arms accidentally unhooking the mother's skin. It fell to the ground, and Temperance trampled it. Everyone was frozen. Even Temperance hushed and became still.

With a concern that was verging on tender, Goodwill picked up the skin and slotted it back into place. Except the catches had been damaged by Temperance's feet. The skin sat crooked on the mother's face.

As if a spell was lifted, Patience called out to the Silenced, "Clear the area. We have work to do."

And the Shaper Mother and Temperance were led away.

As the Silenced removed them, Constance dismounted from the stage. Shaken, concerned to protect her babyfusion, and needing to rest, she intended to slip away home. But she had to pass Gracious leaning against a wooden support, head bowed beneath the transparent veil. She should have looked like an aged elder. But, even now, the nimbus of the Nine suffused her with a bloom. Innocence, also rosy amid the disorder, was talking to Gracious, while members of the Silenced hovered at a respectful distance.

"There isn't time to convene a meeting of the Nine, or to vote. Emergency powers must be adopted by the first three," said Innocence. "Gracious, you must join with me and Temperance. It's imperative that Silence becomes a forgotten woman. We can delete her memory. Not just from Constance 500, but by a general, Statewide unmapping. It will be as if she never existed."

"No!" cried Constance.

"You again!" said Innocence.

"Silence did exist! I won't let you have her unmapped."

"Silence set a bad example – she harmed her child. It's absurd to hold her up as a role model. Sisterland is diminished by her."

"Is that what you think?" Constance challenged Gracious.

Gracious shaded her eyes from the light. "What I think . . . What I think . . ." Stuttering, she was unable to finish.

"Sister, we need to deal with this," snapped Innocence. "It's the only way to weather the storm. Silence must be erased from every mindmap."

"You whipped up the storm with your inflexible rules," said Constance.

Innocence's eyes flashed. "Insolence!" She twisted her head, hunting for peers to summon, and spotted the Peer Mother with a clutch of them. "Remove this sister!" she cried.

The peers looked to their mother, who shook her head.

Innocence deflated.

Gracious held up a hand. "I didn't know this sister named Silence. She doesn't occupy my thoughts the way another sister does. Honour, that's who concerns me. Honour – and her father."

"We have no fathers in Sisterland," said Innocence.

Gracious strained towards Constance, who became conscious of the sister tapping at her mind. She did not resist. Instead, she dipped her head to Gracious, and a charge passed between them.

Turning, Constance remounted the steps and walked out to the centre of the stage.

"Constance!" chanted the crowd.

Its clamour was an adrenaline shot. She began to speak.

"I love a man. His name is Harper."

Those eight words of Constance's caused an eruption. Some members of the audience rose to their feet, incredulous. Constance was almost unnerved by how quickly an audience's admiration could transform to dislike, but stood her ground. A knocking came at her mind – Patience again.

We want you to promote change. But that's too radical! Stay on message, or leave the stage.

A thought-shaper is permanently on message: Constance remembered her training. So everything about the old order wasn't about to be discarded.

She raised a wall against Patience, waiting for the turbulence to subside. Next, she cleared her throat, and readied the words to pour out in a stream. She knew she wouldn't have much time to present her case, and had to be ready to take advantage of a lull.

"Love between a woman and a man was common in PS days. It wasn't harmful. Or wicked. Or deviant. It was natural," said Constance.

"Shame on you!" cried a voice.

"Shame!" echoed from row to row.

"There were many kinds of love between women and men. Romantic love was only one. There was also love between sister and brother. Between source and son. And between daughter and father."

"Impossible!" voices called out.

"Not impossible. The memory-keeper, Honour 19, knew it. She never forgot it. Before she discontinued, Honour shared one final memory with me. It was about her father, who loved her. As she loved him back."

Constance described the cakes Honour's father baked, the way he took pains to pass on his skills to his daughter, and the bond between them.

"Women and men lived together with their children," she said.

Her audience tested the words. "Women and men. Together."

"Yes, it was a system which worked. It gave them satisfaction. They raised contented children. The Nine tells us community child-rearing is more efficient. But who wants to give up their baby? Even for Sisterland? Every source loves her child, and longs to keep it. Whether a daughter – or a son."

A woman near the front stood up. A spotlight moved to her, and the crowd could see she was in the late stages of babyfusion. "I won't let them have my baby. Girl or boy, I'm keeping it!"

"Me too!" cried another woman with a protruding belly.

The audience surged to its feet, en masse. "*We'll keep them all!*" it roared.

Constance signalled for quiet. "And what of men? Do we carry on as before, with men? Or do we share the riches of this wonderful land with them?"

There were mutterings. Reading their unease, Constance understood that boy-babies were defenceless, and inherently appealing – but men fell into another category.

"Remember, sisters, boy-babies will grow into men," she cried. "What's loveable as an infant remains loveable in adulthood."

The rumbles continued, however, and she gave way. She'd try again on another occasion.

Scenting her surrender, Patience's voice soared out from the voicebox. "*We thank Constance for pointing the way towards a new Sisterland. Change is essential. But it must be gradual. Now, sisters, brace yourselves for the release of a synchronised moe: a G has been made available. All of us can share in gratitude for the golden era that's about to unfold for our dearest Sisterland.*"

A chocolate-brown canopy was lowered over the audience, a hissing sounded, and the moe was set loose. Inhaling, the audience sighed with pleasure.

Patience, holding a mesh bowl over her nose and mouth to obstruct the moe, pulled Constance off-stage. "You went too far. Nobody authorised you to push the Silent Revolution's aims as far as you did." Even though her voice was muffled, there was no disguising her aggrieved air.

"Leave her alone." It was Goodwill, also holding a mask. She handed one to Constance.

Constance's neck was flushed, and she could feel the blood pumping beneath her skin. "Doesn't anyone understand? We can't love our boy-babies, and carry on as before. Everything has to change now. Not somewhere down the line. *Now.*"

"Hold up your bowl," said Goodwill, "otherwise you'll be overcome with thankfulness. There's a time and a place for it. But not right now."

Constance did as she was told, but the moe wasn't affecting her in any case.

Goodwill turned to Patience. "Constance is still finding her feet. You have to make allowances for her. She doesn't belong to the Silenced."

"Any more than Silence does," said Constance. Breathing shallowly, she walked away.

As she dismounted from the stage, she saw the Peer Mother talking purposefully with the Scrutineer Mother, both with bowls over their noses. Constance halted to stare. Each had a red scarf knotted at her neck.

Chapter 34

ALERT! VILE NEWS ABOUT THE CORRUPT HABITS OF THE NINE HAS BEEN TRANSMITTED TO EVERY COMTEL. WE CANNOT GUARANTEE IT WILL STAY VISIBLE FOR LONG. SISTERS ARE URGED TO READ IT AT ONCE. DO NOT DELAY! THE SAFETY OF SISTERLAND'S BABIES DEPENDS ON IT!

The flashing message was posted on every public and private entscreen. It was impossible to miss. Constance was napping in her oneser when the entscreen sprang into life, posting the notice. Still groggy, she checked her comtel, and was invited to download a communication. It was a voice message – not the typically bland automated voice, but Goodwill's. At first, Constance thought it was intended for her ears alone. But when she replayed it, she realised this was a mass communication.

"*Dear sisters, you must brace yourselves for sorrowful news,*" it began.

Absorbing the contents, Constance began to tremble. As the shudders continued, she found herself unable to stay indoors, and threw on some clothes.

In the unit courtyard she passed sisters looking about in wide-eyed uncertainty, or standing in knots talking in hushed

312

whispers, but Constance did not stay to join in their discussions. She needed the closest equivalent to fresh air that Harmony could muster. She made for the riverbank, where more sisters were clustered, staring at their comtels or muttering together. The aftershock was palpable.

The message on every comtel came from the Silenced leadership. It revealed the discovery of a horrific practice involving the Nine. They harvested blood from babies to keep them youthful: that was the wellspring of their extraordinary glow. A girlplace mother had exposed the appalling habit, confirmed by Gracious, who could no longer condone the abuse.

Upon admission to girlplace at the age of one, each baby was drained of a quarter pint of blood gradually during her first month – the maximum it was safe to extract. That was why sources were denied permission to visit. The blood was accumulated and stored for the exclusive use of the Nine, whose members underwent regular transfusions.

All at once, the storm broke.

"*Blood-suckers*!" howled a band of women.

From one side of the riverbank to the other, the reaction bounced.

"*Leeches*!"

"*Predators*!"

It was a spontaneous, communal moe-eruption.

Constance stroked the bulge caused by the child inside her. You didn't have to be babyfused, or a source, to be filled with implacable fury against the Nine. But it helped. The nimbus encasing the state's leaders – a defining characteristic – was caused by extracting the life-blood from Sisterland's babies. There could be no excuse for their actions. The Silenced had unleashed a weapon against the Nine which, for all their power, those sisters were powerless to deflect.

The Nine was finished. Sisterlanders would never forgive this.

Modesty and Constance drank ocean tea in a corner of an eat-easy off Eternity Square.

"You're enormous!" were Modesty's first words. "You've ballooned since Memoryday."

"I'm at an advanced stage of babyfusion," Constance protested. "But feel free to make me feel self-conscious."

"That's only a minor moe. Nothing to lose sleep over."

"It's not a moe that ever troubled you, Modesty."

"True. Thanks for meeting me. I know how busy you are."

"Everyone's busy. Setting up a new regime takes time and energy."

Modesty lowered her voice. "Especially when the old regime isn't willing to go quietly. Despite the baby-harvesting story, and blood banks in every girlplace raided by the peers. With the proof posted on entscreens. Remember the time we spoke about a miracle drug reserved for the Nine? And how supplies had dried up? Turns out, baby blood was the drug. That's what they were missing. And that's why they started losing their grip."

"Gruesome! It makes me feel nauseous."

"Me too. They started with the blood of boy-babies. And when that wasn't enough, because boy-baby numbers were falling and their need kept growing, they started harvesting baby girls, too."

"Modesty, did the Shaper Mother have baby-blood transfusions?"

"I don't believe so. It was a Nine perk – the Sisters were greedy about it. You know, Constance, the day sisters tried to storm Sistercentral, I really thought some of the Nine would be torn limb from limb. I have to hand it to Patience and Goodwill – if they hadn't calmed the mob it would have turned ugly."

"Sisters aren't prepared to tolerate the Nine any longer. They want new leaders, with a new vision for Sisterland. We're starting to give sisters what they deserve, Modesty. Don't you ever feel like pinching yourself? We're living through an extraordinary cycle in Sisterland's history."

"It helps that so many mothers are jumping ship to join the new order. I wonder what inducements the Silenced are offering them?"

"Perhaps some of them believe in the Silenced Revolution. Or they're just as offended by babies' blood being harvested as everyone else."

"Such a pearl, even now!"

Constance ignored the prick – the odd jab was inevitable from Modesty. "It's too bad some of the mothers are still holding out. The Buzz Mother remains stubborn. And the Sigs Mother. But the Comtel and Scrutineer Mothers have come over to our side. So have the Thought-hatcher and Crafter Mothers. Most of the Mating Mothers are holding out. But the Peer Mother joined before Memoryday – that's how the celebration was hijacked. The important thing, though, is ordinary sisters are behind us. The tide's turning in our favour."

"There's a lot of 'us' going on here. You really have gone over to the Silenced, haven't you, Constance?"

"They've been good to me." Constance was defensive, and it occurred to her that she didn't have to put up with Modesty's impertinence. She had a position now, whereas Modesty was still jockeying for one.

"Are you one of the leadership?" continued Modesty.

"No. I do as I'm told."

"I have to hand it to Patience and Goodwill: they make an effective team. Patience's one determined sister, isn't she? She kept that side well hidden in Shaperhaus. I wonder what it is she really wants."

"A reformed Sisterland, of course. You're always looking for the angle, Modesty."

"Because usually there is one."

"Here's an angle you haven't taken account of: Gracious. She's onside with the Silenced. She's the hinge opening the door to change."

As if to prove her point, an announcement made over the

entscreen in Eternity Square was carried into the eat-easy. *Calling all sisters. Gracious will make a public address on Wednesday at three o'clock. Sisters are advised to listen with the utmost care. Her speech concerns matters of national importance to Sisterland.*

"Not another public address. No harm to your lot, Constance, but they're obsessed with them."

"This is different. Gracious is going to point the way forward."

"We've had nothing but sisters pointing the way forward! For a Silent Revolution, you do no end of talking."

"Not Gracious. She's allowed her name and image to be used, but she hasn't spoken publicly before. We haven't heard Gracious in her own words. This will be a keynote speech. Patience is thrilled – Gracious represents continuity. A stepping stone between old and new."

"That's not all she represents. Gracious legitimises the Silenced. Though she can never lead them – not after the baby-blood scandal. She can keep issuing statements dripping with apology, but she'll never truly be forgiven for it." A hesitation, followed by a change of tone. "The scrutineer rumour-mill is buzzing with stories about differences of opinion between Gracious and Patience."

Constance blinked. Modesty was well-informed. Then again, she always had been. "Don't believe everything you hear on rumour-mills."

"Only believe the entscreen, is that it?"

"I suppose it might seem as if the entscreen is overused. But it's a way of explaining the various improvements in hand. We know this is a confusing time for sisters. We want them to feel reassured, and go about their business as usual."

"*Smile All The While*," offered Modesty.

Constance's lips twitched, and Modesty pressed on.

"Patience versus Gracious. I don't know how evenly matched they are."

"Patience and Gracious are on the same side. Their differences are about the pace of reform, not the need for it. Gracious advises watchfulness and consultation, to ensure sisters are fully behind each new initiative. Patience believes there's a time for caution – and a time for action."

"I always saw Patience as an icon-polisher, not an iconoclast."

"Perhaps she's tired of icons."

Modesty's glance at Constance was sly. "Perhaps she's becoming her own icon."

Constance gasped. "Modesty, watch what you're saying!"

"Just joking, Constance. Of course, Patience is making a superb contribution. She's farsighted, but with the organisational skills to make it happen. She's neutralised the Nine, hasn't she?"

"Yes, confined them to their homes – unable to communicate. No Sistercentral, no comtels, no access to one another."

Modesty dabbed at some moisture on the sleeve of her scrutineer's uniform. "I suppose you know Patience, Goodwill and others in the Silenced have made Sistercentral their headquarters now. The Queen is dead, long live the Queen." From under her eyelashes, she watched Constance.

"It would be wasteful not to use the building. Its facilities are better than the Shaperhaus ones. Though Patience is often in Shaperhaus."

"Keeping an eye on the Shaper Mother. Who seems to be trying for a foot in both camps. Is she succeeding?"

"We're giving her leeway. We'd like to have her as part of the Silenced Revolution. But it will proceed. With or without her. Patience is exasperated at her dawdling – she's had to take control at Shaperhaus. Patience wants shapers sent around Sisterland, using silkenspeak to promote the Silenced vision. But the Shaper Mother keeps finding reasons not to cooperate. Patience taking over at Shaperhaus isn't a power grab. It's necessary to counteract the mother's –" She searched for the word.

"Loyalty?" suggested Modesty.

"Wrongheadedness," said Constance. "Which is delaying reforms. Still, a public address from Gracious will be helpful. Our sisters in other cities and belts will be reassured when they see she's part of the emerging order."

Modesty's laughter set her topknot quivering. "An order which continues to use silkenspeak. The Nine isn't being toppled, its members are resting. The Silenced aren't against anything, they're for something: Sisterland. '*No cause for alarm, dear sisters. On the contrary: rejoice. A new era is dawning. But don't expect radical change.*'"

Constance looked troubled. "All the same, the Silent Revolution will make conditions better. For sisters, and for men."

"Yes indeed, men. That's what I wanted to talk to you about. I'd like to offer my services to the Silent Revolution. I'm on your side, you know."

Constance bit back a smile. Modesty was on only one side.

Modesty pretended not to notice. "I know you want to break down barriers between the genders. I have some ideas for progressing that."

"I'll certainly pass on your offer."

"Can you recommend me for work in that field?"

"Surely your Scrutineer Mother is the person to make a recommendation on your behalf?"

"She wants to keep me on Sistercentral's staff. But I think opportunities lie elsewhere. Why wait to be discovered when I have a friend with access-all-areas? You're connected, Constance, you know you are. You've advanced almost despite yourself. Take me with you."

Constance liked Modesty, for all her faults. "I'll do what I can."

"I'd appreciate it." Shyly, Modesty rummaged in a pocket

and set a gift-wrapped package on the table in front of Constance.

"What's this?"

"For the baby."

Constance pulled the bow, and the tissue paper fell open to reveal mint-green bootees with a tiny tree appliquéed on the front of each. She gave a gasp of pleasure. "My first present for the baby! Oh Modesty, I'm touched!"

"I thought that forester of yours would like the trees. I ought to walk you to the Buzz, Constance. You're looking tired, all of a sudden. How long before the baby comes?"

"A week."

"It must be exhausting. But at least you're not alone."

Constance's hand, rewrapping the bootees, stopped moving. "You know?"

Modesty nodded.

"Is it widely known?"

"Not widely. Is it a secret?"

Constance finished packing away the gift before answering. "No reason why it should be. I'm not ashamed. Neither is he."

"One day, I'd like to share a unit with a man."

"It's a natural desire."

"It's a perk, Constance. I can't expect it unless I perform stellar service for Sisterland."

Defensive again, Constance said, "Harper's not the only man in the unit. Another moved in soon after him."

"Really? Who does he live with?"

Constance thought of Leaf, the young man chosen by the Peer Mother to share a twoser. "Perhaps I shouldn't say. But I'm glad he's there. He's a friend for Harper."

When they had free time, the two men liked to stroll together in the private grounds attached to the unit. Leaf had told Harper that the Peer Mother was kind to him, and although she would soon wind down towards retirement, she was young at heart. He was fortunate to be chosen by her, according to Leaf.

"Two men in your unit. They must be exceptional specimens. How do I wangle an introduction? Are you planning a party?"

"Not in this condition. Though I did have the man, and the sister who chose him, over for a couple of glasses of setting-sun wine. I want to help Harper put down roots in Harmony. I thought it might help."

"And was your soirée a success?"

"Of course. Devotion's sunset wine is legendary."

"So why did you pull a face?"

"I didn't."

"You did."

Constance knew she was being indiscreet, but Modesty had a knack for ferreting out information. "It wasn't a success, to be honest. Leaf was deferential to the sister he lives with, and Harper didn't like it. I tried to explain Leaf is only protecting his position. But Harper thinks some sisters are treating men as toys."

"Aren't they for playing with? Surely that's why you have them?"

"No! Absolutely not! Men like Harper and Leaf are intelligent. They think. What they say is worth hearing. I talk things over with Harper. We discuss what's happening in Sisterland. He's in the first intake of men learning to read and write, and Leaf is waiting for the next free place on the programme. Harper says men have a hunger for learning."

"OK, if you hear of any more men like Harper and Leaf up for grabs, I mean looking for a good home, let me know."

The baby was kicking, and Constance didn't have the energy to tell Modesty that men weren't up for grabs. Especially because she knew they were. If a sister was useful enough, or senior enough.

They parted, and Constance went to her new home, not far

from her old one in the riverbank unit. She had been given space in a complex set aside for VIPs. Harper had been plucked from Hutchtown and the eat-easy, just as Patience had promised, and lived with Constance. Occasionally, they attracted curious glances in the street, despite being careful not to parade their affection. It left Harper touchy, but Constance was convinced their curiosity value would evaporate, in time. Partnering with a man was a rarity, but that was bound to change.

In the meantime, she was unprepared for how rewarding it proved to be, spending her days and nights with Harper. She had known it was painful to be apart from him, but had not anticipated how pleasurable it would be to live with him. To take the sight of him for granted, the touch, the sound of his voice. To converse without the fear of being overheard. To eat a meal together. To make plans. To sleep curled up beside him, and to see him beside her when she woke. To enjoy Himtime with him whenever they liked.

Sometimes, she longed to close the door on their new home against Sisterland, and concentrate on knowing Harper. But she accepted that she had to pay for the privilege of sharing her life with him. She was no longer a private citizen. The Silenced had expectations of her. And she found herself enjoying the role she performed. Especially with Harper waiting at home.

But while Constance was delighted by the spacious threeser they shared – a threeser! who knew they existed! – Harper felt cooped-up in it. Initially, he had paced its rooms, as skittish as the wild creatures he talked about constantly. Recently, she had managed to have him assigned to the Harmony Parks division, and his outdoors work had put an end to the restless walking, walking, walking. But it did not eradicate his longing for the forest. And not all his co-workers welcomed him.

He complained to Constance about one woman on the

same team who was intent on needling him. "She says men can't appreciate beauty so how can they create it?"

"You'll just have to show her she's wrong, Harper."

"You expect a lot from me, Constance."

"I didn't mean it like that. I meant I have faith in you. You have to believe I'm on your side, Harper. Always."

He had apologised, and peace had been restored. But Constance was forced to admit to herself that life in Sisterland was not easy for Harper. Even the new, improved Sisterland.

At least when they used their bodies to communicate, there was no misunderstanding. The mating ritual gave pleasure and comfort to both of them. Body slotted into body, with the magic of a flame catching, and they achieved a state of grace that often eluded them verbally.

Chapter 35

Constance sat at home doing a last run-through of her introduction to Gracious's speech.

"I hope I remember what I'm supposed to say," she fretted. "Babyfusion's turned my brain to ocean tea."

"I wish you weren't going," said Harper. "What if you get jostled by the crowd?"

"I have to go. At least introducing Gracious is my last job before sourcingplace."

"Try to stay sitting down as much as possible. Otherwise your ankles will get bloated again. I'll have a fresh batch of peppermint foot rub ready when you come home. Are you certain this is still going ahead? The rehearsal was called off at the last minute. The speech could be cancelled, too. It's unfair to drag you over to Beloved Park if there's any doubt."

"There's no doubt. Patience has backed down."

"She didn't vet an advance copy of the speech?"

"No. She had to give in. It was the only way to end the stand-off."

Harper knelt to help guide her feet into shoes, and Constance stroked his hair.

"I hope our baby has your colouring."

He smiled at her. "Push. Your feet aren't going in."

Constance wrestled her way into them. "Goodwill smoothed everyone's ruffled feathers in the end. But Patience should have known better than to ask for script control. Gracious looks fragile, but she isn't afraid to make a stand. She says she's nobody's mouthpiece."

Harper pulled Constance to her feet. "From what you tell me about Patience, this isn't surrender. It's a ploy. As soon as Gracious serves her purpose she's out. Just like the rest of the Nine."

"Maybe. I'm sorry you aren't allowed to come with me to Beloved Park, Harper. I know you have hopes for this speech. Imagine if you could be there to hear her deliver it. But those restrictions will vanish, in time."

"It seems odd to make a speech about men with no men in the audience."

"Lots of women won't be there, either. Modesty can't get a ticket. And Devotion can't be bothered going. Be patient, Harper. Please. For my sake. What does it matter, really, where you hear Gracious announce the unhooding policy? So long as you hear it?"

"Leaf and I were talking yesterday. He wonders when men will be able to propose changes, rather than wait for women to do it for them."

"I bet he hasn't said that to the Peer Mother. He knows to keep on her right side." Harper's face tightened, and Constance said hurriedly, "Harper, try to bear in mind how much has changed already, rather than worry about what hasn't."

"I know, I get edgy. The women I work with in the public parks are keyed-up around me, and it makes me feel like an object of suspicion. The animals in the forest were quicker to trust me."

"They'll get used to you. It takes time." She twined her arms round his neck, and his frown softened.

"Leaf and I are watching the speech on the entscreen in his twoser. We'll be cheering for you."

"I'm only the warm-up act."

"Are you kidding? You'll steal the show."

A purpose-built dais in front of Beloved's statue had been set up for Gracious's speech before a hand-picked audience. Goodwill took a seat beside Constance on the platform, and Constance was glad of her friendly support. She stood up to introduce Gracious.

"Prepare to experience history in real time," Constance announced. "This moment marks the dividing line between the old Sisterland and the new."

Gracious's entrance music swelled, and Constance walked backwards towards her seat, lowering herself gingerly into it. Gracious appeared from behind the giant statue of Beloved. Two members of the Silenced followed, and helped Gracious to reach the front of the dais. Constance tried not to think it, but the thought came anyway. Gracious was older-looking, tired-looking, more ordinary-looking, cut off from her baby-blood supplies. The Nine aura of grace and radiance was gone. She had authority still, however.

Gracious stood without speaking, her eyes sweeping over the spectators, who waited for her to be ready. When utter stillness had settled, she reached up to her veil. With slow deliberation, she unhooked it with both hands, opened them wide, and tossed the veil away.

"Enough of veils. Enough of hiding behind symbols, sisters! Let's try again. Let's do better this time!" Her oration was under way.

At times, it had the ring of a public confession. She taxed the Nine with being dictatorial: "We treated dissent as disruptive. Debate as harmful. The truth as negativity. We must no longer sacrifice Sisterland on the altar of denial. Let us celebrate, sisters, because mistakes have been recognised! And now we're correcting them. Sisterland belongs to all of us, and not to the Nine!"

When Gracious apologised on behalf of the Nine for past shortcomings, Constance wished Harper was beside her. She would have turned to him and made a joke about how well that would go down with the rest of the Nine. She knew each of them was watching Gracious speak on an entscreen – Patience believed it might prick other members of the Nine to throw in their lot with the Silent Revolution.

As the speech wound to a close, Constance was disappointed to realise there was going to be no mention of hoods. She bit her lip: Harper would be deflated. She had assured him the policy was about to be overturned.

"Why did Gracious not mention the new unhooding action plan?" she whispered to Goodwill, during the standing ovation.

"Patience pushed her too hard about it. I suspect she left it out to teach her a lesson."

"But what about all the men who have to wear hoods? They're caught in the crossfire."

Goodwill shrugged. "Some of our number believe sisters need time to adjust to unhooded men. Gracious says sisters must grow accustomed to seeing men on the Buzz, and in shops and eat-easies. Then the sight of unhooded men won't be such a shock."

"Do you really believe our sisters are so easily shocked?"

Goodwill wrinkled her nose. "Maybe. Maybe not. Look on the bright side. At least boy-men aren't hooding any more."

Harper was not just dissatisfied but indignant. His resentment was waiting for her when she walked through the door. "You keep telling me to believe in the Silenced Revolution. But it's all about women, still."

Constance sank heavily into a chair, massaging the small of her back with the heel of one hand. "I know it's frustrating, Harper. Everyone is arguing over the pace of reforms. But hoods will go – there's no doubt about it." She took off her skin, and held both hands out to him. "If our baby is a boy, he won't have to wear one. Let's be glad about that."

He softened at the mention of their child, and allowed her to mollify him.

Later, she asked, "Don't you have a babycare class?"

"It was postponed because of Gracious's speech. I'm going tomorrow instead. We're learning how to bath a newborn."

"Excellent – bathtime duties are hereby delegated to you."

"You know I'm the only man in the class? But at least I'm there," he added. "Don't think I'm ungrateful. I just get impatient with all the restrictions still in place. It's not just hoods. Why can't I go to sourcingplace with you when you have our child? Why can't I visit my forest?"

"Harper, I'm about to have a baby. I can't travel right now. Would you really leave me behind? Even to see your trees?"

"Of course not." He folded her against his chest, where his heartbeat reassured her. "I know I owe it to you that my memory of trees was restored. I owe everything to you."

"Don't say that – I don't want you thinking you're in my debt. I'm sorry I couldn't change Patience's mind about sourcingplace. She said sources shouldn't be troubled at such a delicate time. And I know you feel aggrieved about wearing a hood. I would, too. But you don't have to wear one indoors with me. Or in the grounds of the unit. Or in the dine-all here. Remember, you can go in there and eat on your own – no need for me to be with you. Women take your order for food. All these steps are improvements. More will follow, Harper."

"Women take my order in the dine-all, but they don't like it. And it shows."

"They do it, though."

"OK, you win." He gave a short laugh. "Sisterland is now a paradise."

"I'm not saying that. I'm just saying it's better than before. Small children aren't segregated any more. Girls and boys will grow up knowing each other. Think of the dividends reaped there in future years." He rested his cheek on the crown of her head, and she felt him relax. "You will be patient, won't you, Harper?" He made no reply. "Harper?" she tried again.

He cleared his throat. "What makes you so certain, Constance, we'll be allowed to keep our baby?"

"Don't worry, I'll do anything they want me to, so we can."

"Propaganda work."

"How can it be propaganda if I believe what I'm saying? Besides, you benefit as much as me."

He raised his head. Sorrow lodged in his eyes.

She looked away.

Chapter 36

Devotion arrived on Constance's doorstep unannounced.

"I know I should have comtelled you. But I was too impatient to see this shiny bauble of a unit where you live. Goodwill told me about it. She talks about the man you share it with, too. But I'm not ready to meet him yet. Changes are happening too fast for my liking."

"He's at work."

"I know. I had Goodwill check his assignments today. That's why I'm here now."

"Then you'll know he's planting flower boxes along Courtesy Avenue."

"Autumn-flowering snowdrops. They'll never be noticed among the crowds that shop there. Still, they have charm." She stretched her neck to inspect the view. "A private garden – you've landed on your feet."

"You have one, too. Goodwill arranged it."

"Not like this – a pleasure garden, to walk in. Mine is a working garden. It earns its keep. It's a block away from our unit. I brought you some herbs, ladybird. And a blanket for the baby."

At the sight of the downy lilac strip of fleece, Constance capitulated. "I recognise that – it's mine, isn't it?"

"Yes, it was yours when you were a baby. I kept it safe for you. You chewed a corner, see? But it's in good condition overall."

Constance accepted the gifts, and gave her source a tour of the threeser. Afterwards, they sat over beakers of ocean tea, and talk turned to the Silent Revolution.

"Goodwill keeps me up-to-date, whether I'm willing to hear or not," said Devotion. "One by one, the Nine is retreating before the incoming Silenced tide."

Constance counted them off. "One has asked to retire to private life: she no longer believes herself competent to have a public role. Another stepped down on health grounds. A third asked for permission to work with small children."

"I heard about her. Goodwill says she's being kept under supervision, but appears to have no ulterior motive. She's interacting well with the little boys. Which still leaves five."

"Yes, there are five who won't cooperate. Innocence and Temperance – no surprises there. Also Perseverance, Dedication and Tranquillity. I know Goodwill has been making the case for them to Patience. She says they can't be kept under house arrest indefinitely."

Devotion picked up a hood belonging to Harper, lying on the arm of a chair. She dangled it from a fingertip. "Doesn't he need this?"

"He has more than one."

"How prudent. Goodwill told me there's been discussion about committing the five to Safe Space. Some say it's necessary. Others think it's repressive and smacks of the old order. What's your view, Constance?"

"I think they should be granted safe passage out of Harmony in return for a promise to live quietly in one of the remote belts."

"Would you trust them to keep their word?"

Constance considered. "Everyone deserves a second chance."

"Speaking of second chances, Goodwill's told me about the

Shaper Mother." Constance winced, but Devotion continued. "Confined to her unit, isn't she? So much for a new Sisterland."

Constance reddened. "I'm doing my best to speak up for her. I've begged for leniency. We might be able to hammer out a compromise." It distressed her to consider the Shaper Mother's plight. After all, this was a woman she had admired. Perhaps loved.

"Goodwill says the Shaper Mother provoked the new leadership, pretending to work with the new order but undermining it at every opportunity."

"She doesn't buy into the Silenced Revolution."

"And you do?"

"I have to: for the baby, and for Harper."

Devotion made an impatient noise. "This man has dazzled you, Constance." She was about to say more, but was arrested by a pinched look on Constance's face. Constance was holding her stomach. "Are you all right, ladybird?"

"Just something I ate. I'll be fine in a minute."

"Is the baby coming?"

Constance shook her head. "It's not time. Two more days, that's what I've been told. The date's fixed."

"You need to lie down. Sometimes babies make their own time." Devotion guided her into the next room, and helped her onto the pop-up.

Constance couldn't settle. "I want Harper," she moaned.

Devotion pretended not to hear. "I'll send for a medico. Just to be on the safe side."

"No! Harper!"

Devotion kept a close eye on her as she tapped out a comtel alert for a medico. Constance continued to whimper his name. Devotion relented. "All right, I'll send for this Harper of yours."

Constance tried to lift her hand with the comtel on the thumb, but it flopped back beside her. "His chip signal's stored on my comtel."

"I'll find it. You rest, ladybird. He'll be with you soon, I promise."

Constance's twinges were a false alarm, but Modesty was delegated to sit with her the next day. Constance had tried to protest that Harper would look after her, but had been told it was too weighty a duty for a man, and that she was too precious to Sisterland for chances to be taken. Either she let a responsible sister sit with her, or she'd be sent at once to sourcingplace.

Constance lay like a beached starfish on the couch, only half-listening to Modesty talking about a job she was due to start.

"I know you recommended me – I'm grateful," said Modesty. "Someone called Unity, from the Tower matingplace, is assigned to work with me. I hope she understands I'm the boss."

The word 'matingplace' snagged Constance's attention. "What exactly is your new job, Modesty?"

"I'm on the team overseeing the closure of matingplace."

"It's really happening?"

"No more babyfusion permits," said Modesty.

Harper emerged from the bedroom, where he had been making preparations to leave for work. Head tilted to the side, Modesty made a leisurely examination of him from tip to toe. He ignored her as he hunkered down beside Constance.

"I'm off now, Constance. Make sure you rest today. There's food in the cupboard if you don't feel like going to the dine-all." He lifted one of her hands, and kissed it.

"Introduce us, Constance," said Modesty.

"Modesty, meet Harper. Harper, this is Modesty. My friend." Constance liked having someone she could call a friend. She felt blessed.

Her friend and her lover exchanged glances – cautious on Harper's part, curious on Modesty's. He stood up and moved about the room, putting items in a bag.

"There are no men in my unit yet," said Modesty.

"Really?" Constance adjusted her position, and rubbed at the small of her back. "I thought integration was beginning."

"Unlicensed mating isn't happening yet, either. It's allowed in theory. In practice, it's difficult to arrange."

"Difficult, how?"

"How are sisters supposed to find meets? At least everyone knew what was expected of them at matingplace."

Harper's expression puckered during this exchange. "If you need me, Constance, I'm working in a park near the planetarium. I can be home quickly."

"Harper's been assigned to a project to make parks more hospitable to wild birds," said Constance.

"He used to work in matingplace, didn't he?" said Modesty.

"Ask him yourself."

Modesty raised her eyes to Harper's face. "Didn't you work in matingplace?"

He took his time about answering. "Yes. In the Tower."

"Did you enjoy your work?"

"No."

"Why not?"

"Harper was thrown out of matingplace for refusing Himtime on demand," said Constance.

"I'm all for unlicensed mating. But how does a woman find suitable meets?" said Modesty. "Harper, are you in touch with any of the matingplace men? Could you act as a go-between?"

Harper bridled, and Constance said quickly, "Modesty, leave him alone. He doesn't like being reminded of his time there. I'm sorry, Harper. She doesn't mean any harm."

Modesty was mystified. "Being a meet was a plum job. What's not to like?"

"You really want to know? Everything about Himtime

chipped away at us." Harper used his fingers to tap off a list. "Being expected to do it night after night. Being given drugs to make sure we did. Drugs which shortened our lives. Doing it with strangers. Not having the right to say no. Or to choose who we mated with."

Modesty held up her hands. "OK, I surrender. No offence, Harper. Sometimes, I speak first and think afterwards. I have some good points, too, all right?"

"I'm used to women's ignorance about what life's like for men."

"So, if you happen to know any former meets who miss their old life . . ."

"She's incorrigible, Harper," said Constance. "Take no notice. She also has a weird sense of humour."

"I'll be late for work. There's a spare cushion for your back in the bedroom, if you need it. Are you sure babyfusion won't happen today? I worry about you when I'm out at work."

"No need to fret. Honestly. The medico Devotion sent for yesterday tested me. The date selected for birth activation hasn't been overridden. She gave me a shot, just to make sure."

He kissed her on the lips, while Modesty stared open-mouthed.

"Don't forget your hood," Constance reminded him.

"In my pocket."

He nodded at Modesty, and turned towards the door.

As it opened for him, Modesty said to Constance, "You know, he's the first man I've had a conversation with. A real conversation, I mean. I suspect it's because he wasn't wearing a hood. Hoods create distance."

Harper stopped. "They do more than that. They create suspicion."

Modesty shrugged. "I prefer no hoods."

"Why?"

"I like to see men's faces. Some are handsome. It's a

pleasure to admire beauty. I appreciate flowers. Why not men?"

Against his will, he laughed, and the door closed behind him.

Thoughtful, Modesty said, "He thinks for himself. How does Patience get on with him?"

"Hasn't met him yet. Too busy being the instigator of the Silent Revolution."

"Does she have an other?"

"No, she's a workaholic."

"We all have to make time for relaxation, Constance. It's time I found an other."

"Female or male?"

"Can men be others? Surely that's a step too far."

"I think of Harper as my other. I'm not the only one. I know of several sisters, well-connected, with male others, too."

"Even if I wanted one, I can't get to know any men. Not properly. And definitely not improperly. How did women and men meet in PS days?"

"Social activities."

"Ah, that's where we're going wrong. There's no inter-gender socialising."

"Well then, Modesty, you could always nominate yourself to start some. In the meantime, look around you. You'll see plenty of men. They travel on the Buzz now: that's one place to get to know them. They walk in parks. That's another. And they receive payment for their work, so they can afford to go into eat-easies. You can sit at their table and talk to them. Sooner rather than later, women and men will become better acquainted. It's inevitable."

"I suppose. But women will have to do all the running – men are nervous of us. You've no idea how cagey they look when I approach them."

"Come on, you're well able to do the running, Modesty!"

"I know I'm able for it, but that doesn't mean I want to do it. At least, not all the time." Modesty was wistful. "I might want someone to run after me, for a change."

"That's possible, in this new version of Sisterland. It was never likely under the previous one."

"Why, Constance, you're promoting the Silent Revolution. You told me you only did that on public forums."

Constance was startled. Modesty was right: she'd gone native.

That night, Harper sat Constance on a high stool in the bathroom, and washed her hair at the sink, because she could not manage to bend over the basin by herself. As he massaged her scalp, she asked him what he made of Modesty.

"That woman is a force of nature. She wants to have it all. She's going to be our neighbour in this unit one of these days, with a male other in tow. If not a pair of them."

"It's only a matter of time," agreed Constance. "But why shouldn't she have it all? As a woman getting her hair lathered up, I'm in no position to point the finger!"

"You're babyfused. And due into sourcingplace tomorrow. You deserve to be pampered tonight."

His movements were tender as he wrapped a towel round her head, and helped her off the stool.

"All the same," Constance added, "why shouldn't Modesty have it all?"

Hand under her elbow, he guided her into the bedroom. "If she has it all at somebody else's expense, that's why not."

"A man's, I presume?"

He helped her into the pop-up, propped pillows behind her back, and returned to the bathroom. Constance knew he was turning over what they were discussing, and did not press him. Finger-combing her damp hair, she watched him through the open door. He funnelled the used water from the sink into a basin, and carried it outside to water the garden. Harper was growing vegetables in a patch Constance had secured for him in the communal green area.

On his return, he said, "Some women aren't making space for men in this new world of theirs."

"I'm making space."

"You're in a minority."

"No, I'm not. You, Harper the Forester turned Vegetable-grower, are impatient. But I love you anyway."

She waited. He didn't say he loved her back. But he found a cushion for her feet, tweaking her toes as he lifted them. Her playful protest brought a smile to his face. She wished he could accept that improvements had happened, and more would follow. Harper's scepticism about the changing face of Sisterland made her anxious.

For him, and their baby. Constance had to believe the three of them had a future together here. She had too much invested in the new Sisterland.

"Patience came to see me today," said Constance. "While you were at work. She offered a peer escort and private vehicle to take me to sourcingplace. She said I was in a sacred condition, and every care had to be taken of the baby."

"What did you say?" Harper stopped what he was doing, waiting for her answer.

"I said no, I mustn't set myself apart. I thought Patience was going to insist. But she told me she approved of this act of self-denial, and she'd make sure other sisters heard about it. It's proof we're all treated equally in the new Sisterland."

Harper didn't reply. Uneasy, Constance read his thoughts without mindmapping him. She lived in a threeser in private grounds with a man. She wasn't treated the same as her sisters.

Chapter 37

Constance, Devotion and Goodwill waited for a Buzz to take them to sourcingplace. Devotion and Goodwill had insisted on accompanying her, which pleased Constance.

"I hope you're up to raising a baby, Constance," said Devotion. "Personally, I was relieved when you went to girlplace."

"Though you'd never have let her go if you'd known about the Nine's blood-harvesting," said Goodwill.

"Of course not," said Devotion. "Still, it's a big responsibility to care for a child. I always thought the Nine was right about it – it's too important to let it be an amateur occupation."

"I have Harper to help me."

Devotion looked sceptical, but at a nudge from Goodwill she let it pass.

Behind the women, the station wall was covered by a hologram: a stylised representation of the Silenced in black, white and red. In the first image, scarlet scarves bound their mouths. But the hologram flickered to show the Silenced untying their scarves. And in the final image, each of the Silenced held her scarf aloft, its tail streaming behind. Impossible to miss, the tableau was lasered onto the sides of public buildings, onto Buzzes, onto bridges – all except the Hope Bridge, reserved for Silence's face.

"Personally, I'm tired of this image cropping up everywhere." Devotion jerked her head towards the Silenced hologram writhing the length of the oncoming train. "I liked the Buzz better with nothing on the side."

"These images give substance to our new Sisterland," said Goodwill. "Images stop time – they become eternal. And eternity is the message we seek to convey. Sisterland will continue. Its future is in no doubt."

Constance kept her attention on her bump. That was the future she was interested in. The all-pervasive imagery of Silence and the Silenced in the new Sisterland surprised her – she thought Patience had gone overboard on it. But Patience argued that Silence helped them achieve their goal of easing the transition, and Constance accepted that. Mostly.

She allowed her gaze to meander about the carriage. A hooded man, accompanied by a senior Sistercentral official, sat at the back. He never lifted his eyes from the ground. Space was left around the couple, some sisters preferring to stand rather than sit beside them. But Constance saw the woman travelling with him stroke his arm in reassurance.

The train began slowing into a station.

"Excuse me, aren't you Silence's other?" a sister waiting to disembark said to Constance.

"I was."

The passenger was reverent. "They say your baby will be Silence reincarnated. Sisterland thanks you for it. We celebrate your fertility." The woman gave a radiant smile, and stepped onto the platform.

Constance sighed, resigned. Sisters were expecting too much from her baby. But Patience was keen on the reincarnation theory – she said it would be another stepping stone in fostering a sense of continuity. And Constance didn't want to challenge her on it – what if Patience reneged on letting her keep her baby?

"You ought to put a stop to that story, ladybird," said Devotion. "Why didn't you say something, Goodwill?"

"It could be useful."

Devotion snorted.

Goodwill and Constance exchanged glances, guilty but complicit.

"I felt sorry for Harper this morning," said Goodwill. "He looked left out."

"You won't forget your promise?"

"I won't."

That morning, trying to mask his hurt, Harper had walked her to the Buzz station where Goodwill and Devotion were waiting. Goodwill had spoken to him, but Devotion had kept her distance, turning away pointedly as Harper had hugged Constance.

"I'll make sure you're told about the baby as soon as we have news, Harper," Goodwill had offered. "And don't worry, we'll see good care is taken of Constance."

Harper had been reluctant to say goodbye. Even after he did, he had retraced his steps to hold her once again, resting his forehead against hers, sharing her breath. A ripple of puzzlement had managed to work its way onto Devotion's skin.

Now, the Buzz wended its way to sourcingplace, past Hope Bridge.

Devotion looked out at the Silence hologram, its face ethereal. "You never really know someone, do you? Such a waste."

"It wasn't wasted. Silence is the match that lit the flame," said Goodwill.

"Silence should have taken up gardening or winemaking. They'd have soothed her troubles."

"Patience is in awe of Silence," said Goodwill. "At one stage, planning the Silent Revolution, she considered copycat episodes at the Hope Bridge. I've no doubt volunteers would have queued up to do it, too. 'Think of the symbolism!' said Patience. 'Think of the losses!' I told her. Thankfully, she listened." She noticed Constance shudder, and said quickly, "What a treat to have a new baby among us. Were you never tempted, Constance, to discover the gender in advance?"

"Never." Constance stroked her belly. "Thank you for coming to sourcingplace with me."

"We know you'd prefer that man beside you," said Devotion.

"Harper."

"Yes, him."

"His name is Harper, Devotion. Can't you bring yourself to say it?"

"Harper. There! Satisfied?"

"We're here with you, since Harper can't be," Goodwill intervened. "Naturally, we wouldn't dream of letting you go on your own."

"You'll keep your promise, Goodwill? The minute the baby arrives? He'll be fretting."

"He'll be the first person I tell. After Patience, obviously."

"You like him, don't you, Goodwill?"

"Yes, I do. He made a good job of the baby's cradle."

"Men have a knack for repetitive work," said Devotion.

In sourcingplace, still weak from the birth, Constance watched Devotion clucking over the baby. She rearranged the lilac blanket under the minuscule chin, and checked the temperature control on the wall panel.

"Such a teeny-tiny scrap," said Devotion. "It's hard to believe she weighs more than you did, Constance. She looks so delicate. Such a button of a nose. Look at her wrinkle it up, Goodwill. Isn't she adorable?"

"Harper knows you have a daughter," said Goodwill. "I transmitted an image to the unit-minder's comtel, and she called up to him."

"Did he say anything?"

"He said she was beautiful. And he asked how you were. I told him you took to sourcing like a fish to water."

Devotion poked the tip of her smallest finger into the baby's fist. "You know, Constance, I think she looks like me."

"I see Goodwill in her," said Constance.

"Impossible." Devotion bent low, smelling the milky breath.

"You see what you see and I see what I see."

Goodwill's eyes were luminous as they made contact with Constance's.

Immediately after the birth, Constance had been disappointed to learn her baby's gender: she had longed to be in the vanguard of sisters refusing to relinquish a son. Her hope was that it might help Harper to feel valued, in turn. They'd bring up a son in exactly the same way as they'd raise a daughter, and he'd understand Sisterland had changed beyond recognition. But as soon as her daughter was placed in her arms, Constance knew that a girl was exactly what she wanted. And not just any girl, but this one.

On the third day, eager to let Harper hold their baby, she told the sourcingplace staff she wanted to go home. They tried to dissuade her, but she explained she would avail of special transport for her daughter's sake.

"It takes time to recover from birth-activation procedures," said the medico who delivered her. "You're one of the fortunate few with a private room, and help at the touch of call-screen. Avail of it while you can."

Privileges were seductive – there was no doubt about it. It was something Constance told herself she'd guard against when she was in the whole of her health. Right now, allowances had to be made.

"Stay on in sourcingplace for a third night," Goodwill urged, while Devotion was out buying snacks for them.

"I can't. Harper will be miserable. He's separated from me and his daughter."

"If he cares about you, he'll understand."

"I must admit, my body aches."

"How about if I stop by the threeser and answer all of Harper's questions in person? Would that persuade you to stay in sourcingplace for another night?"

"Would you? That would make me feel a little bit better about him. He's being left out. It isn't fair. He hasn't even seen our baby yet – just a tiny image on someone else's comtel screen."

"Of course I would. I'll go now if you like. I can't see Devotion coming with me, though."

"She thinks it's none of Harper's business," said Constance.

"In fairness, Devotion can't tear herself away from sourcingplace – she's fallen unconditionally in love with the baby. Who'd have predicted it?" Goodwill pulled a comical face.

Constance couldn't help laughing, although she winced at the spasm it shot through her body.

"I'll go to see Harper now, before Devotion comes back and tries to talk me out of it. Although the way she's going, all we can expect out of her is babytalk from now on."

"Tell him I love him," said Constance.

Goodwill tried to hide it, but a scandalised expression settled into the grooves on her skin.

Just then, Patience arrived to inspect the new arrival, Devotion entering the room behind her.

"Your daughter will be an icon, Constance," said Patience.

"She's a baby," said Devotion. "Time enough for anything else."

Patience paid no attention. "What will you call her? Silence has an appropriate ring."

"I'm leaving our daughter's name to her father," said

Constance. "He's choosing it."

Patience arched an eyebrow.

"Have you met Harper, Patience?" Goodwill intervened. "He's an impressive man. I believe we could work with him."

"Not just yet, Goodwill. Our focus must be on consolidation. Cooperation will follow, in due course. When do you suppose you'll be well enough to speak again in public, Constance?"

"Soon. I have ideas I want to share."

"Such as?'

"Skins. I don't want my daughter to grow up wearing one."

"But what about her face?" protested Devotion. "She'll get wrinkles!"

"It's a cage. I don't believe we need them. They stop us reading moes on one another's faces. Some women are already going without skins. And the sky hasn't fallen in."

Patience touched her bare face with her fingertips. "Going skinless feels odd to me, still. I don't feel able to do without it every day. But I'm building up to it. It's important to lead by example."

Devotion struggled with what she was hearing. "But their faces!"

"Will age. In line with the rest of their bodies. It's natural," said Patience. "Skin removal won't be mandatory, Devotion. In time, we hope sisters will see the benefits outweigh the disadvantages. Goodwill isn't convinced yet, are you?"

"Not yet," said Goodwill. "But it's wonderful to see women taking personal responsibility."

"Without skins, we'll become more experienced at channelling moes," said Constance. "I'm going to deliver my next speech without a skin on. In fact, I'm leaving it off permanently from now on. I took it off when I arrived in sourcingplace, and haven't had it on again since. My baby's first day in Sisterland was day one of my new skin-free life."

"Skin removal is certainly something you could discuss in your speech," said Patience. "Though your audience may not be as big as previous ones. Our sisters seem a little weary of public addresses."

"That's because you have so many of them," said Devotion.

"I'll stand on park benches to talk about skins if that's the only audience I can reach," said Constance. "Sooner or later, I'll get through to them. I know I will."

Patience nodded. Then, as if the idea had just struck her, she suggested, "You should bring your daughter along. What a compelling image that would make!"

"She's too young yet for public events – she needs time to grow."

"It's never too soon to serve Sisterland."

"Patience, she's a few days old!"

"Our children aren't intended for our own personal enjoyment. They're only on loan to their sources."

Constance heard a ringing in her ears. She cuddled her daughter closer, conscious that if Patience said the word, she could be snatched away. Eyes tight shut, the baby stirred and nuzzled towards her. Protectiveness rose up in Constance. But fear nudged into its slipstream.

"Constance's just had a baby," said Goodwill. "Time enough for such talk."

Patience held up her hands in mock-capitulation, before saying she had to leave. Goodwill asked for a lift to Constance's threeser, since Patience had a private vehicle permanently at her disposal. "To pick up some bits and pieces for Constance," Goodwill explained. Harper wasn't mentioned.

Devotion lingered after the others had gone. "They'll be talking about you," she told Constance.

"I can't bring my baby along when I speak in public. She's too small."

"Of course it's wrong. But they won't see it that way. Isn't turning her into a symbol part of the plan?"

"I guess. But I didn't think it would happen so soon. I just thought of it as a way to be with Harper, and now our daughter."

"A high price, ladybird. Take care your daughter doesn't feel used, when she's older."

Chapter 38

Harper was showing his daughter an apple tree in the private garden attached to the unit. "See the shape the branches make? Isn't that prettier than all the bangles and earrings those women who visit you wear?" She cooed in her father's arms. "In springtime, there'll be white blossom. But no apples on this tree, I think. Why don't we plant a fruit tree of our own? We could watch it grow, from a sapling to a tree that's as tall as the roof. Would you like that?"

A vehicle pulled into the courtyard, and he stepped out of sight. A woman he didn't recognise emerged, followed by Devotion and Goodwill. They were attentive to a fourth woman, who creaked as she moved, like the apple tree. He recognised her from the entscreen: it was Gracious. The first woman appeared to have high status, judging from the way the others behaved towards her. Even Devotion approached her with wary respect. She must be a member of the Co-Equals, thought Harper – the ruling body which had replaced the Nine.

He heard them discuss a woman who had shaken her fist at their vehicle.

"Too much moe – they're not used to it. It makes them giddy. Disobedient, too. I can't believe she didn't apologise.

She said she just didn't think personal carriers were fair," said the sister he didn't recognise. "Moe deregulation happened too suddenly. We ought to add suppressants to the water, the way the Nine did."

"But spontaneity has come back to us," said Gracious. "Surely some impulsive behaviour – a little recklessness – is a small price to pay?"

The unfamiliar sister sniffed. "Yesterday, I saw a sister walking along the street crying uncontrollably. When I asked her what the matter was, she said she didn't know. She just felt sad."

"Sometimes people do," said Goodwill. "It's not the end of the world. It's abnormal for people to be contented all the time – that's one of the wrong turns the Nine took."

"Too much moe slows productivity." The tall sister was disapproving. "We'll have to take action. When people are emotional they can do rash things. Surely you see that, Goodwill?"

"I've heard some sisters are starting to turn up late for work, or question their superiors' decisions," admitted Goodwill. "I've also noticed more sisters skipping queues."

"Our unit is noisier," said Devotion. "But I can't say I object. Sometimes it was too quiet."

Gracious spoke up. "Patience, has the Silent Revolution changed its mind about free, limitless access to moes? Already? That didn't take long!"

So, the important sister was Patience, thought Harper. Instinctively, he drew the baby closer to the shelter of his body.

"We believe in deregulation in principle," said Patience. "But some of our sisters need to learn how to deal with moes. Perhaps moe-handling lessons. I'll raise it at the next Co-Equals meeting."

"Gracious, we shouldn't keep you standing around," said Goodwill. "Let's go inside to Constance. Lean on my arm."

Harper knew he ought to go indoors so they could meet the

baby – that must be the reason why these dignitaries were calling. But he lingered outside, still talking to the tiny girl in his arms about the tree they sheltered under – a dwarf compared with the ones in his forest, but just as beautiful, he told her. Prominent Sisterlanders held no interest for Harper. Nor did he care for the thought of his daughter being exposed to them. Though he knew he'd fight a losing battle to prevent it.

Constance appeared in the garden, calling his name. "Gracious wonders if she could meet our daughter, Harper."

"I saw her with the one who calls herself the First Co-Equal."

"Yes, Patience is here, too. You need to be polite to her, Harper." He scowled. "Sorry, I didn't mean that the way it sounded. But she matters. Don't antagonise her. Please. For me."

"If she's the First Co-Equal, what does that make Goodwill?"

"Her deputy."

"Second Co-Equal?"

"Don't be mischievous, Harper. You know very well there's no such title. Only Patience is numbered – the rest of the eighteen are Co-Equals. Plain and simple."

"Not quite equals, then. Just like you and me." Harper stretched out his arms to pass the baby to Constance, intending to stay outside.

But she shook her head. "No, you carry her up. I want everyone to see how much our little girl loves her father."

"Including Patience?"

"Especially Patience."

As they walked indoors, Constance remarked, "I haven't seen Gracious since the baby. She's ageing visibly. I don't know how long she'll be able to carry on working with us."

He didn't reply. But in the foyer, he hesitated. "Do I need to put on a hood?"

"Not in your home." She laid a hand between his shoulder-blades, encouraging him forward.

"Here she is," Devotion sang out. "Here's my angel!" She hurried forward to tickle the baby in her father's arms, and was rewarded with a gurgle.

Harper inclined his head to the visitors but kept his distance, until Gracious spoke directly to him.

"You've bonded with your daughter," she told him.

"I'm her father," he answered.

She was older than any sister he had met before, yet her eyes glowed at his answer, and he couldn't tell if she approved or disapproved of it. Nor did he care. She beckoned, and he carried the child over to her.

Gracious rested her palm against the velvet skull, and closed her eyes, smiling. Everyone watched her. Abruptly, her eyes flew open, and the smile collapsed into a semi-circle of surprise. But she recovered herself, and trailed an index finger along the baby's cheek.

"What?" demanded Patience.

"Nothing. She'll lead a fascinating life," she said. "The sights this tiny creature is destined to see!"

"Surely you can intuit something about her future?"

"I told you what I sensed, Patience."

"I get the impression you know more than you're saying." Patience turned her attention to Harper. "Why doesn't he give the child to someone else to hold? Why must he keep her in his arms?"

"He can't bear to let our daughter out of his sight. He's taken to childcare far better than me," said Constance. Patience pursed her lips, and Constance found herself gabbling. "Even when she sleeps, he hovers by her cradle listening to her breathe, or marvelling at the way her hands curl and uncurl. He's absolutely besotted with our baby."

"She's not just your baby, you know," said Patience. "She belongs to Sisterland."

Harper stiffened, but was sidetracked by a question from Gracious.

"I understand Constance is granting you the privilege of naming the child. Have you reached a decision?"

Patience answered for him. "It would be fitting to call her Silence."

Harper's face grew stony. "She has a name. It's not Silence. That was never considered."

"I see." Patience was equally unyielding. "You must have an exceptional name in mind, to reject Silence. May we know it?"

"Faithful."

Constance was surprised. Nothing had been settled – they had discussed several possibilities, but Faithful hadn't figured. All of the possible names they had talked about were associated with plants and creatures in the Brown Convolution forest.

Patience made latticework of her fingers, and examined the shape. "Faithful. Not what we were expecting at all."

"It's perfect," said Devotion.

"It's a wasted opportunity." Patience turned to Constance. "Has it been sigged yet? If not, there's still time."

"It hasn't been sigged," said Constance. "But Harper has chosen Faithful, so Faithful is her name." She went to him, and leaned over the baby in the crook of his arms. "Hello, Faithful. Your name suits you." She touched their daughter's dimpled fist. "We'll go together today and sig her name."

Constance could log it without Harper, but he was not permitted to do it without Constance. She hoped he wouldn't raise this discrepancy in front of Patience. At least now his name would appear on the registration, after Constance's.

"Well, of course, it's entirely down to you, Constance. I mean, to both of you," said Patience. "But what if there are tens of thousands of Faithfuls logged ahead of her? You don't want her to have a long list of numbers after her name."

"Does she need numbers after her name?" asked Constance. "Couldn't we come up with another solution?"

Gracious tilted her head to one side. "It's a point worth discussing. Isn't it, Patience?"

"We could consider alternatives at our next meeting of the Co-Equals," agreed Patience. "I've never much cared for the 66003 after my name."

"Two Co-Equals in the family: Goodwill and Constance," said Devotion. "We're rising at a dizzying pace. I hope nobody here suffers from altitude sickness."

"You misunderstand Constance's role. She's not exactly a Co-Equal, but she attends meetings and we like to consult with her," said Patience.

"Her voice is influential," said Goodwill.

"Naturally. Who wouldn't listen to the source who's given us Silence reincarnated?" said Patience.

Constance was used to Patience's attempts to claim a mystical kinship between the baby and Silence, but this was the first time for Harper. Shock, followed by dismay, chased away by anger, criss-crossed his face. He slanted a challenge at Constance. Her eyes pleaded with his: *Don't say anything, I can explain*. Rigid, Harper turned his back on her, and took a few paces towards Patience. Constance braced herself for a storm.

Unexpectedly, Devotion saved the day by voicing the protest Patience would never have tolerated from a man.

"What mumbo-jumbo! My granddaughter's nobody's reincarnation. She's a baby. Herself, and nobody else. Besides, that's a ridiculously heavy burden to place on any child. Those sorts of expectations will gobble the wee mite whole. Don't you think so, Goodwill?"

Goodwill's eyes slid away. "It's only a name."

"It's more than that and you know it, Goodwill!"

Gracious spoke up. "Why don't I hold Faithful, Harper? She must be getting heavy."

Harper stayed where he was, chin jutting out.

"You must learn to share her," said Patience. "She might not always be in your care."

His eyes splintered at Patience, and Faithful squawked at the pressure from his fingers on her chubby limbs. Frightened now, Constance moved forward, on the pretext of lifting Faithful out of his arms. Her face was wreathed in warning. She uncoiled his hands from their baby, and transferred the warm, small body to Gracious.

Gracious rested Faithful against her neck, and sighed with pleasure as the baby squirmed against her. "What a clever girl you are, to have a name that suits you so exactly."

Harper folded his empty arms, missing his daughter's weight already. He retreated into a corner and watched Patience, who ignored him.

Shortly after, the visitors took their leave, but the atmosphere did not lighten. On the contrary, Harper rounded on Constance, demanding answers. Why was she allowing their baby to be used as a symbol of Silence? How could she stand by and listen to that ridiculous reincarnation claim?

"It's only a bit of silliness," she tried telling him. But when he continued to argue, she said, "Harper, Patience could have Faithful taken away from us with one snap of the fingers. This is part of the deal that lets us keep her with us. And lets you raise her."

"You used our baby as a bargaining chip?"

"What choice did I have?"

Harper shook his head slowly, silently, sorrowfully. But Faithful squeaked, kicking her feet in the air. And some of his tension ebbed away.

The Silent Revolution continued to put down roots. Baby boys were no longer taken from their sources, while boyplace was closed down and boys were educated alongside girls. Flocks of children, girls and boys, mingled freely: it became commonplace to see them with their teachers on the Buzz, going on educational trips, or walking in crocodiles through the parks, having flowers and plants pointed out. Hutchtown was disbanded, and men began to live in units alongside the ones which housed women, although mixed accommodation was not yet permitted. At least, not officially. However, more senior sisters started asking for male others.

Among these developments came an unexpected shift. With matingplace disbanded, more boys began to be born. It was too soon to call it a trend. There were no guarantees it would continue. Scientists were puzzled by it. But the reversal of rigid mating protocols began to percolate through to the birth statistics.

As agreed, Constance spoke at rallies, polishing the new version of Sisterland, but had no involvement in daily decision-making. She hoped, by influencing audiences, to create a public mood for ongoing change. The risk was that sisters would accept a regime change, but prefer life to continue undisturbed.

"Sometimes, ladybird, I think Goodwill suspects she's created a monster in you," said Devotion. She maintained her refusal to join the work of the Silenced. But she was not at cross-purposes with them, either. She was allowed to retire from thought-hatching, because her department was being dismantled, along with thought-mending and crafting.

There were still shapers, however. Their skills were required. New orders need old hands, as Modesty put it to Constance. She knew it was said tongue-in-cheek. One of these days, she must introduce her source to Modesty – the two of them would get along.

Nowadays, Devotion concentrated on the garden Goodwill had been able to secure for her, not far from their twoser – and on Faithful. She took to bringing Harper some of her wine. Sometimes, after Faithful's bath, she'd stay and share a glass with him, talking about the herbs she liked to grow, and the vegetables she was experimenting with – his green fingers impressed her. When he expressed an interest in how the wine was made, she offered to teach him.

"More than she ever did for me," said Constance, when Harper reported it. She alternated between amusement and irritation at her source's developing relationship with Harper. Of course, it was better to have them on friendly terms. They had not just Faithful, but their love of nature in common. But sometimes they she felt a tiny bit excluded, especially when they were outdoors.

Harper sprang fully to life outside. By the riverbank, he was the first to spot fish or insects, and to point them out. If Devotion was with them, as she often was during strolls with Faithful, her source was always fascinated by what he said – whereas sometimes Constance had to fake an interest, preoccupied with her work for the Silenced regime. Harper could not pass near a tree without drawing attention to the patterns on the bark. "Touch it," he'd invite. "Doesn't it feel more real than anything you've ever put your hand on?" It felt appealing, of course. But reshaping Sisterland – that was what truly felt real to Constance.

One day, when Faithful was about eighteen months old, Harper suggested a family daytrip, just the three of them – a visit with Faithful to a copse of trees at the end of the Buzz line. Constance had to cry off at the last minute because of a hastily convened Co-Equals meeting, but Devotion volunteered to take her place.

That night, when Constance returned home to the threeser, she found Faithful in her pop-up, and Devotion still lingering, chatting with Harper.

"We saw copper beeches. Faithful clapped her hands at their blaze of colour," Devotion reported. "Didn't she, Harper?"

"Her face, at the sound of the leaves underfoot! I thought she was going to jump out of my arms!"

"And the way she crunched leaves between her fists, trying to cram them into her mouth!"

The warmth between them was unmistakeable. Constance knew she should feel pleased. And she did. But she also felt left out.

When Devotion went home, Harper said, "Devotion loved the crackle of twigs underfoot – she said it was a forgotten sound in Sisterland. Nothing's ever allowed to lie where it falls here. I've tried to suggest it at work, in the parks, but nobody listens. I told Devotion, and she says the tidiness impulse has been carried too far."

"Sounds as if you and Devotion had plenty to talk about. All she ever does is scold me for overwork."

"You do work too hard. You'd have had fun if you'd come with us, Constance."

"I'd have liked to go. But duty before fun, I'm afraid. I can't miss Co-Equal meetings."

"Come and sit down. You look tired." He perched beside her, and began to rub her shoulders. "Have you eaten?"

"Goodwill always makes sure there's food at the meetings."

The kneading slowed. "Constance, do the Co-Equals ever discuss Outsideland?"

"No, we're too busy with Sisterland. I did ask about the man from Outsideland. I thought I might have been able to do something for him. Too late. He'd been discontinued. Don't stop, Harper, I'm stiff from sitting in meetings all day." She rotated her neck, relaxing under his massage. "There's been a setback. That's why the meeting was called. I'm not supposed to talk about this – it's top secret. To do with the Nine."

"I thought the five who held out were relocated to one of the outer belts? Didn't they give guarantees about living quietly there?"

"That's what they promised to do. But Innocence and Temperance doubled back from Grey Disjoint. They headed for Righteous, they're trying to form a rival government there."

"Is it really a threat?"

"It's a thorn in the flesh, more than a threat. All the key institutions are based in Harmony, so they can't disrupt the machinery of the State. But it's disloyal. And dishonest. Patience says it's treacherous, and can't be tolerated. A solution will have to be found to deal with them. I suppose they'll be put under some sort of restraint."

"You mean Safe Space? Like the woman you talked about in your sleep last night?"

Startled, Constance asked, "Who did I talk about?"

"You called her 'mother'."

"The Shaper Mother. She's on her way to Safe Space, for subversive activities. While she was under house arrest, she tried to slip away and join the remnants of the Nine in Righteous. What did I say about her?"

"'Forgive me, mother'. You said it over and over. I wiped away a tear on your cheek."

"I did my best for the mother. I spoke up for her when the Co-Equals were trying to decide what to do with her. I'm sorry she's gone to Safe Space. I wish it could have been different."

"Maybe you should have seen her before she was ordered to Safe Space."

Constance hesitated. "I didn't want to," she admitted.

"Because she makes you doubt what you're doing?"

"She has a particular way with her. She puts me on the back foot. Harper, how do you think the Co-Equals ought to deal with these remnants of the Nine? There was division at our meeting."

"In the forest, I saw how the hungriest took chances. Their teeth weren't the sharpest, neither were their claws, but they were the most dangerous animals. They had nothing to lose."

Constance shivered. "We can't use force – that's contrary

to everything Sisterland believes in. Yet some kind of action will have to be taken against them. Patience thinks they ought to be arrested, and given treatment to make them understand the importance of obedience. But that sounds like MUM – a barbaric place. We closed it down. You see, Harper, there's still so much to be done in Sisterland. So much to be decided. Outsideland can wait."

"It can't wait. Sisterland has to start reaching out to neighbours. Otherwise, this new Sisterland will be just as inward-looking as the old one."

Constance stood up, and stretched. "Contact is a good idea, in principle. But not yet."

"Have you any idea, Constance, how often you say 'not yet'?"

Despite this minor disagreement, Harper was upbeat for days afterwards. His pleasure in the trip away from Harmony reminded Constance how much sustenance he drew from his forest, but she pushed away the thought. Harmony was their home, and her work lay there. She was helping to shape the future.

Chapter 39

For days, the Shaper Mother's fate troubled Constance. Try though she might, she couldn't ignore it. She told herself the distance to Safe Space, thousands of miles away in Black Particle, was an impediment. But she knew she could apply for transport, provided the visit was approved. *Stay away*, said the voice of reason in her head. *You must see her*, argued her residual sense of loyalty.

Finally, she requested a travel permit, and a day pass into Safe Space. Both Patience and Goodwill questioned her about her reasons. However, they were satisfied with her explanation: she had enjoyed a special relationship with the mother. If anyone could reach her and persuade her to accept the error of her ways, it was Constance.

"And who knows? I might be able to bring her round to our way of thinking," Constance said to Harper, when she told him she had been authorised to go.

He looked resigned, and she couldn't resist tiptoeing into his mind. She wanted him to be happy. She was mindmapping him for both their sakes.

Your way of thinking? It's the Co-Equals' way – not yours, Constance.

"Don't do that!" he snapped.

359

"I'm sorry. I only did it because I'm worried about you."

"Not as worried as I am about you."

Constance told herself they just needed to spend some time together – that would ease the tensions between them. Impulsively, she suggested, "Why don't you come with me? It would do us both good to get out of Harmony. I know Black Particle's not supposed to be all that appealing, but maybe we could stop off somewhere on the way home. In your belt, perhaps? Why not? You could show me your forest."

His face lightened. "The butterflies will be out now. Think of Faithful's face when she sees them!"

She hesitated, unwilling to dampen his enthusiasm, and yet doubtful that the Co-Equals would give their daughter a travel permit. There was a grand design involving Faithful – which she hadn't told Harper about – to take her on a procession through Sisterland, to present her to the people, when she was three years old. It was to be a choreographed unveiling of the figurehead child who represented Sisterland's future. The Co-Equals intended to be alongside her when it happened. "Wouldn't it be too much for her? Why don't we leave Faithful with Devotion, and spend some time together, just you and me? There'll be other trips we can take with Faithful."

"We'd be gone for a couple of weeks, Constance. It's too long to leave her. Even with Devotion. Please. Ask for a permit."

As Constance had suspected, the Co-Equals regretfully declined permission for Faithful to go with them. Harper's anger shook Constance.

"Even if you don't mind for yourself, doesn't the level of control they have over Faithful's life bother you?" he asked.

"They're just worried something might happen to her."

"I'll tell you what really bothers them. They're afraid if they let the three of us go away together, we might make a run for it. They have plans for Faithful. You know they do."

"I suppose they see her as some kind of totem. I try not to think about it. I'm just glad we can keep her with us."

"How long before she's given a formal role? How long before she's taken away from us?"

"Harper, I'm doing my best here. For all of us. Where's the harm in letting Patience include Faithful in some of the Co-Equals' plans? Not now, of course. But later, when she's older. I can protect her. Goodwill will help me."

"Do you really believe there's no harm, Constance? Or have you tricked yourself into believing it?"

Black Particle was not an easy place to reach, even for a sister as important as Constance. She was flown there, in a plane previously reserved for use by the Nine, craning her neck at take-off and landing to see Sisterland from the air. Black Particle was as different from Harmony as night from day. After landing in the most remote belt, she was glad of a personal carrier and guide to take her to Safe Space. No wonder the cities had grown up elsewhere.

Despite its gloomy setting, Safe Space was a well-lit complex of buildings humming with purpose. Those committed there couldn't leave – but that didn't mean it should be defined as a prison, according to the scrutineer who admitted her. It wouldn't be practical to let them wander outside into such an inhospitable environment. They'd die of exposure. The locks were for their own protection.

She was brought into an area throbbing with activity. Safe Space was composed of fitness areas where constant exercise was encouraged and rewarded, to wear down excess energy. "It's for the best – our residents have to be kept too busy to think," said the scrutineer. "Thinking damaged them in the first place."

Constance found the Shaper Mother in the rowing-machine section, resplendent in a bodysuit. No environment could diminish her. She showed no surprise at Constance's arrival, although she hadn't been informed in advance. Standing up and stretching, she led her to a refreshment zone, where they were the only occupants: everyone else was focused on working out.

"No skin, Constance? Your face won't thank you for it, in future years."

"I always loved the onyx box you kept yours in, mother. I hope they let you take it to Safe Space? I wouldn't like to think of it going astray."

"I kept the box. You look different without your skin. Younger, oddly enough."

"You look different, too," said Constance. The Shaper Mother had lost weight, and no longer shaved her head, which was covered in a moss of cinnamon hair. It matched her eyes. "No shawl, mother? You barely seem dressed."

"Shawls tangle in the oars."

Constance laughed. "That's a disadvantage. Still, Safe Space agrees with your health. You look more rested than when I last saw you."

"I sleep like a baby here. Speaking of which, I believe you're a source. Congratulations. My idea, so I claim some of the credit."

"Yes, I owe my daughter partly to you."

Just then, a bell pinged.

"Covenant Time." The mother stood up. "The new Sisterland hasn't abandoned all the old ways." She joined hands with Constance, and together they chanted, "*To universal sisterhood! And brotherhood!*"

"Some of our sisters are reluctant to add the final part," said Constance.

"Change can be troubling."

"Unless it's handled properly. Mother, my daughter isn't the only debt I owe you. You shouldn't be in Safe Space. Isn't there some compromise we can agree that will allow you to leave?"

"It's not disagreeable. It operates on physical fitness principles, as an antidote to brooding."

"Does it work?"

"It tires you out. They have a team of bodies who train us on the machines, laden down with whistles and stop-watches and heart-monitors. They're relentless pearls. See that one over there?" She indicated a woman jogging on the spot. "She's one of the bodies. Zealous. Like all of them."

"That's Benevolence! I knew her in matingplace. She used to be a thought-cruncher."

The mother shrugged. "She's a body-cruncher now. Devoted to that whistle of hers. She operates the cycling machines."

"Benevolence!" Constance waved.

The woman ignored her.

She went across to her. "Benevolence, don't you know me?"

Benevolence looked at her without a trace of recognition. "Have we met?"

"At the Tower. The old matingplace in Oblong."

"You're mistaken, sister. I was never licensed to babyfuse."

Chilled, Constance returned to the Shaper Mother. "She doesn't know me."

"In Safe Space, some people forget."

"Their memories are deleted?"

"No, they choose to forget. Nobody is forced to do anything here. Even this exercise regime isn't mandatory. We can sit in our rooms all day if we prefer. But you start on the running machine to pass the time, and before you know it you're rowing, swimming and cycling. The only disadvantage with Safe Space is the obvious one. You can't leave. Well, that and the bodies. Their endless chirpiness would drive you to distraction, if you didn't block them out. Sometimes, I take a tiptoe round their minds. Just to see if they're as empty as they seem to be."

"Are they?"

"Oh yes. Apart from Benevolence's. Hers has a locked section. You'd never know it from her behaviour, though. She toots away on that whistle of hers, urging us all to go-go-go. At first, I didn't like them telling me what to do. But then I realised they knew their business. And I didn't have a business any more."

"But you could if you wanted, mother."

"I'm not a mother any more, I'm Honour 42."

"You'll always be mother to me."

"I hear you bring your daughter onstage with you now at rallies."

"It's to illustrate the new Sisterland. To point the way forward. Faithful helps me to show sisters how rewarding it is to keep your child, and raise her yourself. Under the old system, she'd be in girlplace by now."

"Faithful is being used, sweet child. Just like you're being used."

"I don't mind taking her with me. I can keep her safe. Sisters like to see her." Constance found she had to drop her eyes under the mother's steady attention.

"And so the transition from Sisterland Mark I to Sisterland Mark II continues, with everyone grist to the mill. I'll watch your new Utopia's progress with interest. No sign of any men being invited onto your Co-Equals group, so far. You still don't have total confidence in them, do you?"

"We have to be realistic."

An arc of teeth flashed. "That's what the Nine used to say."

"You see why we need you? You challenge us. Come and work with us. Help us. Help me."

The Shaper Mother shook her head. "There's too much change. I prefer it here in Safe Space, where stability's guaranteed."

"Oh, mother, you weren't born for stability. Think of what we could achieve, the two of us. Imagine the Sisterland we could build!"

"You really could get me out of here?"

"I think so, if I acted as your guarantor. I could ask – they like to keep me happy. I have something the Co-Equals prize."

"You'd be taking quite a chance on me. How do you know I wouldn't try to slip away?"

"I don't know. But I don't believe you'd do anything that would bring harm to me."

"Once, you were released into my care."

Constance sighed, and watched the exercising women for a few moments. "Tides turn. Change isn't always for the worse." She shifted her gaze back, moving closer to the Shaper Mother. "Why not help me with my work on behalf of Sisterland? I know you haven't been a believer in the Silent Revolution. But you must see now that its work matters – we're correcting the mistakes of the Nine."

"Aren't you falling into errors of your own?"

"Naturally, we're getting things wrong. But we're making progress, too. We could advance faster and further with your wisdom. Your tuition, and intuition. Together, we could make a difference. Will you help? Will you collaborate with me?"

"I'll think about it, Constance."

"Think hard. Remember, here you're an exile in your own land."

"But I choose to be that exile." She laid a single finger on Constance's wrist, light yet insistent. "Be careful when you speak in public, Constance."

"I don't know what you mean."

"I've watched you make speeches. It can be an elevating experience – the orator is swept along on a tide. Take care the euphoria doesn't become addictive."

It was gratifying, she couldn't deny it: the warmth of the approval, the sense of empowerment. "I do it because the leadership wants me to – and they make it worth my while. They've let me form a family."

"We all strike bargains of one sort or another." The mother

365

fell quiet, lost in reflection. By and by, she looked Constance in the eye. "Bring your daughter to see me, if you can. Regret is not a moe I ever bothered with, but I should have liked to spend time with at least one child. I never knew any. There never seemed to be the time. And time trickles out eventually."

"You're still young, mother."

"There's only so much of it to do what counts most in life, Constance."

"How we spend it?"

"Who we spend time with. When time starts to run short, we wish we'd spent more of it with the people who matter to us."

Constance thought of Harper and Faithful, and how limited was the time she could devote to them because of her work for Sisterland.

"It's good to have choices. But they bring their own challenges. Don't they, Constance?"

A surge of irritation shot through Constance. The mother was mindmapping her again.

"Old habits die hard, sweet child." The mother placed a hand on her breast and bowed in apology.

But, as her head dipped, Constance saw that blinding smile transfigure her face.

Harper grew thinner and more remote. One day, Constance noticed a matching pair of lines carved on his face alongside his mouth. When had that happened? He seemed content when he was occupied with Faithful. But when the little girl was taking a nap, or if Devotion borrowed her for an excursion, as she often asked to do, the strain of living in Harmony was visible. He could spend hours locked in thought, staring through a window towards the treetops on a nearby boulevard. He stopped asking Constance about her work with the Co-Equals. When Leaf became the first man licensed to teach literacy to other men, he showed minimal interest. It was the same when the remnants of the Nine were removed from power in Righteous, allowing the Silent Revolution to spread unchecked throughout Sisterland. Not even the reversal of the hooding policy could engage him. He lived only for Faithful.

There were times when he retreated to a place where Constance could not follow. Sometimes, she accepted it – work kept her busy. At other times, she missed the closeness they had enjoyed in their early days together. Then, she would go to him, put her arms about him, and will him back to her. He never failed to respond. But she feared that one day he might.

"I know you never wanted to come to Harmony. But you have Faithful and me now. There are people who love you here." She caressed him, trying to convey the depth of her feelings for him.

"You make sense of me being here. You and Faithful. You make it –" He pulled up short.

"What were you going to say, Harper? Why did you stop?"

He wouldn't answer. Constance was at a loss. If he wouldn't communicate with her, how could they solve problems? She mindmapped him, although she knew it was trespassing and he resented it. That was how she learned what he suppressed for her sake.

You make it bearable.

She could not ignore his pain. And yet she did.

One day, she brought him back a gift of a bonsai tree in a pot. Watching him turn it round and round in his hands, she knew it was a mistake. This miniature compared unfavourably with the towering jack pines that had been his daily companions. She had never expected the forest to wilt from his memory. But his attachment to it was beyond anything she had anticipated.

"Why don't you take Faithful to the forest for a visit,

Harper? You can show her where to look for those butterflies you keep telling her about. She's only seen pictures of them in books. She'll be enchanted!"

"You can't come with us?"

"You know I can't."

His eyes were as cloudy as the skies above Sisterland.

Devotion was in the threeser when Constance arrived home, drained from the post-euphoria of addressing an audience. Momentarily, she resented her presence. Yet something about the scene made her reconsider. Unnoticed in the doorway, Constance watched. Devotion was sitting on the floor close to Faithful. With a pang, Constance recognised that Devotion had more time for the little girl than she had ever spared for Constance herself. Faithful was clinging to Harper's leg, uncharacteristically shy. And then Constance realised what was causing her bashfulness.

"Don't you want to stroke it, Faithful?" Devotion extended her arms to full stretch, and Constance saw a robin perched between her hands. She opened them flat, and the robin blinked and tilted its head. Faithful's fist loosened its grip on Harper's leggings, and she moved closer.

"You can pet him, if you like," said Devotion. "Very gently. He won't hurt you. He's tame."

The tiny hand inched out and touched the bird on its rust-coloured breast. The hand retracted quickly. But after another moment, it risked contact again. Grandmother and granddaughter's heads bent close to one another.

Harper caught sight of Constance and smiled, lighting up for her. She went to him, and his arm circled her waist, drawing her close. But she had glimpsed the sadness in him, watching their daughter with this robin doctored so that it would stand a human's touch. Even so, it would not survive for more than a few months. It could not live in captivity. Sisterland's scientists could achieve much, but not that.

"Where did you get the robin, Devotion?" asked Constance. "I thought Goodwill talked you out of having caged birds years ago."

"There's space in your threeser. It's not as cruel to keep one here. Besides, see how much Faithful likes it."

On cue, Faithful crowed, raising a rosy face to her parents.

"We can't keep it, Devotion. It wouldn't be right. Harper?"

"No. But perhaps we could all go somewhere and release it. How about that, Devotion?"

"It won't live as long. That isn't kinder really," said Devotion.

"Kindness can be misplaced." He looked at Constance as he spoke.

After Faithful was asleep and Devotion had gone home, Harper decided to take a walk in the unit garden. He didn't invite Constance to accompany him. By and by, she went looking for him, and found him hunkered down, letting soil spill through his fingers.

"What's the matter, Harper?"

"I broke a co-worker's machine today. The one for sucking leaves off the trees. I took it off her, and hurled it on the ground – it smashed into pieces. I said leaves should be free to fall, the way nature intended. She reported me to my progress-monitor."

"I suppose you're in trouble now. Don't worry, Harper, we'll sort something out."

"Surprisingly, the monitor agreed with me. She said she'd make a recommendation to the Parks Mother."

"Well done. Perhaps you've started something. Maybe next year leaves will be allowed to fall off the trees in Harmony. Won't Faithful have fun trying to catch them as they fall!" She studied his face. "But I don't understand why you're so upset. You made your point."

He dug his hands into the soil and left them there, staring at the earth.

369

Constance wanted to tell him that she had made sacrifices to be with him – some of the Co-Equals regarded Harper as her little weakness. But she held back. After all, his life was constructed round a more complicated set of compromises.

Pain crouched inside him, she knew that. And she regretted it. But she had convinced herself that his pain was tolerable. It would uncoil and stretch if he went back to live in his forest – after all, he'd have to leave her and Faithful behind. The pain wouldn't vanish then, but would bite in a different way.

If only Harper could learn to enjoy his life in Harmony. After all, he had learned to work alongside women in the parks' division, in a part-time role that gave him time to care for Faithful. He had learned to rub along with Goodwill, to appreciate Devotion. He had learned to negotiate Harmony, not just geographically but in the myriad ways he had to deal with the city. But he had never learned to accept his life there. Always, even on the best days, he did no more than tolerate it.

Constance and Harper never talked about this in any meaningful way. If she raised the subject, he insisted that he was satisfied. But she was aware that Harmony did not supply what he truly needed for happiness. His pleasure in being with Constance and Faithful could not overcome his pull to the forest.

Constance blanked out her concerns. She was happy with this life. She had exactly what she wanted.

Chapter 40

Harper arrived home from work, his gardening tools in a bag slung over his shoulder. Constance could hear the breath tear through his body.

"You're shaking, Harper. Did something happen?" All at once, she realised he was alone. "Where's Faithful? I thought you were collecting her."

"Devotion is keeping her overnight. I said we needed to talk."

"This sounds serious." She could see a tic throbbing above his jawline. "Let's take a walk and discuss whatever's troubling you. We could go down by the riverbank – you like it there."

"Stop it, Constance. Just listen, for a change. Devotion told me what you're up to. She overheard Goodwill and Patience."

Caught out, Constance backed away. She'd hoped for more time, to prepare a reason for Harper. He followed, eyes turned to flint.

"How could you even consider it? She's only a little girl. It was bad enough when you started having her onstage with you. I told you I didn't like it. But you did it anyway. Even though you know it's propaganda. But this is so much worse! It's a mass lie!"

371

"Maybe Devotion explained it wrong."

"And maybe you're the one in the wrong. Constance, this is our daughter. A child. Not a tool to be used in your cause."

"Harper, you need to understand. This is about leadership. And leaders have to harden without losing tenderness."

"What kind of brainwashing is that! You were able to think for yourself once, Constance. Back when we first met. But you've let yourself be indoctrinated. Can't you see the risks with this hideous scheme? It's inexcusable!"

Constance's brain was teeming. She bent down and picked up a small object from the floor. It was one of Faithful's toys – a furry fawn with a dappled stomach. She remembered the day they had chosen it. Her eye lit on the lilac baby blanket that was once hers. She remembered how touched she had been because Devotion had kept it for so many years. Memory was important, she'd always known that.

Harper took the fawn off her, and threw it aside. "It's true, isn't it? The Co-Equals want to plant a false memory in everyone. To make them believe Faithful is Silence's child. A daughter who survived Silence's fall from the bridge. And you're only her guardian. As for me – I'm nothing."

Constance didn't speak.

He crowded in on her. "I'm not surprised you can't bring yourself to admit it. But I want to hear it from your mouth. You've agreed to this. Haven't you?"

"Yes."

"Why, Constance?"

"It's the final part of the strategy." The words came out in a rush.

"That's not what I'm asking. Why would you go along with it?"

"I can't stop them. At least this way I have some influence. Patience won't always be in charge. Some of us are talking about replacing her. I'm playing a long game here, Harper."

"You're playing a dangerous game. The stakes are too

high. Pull out – now."

She shivered, and wrapped her arms around herself.

He watched her with compassion. But there was an air of finality in his gaze, too. "We have to leave this place, Constance. We have to take Faithful away with us."

"To your forest?"

"Not the forest. It's a long way from Harmony, but it's still in Sisterland. We have to get right away from here. From this society you think is close to perfect. But I know is bogus. Just as controlling as it was under the Nine. We need to leave Sisterland. This false-memory plan sickens me to the core. But even without it, I can't stay here any longer. I'm desperate to be somewhere real. Where leaves fall, and rot, and sink back into the land. Where slugs crawl over flowers, and take bites out of them. Where birds live in the wild – not in cages. Where they find twigs lying about, and use them to make nests. Where animals burrow into the earth. You sisters talk about the beauty of the world you've created. But it's artificial – quality-controlled, weighed, and distributed in line with some group-agreed directive. I've tried. For your sake, and for Faithful's. But I can't survive in this fake world a day longer. I have to leave or I won't be able to carry on breathing. You have to leave because you'll become something misshapen and ugly if you don't. And Faithful has to leave because they'll twist her, too. But if you won't come with us, we'll go without you."

Her vision blurred. She stared at Harper, trying to separate out his features, and put them back together again – struggling to recognise her lover in this stern stranger. "You'd leave me? After everything we've been through together?"

"I'm leaving Sisterland. Not you." Harper's silvered eyes fastened onto hers. "Come with us, Constance. Let's all go away together. You, me and Faithful. We could make a life somewhere else. Away from here. In Outsideland."

Constance flinched. Outsideland was a drastic step. If she

went with him it would be impossible to return. She might never set eyes on Devotion again, or Goodwill. She would never see the nooks and corners of Harmony which reminded her of Silence. And she'd lose any chance of helping to give shape to Sisterland. He was asking too much of her.

"I can't, Harper. Don't you know how important my work is here?"

"You're useful for now. But you'll be shucked off as easily as Gracious."

Constance thought of the Co-Equals dinner they had organised for Gracious, and the presentation. Gracious had looked bewildered. It had happened so suddenly. Patience had sneered behind her back about her intuition having failed Gracious. But Constance found herself defending Patience now.

"Patience explained why we needed to stand her down. She said Gracious had served Sisterland for many years, but it was time to give others a chance to be agents for change."

He made an impatient gesture. "There's nothing here for us, Constance. Nothing here for Faithful. Let's just go. While we still can."

"How?"

"Use your silkenspeak. Tell them you have a request, in return for the sacrifice Sisterland asks of you. We need a few days away together: one last time as a family before the memory implant. They won't refuse you. It's not in their interests. We'll choose somewhere near the coast. That's when we'll make a run for it."

"What if we don't make it? We'll lose everything!"

"What if we do make it? Think what we'll gain!"

"I'm frightened, Harper. I don't know what's out there."

"Me neither."

"But it might be a better place for you. It won't be better for me." Uncertainty threaded her voice. "I'm needed here. Outside, I'll have nothing."

"You'll have me." He seized her by the waist, animated in a way he hadn't been in a long time. "Imagine what the world might be like outside Sisterland. No barriers. No demands. No lies. It might be harder in some ways, Constance. But it would be a free life. That's worth something."

"We're free here."

"I know I'm not. I know Faithful won't be. And if you believe you're free, you don't understand what freedom is."

She recognised the truth in his words. Temptation and fear assailed her in equal measure.

"You think it will be like your forest. There's no guarantee. It might be desolate. It might be violent. You think you'll be surrounded by nature – you see yourself breathing in air so pure it slices your lungs. How do you know Outsideland will be anything like that? How do you know it even has trees?"

"I don't. But I'm willing to risk it."

"What about Faithful?"

"She'll be happy with us. I don't want her growing up here. Being part of this. Turned into a living lie."

"Couldn't you wait for things to improve? Sisterland is still evolving."

His hold on her loosened, but he tried once more in a voice grown weary. "Imagine what it might be like for the three of us in Outsideland. Use your imagination, Constance. Don't let it wither."

"How can you be sure you want what's out there more than this?"

"I don't know anything for sure." He let his arms fall to his sides, and took a step back from her. "I had a pet squirrel in my forest. I fed it, stroked it, loved it. But it was still my pet. Here, I'm yours."

"Don't say that, Harper. Don't be so hard on yourself. On us. Look, let's take that trip to your forest we used to talk about. I promise I'll make it happen this time. We could stay for a few months. Maybe we could even arrange to split our time between the forest and Harmony. I'll talk to the Co-Equals about it."

Shoulders hunched, he walked to the window, straining for a glimpse of the treetops. "They wouldn't let us stay in the forest. They'd tell you they couldn't manage without you. And you'd believe them. You haven't been listening to me, Constance. We're not free here. Every day, we fade a little more."

She threw an arm over her eyes, blocking out the sight of him. "I don't want to leave. I'm making a difference here."

No further words were spoken for a time.

At last, he looked back into the room at her. "I love you, Constance, but I can't stay in Sisterland with you any longer."

It was the first time he had said he loved her. Always, Constance had wanted to hear him speak of it. Now, his love had the finality of farewell.

"What will I do?" she wailed.

He trained his eyes on her in a look which did not waver. Even now, the hope in them was a gift to her. She understood what he was telling her.

Choose.

"If it wasn't for Faithful, I'd go with you," she whispered. "How can we take a child to Outsideland?"

"It's because of Faithful we must go."

Constance tried to picture what living in Sisterland without Harper would be like. She'd have Faithful – no matter what he said, he wouldn't be able to take their daughter away unless Constance was willing to let her go. And she never would. She'd have her work. She'd have Devotion and Goodwill. Life would go on. There'd be compensations.

Then she dared to imagine the world he was conjuring up. A world beyond Sisterland. Unknown. Foreign. Terrifying. But with possibilities.

Harper sensed her indecision. He left the window, moved towards her and cupped her chin in his palm. "Say yes."

And it hit her, with the power of seduction and the directness of truth. There was no choice but to leave Sisterland. Not for Harper's sake, or even Faithful's, but for her own. Constance hovered at the point of no return, and tumbled in.

"Yes."

It did not feel like a departure. Rather, an arrival.

GLOSSARY

Babyfusion: pregnancy

Beloved: Sisterland's founder

Beloved's Pearls: A book advising children how to be good Sisterlanders

Blankout: blinds

Bodies: fitness instructors

Boyplace: training camp for boys

Buzz: light rail system

Co-Equals: Ruling body which replaced the Nine

Co-keeper: a new class of memory-keeper without personal experience of the memories they share

Comtel: a communications tool with a small screen worn on the left thumb. It acts as a messaging service and is also a security device, admitting wearers to work and the home

Egglight: egg-shaped, portable source of light

Els: elements, the unit of currency

Entscreen: TV with channels controlled by the Nine

Flicker: someone who works in Moe Express dispensing emotions

Girlplace: school and living quarters for girls

Himtime: mating

Keeper (also memory-keeper): a cohort of the oldest people in Sisterland who pass on authorised memories

Listeners/Listening: counsellors/counselling sessions where indoctrination is reinforced

Matingplace: where women mate with men

Meets: men chosen to mate

Medshop: pharmacy

Mindmap: read minds

Moe: emotion

Nine: Sisterland's ruling body

Oneser: apartment for one person

Other: life partner

Pearl: someone who is prim and proper

Peers: Sisterland's police

Pop-up: a bed

PS days/era: Pre-Sisterland

Scrutineer: guard

Shadow-moeing: flashbacks to emotions no longer freely available

Shaper: a thought-shaper, part persuader and part propagandist, trained to put the most positive spin on all Nine decisions

Shaperhaus: shaper headquarters

Sig: a signifier or identity strip lasered onto the outer wrist of a woman's right hand which gives details such as name and occupation

Silkenspeak: Sisterland propaganda

Sistercentral: seat of government

Skin: face mask worn to protect women from the environment

Source: mother

Sourcingplace: maternity hospital

Stifstat: weapon which sends electric shot into the brain, causing temporary paralysis

Threeser: three-person apartment, extremely rare

Thought-cruncher: someone who disposes of unsuitable thoughts

Transer: electric-powered carriers in which men are transported

Twoser: apartment designed for two people

Voicebox: loudhailer

Wheeler: a tricycle

Interview with the author

Q: Can you reduce *About Sisterland* to one sentence?
A: I can reduce it to one word: extremism.

Q: Where did the idea for the novel come from?
A: It sprang from a book called *Herland* by Charlotte Perkins Gilman (1860-1935), an American writer, feminist, social activist and lecturer who urged economic independence for women. Her ideas were radical and ahead of their time. She also wrote a chilling short story about madness called *The Yellow Wallpaper*. She isn't particularly known for humour, but *Herland* is a satire, and very funny. It was written in 1915, and tells the story of three male explorers who stumble on an all-female community in the Amazon jungle and are amazed to discover it's a utopia. Anyhow, it set me to thinking. And the more I reflected, the more I decided that an all-female community wouldn't be utopian. Quite the reverse. And then I had to explain why.

Q: Why did you position men as a secondary gender in the story rather than just do away with them altogether?
A: I wanted to explore extremism in action, and needed men to show them being treated as slaves – and how this diminished women as well as men. I'm also conscious of what happens when communities or tribes or are kept

apart because I grew up in the north of Ireland during the Troubles. It's never a sound principle to segregate people, or to allow them to self-segregate, because the other side becomes reduced to stereotypes.

Q: Did you set out to write a sci-fi novel?
A: Not at all, although as a student I read Philip K Dick's *Do Androids Dream of Electric Sheep?* which was the basis for the film *Blade Runner*, and was hooked in by his vision. And who doesn't love Margaret Atwood's *The Handmaid's Tale?* I had no choice but to set the novel in the future because I wanted to show what a society would be like where women had been in power for a century or so. However, I made a deliberate decision not to have too much by way of futuristic trappings, bar practical odds and ends like the comtel.

Q: Why does your world mistrust emotions or 'moes'?
A: Women are always being told they are too emotional and the implications are that it holds them back. Successful women seem to be better able to keep a rein on their emotional responses. I wondered what would happen if emotion suppression was taken to extremes.

Q: Did you set out to make the Nine so totalitarian?
A: Yes, because when I look about the world I see how power corrupts people. Even relatively mild-mannered people undergo a transition and start to inhabit ivory towers. They become convinced they are incapable of being wrong, and stop taking advice. I wonder if they don't become afflicted with temporary insanity?

Q: Your characters have unusual names such as Innocence, Goodwill and Devotion. Is there a reason for that?

A: I wanted them all to have so-called virtue names. But I also chose Constance because of the revolutionary countess, Constance de Markievicz, a woman ahead of her time. Silence came about because I've never forgotten meeting a little girl called Silence in the US at a wedding: it occurred to me that her name would be perfect for a character in a book, but it had to be the right character and the right book. I spend a lot of time thinking about names and often change them several times during rewrites.

Q: How did you dream up terms such as peers, meets, Himtime, and so on?

A: Sometimes friends who read early drafts suggested them, sometimes I fiddled about with various words shunted together until I came up with them myself. It was a wonderful distraction from writing. With MUM I was thinking of the antithesis to motherhood, and hoped the juxtaposition would make it more chilling; the same goes for all the mothers like the Mating Mother, and so on. Motherhood has always been regarded as such a sacred condition, so I wondered how would it be if these mothers didn't have the best interests of citizens at heart? But insisted they did?

Q: Do you have a favourite character?

A: Modesty – she started life as a minor character but her role became more important with each rewrite. She just muscled her way into the story. I expect she's on course to run some future version of Sisterland. I also became fond of the memory-keeper, *Honour*, and was sorry to have to kill her off. But she had to go. No room for sentiment when it comes to plot.

Q: What were you trying to convey with the memory-keepers?
A: That memory is highly selective. We all choose what to retain and what to suppress of our own memories, to some extent. But what if the State undertook to do it for us? What kind of society would that produce?

Q: Two dates are mentioned in your novel: June 29 and August 24, Memoryday and Sisterday respectively. Is there any significance?
A: They are the dates of my parents' birthdays. I like to slide family references into my books. Both my parents are dead so they'll never know I did it. But I know. It's also a way of testing whether my brothers read through to the end – I'm presuming my sister will.

Q: Do Harper and Constance escape to Outsideland?
A: I really don't know – I have an open mind about it. It's possible they do. Equally, it's possible they are captured, in which case Faithful would be taken away from them and they'd be discontinued. I don't think Constance would be given another chance: it would be regarded as too great a betrayal. We'll never know which outcome met their escape plan, but what matters is they had one.

Book Club Topics

1. How easily did you enter the fictional world of *Sisterland*?

2. Are there any characters you particularly disapprove of or admire? How did you feel about the Shaper Mother? The Nine? Silence? Harper?

3. How does Constance change during the course of the book?

4. What did you notice about Constance's evolving relationship with Harper? In matingplace? After the Silent Revolution?

5. Why do you think the author decided to tell the story through Constance's eyes? Who else could she have chosen?

6. Which themes are being explored?

7. What is the author saying about memories? And emotions?

8. Some of the characters discuss symbols during the narrative. Which symbols does the author use and why?

9. Do you have a favourite passage and why?

10. What did you make of boyplace/girlplace, matingplace and segregation of women and men, with permits needed to attempt babyfusion?

11. Did you find the end satisfying or how would you change it?

12. How does this book compare with other books by the same author?

Also by Martina Devlin

THE HOUSE WHERE IT HAPPENED

It is 1711, and the Ulster-Scots community in a remote corner of Ireland is in turmoil. A pretty young newcomer is accusing one woman after another of witchcraft. But Ellen, the serving girl in the house where the visitor is staying, is loyal to the family – and over-fond of her master. Yet she knows that Knowehead is a house like no other.

And so she watches and ponders, as a seemingly normal girl claims she is bewitched – as a community turns against eight respectable women – and as malevolent forces unleashed more than half a century earlier threaten a superstitious people beyond their understanding.

Martina Devlin has fictionalised a compelling episode from history, transforming it into a spine-chilling tale.

Praise for *The House Where It Happened*

"Martina Devlin is an immensely skilled storyteller and I was utterly gripped by this book's power. Its sulfurous shadows and air of suppressed menace remind you that the author of *Wuthering Heights* had Ulster blood, like Devlin" – JOSEPH O'CONNOR

ISBN 978178199-930-1

www.wardriverpress.com

WARD RIVER PRESS

Praise for THE HOUSE WHERE IT HAPPENED

"An immensely skilled storyteller and I was utterly gripped by this book's power" *Joseph O'Connor*

"This is a creepy, absorbing tale. The eerie world of Knowehead House is vivid and convincing, layered with authentic detail and lit by striking turns of phrase. Martina Devlin has given us scenes we want to look away from but can't, a whiff of the past that lifts from the page and stays with you, once the story's told"
Lia Mills

"Absorbing" *Irish Times*

"Compelling" *Sunday Business Post*

"A cracking good story" *Irish Examiner*

"A memorable and spirited narrator" *Irish Independent*

"Gorgeously atmospheric and gripping . . . meticulously researched" *Claudia Carroll, Irish Daily Mail*

"Brilliant" *Belfast Telegraph*

"An astonishing achievement . . . a wealth of scholarship and research" *Nell McCafferty*

"Completely bewitched" *The Sunday World*

"Great read, a proper ghost story based on real events and research" *Susan Lanigan, author*